NOVELS BY SANDRA BROWN

Sting
Friction
Mean Streak
Deadline
Low Pressure
Lethal
Mirror Image
Where There's Smoke
Charade
Exclusive
Envy
The Switch
The Crush
Fat Tuesday
Unspeakable
The Witness
The Alibi
Standoff
Best Kept Secrets
Breath of Scandal
French Silk
Slow Heat in Heaven

SEEING RED

SANDRA BROWN

GRAND CENTRAL
PUBLISHING

LARGE PRINT

Copyright © 2017 by Sandra Brown Management, Ltd.

Jacket design by Kathleen Lynch
Digital illustration by Elizabeth Turner
Jacket photograph of woman by George Kerrigan
Author photograph by Andrew Eccles
Jacket copyright © 2017 by Hachette Book Group, Inc.

Grand Central Publishing
Hachette Book Group
1290 Avenue of the Americas, New York, NY 10104
grandcentralpublishing.com
twitter.com/grandcentralpub

First Edition: August 2017

Grand Central Publishing is a division of Hachette Book Group, Inc. The Grand Central Publishing name and logo is a trademark of Hachette Book Group, Inc.

The publisher is not responsible for websites (or their content) that are not owned by the publisher.

The Hachette Speakers Bureau provides a wide range of authors for speaking events. To find out more, go to www.hachettespeakersbureau.com or call (866) 376-6591.

LCCN: 2017941268

ISBNs: 978-1-4555-7210-6 (hardcover), 978-1-4555-7207-6 (ebook), 978-1-4555-7206-9 (large print)

Printed in the United States of America

LSC-C

10 9 8 7 6 5 4 3 2 1

SEEING RED

Prologue

———⊰◦⊱———

Did you think you were going to die?"

The Major pursed his lips with disapproval. "That question wasn't on the list I approved."

"Which is why I didn't ask it while the cameras were rolling. But there's no one here now but us. I'm asking off the record. Were you in fear of your life? Did dying cross your mind?"

"I didn't stop to think about it."

Kerra Bailey tilted her head and regarded him with doubt. "That sounds like a canned answer."

The seventy-year-old gave her the smile that had won him the heart of a nation. "It is."

"All right. I'll respectfully withdraw the question."

She could graciously pass on it because she'd got

what she'd come for: the first interview of any kind
that The Major had granted in more than three years.
In the days leading up to this evening's live telecast
from his home, he and she had become well acquainted. They'd engaged in some lively discussions,
often taking opposing views.

Kerra looked up at the stag head mounted above
his mantel. "I stand by my aversion to having the
eyes of dead animals staring down at me."

"Venison is food. And keeping the herd thinned
out is ecologically necessary to its survival."

"Scientifically, that's a sound observation. From a
personal and humane standpoint, I don't understand
how anyone could place a beautiful animal like that
in the crosshairs and pull the trigger."

"Neither of us is going to win this argument," he
said, to which she replied with matching stubborn-
ness, "Neither of us is going to concede it, either."

He blurted a short laugh that ended in a dry cough.
"You're right." He glanced over at the tall gun cabinet in the corner of the vast room, then pushed
himself out of his brown leather La-Z-Boy, walked
over to the cabinet, and opened the windowpane
front.

He removed one of the rifles. "I took that particular
deer with this rifle. It was my wife's last Christmas
present to me." He ran his hand along the bluish barrel. "I haven't used it since Debra died."

Kerra was touched to see this softer side of the former soldier. "I wish she could have been here for the interview."

"So do I. I miss her every day."

"What was it like for her, being married to America's hero?"

"Oh, she was super-impressed," he said around a chuckle as he propped the rifle in the corner between the cabinet and the wall. "She nagged me only every other day about leaving my dirty socks on the floor rather than putting them in the hamper."

Kerra laughed, but her thoughts had turned to The Major's son, who'd made no bones about his aversion to his father's fame. She'd felt an obligation to invite him to appear on the program alongside The Major, perhaps just a brief appearance in the final segment. Using explicit language that left no room for misinterpretation, he had declined. *Thank God.*

The Major crossed to the built-in bar. "So much talking has made me thirsty. I could use a drink. What would you like?"

"Nothing for me." She stood and retrieved her bag from where she'd set it on the floor beside her chair. "As soon as the crew gets back, we need to hit the road."

The Major had ordered a cold fried chicken picnic supper from a local restaurant for her and the five-person production crew. It was delivered to the house, and, after they'd eaten, packing up the gear had taken an hour. When all was done, Kerra had asked the others to go gas up the van for their two-hour drive back to Dallas while she stayed behind. She had wanted a few minutes alone with The Major in order to thank him properly.

She began, "Major, I must tell you—"

He turned to her and interrupted. "You've said it, Kerra. Repeatedly. You don't need to say it again."

"You may not need to hear it again, but I need to say it." Her voice turned husky with emotion. "Please accept my heartfelt thanks for...well, for everything. I can't adequately express my gratitude. It knows no bounds."

Matching her solemn tone, he replied, "You're welcome."

She smiled at him and took a short breath. "May I call you every once in a while? Come visit if I'm ever out this way again?"

"I'd like that very much."

They shared a long look, leaving the many insufficient words unspoken, but conveying to each other a depth of feeling. Then, to break the sentimental mood, he rubbed his hands together. "Sure you won't have a drink?"

"No, but I would take advantage of your bathroom." She left her coat in the chair but shouldered her bag.

"You know where it is."

This making the fourth time she'd been to his house, she was familiar with the layout. The living area looked like a miniature Texas museum, with cowhide rugs on the distressed hardwood floor, Remington reproductions in bronze of cowboys in action, and pieces of furniture that made The Major's recliner seem miniature by comparison.

One of the offshoots of the main room was a hallway, and the first door on the left was the powder room, although that feminine-sounding name was incongruous with the hand soap dispenser in the shape of a longhorn steer.

She was drying her hands at the sink and checking her reflection in the framed mirror above it, making a mental note to call her hairdresser—maybe a few more highlights around her face?—when the door latch rattled, calling her attention to it. "Major? Is the crew back? I'll be right out."

He didn't respond, although she sensed someone on the other side of the door.

She replaced the hand towel in the iron ring mounted on the wall beside the sink and was reaching for her shoulder bag when she heard the *bang*.

Her mind instantly clicked back to The Major taking the rifle from the cabinet but not replacing it. If he'd been doing so now and it had accidentally discharged...*Oh, my God!*

She lunged for the door and grabbed hold of the knob, but snatched her hand back when she heard a voice, not The Major's, say, "How do you like being dead so far?"

Kerra clapped her hand over her mouth to hold back a wail of disbelief and horror. She heard footsteps thudding around in the living room. One set? Two? It was hard to tell, and fear had robbed her of mental acuity. She did, however, have the presence of mind to reach for the switch plate and turn off the light.

Holding her breath, she listened, tracking the footsteps as they crossed rugs, struck hardwood, and then, to her mounting horror, entered the hallway. They came even with the bathroom door and stopped.

Moving as soundlessly as possible, she backed away from the door, feeling her way past the sink and toilet in the darkness, until she came up against the bead board wall. She tried to keep her breathing silent, though her lips moved around a prayer of only one repeated word: *Please, please, please.*

Whoever was on the other side of the door tried turning the knob and found it locked. It was tried a second time, then the door shook as an attempt was made to force it open. To whomever was trying to open it, the locked door could only mean one thing: Someone was on the other side of it.

She'd been discovered.

Another set of footsteps came rushing from the living area. The door was battered against with what she imagined was the stock of a rifle.

She had nothing with which to defend herself against armed assailants. If they had in fact fatally shot The Major, and if they got past that door, she would die, too.

Escape was her only option, and it had to be *now*.

The double-hung window behind her was small, but it was the only chance she had of getting out alive. She felt for the lock holding the sashes together, twisted it open, then placed her fingers in the depressions of the lower sash and pulled up with all her might. It didn't budge.

Bambambam! The rapid succession of blows loosened the latch and splintered the wood anchoring it.

Because silence was no longer necessary, Kerra was sobbing now, taking in noisy gulps of air. *Please, please, please.* She whimpered the entreaty for salvation from a source stronger than she because she felt powerless.

She put all she had into raising the window, and it became unstuck with such suddenness that it stunned her for perhaps one heartbeat. Another violent attempt to break the latch separated metal parts of it. She heard them landing on the floor.

She threw one leg over the windowsill and bent

practically in half in order to get her head and shoulders through. When they cleared the opening, she launched herself out and dropped to the ground.

She landed on her shoulder. A spike of pain took her breath. Her left arm went numb and useless. She rolled onto her stomach and pushed herself up with her right arm. After taking a few staggering steps to regain her balance, she took off in a sprint. Behind her she heard the bathroom door crashing open.

A blast from a shotgun deafened her and sheared off an upper branch of a young mesquite tree. She kept running. It fired again, striking a boulder and creating shrapnel that struck her legs like darts.

How many misses would they get before hitting her?

There were no city lights, only a sliver of moon. The darkness made her a more difficult target, but it also prevented her from seeing more than a few feet ahead of her. She ran blindly, stumbling over rocks, scrub brush, and uneven ground.

Please, please, please.

Then without warning, the earth gave out beneath her. She pitched forward, grabbing hold of nothing but air. She was helpless to catch herself before smashing into the ground and rolling, sliding, falling.

Chapter 1

———◆———

Six days earlier

Trapper was in a virtual coma when the knocking started.

"Bloody hell," he mumbled into the throw pillow beneath his head. His face would bear the imprint of the upholstery when he got up. *If* he got up. Right now, he had no intention of moving, not even to open his eyes.

The knocking might have been part of a dream. Maybe a construction worker somewhere in the building was tapping the walls in search of studs. An urban woodpecker? Whatever. If he ignored the noise, maybe it would go away.

But after fifteen seconds of blessed silence, there

came another *knock-knock*. Trapper croaked, "I'm closed. Come back later."

The next three knocks were insistent.

Swearing, he rolled onto his back, sailed the drool-damp pillow across the office, and laid his forearm over his eyes to block the daylight. The window blinds were only partially open, but those cheerful, skinny strips of sunshine made his eyeballs throb.

Keeping one eye closed, he eased his feet off the sofa and onto the floor. When he stood, he stumbled over his discarded boots. His big toe sent his cell phone sliding across the floor and underneath a chair. If he bent down that far, he doubted his ability to return upright, so he left his phone where it was.

It wasn't like it rang all that often anyway.

Holding the heel of his hand against his pounding temple, and with one eye remaining closed, he managed to reach the other side of his office without bumping into the bottom drawer of the metal file cabinet. For no reason he could remember, it was standing open.

Through the frosted glass upper half of the door, he made out a form just as it raised its fist to knock again. To prevent the further agony that would induce, Trapper flipped the lock and opened the door a crack.

He sized her up within two seconds. "You've got

the wrong office. One flight up. First door to the right off the elevator."

He was about to shut the door when she said, "John Trapper?"

Shit. Had he forgotten an appointment? He scratched the top of his head, where his hair hurt down to the follicles. "What time is it?"

"Twelve fifteen."

"What day?"

She took a breath and let it out slowly. "Monday."

He looked her up and down and came back to her face. "Who are you?"

"Kerra Bailey."

The name didn't ring any bells, but it would be hard to hear them over the jackhammer inside his skull. "Look, if it's about the parking meter—"

"The one in front of the building? The one that's been flattened?"

"I'll pay to have it replaced. I'll cover any other damages. I would have left a note to that effect, but I didn't have anything on me to write—"

"I'm not here about the parking meter."

"Oh. Hmm. Did we have an appointment?"

"No."

"Well, now's not a good time for me, Ms...." He went blank.

"Bailey." She said that in the same impatient tone in which she'd said *Monday.*

"Right. Ms. Bailey. Call me, and we'll schedule—"

"It's important that I talk to you sooner rather than later. May I come in?" She gestured at the door, which Trapper had kept open only a few inches.

A woman who looked like her, he hated turning down for anything. But, hell. His head felt as dense as a bowling ball. His shirt was unbuttoned, the tail hanging loose. He hoped his fly was zipped, but in case it wasn't, he didn't risk calling attention to it by checking. His breath would stop a clock.

He glanced behind him at the disarray: suit jacket and tie slung over the back of a chair; boots in front of the sofa, one upright, the other lying on its side; one black sock draped over the armrest, the other sock God only knew where; an empty Dom bottle precariously close to rolling off the corner of his desk.

He needed a shower. He really needed to pee.

But he also really, *really* needed clients, and she had "money" written all over her. Her handbag, literally so. It was the size of a small suitcase and covered in designer initials. Even if she had been looking for the tax attorney on the next floor up, she would have been slumming.

Besides, when had he ever been known to say no to a lady in distress?

He stepped back and opened the door, motioning her toward the two straight chairs facing his desk. He kicked the file cabinet drawer shut with his heel and still got to his desk ahead of her in time to relocate an empty but smelly Chinese food carton and the latest issue of *Maxim*. He'd ranked the cover shot among his top ten faves, but she might take exception to that much areola.

She sat in one chair and placed her bag in the other. As he rounded the desk, he buttoned the middle button of his shirt and ran a hand across his mouth and chin to check for remaining drool.

As he dropped into his desk chair, he caught her looking at the gravity-defying champagne bottle. He rescued it from the corner of the desk and set it gently in the trash can to avoid a clatter. "Buddy of mine got married."

"Last night?"

"Saturday afternoon."

Her eyebrow arched. "It must have been some wedding."

He shrugged, then leaned back in his chair. "Who recommended me?"

"No one. I got the address off your website."

Trapper had forgotten he even had one. He'd paid a college kid seventy-five bucks to do whatever it was you do to get a website online. That was the last he'd thought of it. This was the first client it had yielded.

She looked like she could afford much better.

"I apologize for showing up without an appointment," she said. "I tried calling you several times this morning, but kept getting your voice mail."

Trapper shot a look toward the chair his phone had slid underneath. "I silenced my phone for the wedding. Guess I forgot to turn it back on." As discreetly as possible, he shifted in his chair in a vain attempt to give his bladder some breathing room.

"Well, it's sooner rather than later, Ms. Bailey. You said it was important, but not important enough for you to make an appointment. What can I do for you?"

"I'd like for you to intervene on my behalf and convince your father to grant me an interview."

He would have said *Come again?* or *Pardon?* or *I didn't quite catch that*, but she had articulated perfectly, so what he said was, "Is this a fucking joke?"

"No."

"Seriously, who put you up to this?"

"No one, Mr. Trapper."

"Just plain Trapper is fine, but it doesn't matter what you call me because we don't have anything else to say to each other." He stood up and headed for the door.

"You haven't even heard me out."

"Yeah. I have. Now if you'll excuse me, I gotta take a piss and then I've got a hangover to sleep off. Close the door on your way out. This neighborhood, I hope your car's still there when you get back to it."

He stalked out in bare feet and went down the drab hallway to the men's room. He used the urinal then went over to the sink and looked at himself in the cloudy, cracked mirror above it. A pile of dog shit had nothing on him.

He bent down and scooped tap water into his mouth until his thirst was no longer raging, then ducked his head under the faucet. He shook water from his hair and dried his face with paper towels. With one more nod toward respectability, he buttoned his shirt as he was walking back to his office.

She was still there. Which didn't come as that much of a surprise. She looked the type that didn't give up easily.

Before he could order her out, she said, "Why would you object to The Major giving an interview?"

"It's no skin off my nose, but he won't do it, and I think you already know that or you wouldn't have come to me, because I'm the last person on the planet who could convince him to do anything."

"Why is that?"

He recognized that cleverly laid trap for what it was and didn't step into it. "Let me guess. I'm your last resort?" Her expression was as good as an admission. "Before coming to me, how many times did you ask The Major yourself?"

"I've called him thirteen times."

"How many times did he hang up on you?"

"Thirteen."

"Rude bastard."

Under her breath, she said, "It must be a family trait."

Trapper smiled. "It's the only one he and I have in common." He studied her for a moment. "You get points for tenacity. Most give up long before thirteen attempts. Who do you work for?"

"A network O and O—owned and operated—in Dallas."

"You're on TV? In Dallas?"

"I do feature stories. Human interest, things like that. Occasionally one makes it to the network's Sunday evening news show."

Trapper was familiar with the program, but he didn't remember ever having watched it.

He knew for certain that he'd never seen her, not even on the local station, or he would've remembered. She had straight, sleek light brown hair with blonder streaks close to her face. Brown eyes as large as a doe's. One inch below the outside corner of the left one was a beauty mark the same dark chocolate color as her irises. Her complexion was creamy, her lips plump and pink, and he was reluctant to pull his gaze away from them.

But he did. "Sorry, but you drove over here for nothing."

"Mr. Trapper—"

"You're wasting your time. The Major retired from public life years ago."

"Three to be exact. And he didn't merely retire. He went into seclusion. Why do you think he did that?"

"My guess is that he got sick of talking about it."

"What about you?"

"I was sick of it long before that."

"How old were you?"

"At the time of the bombing? Eleven. Fifth grade."

"Your father's sudden celebrity must have affected you."

"Not really."

She watched him for a moment, then said softly, "That's impossible. It had to have impacted your life as dramatically as it did his."

He squinted one eye. "You know what this sounds like? Leading questions, like you're trying to inter-view *me*. In which case, you're SOL because I'm not going to talk about The Major, or me, or my life. Ever. Not to anybody."

She reached into the oversize bag and took out an eight-by-ten reproduction of a photograph, laid it on the desk, and pushed it toward him.

Without even glancing down at it, he pushed it back. "I've seen it." For the second time, he stood up, went to the door, opened it, and stood there with hands on hips, waiting.

She hesitated, then sighed with resignation, hiked the strap of her bag onto her shoulder, and joined him at the door. "I caught you at a bad time."

"No, this is about as good as I get."

"Would you consider meeting me later, after you've had time to . . . " She made a gesture that encompassed his sorry state. "To feel better. I could outline what I want to do. We could talk about it over dinner."

"Nothing to talk about."

"I'm paying."

He shook his head. "Thanks anyway."

She gnawed the inside of her cheek as though trying to determine which tactic to use to try to persuade him. He could offer some salacious suggestions, but she probably wouldn't go that far, and even if she did, afterward he'd still say no to her request.

She took a look around the office before coming back to him. With the tip of her index finger, she underlined the words stenciled on the frosted glass of the door. "Private Investigator."

"So it says."

"Your profession is to investigate things, solve mysteries."

He snuffled. That was his former profession. Nowadays, he was retained by tearful wives wanting him to confirm that their husbands were screwing around.

If he managed to get pictures, it doubled his fee. Distraught parents paid him to track down runaway teens, whom he usually found exchanging alleyway blowjobs for heroin.

He wouldn't call the work he was doing mystery-solving. Or investigation, for that matter.

But to her, he said, "Fort Worth's own Sherlock Holmes."

"Are you state licensed?"

"Oh, yeah. I have a gun, bullets, everything."

"Do you have a magnifying glass?"

The question baffled him because she hadn't asked it in jest. She was serious. "What for?"

Those pouty pink lips fashioned an enigmatic smile, and she whispered, "Figure it out."

Keeping her eyes on his, she reached into an in-side pocket of her bag and withdrew a business card. She didn't hand it to him, but stuck it in a crack between the frosted glass pane and the door frame, adjacent to the words that spelled out his job description.

"When you change your mind, my cell number is on the card."

Hell would freeze over first.

Trapper plucked the business card from the slit, flipped it straight into the trash can, and slammed the office door behind her.

Eager to go home and sleep off the remainder of

his hangover in a more comfortable surrounding, he snatched up the sock on the armrest of the sofa and went in search of the other.

After several frustrating minutes and a litany of elaborate profanity, he found it inside one of his boots. He pulled on his socks but decided he needed an aspirin before he finished dressing. Padding over to his desk, he opened the lap drawer in the hope of discovering a forgotten bottle of analgesics.

That damned photograph was there in plain sight where he couldn't miss it.

But whether looking at it, or acknowledging it in any manner, or even denying its existence, he was never truly free of it. He had lied to Kerra Bailey. His life was never the same after that photograph went global twenty-five years ago.

Trapper plopped down into his desk chair and looked at the cursed thing. His head hurt, his eyes were scratchy, his throat and mouth were still parched. But even realizing that it was masochistic, he reached across the desk and slid the photo closer to him.

Everyone in the entire world had seen it at least once over the past quarter century. Among prize-winning, defining-moment editorial photographs, it ranked right up there with the raising of the flag on Iwo Jima, the sailor kissing the nurse in Times Square on V-E Day, the naked Vietnamese girl running from napalm, the twin towers of the World Trade Center aflame and crumbling.

But before 9/11, there was the Pegasus Hotel bombing in downtown Dallas. It had rocked a city still trying to live down the Kennedy assassination, had destroyed a landmark building, had snuffed out the lives of 197 people. Half that number had been critically injured.

Major Franklin Trapper had led a handful of struggling survivors out of the smoldering rubble to safety.

A photographer who worked for one of Dallas's newspapers had been eating a Danish at his desk in the city room when the first bombs detonated. The blast deafened him. The concussion shook his building and created cracks in the aggregate floor beneath his desk. Windows shattered.

But like an old fire horse, he was conditioned to run toward a disaster. He snatched up his camera, bolted down three flights of fire stairs, and, upon exiting the newspaper building, dashed toward the source of the black plume of smoke that had already engulfed the skyline.

He reached the scene of terror and chaos ahead of emergency responders and began snapping pictures, including the one that became iconic: Franklin Trapper, recently retired from the U.S. Army, emerging from the smoking building leading a pathetic group of dazed, scorched, bleeding, choking people, one child cradled in his arms, a woman holding onto his coattail, a man whose tibia had a compound fracture using him as a crutch.

The photographer, now deceased, had won a Pulitzer for his picture. The act of heroism he had captured on film immediately earned him and the photo immortality.

And, as Trapper well knew, immortality lasted for fucking ever.

The story behind the photograph and the people in it wouldn't come to light until later, when those who were hospitalized were able to relate their individual accounts.

Though, by the time the tales were told, the Trappers' front yard in suburban Dallas had become an encampment for media. The Major—as he came to be known—had been ordained a national symbol of bravery and self-sacrifice. For years following that day in 1992, he was a sought-after public speaker. He was given every honor and award there was to be bestowed, and many were initiated and named for him. He was invited to the White House by every subsequent administration. At state dinners he was introduced to visiting foreign dignitaries who paid homage to his courage.

Over time, new disasters produced new heroes. The fireman carrying the toddler from the Oklahoma City bombing overshadowed The Major's celebrity for a time, but soon he was back on TV talk show guest lists and the after-dinner speaker's circuit. September eleventh gave him a new slant to address: his random act of heroism compared to those performed every day by unsung heroes. For more than two decades he kept his story timely and relevant.

Then three years ago, he stopped cold turkey.

He now lived very privately, avoiding the limelight and refusing requests for public appearances and interviews.

But his legend lived on. Which was why journalists, biographers, and movie producers emerged now and again, seeking time with him to make their particular pitch. He never granted them that time.

Until today none had ever sought out Trapper's help to gain access to his famous father.

Kerra Bailey's audacity was galling enough. But damn her for snagging his interest with that remark about the magnifying glass. What could he possibly see in that photograph that he hadn't seen ten thousand times?

He longed for a hot shower, an aspirin, his bed and soft pillow.

"Screw it." He opened his desk's lap drawer and, instead of reaching for the bottle of Bayer, searched all the way to the back of it and came up with the long-forgotten magnifying glass.

Four hours later, he was still in his desk chair, still reeking, head still aching, eyes still scratchy. But everything else had changed.

He set down the magnifier, pushed the fingers of both hands up through his hair, and held his head between his palms. "Son of a bitch."

Chapter 2

⸺◈⸺

I t's called Gringos, so you should fit right in."

John Trapper's remark had been snide, but after the terse phone call when he'd given Kerra a place and time to meet him, she dressed down, replacing the pantsuit she'd worn earlier to his office with a pair of jeans and a plaid wool poncho.

She hoped he would at least shower.

She arrived at the restaurant early, put her name on the wait list for a table, and claimed a stool at the bar where she had a view of the entrance. She hoped for an opportunity to observe him before he became aware of it.

But the instant he walked in, he homed in on her as though by radar with eyes that belonged in a spectrum of blue all their own. Electric. Like neon light. And when he looked at her, antagonism radiated from them.

The hostess greeted him. He gave her a slow grin and said something that made her giggle. She indicated Kerra. He nodded and walked toward her.

He had swapped the wrinkled suit pants he'd obviously slept in for a pair of jeans with knees almost worn completely through. The hems were stringy against the vamp of his cowboy boots. He had on a black leather jacket over a white western-cut shirt with pearl snaps instead of buttons. He wore the shirttail out.

When he reached her, he didn't speak, just stood there looking down at her. He wasn't clean-shaven, but he had showered. He smelled of soap. And leather. His dark hair was clean, but he hadn't tried to tame its natural growth pattern. The thick swirls were as tousled as they had been this morning, and Kerra found herself thinking: *Why mess with a good thing?*

They continued to stare each other down until the bartender approached. "I'm fixin' the lady a margarita rocks. How 'bout you, cowboy?"

"Dos Equis, please."

"Want 'em brought to your table?"

Before she could reply, Trapper said, "That'd be great. Thanks."

He wrapped his hand around Kerra's elbow, hauled her up off the barstool, and propelled her toward the hostess, who was waiting with menus the size of overpass signs. She led them to a table for two.

"Do you have a booth?" Trapper asked. "Where we can hear ourselves think?" He gave her a wheedling smile, and she smiled back, and without delay they were led deeper into the restaurant where the lights were dimmer and the mariachi music wasn't blaring.

Once they were seated across from each other, Kerra said, "Still hung over?"

"The beer should help."

"Do you get drunk often?"

"Not near often enough."

To avoid meeting his hostile gaze, Kerra looked around, taking in the strands of Christmas lights strung across the ceiling and trying to think of a topic of conversation neutral enough to alleviate the tension. "When did you move from Dallas to Fort Worth?"

"When Dallas got too far up its own ass."

The topic wasn't the problem, she decided. He was. Anything she said would rub him the wrong way. As soon as the cocktail waitress delivered their drinks, she figured she had just as well skip cordiality and get on with it. "You saw it?"

"I wouldn't be here otherwise."

"Did you actually use a magnifying glass?"

Before he could answer, a waitress arrived with a basket of tortilla chips and a bowl of salsa. "Ready to order?"

Daunted by the scope of the menu, Kerra opened it and scanned the first page. "So many choices," she murmured.

"You eat meat?"

He asked as though she would get demerits if she didn't. She bobbed her head once.

He took her menu from her and handed it along with his to the waitress. "Double fajitas, half chicken, half beef, all the trimmings, split the tortillas fifty-fifty, and I want a side of beef enchiladas, chili on top. Queso's okay, but don't come near me with the ranchero." Then he smiled at her, winked, and added, "Please."

After the simpering waitress withdrew, he folded his forearms on the tabletop and leaned toward Kerra. No smile, no wink. "I want to know two things from you."

"Only two?"

"Why'd you come to me?"

"The reason should be obvious. You're his only living relative."

"Well, what isn't obvious, at least to you, is that I'm a dismal disappointment to him. If you're thinking that my intervention on your behalf will make a dent, you're sadly mistaken. In fact, my involvement would work against you."

"That's a chance I have to take. I don't have a choice."

"How's that?"

"His property is posted. If I showed up on his doorstep unannounced and unaccompanied, he could have me arrested for trespassing before I even introduce myself. If you're with me—"

"He'll kick you off his place twice as fast."

"He can't. Your name is on the deed. When your mother died, her share bypassed him and went straight to you. You share ownership of the land."

With anger, he plucked a chip from the basket, dunked it in the salsa, and popped it into his mouth, chewing as he studied her. "You did your homework."

"You're damn right I did."

"By bringing your secret to light, what do you hope to achieve?"

"Achieve?"

"Come on," he said. "You caught me drunk, but I'm not dense."

"Is that the second thing you want to know? What I hope to *achieve*?"

"No. I've got that figured."

"I doubt it."

"You want to rock the world."

They were interrupted again when the waitress

returned with a sizzling platter of grilled meat, which she set in the center of the table then crowded the side dishes around it. Kerra passed on his offer to share the enchiladas, but they each built a fajita.

"Delicious," she mumbled around the first bite.

"You oughta come to Cowtown more often. In Dallas you get Tex-Mex with mushrooms." He wiped his mouth with his napkin. "Second thing I want to know."

"I'm listening."

"How long have you been sitting on this?"

"A while."

"A while. That's vague enough. Why jump on it now?"

"It's not as sudden as it seems," she said. "I've been trying for months to contact The Major. He wouldn't have it, and now I'm out of time. This coming Sunday is the twenty-fifth anniversary of the bombing. Perfect timing. It would make for amazing television."

"Ratings, all that shit."

"Shit to you maybe, Mr. Trapper. Not to me."

"Just plain Trapper." He ate for a time, then, "You realize that Sunday is six days from now."

"The clock is ticking. When The Major hung up on me yesterday for the thirteenth time, I looked you up. I'm desperate."

He stopped eating. "Well, that explains what brought you tap-tap-tapping at my chamber door.

Desperation." When she didn't deny it, he made a scornful sound and went back to his food. "I already told you, nothing I say will sway him."

"Fair enough. Escort me as far as his threshold. You do that, I'll take it from there."

He bounced his fork against his plate and looked her over in a way that made her feel uncomfortably hot inside her clothes. She reached for her margarita and sipped through the salt rim. "How long did it take you?"

"To figure it out, you mean?"

She nodded.

"Longer than it should have. I'm out of practice."

Despite the mule's kick of the margarita, she took another sip for courage. She was approaching a slippery slope. Or more like reaching for the lion's tail dangling from between the bars of his cage. "There's quite a bit about you online."

At first he didn't act as though he'd heard her. He finished a bite, washed it down with a swig of beer, then looked across at her, his eyes like blue flame. "Well, don't keep me in suspense."

"You were with the ATF."

"Um-hm."

"For five years."

"And seven months."

"Before your anger issues got you fired."

"I *quit*."

As the waitress passed by, she paused and asked if they needed anything. Without taking his eyes off Kerra, Trapper thanked her, but gave an abrupt shake of his head.

After she moved on, Kerra said quietly, "You told me today that The Major's overnight celebrity had no effect on your life. But it did, didn't it?"

"Yeah. Huge. I was the only kid in my grade who got fifty-yard-line tickets to all the Cowboys' home games. Couple of times we were invited to the owners' suite."

"If you weren't influenced by the Pegasus, why did you choose a career with a federal bureau that investigates bombs and explosions?"

"The group insurance. Most plans don't include dental."

She frowned. "Please stop joking. I'm serious."

"So am I," he said in an angry whisper. "Stop interviewing me. I've got nothing to say to you about this."

"Then why'd you call and meet me tonight?"

He didn't have a ready response. *Score!* She mentally high-fived herself. "You're an investigator by profession and inclination. You like puzzles and can't tolerate one going unsolved. When you were with the ATF, you worked cases tirelessly until you had the answers, found the culprits. You were let go because of insubordination, not for lack of talent or initiative."

"My, my. For somebody who's never laid eyes on me

until a few hours ago, you sure know a lot. Or think you do, anyway."

"I know that you couldn't help but be intrigued by the challenge I left you with today. I also know that what you discovered was much more significant than what you bargained for. Wasn't it? Trapper? Correct me if I'm wrong."

He didn't say anything, just took a drink from his beer and held on to it when the busboy arrived to clear away their plates. Kerra used her credit card to settle the tab as soon as the waitress brought it.

Through all that activity, a hostile silence teemed between them. When they were left alone again, Kerra shook the ice cubes in her glass. She used the wedge of lime to draw circles around the rim of it. When she next looked across at Trapper, his eyes were tracking the motion, and it made her feel...funny. She placed her hands in her lap under the table and took a moment to get grounded. "What were you angry about?"

"When?"

"When you got fired."

"I *quit*."

"Before they could fire you. What was it over?"

"Didn't you research that part?"

"I didn't get to the specifics."

"Nobody else did, either." He mumbled that as though to himself. Then he shifted his legs beneath the table and leaned forward again. "I got really specific the day I walked out. I told my boss where he could shove his job."

She could believe it. He looked coiled and ready to strike now. Speaking softly, she said, "I think you still have anger issues."

"I do. Big time. And what pisses me off quicker than anything is being played by somebody who thinks she's real cute and clever. Why didn't you just come out and tell me?"

"Did you actually use a magnifying glass?"

He scowled at the taunt and tipped his head toward her drink. "You gonna finish that?"

"No."

He picked up the glass, tossed back what remained of the margarita, then pointed her out of the booth. His wide hand stayed at the small of her back as they wove their way through the crowded restaurant. Kerra felt as though she was being herded but didn't make an issue of it, not wanting him to know she was even aware of his hand.

As they walked past the hostess stand, the young woman gazed at Trapper dreamily and wished them a good night. Outside Kerra inhaled a deep breath to counteract the effects of the tequila.

"Thanks for dinner," he said.

"You're welcome."

"Where's your car?"

"We haven't settled anything."

"Hell we haven't. Where's your car?"

"I Ubered here."

He took his phone from the pocket of his jacket and pulled up the app.

"I can order my own car."

Ignoring her protest, he asked for her address. She gave it to him. He ordered the car.

"He'll be here in two minutes. Ralph in a silver Toyota. Let's wait over there out of the wind."

Taking her elbow, he guided her around the corner of the building. "This is better," she said, shivering inside her poncho. "The temperature has dropped—"

She broke off when he placed his hands on her shoulders and backed her against the exterior brick wall. Before she recovered from the shock of that, he leaned in, and she forgot all about being cold. But she struggled less against his hold on her than she did against her reaction to it. "What the hell are you doing? Get away from me."

He lowered his face close to hers. "You listen and learn," he said in a low thrum. "I'm not him. I'm not noble, not a gentleman, not a hero, understand?"

"That wasn't so hard to deduce."

She thought the putdown would anger him, but he retaliated by gently placing his palm against her cold cheek. He brushed his thumb across her beauty mark.

"I noticed this right off, and the whole time you were

sitting there in my shabby office, wearing your city get-up, acting all sassy and know-it-all, you want to know what was going on in my mind?" He ceased the stroking motion of his thumb, stopping it right on the small mole. His mouth lowered to within a hair's-breadth of hers and he whispered, "Figure it out."

Then he released her and said over his shoulder as he sauntered away, "Ralph's here."

———

The minute he got to his apartment, he went into the bedroom, tugged off his boots, stripped down to his jeans, and, sitting on the edge of the bed, called his friend Carson Rime.

The defense lawyer had a ground-floor office in the same building as Trapper's. His practice was on the wrong side of the freeway to attract criminals who bathed regularly and stood accused only of white-collar malfeasance. But being close to the court-house, county jail, and bail bondsmen, the location was convenient for Carson's clients who were unwashed and felonious.

Trapper had to call him three times before he answered. "What the hell, Trapper? Stop calling me. I'm on my honeymoon, for crissake. Or have you forgotten I got married last Saturday?"

"Like that's a big deal. Isn't this your fourth?"

"Fifth. Have fun at the wedding?"

"Not the wedding. The reception."

"What I meant. Quite a blowout, huh? You catch the garter?"

"No, the bridesmaid."

"Which one?"

"She was blond."

"Big tits or the skinny one?"

"I can't remember. Have you ever heard of Kerra Bailey?"

"The one on TV?"

"You know who she is?"

"Sure. She's a local reporter, but she also shows up every once in a while on that—"

"She came unannounced to my office today."

After a stunned silence, his friend chortled, "Holy shit! Are you kidding?"

"No."

"She came to see *you*?"

"Yes."

"What for?"

Trapper withheld mention of the photograph and its startling revelation. He told Carson only that Kerra wanted to interview The Major. "She asked me to pave the way for her."

"To which you said?"

"Several expletives that boiled down to *no*. But she's not done asking."

"How do you know?"

"She gives off a vibe."

"She vibrates? This just got interesting. Hold on." Trapper could hear Carson murmuring an apology to the new Mrs. Rime, followed by several seconds of rustling, then a closing door. "Tell me everything."

Over the sound of Carson noisily peeing into the toilet, Trapper gave him a condensed version of Kerra's unexpected arrival. When he finished, Carson asked, "Does she understand that you and the pater aren't exactly simpatico?"

"She does now. But that didn't sway her. She still believes I could be useful."

"Are you going to help her?"

"Depends."

"On?"

"Look, Carson, I realize it's your honeymoon and all, but if I hadn't taken you to happy hour at that topless club, you and your bride never would've met."

Carson was quick on the uptake. He sighed. "What's the favor?"

―――◈―――

After he and Carson disconnected, Trapper shucked his jeans and got into bed, but he took his laptop with him.

He went on to YouTube and watched every story

and interview featuring Kerra Bailey that he could locate. He had wished to find fault, had hoped to see a struggling amateur. But on camera she came across as poised, smart, and informative, but also warm and personable. She had a sharp wit, an incisive toughness without meanness, but she didn't allow professionalism to overshadow compassion.

After watching clips for almost two hours, Trapper paused a video on a close-up of her face and stared at the beauty mark, the giveaway, the thing he'd seen ten thousand times, but had never really looked at until it had been magnified ten thousand times on his computer screen.

Though he hadn't known her name until today, he had resented her since he was eleven years old when she had replaced him as the most beloved child in his father's heart.

Because of her, Trapper had lost his dad to the world.

Because of her, his life had become one long game of catch-up at which he continually lost.

Because of her: the little girl his father had carried from the burning ruin of the Pegasus Hotel.

Chapter 3

Kerra was switching between networks to get a sampling of the morning news shows when her cell phone rang. "Hello?"

"I'm outside." Those two words, and Trapper hung up.

Kerra tossed her phone onto the bed, muttering, "Rude jerk."

She had already showered, so it didn't take her long to dress. But she dawdled an extra five minutes, not wanting it to look like she'd rushed down in response to his ill-mannered summons. She should ignore him altogether and find some other way to breach The Major's self-imposed seclusion.

But she'd already lost another day. Between now and Sunday, every minute counted.

Besides, she couldn't let Trapper think that he'd intimidated or scared her off with his manhandling last night.

The condo building's revolving door emptied her into brilliant sunlight and a frigid north wind that made her eyes water. Even so, she couldn't have missed Trapper. Directly across the street from the building, he was leaning against the passenger side of his car, recognizable by the deep dent in its grill roughly the size of a parking meter post. He exuded supreme confidence that she would appear as summoned.

He was dressed as he'd been the night before except that, beneath the leather jacket, today's shirt was blue chambray, and he'd added a pair of sunglasses. Ankles and arms crossed, he looked impervious to the wind whipping his dark hair.

She amended her earlier summation: He was a *sexy* rude jerk.

She waited for a delivery truck to lumber past, then crossed the street mid-block and walked straight toward him. "Isn't Texas supposed to be hot?"

"Not in February."

"I moved here from Minneapolis–St. Paul to get away from winter."

"Live here long enough, you learn we have weather

extremes." He opened the passenger door and motioned her in, then went around. In order to get in on the driver's side, he had to squeeze past a no parking sign.

Kerra called his attention to it. "Your car could get towed."

"They're welcome to it. Smoke has started coming out from under the hood. I figure the radiator's busted."

"It fared better than the parking meter."

He didn't comment on that as he propped his left shoulder against the driver's window and turned toward her. After looking at her for what became an uncomfortably long time, he said, "For twenty-five years people have been trying to identify the little girl in that picture."

"You were so annoyed last night, you never told me exactly how you discovered the birthmark."

"I took a picture of the picture with my phone, downloaded it onto my computer, and enlarged it to the max. I went over it a square inch at a time with a freaking magnifying glass. Twice. More than half your face is buried between The Major's chest and arm, but in the part that's visible you can see the speck near your eye."

"Eureka!"

"That wasn't my first reaction," he said. "My first thought was that you'd doctored the print."

"You doubted my integrity?"

"Doubted? No. You drop out of nowhere and hit me with this? I was *sure* you were a fraud."

"What convinced you otherwise?"

"I checked other prints, early ones, including the cover of *Time*. If you know to look for it, the mark can be seen on every reproduction of the photo. Not as large or as dark as it is now, but there. You're about to put an end to all the speculation about the mystery child."

"Some of the theories regarding my identity were pretty wild," she said with a soft laugh. "I heard a TV preacher once say that I wasn't flesh and blood. That I was an angel who'd been miraculously captured on film. That I'd been sent to escort home all the children who'd died in the explosion. Can you believe that?"

"I don't believe in miracles." He paused, then added, "You're definitely flesh and blood, and I'm also willing to bet that you're no angel."

She hadn't expected an answer to her rhetorical question. She certainly hadn't expected his answer to feel like he'd lightly scratched her just below her belly button. Because of the dark sunglasses, she couldn't read in his eyes whether or not he'd meant the remark to be suggestive. She was probably better off not knowing.

He continued. "It didn't irk you when imposters came forward, claiming to be you?"

"Amused more than irked."

"Amused, because you knew they'd have their fifteen minutes and then be debunked. They couldn't prove their claim. You can."

She touched the spot beneath her eye. "It's irrefutable."

"I should buy stock in magnifying glasses. Once you make the big reveal, there's sure to be a run on them."

"Oh, so we've circled back to what I hope to *achieve*."

"Fame and fortune would be my guess."

"Well, you'd be wrong."

"You don't expect to benefit?"

"Naturally I'll benefit."

"No shit."

"But that's not the only reason I'm going public."

"Then enlighten me."

"I want to thank the man who saved my life," she said with heat. "Don't you believe The Major is due my gratitude?"

"Past due. So what's taken you so long? Oh, wait, I know. You've been waiting on the twenty-fifth anniversary for the big ta-da."

"No, I've been waiting till my father died."

Whatever he'd been about to say, he bit back. He looked aside for several seconds, then removed his sunglasses and flicked a glance at her. "Recently?"

"Eight months ago."

He didn't voice regret, but she saw it in his expression.

"It was a blessing," she said. "He had suffered for a long time and had no quality of life."

Trapper settled his gaze on her, a question in it.

"Shall I back up and start at the beginning?" she asked.

"The day of the bombing?"

"Do you want to hear it?"

"Yes."

"Are you going to continue making snide editorial comments?"

"I'll ration them." When she gave him a reproving look, he added softly, "I'm kidding."

"You're so good at sarcasm, it's hard to tell."

"I want to hear your story."

She took a deep breath and began. "It was a couple of weeks past my fifth birthday. We lived in Kansas City. Daddy had to be in Dallas for a business seminar. Mom and I came along so they could take me to Six Flags as a belated birthday present.

"Staying in the hotel was an adventure in itself. I'd never had room service before. Mom let me order our breakfast. After we'd eaten, we all rode down the elevator together. Daddy kissed us goodbye and got off on the mezzanine level for his meeting. Mom had planned a shopping trip for the two of us. She and I got off on the ground floor. I was skipping across the lobby toward the entrance when the bombs went off. The doorman was smiling at me, about to say something. I saw him just . . . disappear."

Trapper turned his head away and looked through the windshield as he ran his hand over his mouth and chin. "Ten-forty-two. The first of them, ten-forty-two thirty-three to be exact."

"How do you know that?"

"Because every ATF agent studies the Pegasus Hotel bombing. It's textbook. All together there were six bombs, set to detonate simultaneously, but they staggered by several seconds."

"It was like one huge blast to me."

"What do you remember most clearly?"

"The fear. I couldn't hear anything. I was unable to see for the smoke and dust. I couldn't breathe without choking. I was screaming for my mother but couldn't find her. Things were falling all around me. Crashing. I was too young to be afraid of death. The terror of being lost is my most vivid memory."

"For a kid, that makes sense."

"My mother was alive when firemen found her, but her chest had been crushed. She had extensive internal injuries and died in the hospital within an hour. My father survived, but his head and spinal injuries were so severe, he was paralyzed from the neck down. He lived hooked up to a respirator in a permanent care facility for the rest of his life."

"Jesus." Trapper looked away again before coming back to her. "None of the casualties were named Bailey."

"Elizabeth and James Cunningham."

"So how'd you wind up with a different name?"

"My injuries were comparatively minor, but I spent two nights in the hospital. Daddy was in ICU and on life support, so I was released from the hospital into the care of my aunt, my mother's sister, and her husband, who'd been notified as next of kin and had flown to Dallas immediately.

"I've been told that there was a frenzy, especially among the press, to identify the little girl in the photo, which had already been reproduced by every news agency in the world.

"My aunt and uncle foresaw additional trauma for me if my identity became known, so they insisted to the hospital staff and the authorities that my name not be released. They wanted to protect me from the onslaught of media attention that The Major, you, and your mother were already being subjected to.

"My aunt whisked me off to Virginia, where they lived. For months after, my uncle commuted back and forth, overseeing Daddy's care here in Dallas until he could be relocated to a place near their home.

"My uncle settled my family's affairs in Kansas City, sold everything to help offset the expense of Daddy's care. There was a memorial service held for my mother, but Daddy wasn't well enough to attend. Because of his infirmity, and predictably short life span, he urged my aunt and uncle to legally adopt me and change my name to theirs. They had no other children. They reared me as their own."

"What was going on inside your head?"

"What do you mean?"

"Were you messed up by all the upheaval?"

"I was too young to fully grasp the magnitude of the tragedy. All I knew was that we'd been through something terrible. Mommy had gone to heaven and Daddy was very sick, and we didn't live in our house any more. In Kansas I'd had a pet parakeet. I never knew what became of it. I missed my swing set until my uncle installed one for me in their backyard.

"Basically, I was a happy, normal child. But whenever I was taken to visit Daddy, he would sob inconsolably. Nothing unsettles a child more than seeing an adult cry. That was the worst of it. And the nightmares."

"You had nightmares?"

"Yes. They subsided over time, but early on they were horrible, harsh reminders of the bombing, although I didn't know to attach that word to it. I dreamed about smoke and choking and seeing blood. My mother was there, saying my name over and over. I would wake up screaming, telling my aunt and uncle that they were wrong, that she hadn't died. She was alive. I could see her, hear her, feel her reaching for me and tightly squeezing my hand until..."

Trapper remained silent and still.

She swallowed. "Until her hand let go of mine. She used it to wave at a man running past us. She was crying, yelling at him to stop. *Please. Help.* He stopped and picked me up."

"The Major."

"I remember being hysterical. Fighting him. Trying to get back to my mother. I remember him clutching me against his chest and telling me that everything would be all right."

"That was a lie, though, wasn't it?"

"Yes, but he lied out of kindness."

Trapper didn't say anything for a moment, then asked her when she had put two and two together. "When did you realize that your nightmare was actually a memory of the 'something terrible'?"

"Not for years."

He gave her a sharp look.

"I can tell you don't believe that, but it's true. No one around me ever referenced the bombing. I was a child. I watched *Sesame Street,* not *60 Minutes.* The Oklahoma City bombing came a few years later, and I remember the grown-ups in my life being terribly upset, but it was irrelevant to me."

"You never matched the date of the Pegasus bombing with the day your mother died?"

"That's precisely how I eventually became aware. I was in middle school, about twelve or thirteen. On an anniversary of the bombing, one of my teachers mentioned it. When I got home from school, my aunt was sitting in the living room, looking at a picture of herself and my mother together. I asked her why she was crying. 'I always get sad on this date,' she said. 'It's the day your mother died.' Suddenly it clicked. I realized why I had such vivid nightmares of smoke and fire, of my mother letting go of me and being carried away from her.

"My aunt and uncle were reluctant to confirm it. Justifiably, as it turned out, because once I knew, I became obsessed with the bombing. I wanted to learn everything about it. I read all the books, watched all the films and interviews with survivors. I'd seen that famous photo, of course, but I'd never paid much attention to it, because, again, it had no relevance to me.

"But when my aunt pointed me out, I saw not only myself, but also the face of the man who'd saved me. The Major became real when, up to that point, he was only the stranger in my dreams who'd responded to my mother's dying plea."

"Why didn't you blurt it to the world then?"

"My aunt impressed upon me what an awful ordeal it would be for my dad. The Major had stepped into the role of hero naturally, as though born to it. But my dad was a soft-spoken, self-effacing man. Given his circumstances and frailty, it would have been cruel to thrust him into the spotlight. I swore to my aunt, and to myself, that I wouldn't go public with it as long as Daddy was alive. I upheld that promise."

"For what? Thirteen years?"

"Roughly. During that time, I went on with my life, a happy, healthy, normal girl. I finished school, entered adulthood, pursued my career."

"You were preparing for the day."

"You make it sound more calculated than it was, Trapper. Unfairly. I didn't want my dad to die. But he did. And yes, by then I had press credentials and an excellent forum. I began reaching out to The Major."

He ruminated on all that, then said, "The name 'Bailey' wouldn't have meant anything to him. You never told him who you were or why you wanted to interview him?"

"He never gave me a chance to speak more than a few words before hanging up."

"You could have sent him an email. A letter."

"I wanted to introduce myself in person. Besides, how many correspondences has he received over time from women claiming to be the rescued little girl?"

"Good point."

"He would have thought I was just another

opportunist." She held up her hand palm out. "Don't say it."

"I won't. Too easy." The comeback had been as quick as all his were, but his dark brows were furrowed and there was no humor in his expression. "How many people know that you're that girl?"

"My aunt and uncle and me. You make four."

"If you go through with this, everybody will know."

"Oh, I'll go through with it, Trapper. With or without your help, I'll find a way to make it happen."

He swore under his breath and looked out the windshield again. He could have read the tow warning sign a hundred times during the amount of time he stared at it. She didn't break his concentration.

When at last he turned back to her, he said, "You'll have to do it without me."

"Trapper—"

"Sorry."

"I'm not giving up until I have a face-to-face with The Major."

"Up to you if you want to try, but I'm having no part of it." He slid on his sunglasses and started the car's engine. "I hope you take rejection well. The Major won't let you get your foot in the door before running you off. Have a nice life, Kerra."

She had thought that hearing about the bombing from the viewpoint of a five-year-old survivor would have softened him. There had been a few moments when she felt that she'd struck a human chord, snagged a sensitive thread in his caustic soul, but apparently not.

He wasn't even angry and edgy as he'd been last night. He was cool and indifferent. Further argument would only provide him more opportunities to be ornery and insulting, and she'd be damned before giving him that satisfaction.

"I wish I could say that it's been a pleasure, Mr. Trapper. But all you've been is crude, rude, and a waste of precious time. Thanks for nothing." She yanked the handle of the car door and pushed it open.

"One thing, though," he said.

She turned back. "What?"

"If I had it to do over, I'd kiss you like you wanted me to."

"Go to hell." She slammed the car door, crossed the street, and didn't look back.

She stormed through the entrance of her building and made a beeline for the resident concierge. The smiling young woman asked how she could be of service.

Kerra requested that her car be brought from the garage. "An hour from now."

"What'd you get?"

"What happened to 'Hello, how are you? I'm sorry for butting in on your honeymoon.'"

"I'm not in the best of moods, Carson, so cut the crap."

Trapper had watched Kerra jog across the street and disappear through the glassy entrance of her apartment building. He then drove away, but only covered a couple of blocks before pulling into an empty loading zone and punching in his friend's number.

Last night the favor he'd asked of Carson was to use every available resource to run a background check on Kerra Bailey.

"I didn't get anything you couldn't have gotten on your own," Carson complained.

"I've been busy."

"Like I haven't?"

"And I have to go through legal channels to get information."

"If you start nitpicking, then—"

"I repeat. What did you get?"

"I emailed it all about thirty minutes ago."

"Thanks, but I'm driving," Trapper lied. "Can you give me the bullet points?"

Carson huffed in exasperation but began. "When she was five years old, she was adopted by her aunt and uncle."

"Do you know what happened to her real parents?"

"Court records of the adoption were sealed."

The aunt and uncle truly had protected her identity and history. "Okay."

"Grew up middle class. Apple pie Americana. No scandal. Straight and narrow and boring, if you want to know the truth."

"Okay."

"She attended junior college in her home town in Virginia before transferring to Columbia."

"South Carolina?"

"No, Columbia University in New York. Graduated with a BA in journalism. She hopped around to various and sundry TV stations, never staying long at one before moving on, always to a larger market, till she landed this gig in Dallas early last year. Local network affiliate. She gets a lot of face time. Network uses her for regional stories that go national. There's a bunch of her stuff on YouTube."

Trapper didn't admit to having watched hours of it.

"I have her car tag and driver's license numbers."

"If they're in the email, I don't need them now."

Carson rumbled on. "She lives in downtown Dallas, one of those glassy condo buildings near Victory Park."

Trapper didn't tell Carson he'd just been there, but he did ask, "Alone?"

"The condo's in her name, and that's the only name

on the mailbox. I made up some gobbledygook and talked to the concierge of her building. No roommate since she's lived there. Let's see...what else? Oh, she was arrested once in Seattle."

"What for?"

"Protest march. There were numerous arrests. At her arraignment, she pled guilty, paid the fine."

"What was she protesting?"

"A colleague was jailed for contempt of court because he wouldn't reveal a source. She was guilty of passion for her profession and First Amendment rights, and that's as sinister as she gets, Trapper.

"She's square with the IRS. No debt other than her mortgage. Pays her bills on time. She's ambitious. She's got the goods. I gather an interview with The Major would be a real plum. End of story."

Like hell it is, Trapper thought. "Anything else?"

"Nothing noteworthy. Bits and pieces. You want details, they're in the email."

"Thanks, Carson."

"Can I get back to honeymooning now?"

"Just one more request."

Carson groaned.

Trapper said, "Do this and then you can screw yourself blind."

Chapter 4

Kerra brought her car to a stop within a few feet of the black SUV parked crosswise in the drive that led up to Major Franklin Trapper's house. She left the motor running as she got out and cautiously approached the driver's side of the truck.

Trapper, watching her through the side mirror, saw in her face the instant she recognized him as the person in the driver's seat. She marched the rest of the way, and when she came even with the door, knocked hard on the window.

He lowered it. "Hi."

"What are you doing here?"

"Testing you, to see if you meant it when you said you'd do this with or without my help. I didn't think you'd be that foolish, but since it appears that you are..." He hitched his head back toward her car. "Follow me."

She hesitated as though trying to decide whether to kill him, yell at him, or take advantage of his being here. She went with option three. She turned and stalked back to her car.

He waited until she was once again behind the wheel before dropping the SUV into forward gear and starting up the gravel drive.

The Major's ranch house sat on a rise surrounded by a grove of trees now bare of leaves except for the conifers. Constructed of limestone and timber, the house was one story with a steeply pitched roof. Square columns supported the overhang above the deep porch that ran the width of the house.

Trapper brought the SUV to a stop a short distance from the front steps and looked at each tall window along the porch. He was certain The Major was watching their approach through one of them, but he couldn't see him because of the glare.

Kerra joined him as he alighted from the SUV. "Whose truck is this?"

"I borrowed it from a buddy." Carson had come through on the second favor, setting Trapper up with a garage and body shop that would loan him a vehicle while his car was being repaired. Mounted on a monstrous set of off-road tires, the truck was tricked out with all the bells and whistles.

Kerra was gawking with appreciation at The Major's house and surrounding landscape. "Would you look at this?" she murmured.

"I've seen it. You ready?"

She tilted her head back and used her hand to shade her eyes against the western sun. "It pains me to say it, Trapper, but I'm glad you're with me. I've suddenly got stage fright. Thank you for coming."

"Don't thank me yet. He could still sic a pack of dogs on us."

"He has a pack of dogs?"

He smiled grimly. "I have no idea."

"When were you last here?"

"Few years."

"What's the quarrel between you?"

"You want to interview him or me?"

She shook her head in frustration and started up the steps ahead of him. Before she could knock on the front door it was pulled open, and there stood The Major.

Trapper could practically feel the sparks when his eyes clashed with his father's. Neither would have backed down or broken the hard stare had it not been for Kerra's intervention.

"Major Trapper?"

He looked down at her, then shocked both Trapper and her by smiling. "Hello, Kerra."

She actually fell back a step. "You know me?"

"Of course. Channel six. I enjoy your reporting."

"I'm flattered." She reached across the threshold
and shook hands with him. "Trapper was kind
enough to escort me here. May we come in?"

Trapper didn't call her on the fib. With only a
slight hesitation, and a glance at Trapper, The Major
backed away to allow them inside.

Kerra went ahead of Trapper. Under his breath, he
said to her, "You didn't need me to get you across his
threshold, after all. Seems he's a fan."

The Major motioned them toward the sofa. Kerra
sat. Trapper perched on the end of the upholstered
arm. The Major asked if they wanted something to
drink.

Trapper said, "No thanks."

At the same time, Kerra replied, "Maybe later."

The Major settled into his recliner. Wearing a
frown of slight disapproval, he took in Trapper from
head to toe, then asked, "How are you, John?"

"Good. You?"

"Can't complain."

After that, they had nothing to say to each other,
and even that amount of compulsory politeness had
been for Kerra's benefit. Trapper would have left
right then, except for his vital need to know how the
next few minutes panned out.

The Major was regarding Kerra with a halfhearted
scowl. "Are you the persistent young lady who's been
calling me these past months?"

"You've been just as persistent hanging up on me."

"Had I known it was you—"

"You wouldn't have hung up?"

"I would have," he said, "but I'd have been more courteous."

She laughed softly. "Well, no matter, I got the message that you didn't wish to speak to me. My only recourse was to seek out Trapper and request an audience with you."

The Major looked at Trapper. "Didn't you explain to her that I don't do interviews anymore?"

"About a dozen times."

"Then why'd you bring her?" He looked at Kerra and softened his expression. "Even though I'm delighted to meet you."

"Likewise."

Breaking up the mutual admiration–fest, Trapper said, "I tried talking her out of it. She wouldn't take no for an answer. Maybe she will from you. Tell her no, I'll see her on her way, and go have one of Del Rancho's chicken fried steak sandwiches. That might make it worth the trouble of having to drive up here."

With annoyance, The Major shifted his attention away from Trapper and back to Kerra. "I don't give interviews anymore."

She held steady. "This would be an extraordinary interview."

"They all say that."

She smiled. "But in this case, it's true."

"How so?"

She bent down, extracted a printout of the photograph from her bag, then got up and carried it over to The Major. "It would be a reunion."

"Reunion?" He took the photo from her but didn't look at it. He was looking up at Kerra waiting for an explanation.

She leaned down and pointed to the girl in the picture. "Look closely at her face."

Several minutes later Trapper left through the front door. Neither noticed his departure.

⸺◈⸺

Trapper drove to the drive-in restaurant that had been there for as long as he could remember. It had withstood the invasion of fast-food chains and still offered curb service. He ate in the truck and listened to country on the radio.

The sandwich wasn't famous for nothing. The battered, tenderized round steak was as big as a hubcap and extended beyond the edges of the bun. It was delicious, but every bite Trapper took went down with a lump of worry over what was happening back at The Major's place, what kind of persuasion Kerra was applying, and how easily, or not, The Major would yield.

When he finished his meal, he drove toward the interstate to start his trip back to Fort Worth, but when he reached a crossroads, literally, he stopped and took out his phone. The number was in his contacts.

The call was answered by a female voice made husky by too many years of Marlboros. "Sheriff's office."

Trapper asked to speak to the head man himself but was told that Sheriff Addison had already left for the day. "Do you want his voice mail?"

"No thanks."

Trapper clicked off and sat staring through the windshield at the rural landscape, now tinted with the lavender of dusk. A small herd of beef cattle dotted the pasture to his right. On his left, dead winter grass bent to the strong north wind.

Mentally he listed all the reasons why he should drive on and take the next entrance ramp onto eastbound I-20. He could be home in time to crack a beer just before the Mavs tipped off.

Ultimately, swearing at himself for being a damn fool, he took his foot off the brake and made a left turn onto a rural road.

A few minutes later he topped a hill, and the Addisons' house came into view. There was a light on in every room, and the house was surrounded by parked cars and pickup trucks. Trapper immediately changed his mind about calling on The Major's long-time best friend.

He was in the process of making a three-point turn when an adolescent girl broke away from a group of kids kicking around a soccer ball in the front yard. She jogged toward him, waving her skinny arms as she directed him to pull the SUV into the dry ditch. Trapper did as directed and lowered the driver's window.

She landed against the door, breathless. "I'm supposed to tell latecomers to park along the road."

She had crazy red hair, redder cheeks, and a mouthful of braces. Trapper fell in love. "Latecomers to what?"

"The Bible study. Isn't that what you're here for?"

Trapper turned off the motor and climbed down. "What do you think?"

She looked him up and down, then grinned and said, "IDTS."

"What's that?"

"I don't think so."

He laughed. "Smart guess."

"You're John Trapper, aren't you?"

"How'd you know?"

"Everybody knows. You're the black sheep."

So, the townsfolk of Lodal talked among themselves about The Major's wayward son. He wondered if they used coded language in front of the children. But the children now had a coded language all their own.

"I'm Tracy," the girl said.

"Pleased to meet you, Tracy."

"You have. When I was about six. It was Thanksgiving. You, The Major, and your mom were here visiting. I got my foot stuck in the commode. You worked it free."

"That was you?"

"Yep," she said with pride.

"I never knew why you put your foot in the commode."

She raised her bony shoulders in a shrug. "I never knew why, either."

Trapper couldn't help but laugh again. "The sheriff at home?"

She glanced toward the house, then came back around and leaned in to speak low. "The front rooms are overflowing with deacons and church ladies learning about Job. But the sheriff's in the kitchen drinking beer."

It wasn't beer, it was Jack Daniel's. Glenn Addison was pouring a shot into a cup of black coffee when Trapper, who hadn't bothered to knock, came through the mudroom into the kitchen.

Astonished to see him, Glenn nearly knocked over his chair as he stood up, rounded the table, and clasped Trapper in a bear hug. "Son of a bitch," he said, thumping him on the back. "What are you doing here?"

"Well, not for a lesson on Job. Hank leading the Bible study?"

"Don't you know it." Glenn shook his head with bewilderment. "Where'd I go wrong?"

"Not a bad thing, having a preacher in the family."

"No, it's a good thing. Just wish it wasn't my family."

Trapper motioned toward the spiked cup of coffee. "I don't think that's going to fool anybody."

"Like I give a flying you-know-what. This is my house, and I'm the law around here, so I'll have me some sour mash, thank you. Pour yourself one."

"No thanks. I've gotta drive back to Fort Worth."

Glenn and The Major had been boyhood friends, had gone through twelve grades virtually inseparable, then had roomed together for four years at A & M. Out of college, The Major joined the army. Glenn returned to their hometown, ran for sheriff and won. He'd held the office ever since, usually running for reelection unopposed.

"The faithful have outdone the dessert buffet at Golden Corral," he said, indicating the array of Tupperware containers on the countertop. "Help yourself. Those brownies are good. Linda made them."

"How's she?" Trapper asked of the sheriff's wife.

"Goes to the gym now. Zumba classes. Tries to get me there."

"No luck?"

"Wouldn't be caught dead." The older man eyed him up and down. "You could use a shave. And a haircut. Boot shine wouldn't hurt. Have those blue jeans ever met an iron?"

"No, and they never will."

"You got a girl yet?"

"Had one Saturday night."

The sheriff frowned with disapproval. "You need a wife, kids."

"Like I need leprosy."

"The Major would like some grandkids."

He tossed the statement out there like a gauntlet. Trapper let it lie for a beat or two, then said, "Not by me."

"I think you're wrong."

Trapper shrugged with feigned indifference. "Doesn't matter. I'm not making babies."

"You didn't come to town bearing an olive branch, then."

"No. I bore something a little more... troublesome."

Glenn's gray eyebrows wrinkled. "To who?"

"To you, Sheriff Addison."

Glenn picked up the whiskey bottle and held it tilted above his cup. "Am I gonna need another hit of this?"

"'Fraid so."

The sheriff poured a generous portion into his coffee cup and took a swig. "What's going on?"

"You ever heard of Kerra Bailey?"

"The girl on TV?"

"How is it everybody has heard of her but me?" Trapper muttered. But he knew why. Except for ESPN, he avoided most television programming. He avoided news in particular, half afraid of what might be on it one of these nights.

"So what about her?" Glenn asked.

"She wants to interview The Major."

Glenn listened with mounting interest as Trapper described to him Kerra's unheralded visit to his office. "I was hung over as hell. She sobered me up real quick by asking would I help her get through to The Major. I had a good laugh, then told her no. Hell, no."

"But here you are."

He skipped telling Glenn about their dinner date but told him they'd met again that morning. "She told me she wasn't going to stop until she had a face-to-face with him. I wished her a good life and washed my hands of it."

Glenn burped whiskey fumes. "I say again, but here you are."

"I was afraid she'd do something stupid, in which case, the blame would probably come back to me. Hoping to head that off, I got here before she did and walked her to his door. Far as I'm concerned, I've done my part. I'm clear. The lady is now on her own."

"Well, good luck to her," Glenn said. "Since he retired, he's turned down every request. Big names, even."

"Kerra Bailey might break him. He greeted her as a fan."

"He was a fan of Oprah, too. He turned her down."

Trapper wasn't going to tell Glenn what made Kerra exceptional. That was her secret to reveal. But he'd seen the immediate effect that learning her identity had had on The Major. He'd looked at her in wonder. She'd extended him the long overdue thank-you for saving her life. They'd clasped hands and had been absorbed in cozy conversation when Trapper left unnoticed.

"When would this hoped-for interview take place?" Glenn asked.

"This Sunday evening."

"*This* this Sunday?" Glenn counted up the days, then flopped back against the slats of his chair. "The anniversary of the bombing."

Trapper gave him a somber nod. "She went gaga over the house and setting, so I predict she may be planning to broadcast from there, not from a studio in Dallas. That's why I stopped by tonight. If The Major consents to do it, your town, the whole damn county, will be overrun. This is a heads-up. Brace for the worst."

Glenn groaned.

No doubt he realized the tactical implications of such an event taking place. And he still didn't know the half of it. If Kerra had her way and she got to drop her bombshell on Sunday night, there would be an eruption of renewed interest in Lodal's favorite son. Keeping the chaos under control would fall to Glenn Addison and his department.

That wasn't at the heart of Trapper's worry, though. His concerns were much more ominous than potential traffic jams.

Glenn looked at him glumly. "It may not happen. The Major may send her packing."

"We can hope." Trapper stood up. "I need to start back."

"Before saying hello?" He hitched his thumb over his shoulder to indicate the living area where a sonorous voice could be heard praying.

"Pass along my apologies to the family."

Glenn leaned heavily on the edge of the table as he came unsteadily to his feet. "I appreciate the warning, Trapper." He hesitated, then said, "Mind me asking what his reaction was to seeing you on his doorstep?"

"Civil but stilted."

"If the girl hadn't been there, it might have been colder."

"If the girl hadn't been there, I wouldn't have been on his doorstep."

"When did you and The Major last speak?"

"The week I left the bureau."

"Tore him up, John, that you were kicked out."

"I *quit*."

"Before they could kick you out. He never said, but I think that's why he went hermit on us."

"Yeah. I tarnished his hero's image. Dulled his halo something awful."

"Don't say things like that. The Major—"

"Go easy on that whiskey."

"Trapper, he—"

"Great seeing you, Glenn." He left.

It had become full dark while he was inside, but as he skirted the yard, he managed to get Tracy's attention and signaled her to meet him at the SUV. When she reached him, she danced a little jig. "I just scored a goal."

Trapper fist-bumped her. "Can I ask a favor?"

"Sure. I owe you for the toilet thing."

"Go inside and whisper to Hank that he needs to check on his dad."

"How come?"

"He's getting shit-faced."

She shot him a grin. "I can do that."

"Be discreet. I don't want anybody embarrassed."

"Got it. You can count on me."

"You know what, Tracy?"

"What?"

"I think I want to marry you."

The metal on her teeth flashed when she smiled. "You're as wicked as they say." Then she fist-bumped him again before dashing off.

As Trapper drove away, he thought how badly he hated tattling on Glenn, the man he'd known since birth, who'd always treated him like a second son.

Because of their shared vocations in law enforcement, Glenn had more in common with Trapper than with Hank, who was idealistic and optimistic, always finding the good in people and situations, never probing gray areas because to people like Hank gray areas didn't exist.

Trapper had no faith in goodness and light. People and institutions were fallible and undependable. Fate was a cruel bastard. If a situation turned out all right, Trapper figured he'd simply gotten lucky, but his tendency was to expect calamity. As he did now.

Chapter 5

Y ou're going to love it!" Kerra said. "It's perfect."

"I'm envisioning Southfork."

"No, more low-slung. Ranchy. Not as formal. His living room has a cathedral ceiling, exposed beams, and a natural stone fireplace that I could stand up in. I want to shoot the interview in that room with him seated in his leather recliner."

Too excited to sit still as she described The Major's house to her producer, Gracie Lambert, Kerra paced the narrow space between the motel room bed and the bureau.

"Keep talking," Gracie said. "I'm taking notes. What's he like?"

"Exactly the way you'd expect. Strong but humble. Kind eyes. He's been on camera so much, he won't need any coaching for that, but he and I are having a couple of getting-acquainted sessions. Come Sunday night, we'll be at ease with each other. The first chitchat is tomorrow morning. I offered to bring doughnuts."

"Doughnuts, chitchat, when no one else has been able to get near him for years."

Gracie didn't do giddy, but she was close to getting there tonight. Kerra couldn't help but feel a little giddy herself.

"I can't believe you pulled it off," Gracie enthused. "How did you manage?"

The reminder of Trapper brought Kerra down from her near-high. She would have succeeded without his help, she supposed. But it wouldn't have been as...interesting. However, she saw no reason to tell Gracie about him. He was a story for another day. Or better yet, never.

In reply to the producer's question, she said simply, "I kept on keeping on."

"Or waved a magic wand."

Identifying herself in the photograph had worked as a magic wand to break down The Major's barriers. He had held himself together. There'd been no tears of joy or even a drawn-out hug. But his voice had become unsteady with emotion.

Gracie, however, would go off like a skyrocket when she was told, which is why Kerra had decided not to break it to her until the final few hours before the interview. The production crew would need some advance notice so they could set up their camera angles for maximum impact when it was televised, but they would learn her secret only shortly before a vast viewing audience did.

"What's the name of the motel?" Gracie followed the question by mumbling, "I can't believe that word is even in my vocabulary, much less that I said it out loud."

Kerra laughed. "It's not The Mansion, but not too bad."

"Indoor plumbing?"

"Only in the executive suites," Kerra teased.

"I'll start assembling a crew tonight," Gracie said, "but when I tell the news director what I want them for, he'll green-light every request. That is, he will after his heart attack, which he's sure to have. I'll try to have us up there by tomorrow night. Thursday midday at the latest."

Kerra said, "In the meantime I'll be busy. The Major—" A knock on the door interrupted her. "Oh, hold on, Gracie. My pizza's here." She pressed the phone against her chest and pulled open the door.

It wasn't her pizza.

She'd never had a pizza delivery man standing with his hands braced high on the jamb, leaning in, filling up the entire opening and looking ready to go to war.

"I'll call you back." Before Gracie could object, she disconnected and silenced her phone. "I thought you were the pizza man."

Trapper's frown grew sterner. "You opened the door without checking?"

"I wasn't expecting anybody but him. I certainly wasn't expecting you."

"Bad things happen when you least expect them."

"How did you know I was here?"

"I called your apartment building to see if you were back yet."

"They wouldn't tell you that."

"The concierge would if you'd flirted with her and confided that you and I had a thing going."

"We don't have a thing going."

"Right, but she'd seen us this morning sitting to-gether in my car for—what? Half an hour? When we said goodbye, she hadn't heard you tell me to go to hell."

"Which you deserved."

"You're right. I did. I said the thing about kissing only to provoke you."

"It worked."

At that, his stern expression relaxed. He almost smiled.

But still provoked, Kerra placed her hand on her hip, as if that stance would block him from entering the room if he was of a mind to. "What happened to you?" she asked. "You disappeared."

"How long did it take you to notice?"

"I didn't," she lied. "The Major did," she lied again.

Trapper seemed to know it. He gave a cynical snuffle. "Whatever. It didn't look like you were returning to Fort Worth tonight, and choices of places to stay in Lodal are limited. This was the second place I checked, spotted your car in the parking lot, and had the desk clerk confirm that you had checked in."

"He gave you my room number?"

"I'm a licensed PI, don't forget."

"That got you my room number?"

"That and a five-dollar bill."

"Does anyone ever say no to you?"

He looked rueful and amused at the same time. "Yes. The people who really count."

She didn't know how to respond to that.

He looked beyond her, his gaze lighting on her open suitcase on the bed, her laptop being charged on the table, her personal belongings already on the dresser. "You came prepared to stay."

"I was optimistic enough to pack a bag and bring it with me."

"Must've gone well with The Major," he said.

"Otherwise you wouldn't be here and all . . . " His eyes scaled downward from her messy topknot all the way to her fuzzy slippers, taking in the flannel pajamas in between. "Settled in."

She told herself that his languid survey had nothing to do with her folding her arms across her chest. "It went exceptionally well. That was my producer I was talking to on the phone. We do the interview live on Sunday evening from The Major's house."

"Can't get any chummier than that. Congratulations."

"Thank you."

Then for several moments they just looked at each other. Finally, she said, "If you'll excuse me, cold air is getting in."

"Sorry." But rather than let her close the door on him as she'd intended, he shouldered past her and came into the room.

"Trapper—"

"Is he looking forward to it?"

Her mind had to backtrack to pick up the thread of their conversation. "The Major? Yes. He is. Surprisingly." She told him about the preliminary meetings they'd scheduled. "He promised to cook me his famous chili."

"That alone ought to send you back to Dallas."

She laughed, asking, "Is it that bad?"

He nodded, but she wasn't sure he was paying

attention. Since coming into the room, he'd been prowling it. He'd peeked into the bathroom, slid the closet door open and shut, looked down into the rumpled contents of her open suitcase. Some articles she'd rather him not see, and those were the ones he seemed most interested in. She went over and flipped down the top of the suitcase.

"I need to finish unpacking, and my food will be here any minute, so—"

She was about to evict him, but the words got stoppered when he went over to the table near the window and opened her laptop. He looked at the screen, then over at her, then turned the laptop around where she could see what was on it, although she already knew: a newspaper article about him with an accompanying picture.

He cocked his eyebrow.

She said, "I was doing research for the interview."

"You're not interviewing me."

"But you're part of—"

"Nothing. Leave me out of it."

"Relax, Trapper. You don't have anything to worry about. The Major stipulated that his family is off limits. I was doing that"—she motioned toward the laptop—"strictly for background."

"Why didn't you just ask me what you wanted to know?"

"Because you wouldn't tell me."

"Depends on what you ask. Give it a shot."

"All right. Tell me about your mother."

"Name, Debra Jane. Date of birth—"

"I already know all that. Tell me what she was like."

"Didn't The Major cover that with you?"

"Some. Enough so that I got a sense of her personality. Is there anything you can contribute without getting your back up and looking for ulterior motives beyond my curiosity?"

He thought it over, then said, "She was a great lady. She didn't sign on to be a celebrity's wife, but when the role was thrust on her, she accepted it. Growing up, I was a handful and—"

"I can imagine."

"—her husband was deployed twice overseas. One year in Kuwait during the Gulf War. When his tour was over and he retired from the army, she was grateful to have him home and out of military life. And then the Pegasus happened."

He shrugged, but Kerra wasn't convinced of the indifference it was meant to convey.

He said, "I suppose being an army wife had prepared her for being left alone a lot of the time to handle house and home and me by herself."

"That's almost word for word what The Major said about her."

"God help me if I start sounding like him."

"No chance of that. The Major doesn't bite my head off when I ask a question he doesn't like. He courteously told me ahead of time the topics I'm to avoid."

"Me and what else?"

"Hunting."

"Hunting?"

"I asked if he would consider removing the mounted trophies from his walls before the interview, and he said, 'Hell, no.' There are several subjects on which he and I have agreed to disagree."

Sardonically, he repeated, "Me and what else?"

"Actually he and I are in total agreement about you. You're sarcastic, defensive, and hostile."

"You left out wicked."

"I wouldn't go so far as to call you wicked."

"Somebody already did."

"Who?"

"A cute redhead."

"When?"

"Tonight."

"Oh," she said, feeling a dart of resentment. "What had you done?"

"Told her I wanted to marry her."

Kerra laughed, although she halfway believed him, and his grin—which was decidedly wicked—said he knew that, too.

There was a knock on her door. This time she did

check the peephole, and it was her pizza delivery. She paid the young man, closed the door against the wind, and nudged her laptop aside to allow room on the table for the box, from which heavenly aromas were wafting. "Want some?"

"No thanks. I'll go and leave you to it."

But rather than move toward the door, he went to the nightstand and bent over it. She couldn't help but notice the ragged hole in the rear pocket of his jeans or the way the leather jacket stretched across his shoulders.

Using the stubby pencil provided by the motel, he scrawled something on the notepad beside the telephone. When he finished, he tore off the sheet and brought it over to her. She read, "Sheriff Glenn Addison." He'd written a phone number under the name.

"The Major's friend for life and all-around good guy," he said. "After leaving The Major's place, I went to see him, told him about you and the interview." He held up a hand when she was about to interrupt. "I didn't tell him everything. If he learns who you are in the context of the bombing, he'll hear it from The Major, not me."

"Initially you were certain The Major would turn me down, yet you went straight to the sheriff as though the interview were a sure thing."

"At that point, it was. The photo made all the difference. I saw his reaction to it. His ego wouldn't let him pass up the opportunity to be a hero."

"He's already a hero."

"But now he's the man who saved Kerra Bailey, TV personality. Anyhow, I felt the sheriff should be alerted to the arrival of a TV crew and the excitement that will generate. Lodal is the county seat but basically a small town."

She'd been in the area for only a few hours, but already she'd gotten a sense of place. The town and surrounding ranch land were far removed from the metropolitan sprawl of Dallas and Fort Worth, not only geographically but in atmosphere and mind-set.

"I'm afraid our presence will create a stir," she admitted.

"News of the interview will spread like wildfire. By noon tomorrow everybody will know. Put the sheriff's number in your phone, so you can call him immediately if you need him."

She laughed. "I doubt there'll be *that* much of a stir."

"I'm not joking, Kerra. Put Glenn's number on speed dial."

Mystified, but subdued by his no-nonsense tone, she promised she would.

He looked like he had more to say, but he glanced at the pizza box. "It's getting cold."

She followed him to the door. "Will you be watching Sunday night?"

"No."

He hadn't given it a moment's consideration, which was unsurprising but disappointing. Feeling awkward and illogically deflated, she said, "I guess this is goodbye, Trapper."

"Guess so."

"Drive safely."

"I'm stone sober. Parking meters can rest easy tonight."

She gave a quick smile and stuck out her hand to shake with him. "For any inconvenience I've caused you, I apologize. I know I was an unwelcome and unexpected intrusion into your life." Then, quoting him, she said, "Bad things happen when you least expect them."

"So do good things." The low pitch of his voice caused heat to blossom in her middle. Rather than shake her hand, his right one curved around the back of her neck and pulled her up until she was on tiptoe. "What I said about kissing you..."

"If you had it to do over?"

"Happens I do."

Her mouth was stamped with all things wonderfully masculine: the agreeable prickliness of scruff, the sureness of lips that knew what they wanted and how to get it, the deft and possessive slide of tongue.

All too soon it was over. He set her away from him but kept his hand clamped around the back of her neck for a few seconds longer, his eyes searching hers.

Then Kerra was struck with a blast of cold air, and he was gone.

Chapter 6

The present

Jesus, who'd've believed it? Only a few hours after that interview, now she looks like she's been run over by a tank, and The Major..."

The whispered words drifted toward Kerra through the fog of semiconsciousness, and she resented the intrusion. She preferred being wrapped in the warm cocoon of oblivion.

The voice continued with a question. "Have you seen him?"

"They wouldn't let me in yet."

"Just as well. He looks bad. I won't shit you."

"Thanks for calling me when you did, Glenn."

"Soon as I got out there, saw the mess. God, it was awful."

"I know it couldn't have been easy for you."

Kerra wanted them to stop talking. She'd been kept in what the medical staff had called a twilight state. She'd been able to respond as they'd assessed and treated her injuries: *Kerra, can you lift your arm? Does this hurt? This may sting a little. Lie still so we can get a good image.*

After what had seemed like hours of torture, she'd been left alone and allowed to sleep. But now wakefulness was encroaching, and she didn't welcome it. She was reluctant to return to the bright, cruel place where horrible memories lay in wait.

But avoidance was cowardly. She pried open her eyes.

Two men stood at the foot of her bed.

The one in uniform was Sheriff Addison. The two times she'd met him this week, he'd been wearing the cowboy hat he was now holding at his side.

Beside him was Trapper, looking directly at her with eyes as piercing and incisive as laser beams.

The sheriff was saying, "After the interview, she'd stayed behind while the rest of them went to fuel up their van. According to her producer, Kerra wanted to say a private goodbye to The Major and thank him for giving her the 'holy grail of interviews.' That's a quote." After a pause, he said, "John, when you came to my house the other night, did you know she was the kid in the picture?"

"Yes."

"Why didn't you tell me?"

"Wasn't my secret to divulge."

The sheriff sighed heavily. "I guess Kerra and The Major didn't want to spoil the surprise."

Trapper said darkly, "They got their surprise, all right."

Kerra's heart constricted. It hadn't been a nightmare, then. The Major was dead, and she'd heard the gunshot that had killed him. She closed her eyes again and wished she could will herself back into the dusky bliss of forgetfulness.

But the disruptive recital continued.

"When the crew came back for her, they found The Major lying across the threshold of his front door. Called 911. First responders told me that when they got there, those people were huddled in their van, freaking out. Not only had they seen what nobody should ever have to see, but for all they knew the killer was lurking around, and they were scared for their friend here, who was nowhere to be found.

"Meanwhile, I was working late at the office catching up on paperwork. A deputy tapped on the door and told me there was an emergency situation out at The Major's place. I asked him the nature of the emergency, and he said he didn't know. But he did, because he couldn't look me in the eye.

"As I walked through the squad room, somebody, I don't even remember who, tried to waylay me, told me that our detectives were already on the scene and would handle things, that I didn't need to go. They said Hank had been notified and was on his way to me.

"But I needed to act, to do something, not hold hands in a prayer circle. I gotta tell you, though, when I walked up the porch steps and saw The Major, the sight nearly brought me to my knees." He made a strangling sound and coughed.

Silently Kerra implored him to please stop there. She didn't want to hear this, didn't want to know.

But once he'd composed himself, he continued. "Dealing with that was tough enough, but along with it was the missing woman. That small bathroom in the hall? The lock was busted all to hell. The window was open. Ground outside showed scuff marks. We hoped she'd managed to get away, but truth is, we were expecting to find her body, because the bastards meant business. One of my deputies—"

"Hold on," Trapper said. "Bastards, plural?"

"We think there were at least two. The Major was shot with a nine-millimeter. But something bigger than a pistol had shattered the door lock. I'm thinking the stock of a shotgun, because it appeared that one took out the top of a tree and blasted a boulder. Probably fired from the bathroom window."

A silence ensued before the sheriff continued. "Kerra was finally spotted by one of my deputies. You know that drop-off behind the house that goes down to the creek bed? Looked like she went sailing right over the edge and didn't stop till she hit bottom, which is essentially a rock pile unless it's rained real hard. She was banged up, near to freezing, but alive." He paused for a few seconds. "She got lucky. Guess we did, too. We have a witness to whoever shot The Major."

Needing to disabuse him of that, Kerra opened her eyes and tried to focus on him. When he realized that she was awake and aware, he took a step closer to the foot of the bed. "Ms. Bailey. Do you know where you are?"

"Hospital."

"That's right. You recognize me?"

"Of course."

"And you've met Trapper here."

"Yes."

Trapper didn't move or speak.

"How long have I been here?"

"Few hours. It's going on four a.m. Monday." The sheriff's voice was gentle, but he got down to business. "Do you remember last evening? The TV interview and what happened after?"

Tears collected in her eyes, and she had difficulty swallowing. She managed to nod, but the head movement made her dizzy.

"Do you feel up to answering a few questions?"

"I'm still muzzy." All she felt like doing was closing her eyes and seeking oblivion, and that was very uncharacteristic of her. Struck by a frightening thought, she asked, "Do I have a brain injury?"

"Not that I've heard," the sheriff replied. "Nothing serious. You're just doped up," he said and gestured toward the IV. "You took quite a tumble and landed like a rag doll. You recall that?"

"Somebody came down on a rope."

"A fireman. We weren't sure until he got down there that you were still alive. We'd been searching for almost an hour, shouting your name."

As after the hotel bombing, memories of the previous night came back to her in snatches with wide gaps in between. Some were vivid, like how badly her shoulder had hurt, how cold she'd been, while others were foggier.

She remembered lying on her back on the hard ground, the fierce wind, sprinkles of cold rain. She recalled trying to respond to the people shouting her name, but she couldn't find the strength to raise her voice.

She'd also been afraid that if she signaled her whereabouts, it would seal her doom, that whoever had killed The Major would appear at the top of the ravine and finish her off from that vantage point.

She remembered fearing that she would die in one

manner or another, from internal injuries, exposure. Her mother had died catastrophically. Her father's death was all too recent. The longer she lay there, the greater the possibility she would die. Surely she wouldn't cheat death a second time.

She was so convinced of that, she became hysterical with relief and thankfulness when rescuers arrived. As they strapped her to a stretcher, she'd begged for repeated reassurance that she had survived. A consoling EMT had pushed a tranquilizing drug into her vein to stop her hysteria.

But now, she felt the scald of fresh tears. "I'm sorry, so sorry."

"You've got nothing to be sorry for," Sheriff Addison said.

Just then a man dressed in scrubs came through the door into the room. He looked surprised to see Trapper and the sheriff there. "What are you doing in here?"

Sheriff Addison replied, "I need to talk to the witness."

"Not now, sheriff. Who's he?"

"John Trapper."

"Oh, well…Sorry, Mr. Trapper." He glanced at Kerra before going back to them. "She'll be going in and out for a while yet. You couldn't trust anything she told you to be sequential, accurate, or thorough. It'll be at least several more hours before she's up to

being questioned. I'll have the deputy outside call
you when I feel she's ready."

"But—"

"With all due respect, gentlemen, I need to exam-
ine my patient." The doctor stood firm.

Glenn Addison didn't look happy about getting
the boot, but he bobbed his head toward her and said
good night, then used his hat to motion Trapper toward the door.

Trapper remained motionless, staring at her in that
silent and predatory way of his, then turned abruptly
and followed the sheriff out without uttering a word.
Kerra followed his exit until the door whispered
closed behind him. Had that cold and remote man
really kissed her? Or had she dreamed it?

"I'm sorry about that." The doctor moved to the
bedside, consulted her chart, then smiled at her
through a neatly clipped door-knocker, and introduced himself. "How are you feeling?"

"Was I shot?"

"No. No spinal cord injury, broken bones, or internal bleeding, which is just short of a miracle. You
were close to hypothermia, but the EMTs had you
back to normal temp by the time you got to the ER.
Your left shoulder was dislocated. I hope you don't
remember us popping it back in."

"No. Thank God."

"We sent the MRI to an ortho specialist, but

several of us here looked at it and didn't see any damage to the rotator. You have a hairline fracture on your left clavicle. Take it easy with that, no strenuous workouts for six weeks, and it'll heal on its own.

"You sustained a lot of scrapes and cuts, and we had to dig out some bits of rock and wood splinters. Most were superficial wounds, but one on your right thigh required two stitches. You're getting IV antibiotics to prevent infection. The worst of it, you took a whack on your head, which gave you a concussion. Is your vision blurry?"

"Yes."

"It's temporary. Do you know what month it is?"

"February."

"Nausea?"

"It comes and goes. As long as I'm lying still, it's okay."

"How's the pain?"

"Not pain, specifically. General soreness and discomfort all over. A headache."

"On a scale of one to ten?"

"Five."

"I'll keep the drip going," he said, making a notation on the chart. "Any questions?"

"How long will I be here?"

"Couple of days. Tomorrow, we'll get you up, see if you can make it to the bathroom on your own. Check your head again. I'd like a neurologist to look at the pictures. We'll know more once he gets back to us, but I think you'll be fine in a day or two."

"Do you know anything about my crew? Are they all okay?"

"Anxious about you. They've been camped out in the waiting room since you were brought in."

They'd been traumatized, too, and she knew their concern for her was sincere. But the thought of being swarmed, even by five well-meaning colleagues, was an overwhelming prospect. "Would you please send word out that I'm fine, but—"

"No visitors. I'll tell them myself. Doctor's orders. Best thing for you now is rest." He switched out the light above her bed. "This may not be the suitable time to say it, but I'm a fan."

"Thank you."

"I caught your interview with The Major. It was outstanding."

"Thank you."

He patted her knee, said, "See you tomorrow," and left.

She settled into a more comfortable position. She closed her eyes. But rather than finding comfort in the grogginess that had protected her earlier, panic overcame her with tsunami force.

She was back in the powder room, only a door between her and certain death. Powerless to move. The walls and ceiling closing in. Heartbeats loud against her eardrums.

Recognizing the panic for what it was, she covered her nose and mouth with her hands and willed herself to inhale deeply and exhale slowly. The concentrated breathing staved off hyperventilation. The resultant tingling in her hands and feet subsided.

But her heart continued to race. Her skin broke a terror-induced sweat.

She relived squeezing through the window and the blinding pain when her shoulder hit the ground. She felt the rush of bitter wind as she ran headlong into the dark chased by gun blasts, striking close. She felt again the earth giving way beneath her.

The falling sensation was so real it made her clutch at the sheet, clawing up handfuls of it in an attempt to stop her plummet. But she kept falling and landed hard enough to knock the wind out of her.

Gasping, her eyes popped open.

Trapper was standing at the side of the bed.

Her throat seized up so completely she couldn't make a sound. Not a peep. Not a scream. She wet her lips, or tried. Her mouth and tongue were dry and her breaths were coming hard and fast.

He picked up the lidded plastic cup of water that had been left for her on the nightstand, held it close to her mouth, and pressed the bendable straw between her lips.

She sipped, then again, then continued to. They didn't break eye contact until the cup was empty and he returned it to the nightstand.

"Thank you." Her voice was raspy in spite of the water.

"You're welcome."

"Where's the sheriff?"

"On his way home to catch a few hours' sleep."

"Did he send you back here?"

"No."

"Does he know you came back?"

"No."

"Why did you?"

"Coming from somebody who interviews people on TV, that's a dumb question."

He was a large, looming, rough-looking, rude presence, but not wholly unwelcome. With him here, who or what could harm her?

She had thought never to see him again. When she had allowed herself to fantasize about an occasion when they came eye to eye for the first time after that kiss, the setting was either rose-scented, rose-colored, and romantic, like a picnic beneath a cherry tree in full bloom, raining pink petals over them. Or the scene was hot and torrid and untamed, twisted bedsheets, naked skin, and sweaty sex.

Never would she have fantasized a tragic circumstance such as this.

He was wearing his standard uniform. His hair was windblown. His scruff was the same as when he'd beat a hasty retreat from her motel room on Tuesday night, but there were dark circles under his eyes as though he hadn't slept since then. He probably wouldn't be sleeping much for days to come.

"Trapper," she said with emotional huskiness, "I'm sorry."

"Like Glenn said, there's nothing for you to be sorry about."

"The nation lost a hero. You lost your father. I don't know how his murder could possibly be connected to the interview, but I feel—"

"Wait. Kerra. You think The Major's dead?"

She inhaled a swift breath.

"He's upstairs in ICU," he said. "Barely alive, but not dead. He has a head wound, worse than superficial, but better than fatal. But that may not matter because a nine-millimeter bullet blew a hole in his left lung. Collapsed like a burst balloon. Massive blood loss. Odds are that he won't make it, but for the present he's hanging on."

Tears of relief began coursing down her cheeks. "But he said...I heard him ask The Major how he liked being dead so far."

Trapper hooked his foot around the leg of a chair, pulled it nearer the bed, and sat down. He planted his elbows on his thighs, tented his hands, and held them against his chin as he studied her. "Who said that?"

"The man who shot him. He thought he'd killed him. So did I."

A tear slid from the outer corner of her eye and trickled toward her hairline. His eyes followed its path then held steady on her face, while her image of him was doubling and quadrupling, making her seasick.

"Tell me everything, Kerra. Talk me through it."

"I can't, Trapper. Not now. I'm dizzy. The doctor said I shouldn't have visitors."

"He didn't say it to me."

"*I'm* saying it to you."

Actually, she didn't want to be alone, but she also didn't want to be pressured to answer questions right now.

He said, "When I came in, you were having a panic attack."

"Yes."

"What brought it on?"

"Nothing specific. I was fully conscious for the first time. Alone and aware of being alone. I got frightened. It all came rushing back, and I . . ."

"Felt you were in mortal danger again?"

"Yes."

"Any flashbacks to the Pegasus bombing?"

"No. It was all about last night. I was in the

powder room again and fearing whoever was on the other side of the door." She thought back to the latch being shaken to test if it was locked. The soft, metallic rattling had been as menacing as that of an unseen diamondback.

Feeling the weight of Trapper's stare, she collected herself. "The panic has passed. I'm fine now."

He looked down at her hand. It was still gripping the sheet. She forced her fingers to relax and let go of the cloth.

"Did Glenn figure right?" he asked. "You escaped through the window?"

"That's when I dislocated my shoulder."

"What were you doing in the bathroom?"

"What one usually does in the bathroom."

"You weren't hiding?"

"Not at first."

"Not at first." His inflection was a prompt for her to elaborate. "You went to use the bathroom and...? Then what?"

"Trapper, please, I don't feel up to talking about it yet. It's too fresh. In a couple of days when I have some distance from it—"

"It will take more than a couple of days for you to gain distance from it, and I don't want distance from it. I want to hear it while it's fresh."

"But my recollections are all jumbled up."

"Did you put Glenn's number in your phone?"

"What?" Her mind was hazy with confusion, then she remembered. "Yes, I did."

"If you were in fear, why didn't you call him?"

Yes, why hadn't she? When she'd added the sheriff's number to her speed dial, she'd done it only to honor her promise to Trapper that she would. He had said, *I'm not joking.* But she hadn't taken the statement as a warning. Not until now. There were disturbing implications to that lurking just beyond her ability to reason them out. She couldn't identify and contemplate them until she had a clearer head.

She said, "I don't feel well. Besides, until I'm questioned by the authorities, I don't think I should talk about it to anyone."

"I'm not just anyone. The man clinging to life upstairs is my father."

"I know this is very personal for you, but there are proper police procedures to adhere to."

"Well, you're half right. There are proper police procedures, but they don't have to be adhered to. In fact, I'm not big on procedures in general, and proper ones in particular."

"Then we can all be glad that you're not investigating the case."

"What gave you that idea?" He stood up slowly, planted his fists on the edge of the mattress, and leaned over her. "Kerra, who did you see out there?"

"No one."

He continued to stare at her, his eyes hard, incisive, unmoved by her firm denial.

"*No one,*" she repeated. "I didn't see anything."

He stayed where he was for a ponderous length of time, then straightened up and headed for the door.

She struggled to lever herself into a half-sitting position. "Trapper, I swear I didn't. Don't you believe me?"

"Doesn't matter if I believe you. Only matters if they do."

"The police?"

"No, the men who were there."

Chapter 7

———⸬———

By the time I got over to the window, she was racing away from the house. You know how dark it can get out there. It was like she was swallowed by it." Petey Moss's knee was jiggling beneath the table on which were strewn the contents of Kerra Bailey's shoulder bag.

The man rifling through the articles pulled a plastic card from one of the slits in a flat wallet and flipped it onto the table. "Fitness club membership."

Petey looked relieved. "That explains it. Conditioning. No wonder she can run like a deer."

"I still don't see how she escaped you."

"Well, first, it took us off guard that she was there."

"But when you discovered that she was—"

"We—"

The other man held up his hand. "Start at the beginning."

Petey wet his lips. "Well, The Major came to the front door, opened it, and poked his head out. Didn't expect him to be carrying a rifle. Jenks was on his blind side. Hit him with the stock of the shotgun. Here." He touched his skull behind his right ear. "Major dropped. I shot him in the chest. He never felt it."

"He's feeling it now."

"What?"

"You didn't kill him."

Petey looked like he'd been struck between his eyes with a sledgehammer. "That's impossible."

"He's in county hospital, not the morgue. He's not dead. Neither is the woman, which means you failed on two counts." This was said calmly as the contents of a small pouch containing various cosmetic products were inspected item by item.

He opened a tube of lipstick, sniffed it, replaced the cap, and tossed it back onto the table. "His condition is critical. He probably won't survive. But we can't count on that. He may pull through."

Petey was looking like he might throw up.

"But actually, the woman is more of a worry than The Major. Her injuries aren't that serious. She's able to communicate, and communicating is what she does for a living. So, Petey, I need to know, and know *now*, if she saw you."

He shook his head vigorously. "No. She'd locked herself in the bathroom."

The man played with Kerra's key chain, his expression thoughtful. "How did you come to realize she was in the bathroom?"

"No sooner had I shot The Major, I noticed the light go out under the bathroom door. I went to check. Sure enough, the door was locked. By the time we'd busted it down, she'd gone out the window. Jenks fired at her, but she—"

"Was swallowed up by the darkness."

"That's right."

"Why didn't you chase her down?"

"No time to. We heard a car turning off the main road. Saw the headlights coming up the drive. We went out the back, but not before thinking to grab her bag there."

"Nobody saw you?"

"No, sir. I'd swear to it. She was too busy running for her life to look back, and the house was between us and whoever was approaching in that car."

"It was the TV crew's van. Five of them."

"They couldn't've seen us. Jenks had left his truck at least a half mile from the house. We found our way back to it in the dark. Near froze our balls off on that hike. Anyhow, we drove on back to town and shared a basket of ribs at the barbecue place on the square. Established an alibi, like you told us."

"Which will make no difference if The Major survives."

"No way he could. I'd lay money on that. They must be keeping him alive with machines."

"Kerra Bailey isn't hooked up to machines. Eventually she'll tell everything she knows." He dwelt on that for a moment as he absently jangled the key ring. Then he set it down and motioned for Petey to lean forward as he lowered his voice to a whisper. "I'm nervous, Petey."

"I swear she didn't see us."

"Not about her. About Jenks."

Petey flinched with surprise then threw a look over his shoulder toward the closed door that stood between them and the next room in which Jenks had been told to wait until it was his turn to give his version.

Coming back around, Petey asked in a hushed voice, "What about him?"

"When The Major came to the door, why didn't Jenks blast him with the shotgun?"

"Shocked him to see The Major with a rifle."

"Hmm. That concerns me. If Jenks is so easily rattled, he's unreliable."

"No, sir. Nerves of steel. He's as solid as the day is long. I'd swear to that."

"Your loyalty to him is admirable, Petey. But what about his loyalty to you? Are you willing to bet your life on it? This Bailey woman might not have seen you fire a bullet into an American hero's chest. But Jenks did."

Petey's eyes darted out and back, then up and down. He licked his lips again. He was thinking it over. "He's solid," he repeated, but with noticeably less conviction.

"In order to protect yourself, me, all of us, you know what you have to do."

Petey swallowed noisily. "Not sure what you're getting at."

"Yes you are." He let that rest for a second or two, then said, "Make sure you bury his body deep enough so scavengers can't get to it, or sink it in The Pit with enough weight that it'll never surface. Do you understand?"

Petey understood, all right. His forehead was beaded with sweat. He looked miserable. "When?"

"Now."

"It's coming up on daylight."

"Then you've got no time to waste, do you?"

Petey blinked several times. "Me and him have come to be good friends."

"I know. I also know you understand the gravity of your situation. You said The Major didn't see you. Either of you."

"No. Jenks clouted him before he could."

"And Kerra Bailey didn't."

Petey shook his head.

"Leaving only one person who remains a threat to you. To us. Harvey Jenks. Right?"

Petey nodded but looked on the verge of tears.

The other man reached across the table and gripped Petey's hand hard, like a general commending a volunteer, then motioned him up. "Ask him to come in now."

"How come?"

"It would look fishy if I didn't talk to him, too."

Petey shuffled to the door, opened it, and in a jocular voice that sounded close to normal, said, "Your turn."

For the next twenty minutes, Harvey Jenks was put through the same drill. His account was almost word for word identical to Petey's. "When we ran out of time to take care of her, I thought to grab her bag," he said of the disemboweled Louis Vuitton. "Too bad the fall didn't kill her."

"That is too bad. It's also too bad that The Major's heart is still beating."

Jenks reacted with a start, then rubbed the bridge of his nose as he processed it. "Petey shouldn't have got so trigger happy. Or he should've shot him twice. At least."

"Why didn't you shoot him as soon as he came to the door?"

"He had a rifle."

"So I've been told."

"He might've got off a shot or two, even if it was recoil. If we'd been hit, it would've left blood. Evidence. I disabled him by knocking him out."

"A shotgun blast to the head would have disabled him."

Jenks frowned his regret. "Hindsight."

The man pursed his lips as though thinking it over. "It was Petey's mistake. He should have made certain his shot was fatal. He didn't, and now we're in a fix. This isn't the first time he's messed up. He's excitable and likes to boast. Which makes him a risk we can no longer afford." He then leaned across the table, crooked his finger, and lowered his voice to a whisper.

Several minutes later, Jenks left the room, having been given the same order as his cohort had been issued a few minutes earlier. It would be interesting to see which of the two returned. Whoever did would have proven himself to be blindly obedient and absolutely ruthless.

The man sat back in his chair, fingered the adorned leather case of Kerra Bailey's cell phone. She had made that stunning revelation during the interview, no doubt counting on it to further her career.

Rather than to end her life.

Trapper checked into the motel where Kerra had been staying since Tuesday. Once settled into his room, he called Carson.

"These calls are getting old, Trapper," he growled. "If you need somebody to talk to in the middle of the night, why don't *you* get married."

"The Major's been shot."

After several seconds of silence, Carson blurted, "Gunshot?"

"He's alive, but only by a thread."

More silence, then, "You're not kidding."

"No."

"Jesus, man. This is unreal. My bride and me took a timeout to watch the interview."

"Happened a couple of hours after it."

"We shut off the TV and went to bed early."

He gave Carson a rundown of the chain of events. "I just left the hospital. She looks like Rocky, and he's critical."

"Swear to God, Trapper, I don't know what to say. You see the interview? They dropped quite a bombshell." After a beat, he groaned, "Oh hell, bad word choice."

"It's okay. It was a bombshell."

"Are you all right? I mean, you know, he's your dad and all."

"I'm all right."

"You're compartmentalizing."

Carson must've picked that up from Dr. Phil, but damn if it wasn't accurate.

"Are you gonna stay up there?"

"Yeah," Trapper said. "I need to be here. My car's still not ready, so I had to bring the loaner. If the body shop wants to tack on a few days' rental, I'll understand."

"Okay. I'll let the guy know. I'm sure he's cool with you keeping it for a while longer."

"Thanks."

"Does anybody know what happened? Any suspects?"

"The Major's friend is sheriff, remember. His department is investigating, but the Rangers and feds will probably join in."

"Just as well. You told me this sheriff and The Major are blood brothers. He can't be objective."

"What I told him."

"Especially if The Major doesn't make it."

"If he doesn't, Glenn said he would go caveman on whoever killed him."

"So would you."

Trapper didn't comment on that. "Listen, is the honeymoon over?"

"As of this phone call, yes," Carson said drily. "She's had it with you. But both of us are back to work in the morning anyway."

"It is morning. Almost five thirty. Local TV has

already issued bulletins about the shooting, but the story will start getting full coverage on the morning newscasts. Keep an eye out at the office. Anyone comes poking around, you let me know."

"There'll be media."

"Possibly someone will try sniffing me out there. But I'm not talking about media."

"Then what? Who?"

"Just keep an eye out and tell me if anyone suspicious-looking comes around."

"Besides my clientele, you mean."

"And dig deeper on Kerra Bailey."

"In my spare time?"

"I'll pay you, Carson. Put some of your former clients on it. The hackers. Identity thieves. Whatever you can get on her, I want. Immediately."

"It would help if I knew what you were looking for."

"I don't know."

"Still getting a vibe, huh?"

"Yeah. A bad one."

Terror jolted her awake.

Before Kerra remembered that her body was battered and bruised, she sat bolt upright. Pain shot through her head like a lightning bolt. The fracture in her clavicle made itself known. Her stomach heaved, and she retched into her lap.

Groping for the remote, she rang for a nurse, who took her sweet time responding while Kerra sat shivering in her sweat-soaked gown and clammy sheets.

When the nurse arrived, Kerra apologized for the mess. "I had a nightmare."

"I guess you did, honey. You're shaking like a leaf in a gale."

The nurse called for assistance, and within five minutes, Kerra's gown and bedding had been replaced. When alone again, she used the remote to switch the nightlight back on.

Although she was clean and dry, she continued to shiver so badly her teeth chattered.

In her nightmare, the aftermath of the bombing had been replaced by her isolation in the powder room. An aspect of that nightmare had catapulted her out of sleep and into awareness of something she'd forgotten: Someone had tried to open the powder room door before she heard the gunshot.

That fact had been tucked away in her subconscious. The nightmare had revealed it to her.

The doctor had explained to Sheriff Addison that any account she gave so soon after coming around would be questionable, the sequence of events possibly incorrect. Now she was glad she hadn't remembered that detail. Before telling anyone, she needed time to process what significance it had, if any.

But she *felt* it did.

Someone had tried to open the door *before* the gunshot. She had addressed The Major through the door and said, "I'll be right out." There had been no response. *Then* the gunshot.

Who had been trying to open that door?

Not The Major. He would have responded when she spoke to him, and, besides, why would he have tried the door, knowing that she was using the restroom? Not the would-be killers, who were in the front of the house.

Could an accomplice have been in the back rooms? Perhaps all along? Had he seen her go into the powder room?

Gooseflesh broke out on her arms as one name sprang to mind, the name of the individual who had returned tonight—without the sheriff—demanding to know whom she had seen "out there."

Trapper.

Chapter 8

———◦◦◦———

The sun was coming up by the time Trapper went to bed, and he slept with one ear attuned to his phone, fearing and half expecting a call from hospital staff. None came. He woke up a little after ten o'clock, efficiently showered and dressed, and grabbed a sausage biscuit at a drive-through on his way to the hospital.

When he stepped off the elevator on the ICU floor, he nearly collided with Hank Addison, Bible in hand.

"Oh," Trapper drawled. "You must be the lookout, posted to see if I'm respectable enough to be here."

Hank gave Trapper a disapproving once-over, frowning down at his scuffed boots. "If this is the best you can do…"

"Like I give a fuck."

Hank hadn't inherited much from his father's gene pool. He had a slighter, more compact build than Glenn. He was fair-haired and brown-eyed like his mother, Linda, and had her mild-mannered smile.

Because of the close friendship between their fathers, the two boys had spent a lot of time together during their developmental years. Trapper was the younger, but he'd been the instigator of the general mayhem they created during the vacations and holidays the families spent together. He devised their shenanigans and cajoled Hank into going along.

One saw traces of the mischief-maker in the pastor only on occasion, as now, when he laughed at Trapper's vulgarity. They shook hands then man-hugged, slapping each other on the back. "We held a prayer breakfast at the church this morning. We didn't pray nearly hard enough for you."

"Lost cause," Trapper said. "But I appreciate the thought. And I apologize for cutting out the other night before even saying hello."

"Not exactly your scene."

"Job still enduring trials and tribulations?"

"Sort of like you," Hank said, turning serious. "This is... I'm at a loss, Trapper."

"I know. Me too." He looked beyond Hank in the direction of the double doors that sealed off the ICU. "Have you seen him?"

"No. Only one person allowed in every couple of hours. I stayed with Dad in the waiting room until they came out to tell him he could go in."

"How is he this morning?"

"As shaken as I've ever seen him. Right now, he's caught up in the investigation, the hubbub. But if The Major dies, it's going to hit him hard. All of us. The nation."

Trapper nodded.

"How are you?" Hank asked.

"Stunned like everybody else. Hasn't quite soaked in yet."

"If the worst happens, it'll hit you hard, too. I'm available if you need someone to talk to."

"Thanks. I'll be okay."

Hank looked unconvinced, but let it drop and summoned the elevator. "I've got other church members to visit. The nurse told Dad he could stay for only a few minutes, so he should be out directly."

"Did he mention how Kerra Bailey is faring?"

"No, sorry. A shame about her, too."

"Yeah, it is."

When the elevator came, Hank boarded but stopped the door from closing. "Listen, don't let on that you know anything about Dad's rift with The Major. He hadn't backed down, and Dad was being just as pig-headed. They still weren't speaking right up till Dad got the news last night, which is one reason he—"

Hank stopped, having realized that he'd let the cat out of the bag. He put his hand to the back of his neck and looked down at the floor. "Oh, hell."

"The preacher caught cussing." Trapper *tsk*ed, then asked, "What was their rift over?"

"It was nothing. Really."

"You never could lie for shit, Hank."

The door was trying to close. "If Dad wants you to know he'll tell you. See you later." He lowered his hand and the door slid closed.

"Chickenshit," Trapper muttered.

He'd always had to twist Hank's arm before he would engage in any real fun like sneaking copies of *Playboy,* nipping from bottles of liquor when the grown-ups weren't around, shoplifting a tin of chewing tobacco from the convenience store. Hank had confessed to that particular misdeed before their parents were even aware that the petty crime had been committed. He'd cried and said over and over how sorry he was.

Not Trapper. He'd thought the adventure was well worth puking his guts up later.

The double doors to the ICU opened, and Glenn came through. He was in his uniform, which was as crisp as ever, but his gait wasn't his usual stride and his face was haggard. Seeing Trapper, he motioned for him to follow him into the waiting room. No one else was in there. They sat down in adjacent chairs.

"How is he?" Trapper asked.

Glenn set his cowboy hat over his knee. "Far as his chest, we can thank our lucky stars that the surgeon worked twenty-five years at a trauma center in Dallas. He was on call last night and knew what he was doing. Otherwise, The Major would already be dead."

"What about his head?"

"Cranium's got a depression this big." He made a circle with his thumb and finger. "His pupils were reactive when he was brought in and still are. That's good. Doctor says the main concern now is swelling of the brain. If it gets bad, they'll have to bore a hole in his skull."

Trapper dragged both hands down his face.

"The good news," Glenn continued, "is that his vitals are strong."

"Oh, that's great news," Trapper said. "He could be a vegetable, but he'll live a long life."

"He's got brain function. They just don't know how much yet."

A glum silence fell between them. Trapper broke it by saying, "I caught Hank on his way out."

"He said they had a capacity crowd at the prayer breakfast. Everybody turned out for The Major."

"What was your rift with him about?"

Taken off guard by the question, Glenn looked startled, then annoyed. "Damn Hank."

"He never could keep a secret. Always a tattletale."

Glenn sighed heavily. "John, now's not the time—"

"You don't call me John unless we're talking about something serious, and whatever this is was serious enough to cause a rift between you and The Major that hadn't been patched."

"Which is why it's tough to talk about. Later, when we know—"

"Not later. Now."

Glenn swore under his breath. "One of my CAP detectives has been diagnosed with prostate cancer. Looks bad. He's taking early retirement."

"Shit luck and sad story. What's it got to do with what we're talking about?"

"I've got to replace him. That division needs somebody younger and smarter than him, than *me*. You would be my first choice. I bounced the idea off The Major and . . . " He paused, took a breath, blew it out.

Trapper waited him out, although he could have filled in the blank any number of ways and captured the gist of what Glenn was reluctant to tell him.

"The Major gave me an ultimatum. I could have you living here and working for me."

"Or?" Trapper asked quietly.

"Or I could continue being his friend. Given that choice . . . " He raised his beefy shoulder. "There wasn't a choice. But I was still mad at him over it."

Glenn looked so shamefaced and sad that Trapper

took mercy and let him off the hook. "Don't beat yourself up, Glenn. I would've said no." Yet he thought wistfully, *Crimes Against Persons. Right up my alley.* But wrong time, and definitely wrong place.

"I figured," Glenn said. "But I was going to try. You're being wasted. Private investigator? Come on. Besides, I was hoping that getting you here would be the first step toward a reconciliation between the two of you."

"Not gonna happen, Glenn."

"Not overnight, but given time, maybe." Glenn regarded him for a moment. "When he went from being just Frank Trapper to the hero, things changed for you, too. He took to celebrity and ran with it. I felt sorry for Debra having to either follow in his wake or get left behind altogether. But I felt even sorrier for you. I can tell you that now."

"No boo-hoos for me, thank you."

"That's my point. You rode it out. Finished growing up without any serious missteps and turned out okay. Your life was on track, and things seemed to be fine between you and The Major. Till you left the ATF. Y'all had more than a falling out. It was a severance."

"As you said, it tore him up. He couldn't forgive my failure."

"What did you fail at? What were you working on?"

"That's classified, Glenn. I can't talk about it."

"Bullshit."

"Okay, I *won't* talk about it."

Glenn stared at him hard, not with a friend's or surrogate dad's eyes, but with those of a lawman seeking truth behind a lie. "Your quarrel with The Major was over you leaving the bureau. That's it?"

Trapper tried to keep his expression unreadable. "That's it."

Glenn still looked like he didn't believe him, but eventually he stood and put his hat on. "I'm gonna check in with the office. You staying?"

"Yeah, I'm gonna hang around until they let me see him."

Glenn placed a firm hand on Trapper's shoulder. "The hell of it is, you love him."

Trapper didn't say anything. Glenn nodded understanding, removed his hand, and left him.

When he was out of earshot, Trapper murmured, "That is the hell of it."

Kerra had hoped the dawn would bring some relief from the terrible night.

But the day began with the discovery that her shoulder bag had been misplaced and no one seemed to know what had happened to it.

Using the hospital phone on her nightstand, she called Gracie and explained the situation. An hour later, Gracie Lambert walked into her hospital room, carrying a shopping bag in each hand.

She was a familiar and welcome sight with her nimbus of salt-and-pepper hair and eyeglasses with bright orange frames. Her demeanor could be either maternal or martial, and she could switch between the two in a heartbeat, a skill that made her an excellent producer. This morning she was in motherly mode.

"God, it's good to see you," she said. "We've been so worried. The others wanted to come with me, but I didn't think you needed a mob scene."

"Not this morning," Kerra said. "But I appreciate their concern. Did you ask them about my bag?"

"Yes, and it was unanimous. After the interview was finished, we packed up all the gear and loaded it into the van. You kept your bag with you."

Kerra had known that to be the case, but she'd clung to the faint hope that she wasn't remembering correctly. Now, with the crew members' verification that she'd had the bag with her, she was both disturbed and desolate.

Gracie asked, "Are you sure the hospital staff hasn't stashed it somewhere?"

"Everything I had on me was collected in the ER and put into a plastic bag. The bag accompanied me to this room and was placed in the closet. I buzzed a nurse first thing this morning. My lips were dry, and I asked her to fetch the lip salve out of my makeup kit. No makeup kit, no shoulder bag. Everything else was there, even my ruined clothes and shoes."

"The police must have it."

"Two detectives from the sheriff's office were here earlier. They questioned me for an hour, until the doctor stopped by on his rounds and ran them out. They're coming back after lunch. In the meantime, they promised to check with the first responders, but they didn't hold out hope that my bag would turn up. They have a log of the evidence collected from The Major's house, and the only thing belonging to me is my coat, which was on a living room chair."

"No Louis Vuitton."

Kerra shook her head.

"It's not like that thing could be easily overlooked, either," Gracie said. "It's huge. How much cash were you carrying?"

"Not enough to cry over."

"Anything of real value?"

"The bag is more valuable than anything in it."

"At least you have this." Gracie passed Kerra her laptop. "You did leave it in the van while we were doing the interview. I gather you've got passwords stored for credit cards and such."

Kerra nodded absently. Canceling the cards would

be a tedious project, but far more worrisome was that if the perpetrators had her bag, they had access to her: personal things that she used every day, her calendar, phone, key ring, driver's license and all the information on it. In essence they'd have an open gateway into her *life*.

"Here's your new phone." Gracie handed her one of the shopping bags from a local supermarket. "Not as high tech as what you're used to, but it'll get you through the next few days. The number showed up in the LED, so I have it. Give it an hour or more to fully charge. I also picked up some toiletries."

"Thank you." Kerra placed the sacks aside, too upset over the missing shoulder bag to be distracted by either the new phone or personal hygiene.

"Have you talked to your aunt?"

"Twice." Kerra motioned toward the hospital telephone on the nightstand. "She offered to come down, but my uncle is recovering from a knee replacement. He needs her more than I do. I couldn't ask her to abandon him just to sit here and pat my hand. I assured her that I was surrounded by caring people and that I would be fine."

Gracie gave her a critical once-over and sat down on the corner of the bed. "Okay, enough with the brave face. How are you really? Pain meds not adequate? Or is it something in addition to your injuries that has you upset?"

Trapper. He upset her. The way he studied her without moving or speaking was upsetting. What was he looking for? It was upsetting to her that he'd come back without the sheriff's knowledge, demanding to know if she'd seen the assailants. Her chest grew tight with foreboding each time she remembered his parting words.

But she didn't want to share any of that with Gracie, who still didn't know that she'd been in contact—close contact—with The Major's son. The producer hadn't fully forgiven her for keeping it a secret until hours before the broadcast that she was the girl in the iconic photo. Of course Gracie had been elated over the new dimension it would give the interview. If she knew about Kerra's interaction with Trapper, she'd jump on it.

Kerra shuddered to think what his reaction would be to a media blitz with him as its topic.

In response to Gracie's question, she confessed to feeling overwhelmed. "I'm rarely daunted by anything, but this is my second life-threatening experience."

"That would give one pause."

"Not just that. I get ill when I think of what could have happened to you and the crew." She reached for the other woman's hand and squeezed. "If you had returned for me five minutes sooner, *one* minute sooner, and walked in on them, you could have all been killed."

"I won't kid you, we talked about that among ourselves. Last night I slept in Troy's room on the extra bed. Silly, but I didn't want to be by myself."

Remembering her panic attack and nightmare, Kerra said softly, "Not silly at all."

Gracie said, "We've given our statements and have been cleared to leave."

"So I was told."

The detectives had informed her that the five had been questioned separately. Their accounts were in such accord that they'd freed them to return to Dallas, but had stipulated that they could be subpoenaed later, depending on the progression of the investigation and resultant arrests and trials.

"What time are you leaving?"

Gracie repositioned her eyeglasses and took a deep, bolstering breath. "Our news director made me swear I'd ask you one more time."

Without hesitation, Kerra said, "No. I won't even consider giving an interview now. It would be insensitive, exploitative, and in the poorest possible taste."

"When has the media been sensitive? And the industry thrives on exploitation and poor taste."

"Well, I don't. I esteem The Major. He's fighting for his life. I'm not about to cash in on that."

In a leading tone, Gracie said, "You know he has a son."

Kerra gave a noncommittal nod. "The Major put him off limits."

"Well, The Major is currently comatose. This son is his only family, and in light of Sunday's interview, you have an inroad to him."

"Which I wouldn't dream of abusing."

"I told the news director you'd stick to your guns, but you know him. There's a Nielsen rating where his heart is supposed to be. Besides, this time he's only the mouthpiece. The request is coming from the network. It would be an extraordinary follow-up, Kerra."

"Whose side are you on?"

"Yours," the producer said. "But out-of-the-stratosphere ratings aside, it would be the honorable thing to do."

Kerra gave her a look. "This I've got to hear."

"Don't you owe it to the public to share what The Major said in those last few minutes with you? If he doesn't pull through, and it's looking like he won't, you'll have been the last person on earth who talked to him."

"It was a personal conversation, Gracie. He wasn't in his public persona, and neither was I. Nothing we said would enlighten or edify the 'public.'"

Gracie hesitated, then said, "Promise you won't throw a bedpan at me for saying this."

"But?"

"Are you sure you want to pass on this career leg-up? It's unprecedented. A journalist's fantasy scenario. Some might think you'd be crazy not to take advantage of it."

"Some? What do *you* think?"

"You've been traumatized. You're still reeling from it. Today you're battered and bruised and grateful merely to be alive. But in a week, you'll be recovered, back in the swing of things, business as usual. This could launch you straight to the network, but if you don't seize the opportunity, it's unlikely you'll get another."

"That sounds almost like a warning."

"Not a warning, honey. A reality. I'm just telling it like it is. You can't be squeamish or nice and become a star in this industry."

Suddenly overcome with exhaustion, Kerra laid her head on the pillow and stared up at the ceiling.

Gracie patted her hand before releasing it. "The crew and I have checked back into the motel. The station sent another reporter to cover updates on The Major's condition and the pomp and circumstance of the funeral if he dies. But we're standing by, waiting on a call from *you*, ready to roll whenever you are. Think it over."

Kerra did little else for the rest of the day except for the time spent being questioned by the sheriff's office detectives.

In late afternoon she was brought a dinner tray, but the food was unappetizing, and she wasn't hungry anyway.

She watched the evening network news. Being the subject of the story rather than the reporter gave her a far different perspective. She felt a surge of compassion for all the individuals she had placed in the spotlight while they were in the vortex of a life crisis.

The Dallas–Fort Worth stations covered the story even more extensively, some recapping the Pegasus Hotel bombing. A spokesperson for the sheriff's office assured that the attempted assassins would be identified, captured, and brought to justice. Several reports were broadcast live from outside the hospital, where a candlelight vigil was being held for The Major.

The evening wore on until it neared what she considered to be bedtime.

She'd been given a sponge bath that morning in her hospital bed, but she went into the bathroom to give herself another using the toiletries Gracie had brought her. She cleaned her teeth and brushed her hair.

The harsh bathroom light was unforgiving. She had countless scratches, abrasions, and bruises all over, including her face. A large bruise extended down from the corner of her mouth to beneath her chin, as though she'd taken an uppercut to the jaw.

Another spread upward from her eyebrow and into her hairline. Both were tender to the touch, and she could count on days of discoloration. But the damage was minimal considering what it could've been.

She could be dead.

She pulled on a pair of plain white socks and a fresh hospital gown, tying it at the neck. She switched out the light and opened the door, but drew up short on the threshold.

Trapper was here.

Chapter 9

⟞⟐⟝

Her heart tripped, but she couldn't have specified why. Fear? Or something entirely different?

However, exhibiting anything except annoyance would be a mistake. "Why do you feel at liberty to keep sneaking into my room?"

"Only twice now."

"Kindly leave."

"I don't do anything kindly."

"That I can certify."

He eyed her up and down, making her uncomfortably aware of how short and insubstantial the hospital gown was and also of how defenseless she was. "Are you going to leave or force me to create a scene?"

"Tonight's deputy on guard? He—"

"I have a guard?" She shot a glance toward the door.

"Yes, Kerra, you have a guard." He said it as though he couldn't fathom her not knowing that or grasping the necessity of it. "He's Sheriff Addison's man and knows how thick Glenn and I are, didn't even question me coming in, so I doubt he'll kick me out." He gestured toward her. "No more IV."

The sudden switch in topics threw her for a moment, then she followed his gaze down to her right hand. A bandage covered the spot where the shunt had been. "They took it out this afternoon."

"Then you must be doing okay."

"Okay" was going to take more than a single day, but she pretended to agree. "Have you seen The Major?"

"Twice today."

"And?"

"No better, but no worse. Holding steady. Which at this point is good."

"That's what was reported on the evening news. I'm happy to have it confirmed."

"The weather has taken a turn. It started sleeting about an hour ago."

"The nurses have been talking about it. They're worried about getting home after their shifts. But I'm told the weather hasn't kept the media away."

"No, they're here. Like vultures circling a wounded animal, waiting for it to die."

"That's a distressing analogy."

"But fitting."

She had to agree and guiltily acknowledged that if she weren't inside here, she would be out there competing with her colleagues for a scoop. "Did you have any trouble getting past the throng?"

"No, I have an avoidance technique."

"Which is?"

"I tell them to fuck off."

"You didn't tell me that."

He was about to say something but changed his mind, disappointing her. She would have liked knowing what it was. Instead he asked how much longer she would remain in the hospital.

"Barring any setbacks, I'll be released tomorrow."

"Hmm. You still look puny, though. Here." He rolled aside the table bridging the bed and motioned her toward it. "Climb in."

She stayed where she was.

"Come on," he said. "You look like you're about to faint. If you do, I'll have to scoop you up in that bare-assed gown and call for help. Talk about creating a scene."

This had been the longest stretch of time that she'd been out of bed and, damn him for the accurate observation, she was feeling weak and light-headed. With what dignity she could muster, she reached around to her backside and held the gown together as she minced over to the bed and sat down on the edge of it.

"Need help getting in?"

He reached out to assist her, but she shrank from him. "I'll sit." She tugged a corner of the sheet out from under her hip and arranged it over her lap and thighs. "Why'd you come back tonight?"

"Your interview with The Major is on YouTube. I finally got around to watching it. You did a good job."

"Thank you."

"I brought you those." He called her attention to a cellophane-wrapped bouquet of wilted carnations tied with a garish glitter bow. He'd stuck it into a vase of elegant long-stemmed roses sent by the network.

"Thank you."

"Not that you need more flowers."

The room had been filling up throughout the day. "People have been very thoughtful."

"Who's Mark?"

She looked at him with incredulity. "You read the enclosure cards?"

"Just that one."

She glanced at the elaborate arrangement of calla lilies and white hydrangeas. "Why that one?"

"It's the fanciest bunch. I figured the sender must be someone special."

"He is. He's a very special friend."

"Yeah?" His gaze dropped to her lap, and when it reconnected with hers, he said, "A friend with benefits?"

That split-second glance, coupled with the insinuation, brought heat to her cheeks, which only minutes ago had been abnormally pale in the bathroom mirror. His audacity was insufferable, but her embarrassed reaction to it was even more so. "Not that it's any of your business, but yes."

He didn't smile but there was amusement in his eyes. Maybe he was remembering that when he had kissed her, she'd done nothing to discourage or stop him. He'd ended it before she had.

However, the memory of that swift but potent kiss was immediately elbowed aside by ones of him demanding to know what or who she'd seen before barely escaping The Major's house.

The space around her seemed to shrink, mostly due to Trapper's large presence and his cocky stance: feet apart, jacket spread open because he'd slid his hands into the rear pockets of his jeans. And those damn blue eyes, penetrating and intimidating.

Panic swooped toward her like a bird of prey, blocking out the light with its wide wings, stealing her breath with their noisy flapping. Her hand moved to her throat. "I'm not feeling well."

"Are you going to throw up?"

Immediately he was there, bending over her, holding a plastic basin under her chin with one hand. His other he placed in the center of her back, where the gown was open. Against her hot skin, she felt the cool imprint of each fingertip, the pressure of his wide palm.

A tide of heat spread up from her chest to enclose her head. The rims of her ears caught fire. She broke a sweat from her scalp to the soles of her feet. She kept her head down and prayed she wouldn't retch as she had the night before. Even dry heaves would be humiliating.

"Breathe through your mouth."

She did as he instructed, and that alleviated the nausea. Eventually the encroaching darkness and noise receded and then were gone entirely. The hot flash cooled. "I'm okay." She pushed away the basin and straightened her spine to break the contact of his hand with her bare back.

"Want some water?"

She shook her head.

"Something else?"

Another head shake.

"Why don't you lie down?"

She looked up at him. "Why don't you go away?"

"A few questions, and then I will." He returned the basin to the nightstand then backed up to the chair he'd sat in the night before and struck the same pose, elbows on knees, eyes on her. "Detectives from the SO questioned you?"

"Twice."

"How'd it go?"

"Fine."

"Fine?"

"Fine."

"They clear you to go back to Dallas?"

She looked away from his blue-flame gaze. "Not yet."

"Huh. Then your sessions didn't go so fine."

"Before I sign off on my statement, they want me to go through it one more time with...with Texas Rangers." She rushed on before his arched eyebrow became a smart remark. "Only to make absolutely certain that I haven't forgotten something."

He just stared at her, saying nothing, but his skeptical expression put her on the defensive. "You should remember from your days in law enforcement how it works."

"I do remember. Know what I remember best, Kerra? People lie."

"I don't."

"No?" He tilted his head in the direction of the floral arrangements lined up along the windowsill. "Mark? You and he shared an apartment on West 110th Street when you were both attending Columbia. He's currently a successful architect in his native Baltimore. He's gay. He's happily married. He and his partner just adopted their second child."

Her surprise was such that she barely had enough voice to ask, "How did you know all that?"

"If you lied to me about something as harmless as a college pal, you'll lie to me about a near-murder and what you saw and heard and sensed while it was being committed, and what went down afterward.

"And the investigators must know that you're leaving out chunks of information or they wouldn't be requiring a third go-round with Texas Rangers. Now what are you omitting or glossing over, Kerra?"

"Nothing. And besides, I was ordered not to discuss the case while it's an ongoing investigation."

"With anybody or with me in particular?"

"With anybody."

"Then we've got no problem, because we've already established that I'm not just anybody."

He seemed prepared to lunge from his chair and wring answers out of her. But he must have sensed her apprehension, because he backed down, relaxed his shoulders, and, in a quieter tone asked, "How many were there?"

She determined that he wasn't going to leave until she gave him something. She might just as well get it over with. She looked down at her hands in her lap, clasped together so tightly her fingers had turned bone white. "Two. I'm almost certain."

"Did they say anything?"

"Only that one mocking question."

" 'How do you like being dead so far?' That's all you heard anyone say?"

She nodded.

"You didn't see them?"

She shook her head.

"Kerra?"

Looking across at him, she said, *"No."*

"Any part of them? Clothing? Footwear?"

"No. Nothing. I told you that last night."

"You also told me that Mark was a friend with benefits, when I know damn well that he ain't fucking you."

She shook back her hair, took a deep breath, and looked him straight in the eye. "I didn't see the man or men who shot The Major. I left him alone in the living room. I was in the bathroom when I heard the gunshot."

"Single gunshot?"

"Yes. My first thought was that one of his hunting rifles had misfired."

"Why did you think that?"

"We'd been talking about hunting. Remember, I told you that. He'd opened the gun case to show me a rifle your mother had given him."

"Her last Christmas gift to him."

"Yes. I thought perhaps it had accidentally discharged as he was putting it away. But the shot hadn't sounded as loud as a rifle. More of a pop. All this went through my mind in a millisecond.

"Then I heard the 'so far' question and understood that there hadn't been an accident. I thought The Major had been killed and that if I was discovered, I'd be killed, too."

At the end of that sentence, her courage ran out. She crossed her arms over her middle and hugged her elbows. "They were banging on the door, trying to break the latch. I wanted to live. There was only one way out. I took it. That's what I told the detectives, and it's the truth." The truth minus the part about someone trying to open the door before the gunshot. Instinct told her to keep that to herself.

As though knowing she was withholding something, Trapper continued to stare at her. But after a long moment, some of the tension eased out of him. "Why's your crew hanging around?"

"We touched on that. Lodal is crawling with media."

He said nothing, just tapped his chin with his clasped hands.

She didn't stand up long against his unflinching stare. He'd find out soon enough anyway. "I've been approached to describe those last few minutes I spent alone with The Major."

"You mean on TV?"

"Yes. The network wants the anchor to interview me on the evening news."

"In New York?"

"No, from here. Via satellite. Preferably live."

"Are you going to do it?"

"I haven't decided yet."

"What would decide you?"

"For or against?"

"You have to ask?"

He was taking to the idea exactly as she had predicted he would. With resistance. "I'm sensitive to how you might feel about it. That's the main reason I'm hesitant to do it."

"Oh. Your hesitancy has everything to do with my feelings and nothing to do with the fact that you're a material witness—the *only* one—to the attempted assassination of a public figure."

"I'm also a newswoman."

"Ah."

"Yes, *ah*! I have a career, Trapper. This is what I do."

Now that she'd had hours to consider it, she acknowledged that Gracie's points were valid. Her career could be irreparably damaged if she refused. Since their conversation this morning, Gracie had called twice to ask if she'd thought it over and come to a more sensible decision. "But no pressure," the producer had quipped.

Now Trapper was applying pressure from the opposing side. Challenging him, she said, "Why are you so against it?"

"Common sense. It's a bad idea. Have you discussed it with Sheriff Addison or anyone investigating the case?"

"Not yet. It's only been proposed. I haven't committed."

"If you do it, you should be committed. Going on TV and talking about the minutes leading up to the shooting?" He shook his head in a way that said she was nuts. "I don't think it's sunk in with you the danger you're in, the threat you pose, the—"

She held up her hand to stop him from feeding her fear, which his parting words the night before had engendered, which his presence here now reinforced. "I don't pose a threat to anybody. If I do the interview I'll underscore that I couldn't identify the guilty parties because *I didn't see them*. That'll be the end of it."

"You think so?"

"Yes. I don't know what more I can say."

"Say you've told me everything."

"I've told you everything." She enunciated each word, gave them time to sink in, then gestured toward the door. "Now, I've answered your questions, which you have no authority to be asking. I'm tired. Please leave."

"All right. Just one more question and I'll go."

His capitulation had been too easily won, and her suspicion must have showed, because he added, "I promise."

"What's the question?"

He used the padded armrests to push himself out of the chair and came toward her, not stopping until she could feel the soft denim of his jeans against her bare legs draping the side of the bed. Her eyes tracked up the row of pearl snaps on his shirt, along his throat, to his face. His expression was inscrutable.

She repeated, "What's the question?"

He placed his bent index finger beneath her chin and stroked the bruise there, following it up over her jaw until his knuckle rested against the corner of her lips where the delicate skin was abraded. "Does that hurt?"

"A little."

He lifted his hand to his mouth and kissed the pad of his thumb with slightly parted lips, then brushed it against the injured spot. The unexpected touch was tender and sweet. Yet the thrill it elicited low and deep was purely erotic.

Even after removing his thumb, he continued to stare at the spot his stroking had left damp. Then he reached into his jacket and removed something from the breast pocket. "I believe you're the rightful owner. You were wearing it during the interview." He lifted her hand and dropped the object into her palm.

Dumbfounded, Kerra was held captive by his eyes. Then without another word, he turned and went to the door. Kerra continued to watch him until it closed behind him.

She looked down at her open palm. On it lay a single gold earring, which, after the interview, she had removed and placed with its mate in an inside pocket of her Louis Vuitton shoulder bag.

The deputy on guard duty was at the water fountain at the far end of the hall when Trapper came out of Kerra's room. They'd introduced themselves when Trapper arrived. Now they met at the halfway point of the corridor, and the deputy asked, "She like the flowers?"

"She liked them okay." Trapper was less sure about Kerra's opinion of him. They'd touched tongues. Now she recoiled every time he got near her.

"How's she doing?"

"As well as can be expected, I guess," Trapper said. "She took quite a tumble." Kerra was banged up, but the worst of her ailments was fear. At hiding it, she wasn't as good as she thought.

"She talk to you about what happened to her?"

"No. She's been instructed not to talk about it."

"Ongoing investigation."

"Right. Wouldn't want to hinder that." Trapper rolled his shoulders and popped his neck.

"Pardon me saying so, Trapper, but you look beat."

"I am. But I'm going upstairs and check on The Major one more time before shoving off. I leave you to your duty. Keep a close watch on her."

"Count on that."

"I know I can. Have a good night, Jenks."

Chapter 10

Trapper rolled over and snatched his chirping cell phone off the nightstand. Each time it rang, he feared hearing the worst. After leaving Kerra's room last night, he'd stayed in the ICU waiting room for hours but was allowed to see The Major only once. His condition was stable and unchanged.

The nurse in charge convinced Trapper there was no reason for him to hang around. She got his cell phone number and assured him that if there was any reason to call him, good or bad, she would.

But it wasn't she or anyone from the hospital calling now. He answered by saying, "You're paying me back for those untimely calls."

"You have a naked woman in bed with you?" Carson asked.

Trapper looked over at the empty space beside him and thought about the promised delights he'd detected under Kerra's thin hospital gown. "No."

"Then I'm not quite paying you back. But I'm calling early because one of my contracted associates—"

Trapper chuffed.

"—found something I thought you'd be interested in learning right away."

Trapper scrubbed his face with his hand to wipe away the dirty thoughts he was entertaining about Kerra's topography and how he'd like to explore it. "Listening."

"When you got crosswise with the ATF, weren't you investigating a guy named Wilcox?"

Trapper went absolutely still.

"Thomas Wilcox?" Carson said.

"It was covert," Trapper said. "How'd you know about it?"

"You got drunk one night. Mumbled on and on about this big shot over in Big D."

He didn't recall venting his spleen to Carson, but he didn't doubt that he had. The mere mention of Wilcox's name aroused feral impulses. "What about him?"

"When Kerra Bailey signed on with the Dallas TV station, he was one of her first interviews."

After a sustained silence, Carson said, "Trapper? You still there, buddy? Did you get that?"

Trapper cleared his throat. "I'm here. I got it."

"Don't know if it means anything. But, six degrees of separation. All that."

"Right. Thanks, Carson. I'll be in touch."

"Before you go. About that slick SUV—"

"Did you tell the guy I'll pay him a daily rate? I couldn't get it back to him now anyway on account of the weather."

"But—"

"I gotta go. Somebody's beeping in, and it could be the hospital." It wasn't. The readout said *Glenn*. Trapper didn't want to talk to him, he wanted to ponder what Carson had just told him about Thomas Wilcox and Kerra. But Glenn might have news about The Major, so he answered.

"I was about to give up on reaching you," the sheriff said.

"I had to click over."

"Want to have breakfast?"

"No."

"I'll pick you up in an hour."

"I'm going to the hospital."

"After you've seen him, call me. I'll pick you up outside." The phone went dead.

"*Sssshit,*" Trapper hissed as he slung back the covers. The start of the day didn't bode well for the rest of it.

———◆———

Trapper and the trauma doctor who'd been overseeing The Major's care stood across the ICU bed from each other. Between them lay The Major.

The physician said, "We're a little more optimistic this morning."

Trapper had to take his word for that. He compared the helpless patient in the bed to his father as he'd last seen him. Even though Kerra and he had shown up at The Major's house unannounced, he'd looked company-ready, dressed in starched khakis with a knife-edge crease. His flannel shirt was softly worn, but neatly tucked in behind a wide tooled leather belt with a large silver buckle. His boots had their usual shine. His shave was so close his skin was shiny, too. Not a hair out of place. Fit as a fiddle for a man his age. For a man half his age.

He didn't look like that now. There was an IV port between his shoulder and neck with multiple lines attached. The hospital gown lay loose on his chest. His chin was bristly with white whiskers. A clear hose was emptying his piss into a bag hooked to the bed rail.

The Major was human after all.

"The swelling has gone down considerably from what it was this time yesterday," the doctor was saying.

"So no hole required?"

"Not unless something changes, but I don't anticipate it. He's been moving his hands and feet. Reflexively, but that's still a positive sign. His vitals remain stable and strong. He's not out of the woods," he said with emphasis, "but these incremental improvements are encouraging."

"Have you reported this to the doctors in Dallas?"

From the outset, the doctor had been consulting with a team of specialists, former colleagues of his. "They share my optimism. Your father is stable enough now to be transported to Dallas or Fort Worth, if you'd rather have him there. I could make the arrangements. But with the weather..." He let that hang and looked at Trapper. "It's your call."

"He's improving on your watch. I say leave him be."

"Thank you, Mr. Trapper. I appreciate the vote of confidence."

He detailed a few more aspects of The Major's condition. Most of the medical jargon went over Trapper's head, but the underlying message was that the patient was making progress.

Which is what Trapper told Glenn as he settled into the passenger side of the sheriff's sludge-covered unit and buckled his seat belt. Glenn had driven right up to the hospital exit, emergency lights flashing, allowing Trapper to leave without being hounded by reporters, who'd been restricted to an area behind a barricade. Some stood outside, backs to the frigid wind, stamping their feet in a vain attempt to keep warm. Others sat inside vehicles surrounded by the vapor coughed from their exhaust pipes.

"Lordy, lordy, that's good news," Glenn said as he steered the unit onto the street.

"He's not totally in the clear. The doctor doesn't want to build hopes up. But his outlook is definitely more upbeat. Where are we going?"

"Since you turned down breakfast, I'll just circle the block."

"It's such a nice day for a drive," Trapper remarked, looking through the sleet on the windshield.

"We need to talk uninterrupted," Glenn said. "I brought you some coffee."

Trapper pulled the sleeved cup from the holder in the console, removed the lid and sipped. It was tepid, but he needed the jolt of caffeine.

They drove past the municipal park, where tree branches were becoming glazed with ice.

"Remember that shindig the town threw for your daddy? Right out there," Glenn said, pointing through the driver's window. "Citywide barbecue on the Fourth of July. Texas Tech band. Banners. You remember?"

"Yes." He remembered it well because he'd been required to miss a Little League championship game in order to be standing beside The Major when he received a key to the city and a plaque from the town council. Missing that stupendous event hadn't been an option.

But he doubted a stroll down memory lane was the purpose of this outing that required no interruption. "What's up, Glenn?"

"I heard Kerra Bailey had a visitor last night. Bearing pretty pink flowers."

It came as no surprise to Trapper that Glenn knew about it. Deputy Jenks would've reported back to him. Besides, Trapper hadn't exactly made a secret of the hospital visit.

"Actually, the flowers were red with a butt-ugly bow. I bought them on special at QuikMart when I went in for a six-pack."

Glenn kept driving, saying nothing.

"I had watched the interview," Trapper said, trying not to sound defensive. "I wanted to tell her what a good job she'd done."

"Okay. What about the time before, when you went back after you and I had left the hospital together?"

In response to the implied hand-slapping, Trapper stretched his legs out as far as he could in the confined foot well and drank from his cup of coffee with affected nonchalance. "The doctor ran us out before I'd heard what I wanted to hear."

"What was that?"

"Whether or not she saw the men who shot The Major."

"You ask her?"

"Yes."

"What'd she say?"

"She said no."

Glenn stopped at a traffic light, reached for his thermal coffee container in the cup holder, and eyed Trapper over the cap of it as he drank from the spout. "You didn't tell me you'd talked to her."

"I figured you had enough on your mind."

"When I have enough on my mind, I'll let you know. Okay?"

Trapper made a gesture. *Okay*.

Glenn returned his thermos to the cup holder. "She share anything with you last night?"

"A glimpse of inner thigh, but it was by accident."

"You know what I mean."

"Yes, I know what you mean, but, no, she didn't share anything."

Glenn signaled a left turn and executed it with care. "She tell you her bag is missing?"

Caught unaware, Trapper retracted his legs and set his cup back in the holder with care, but kept his tone casual. "What bag?"

Glenn described the bag as "about so-so," and took his hands off the steering wheel to approximate the dimensions. Trapper knew the bag.

"Most of yesterday was spent going through the chain of custody," Glenn was saying, "but the upshot is that it's unaccounted for, and nobody claims to have any knowledge of it."

He shrugged before continuing. "Expensive and belonging to a TV celebrity would make it worth stealing, so it's conceivable that somebody at the hospital lifted it. You know what the ER's like. But I had a deputy review the videos from hospital security cameras, and nobody was captured toting it out. Besides, the EMTs who brought her in said they never saw it. Logical conclusion, the perps have it."

"What're your detectives saying?"

"About the bag?"

"The investigation in general."

"I've read the highlights of Kerra's two interviews with them."

He recounted them to Trapper, and they matched the highlights that Kerra had given him.

"But have there been any breakthroughs?" Glenn said. "No. Seven people were inside the house that afternoon and evening, and that's not counting the two from the café who delivered the fried chicken dinner. The production crew had been meandering around all afternoon, hauling equipment in and out, stringing cords from outlets in the back rooms to the living area. They were in practically every room of the house at one time or another."

"Meaning there's enough trace evidence in there for a hundred cases."

"Right. What we collected, we sent to the Tarrant County's SO lab. They have better equipment than smaller departments like mine, but that also keeps them busy and backlogged. It could take several days before they even look at the samples."

Trapper understood the frustration of wanting answers and having to wait for them while perpetrators remained unknown and the trail grew colder. "Nothing else shook loose?"

"From the crime scene? Not really. This shit," Glenn said of the weather, "hadn't started yet. The ground was dry, hard to get impressions off dry and rocky ground. I've got personnel working around the clock, and now the Rangers have joined the party. Waltzed in and said they wanted to question Kerra Bailey."

Trapper didn't tell him he already knew that. He leaned back in his seat and stared thoughtfully out the window. "I had her talk me through it."

"Reckoned you had. That's why I called this meeting. You had no authority to do that, Trapper."

"Yeah, I know."

"She was instructed—"

"Don't blame her. I browbeat her into talking about it."

When he stopped with that, Glenn prodded him. "Well? Wha'd she say?"

"She described what it was like for her inside the powder room. Her fear. Knowing she would die if the individuals on the other side of the door got to her. She used nickel words, Glenn."

The sheriff shot him a look. "Fuck does that mean?"

"As opposed to fifty-cent words, which would have led me to believe they were chosen ahead of time and rehearsed, that she was trying to impress me or that she was lying. She wasn't that smooth."

"But what? You're frowning."

"But..." Trapper sighed and shook his head in frustration. He was frowning because he sensed Kerra was holding something back, something that made her afraid. He was frowning because of all the names Carson could have dropped this morning, the name had been Thomas Wilcox. Who had crossed paths with Kerra. Which could be a bizarre coincidence. Or not. In any case, it raised the hair on the back of Trapper's neck.

"You think she saw more than she's telling?" Glenn asked.

"I don't know."

Glenn reentered the hospital parking lot and pulled the patrol car into the fire lane, where he set it to idle. "John, listen to me."

"Stay out of it," Trapper said, anticipating what Glenn had been about to say.

"That's right. Stay out of it. You can't go meddling in this investigation."

"I'm a licensed investigator."

"And the victim is your father. I don't care what your beef was with him, you can't be objective."

"I don't have a need for objectivity, because I have no intention of meddling in the investigation. So where's this lecture coming from?"

"It's coming from private, late-night visits to the material witness that lasted forty-three minutes."

Trapper muttered a swear word. "Good man, Jenks. But for the record, it was only forty-two and a half."

"It took Linda and me a whole lot less time to conceive Hank."

"Really? You're that quick on the draw?"

The sheriff turned in his seat, squeezing his paunch beneath the steering wheel. "John, for once, please—"

"Do yourself a favor," Trapper said, again anticipating the next words out of Glenn's mouth. "You don't call me John unless the subject is serious *or* you're about to impart unsolicited advice."

"Okay, be a smart-ass. But I'm going to say this, and you're going to hear it. Don't rile the wrong people. You did that once, and look what happened."

"I *quit*."

"Whatever, you lost your job. Didn't you learn anything from that?"

"Yeah. I learned that I put up with that bureaucratic bullshit for much longer than I should have."

"Oh, like you're the epitome of happiness in the workplace these days?"

Trapper gnawed the inside of his cheek, then reached for the door latch and popped it. "I've got someplace to be."

"Where?"

"Someplace else."

———

It took all morning for Kerra to be released from the hospital. Five minutes were devoted to the doctor's final physical exam, five hours to signing all the dismissal forms. By the time she'd completed the paperwork, she felt more like crawling back into the bed than leaving under the escort of two deputies.

They drove her directly from the hospital to the sheriff's office in the courthouse, where she was led into an interrogation room. Two Texas Rangers and Sheriff Addison himself were waiting for her there.

She and the sheriff shook hands. "You're looking a lot better than the last time I saw you," he said.

"I'm feeling better. Has there been any change in The Major's condition?"

"Actually, there's good news." He shared what he knew and held up crossed fingers. "Baby steps. But thirty-six hours ago we didn't think he'd live through the night."

She splayed her hand over her chest. "I'm so glad to hear this."

During their exchange the Rangers had been standing by. The sheriff introduced her to them now. All took seats around a table and, after explaining to her that the session was being recorded, one of the Rangers took the lead.

"We've spoken to the detectives, Ms. Bailey, but this time we're hearing it straight from you. For our benefit, please start at the beginning, and tell us everything you remember."

"My story hasn't deviated from the first time I told it," she said. "Except for one detail. Well, actually two details. I'm not sure what significance either has."

Looking interested and mildly surprised, the sheriff clasped his large hands together on the table. "Let's hear 'em. We'll determine their significance."

Her wish was that they would dismiss both as being of no importance. But she didn't believe they would. Her palms turned damp. "One involves the sequence of events."

She related how someone had tried opening the powder room door before she heard the gunshot. "Everything happened in rapid succession after that. Because of the meds, the concussion, when I gave my account to the detectives I got the timing mixed up."

"You only realized this discrepancy later?" the sheriff asked.

"Yes. When I wasn't so woozy." If she told them that clarity had come to her during a nightmare they would think she was crazy. "But now I'm certain that someone tried to open that door before the first shot."

"Must've been the assailants."

"Possibly," she said, "but they approached from the main room after the gunshot, not before. And they weren't stealthy. I followed each footstep."

One of the Rangers said, "You didn't hear approaching footsteps the first time someone tried the door?"

"No. I wasn't aware of anyone being there until the latch rattled."

The same Ranger asked, "Are you suggesting that someone else was inside the house, a third suspect?"

"I'm not suggesting anything. I'm only telling you how I'm remembering it now."

No one said anything for several moments, then the second Ranger addressed her. "After the crew left, how long were you and The Major there alone before you excused yourself to go to the bathroom?"

"Fifteen or twenty minutes."

"You stayed in the main room that whole time?"

"Yes. Neither of us left it until I excused myself."

"So somebody could have come in through a door or window at the back of the house?"

"I suppose."

"Were lights on in the other rooms?"

"No." She gave a faint smile. "Our setup required a lot of electricity. We used several circuits. The Major complained how that would run up his next bill. He was teasing, but the crew was conscientious about turning out lights when we were finished.

"As I left the living room and went into the hall, it was very dark." She told them she had switched on the bathroom light even before shutting the door and remembered turning it off immediately after realizing it would give away her presence.

The sheriff said, "You didn't see anything suspicious, or off somehow, that would make you think now that somebody was in one of the back rooms?"

"Nothing."

Kerra wasn't sure what to make of the look that passed among the three men before the sheriff came back to her. "Kerra, what I'm about to tell you isn't for disclosure."

"All right."

"It's a fact we've been holding back because we don't know what to make of it, and when we have a suspect to question—"

"You want to see if he's aware of it, whatever it is."

"That's correct." He paused, then said, "The Major's deer rifle was within his arm's reach when the first responders arrived."

"He was probably putting it away."

The three men shared another look. One of the Rangers asked, "He had it out of the cabinet while you were there?"

"Yes." She explained The Major's sentimental attachment to the rifle. "After showing it to me, he propped it against the wall and went over to the bar to pour a drink. He was probably putting it away when he was attacked."

The three sat back in their chairs, their body language conveying that was a plausible explanation for something that had intrigued them. Sheriff Addison said, "We conjectured that maybe he had heard something at the back of the house, or heard the culprits coming up the porch steps, and went for the rifle to protect himself. It wasn't loaded, but he could've scared somebody into thinking it was."

In a soft voice, Kerra said, "If only he'd had the chance."

He nodded glumly, coughed behind his fist, then said, "What's the second detail that may or may not be significant?"

She rolled her lips inward, which made the abraded corner of her mouth sore, which reminded her of why she dreaded this so desperately and wouldn't be doing it at all except that it was the right, moral, and legal thing to do. "It concerns my missing bag."

"It's turned up?"

"No, sheriff. But something I'm certain was inside it has been returned to me."

He registered astonishment. "By who?"

Chapter 11

Contrary to the relief Kerra had expected to feel upon being dismissed and allowed to leave the sheriff's office, she hunched in the backseat of the deputy-driven patrol car, feeling despondent and generally miserable.

Her head ached dully but without letup. Her coat had been returned to her, but it was inadequate against the Siberian express, which had hit the plains of North Texas where there was nothing to block it except for barbed-wire fences. Over the course of the afternoon, roads had become increasingly hazardous.

Her car, now encased in ice, was still in the motel parking lot where she'd left it Sunday morning to join the crew in the production van for the short trip out to The Major's spread. That seemed a long time ago.

Gracie had checked her back into the room she'd previously occupied, where a welcome back party was already in full swing when the deputy delivered her. Dazed by the ill-timed surprise, Kerra reunited with the rest of the crew who, despite the inclement weather, had rounded up burgers and beer and helium-filled balloons that bobbed and swayed from various anchors in the crowded room.

She tried to be gracious and get into the festive spirit, but Gracie must have sensed her downcast mood. As soon as the burgers had been demolished, the producer shooed the others out.

"Maybe our celebration was a bit much with you just out of the hospital," she said, plopping cross-legged in the center of Kerra's bed with her tablet in her lap. "But we need to go over some particulars about tomorrow."

"Gracie, if you're referring to the interview, there may not be a 'tomorrow.'"

"I'm betting on a thumbs-up. In which case, we have to be ready."

Kerra had struggled with the decision over whether or not to agree to be interviewed about her private time with The Major. After weighing the pros and cons, she'd decided that Gracie had given her a solid piece of advice. Shouldn't she take advantage of this tragic, yet exceptional, set of circumstances? She hadn't worked this hard, gotten this far, to blow it now. The industry was cutthroat and unforgiving. To pass on this opportunity could amount to career suicide.

But, as Trapper had predicted, neither Sheriff Addison, the Rangers, nor anyone involved in the investigation was enthusiastic when she broached the subject at the conclusion of her questioning.

The officers raised a number of objections and concerns. The discussion went back and forth with compromises being granted by both sides. Ultimately, however, Kerra had come away with only their promise to consider it and inform her of their decision in the morning.

But as though it were a done deal, Gracie proceeded to run down her checklist. "His Highness will want to steer the interview because he's peeved that you got to The Major when he failed to." She was referring to the network's venerable anchorman, who would conduct his end of the interview from the studio in New York.

"But don't give him any wiggle room, Kerra. The nation will be wanting to hear from you. *You*. Your disbelief, your heartache, your...well, you know. Be human. If you can cry on command, a tear or two would be a great effect.

"I thought we'd do it from the first floor lobby of

the hospital," she rattled on. "Make it feel real. A hero's life hanging in the balance. Admirers around the world praying for a miracle. So forth."

She moved from that to wardrobe, which presented a problem because Kerra's suitcase was locked in the trunk of her car, to which she had no keys, and even if she did, the car was sealed in ice.

"I'll figure out something," Gracie said breezily and launched into the issue of Kerra's bruised face. "I'll go out first thing in the morning and try to find some good concealer, but, come to think of it, the bruises will—"

"Gracie, please, take a breath," Kerra cut in. "I know what's expected, and I'll deliver. But let's not lose sight of the fact that a great man is still in critical condition. He may die, and I'll have been there when he was fatally attacked." She bent her head over her hand and pressed her fingers to her forehead.

"That's the kind of emotion I want to see from you tomorrow," Gracie exclaimed. "Just like that. You're distressed to the max. Inconsolable."

Kerra was appalled by her insensitivity.

"Of course I realize that your distress is genuine," Gracie added hastily. "It's just that I'm trying to infuse you with some excitement. Where's the go-getter I'm used to working with? Where's your usual verve?"

"Sorry. I'm fresh out of verve," Kerra said. "Besides,

this conversation may well be pointless. So I'm running you out. I need to rest."

Realizing she'd overstepped, Gracie gathered her things and went to the door. "I'm sorry. I get wound up and lose all perspective."

"It's okay. I do it myself." Kerra hoped she never did it to that degree, but she had said it to get rid of Gracie faster.

"Do you need anything? Will you be all right?"

"After a good night's sleep, I'll be fine." Kerra opened the door.

On her way out, Gracie said, "You know I'm up till all hours, so if you need—*Who* is *that?*"

Kerra turned to see who had Gracie agape.

He had swapped the leather jacket for a heavier one made of shearling sheepskin. The collar was flipped up against his jaw, which was set as hard as granite.

He was coming toward them from across the parking lot, appearing out of the swirling, freezing mist like an avenger in an apocalyptic movie, impervious to the precipitation, sure-footed in spite of the icy pavement, so purposeful in bearing and stride it seemed that no power could have stopped him unless it was divine. Or demonic.

"That's John Trapper."

Gracie's eyes bulged behind her orange glasses. "The *son?*"

"Yes."

"You've met him?"

Kerra swallowed. "Briefly."

He almost had to duck to clear the low overhang. Ignoring Gracie as though she were invisible, he placed his two forefingers against Kerra's sternum and pushed her back across the threshold, then slammed the door behind them.

Trapper stormed past her and took a look around. "Does that beer belong to anybody?" Without waiting for her to answer, he yanked a can from the plastic webbing and opened it.

"Help yourself."

Ignoring her sarcasm, he looked her over while taking a long drink, and when he lowered the can, he said, "You don't strike me as a beer drinker. Or a collector of balloons with goofy faces on them."

"The crew hosted a party."

"Party, huh? If you ask me, you don't have much to celebrate."

"Well, I didn't ask you, did I? I don't want you here, and where do you get off showing up and barging in whenever you feel like it?"

"When I barged in, you didn't put up much of a fight. How come?"

"I'm short on verve."

"Maybe. But that's not it. You're scared of me."

"I am not."

He took in the upward tilt of her chin and defiant stance, and scoffed. "You get credit for at least trying to sound unafraid."

"Why would I be scared of you?"

"Beats the hell out of me." He came toward her until he was close enough for her to see individual ice crystals melting on the shoulders of his jacket and in his hair. "You tell me, Kerra. Why would I make you afraid?"

"I'm not afraid, I'm weary." She edged around him. "Achy. My shoulder hurts. I'm reminded of my cracked collarbone whenever I move a certain way. I have a headache. Occasional dizzy spells. It's been a very long day, and I'm tired. I'm especially tired of you bothering me."

He raised his eyebrows. "I bother you?"

Ignoring that, she said, "I want you out of here so I can go to bed."

"So you'll be daisy fresh for the big interview tomorrow."

That brought her up short. "How did you know I'd consented to it?"

His expression hardened. "I didn't." He drained the beer, crushed the can with one hand, and lobbed it into the wastebasket. "Wild guess."

"Very clever."

"I'm not a private eye for nothing." He waited a beat, then, "Actually, the guess wasn't so wild. I knew you'd do it."

"No, you didn't. *I* didn't. I didn't make up my mind until after thinking about it overnight and all day today. Don't presume to know me, anything about me. You don't."

"Oh, yeah?" he said in a drawl. "Let's see. I know that you use bath powder. I know that you have an old scar about two inches above your left knee on the inside of your thigh. I say old because it's pale, barely visible." His gaze dropped to her chest. "And you get chilled easily." He let that resonate, and when his eyes reconnected with hers, he said, "What else do you want to know?"

It was indignation that caused her to go hot all over. She was sure of it. She should call him on the uninvited suggestiveness, but then he would know that his sexy insinuations had affected her, and that would equip him to intimidate her even more than he already did.

Instead, she turned the tables and put him on the defensive. "How did you get my shoulder bag? When? Where?"

"Funny, we covered a lot of territory last night, but you failed to mention that your bag was missing. Why?"

"Why would I? It was none of your business. Or so I thought."

"Well, it for damn sure is my business now." With a suddenness that made her jump, he whipped off his coat and flung it into a chair. "I was sitting there in the ICU waiting room, waiting to see if The Major's improvement would continue or if he'd tank, my butt going numb from sitting, reading an old copy of *Outdoorsman* for the third time. Ask me anything about the mating rituals of white-tail deer."

The fuse on his temper was burning short. At the end of it, she feared it was going to be explosive. He had started out with his voice at a conversational level, but the volume had steadily increased. "What happened?" she asked.

"In sauntered two deputies who told me that Sheriff Addison wanted to see me. I told them that Glenn had my cell number. If he wanted to talk, he knew how to reach me. Noooo. A phone call won't do, they said. The meeting had to be in person."

"You were arrested?"

"I told them I'd already had a person-to-person meeting with Sheriff Addison today, thank you, and went back to reading about stags in rut. But then one of the officers plucked the magazine out of my hand and said that the summons was more than a friendly invitation. I could follow them in my own vehicle to the sheriff's office, but I had to go, and it had to be right then.

"So I left those poor bucks unfinished and followed the pair of deputies to the sheriff's office, where I was grilled for the next two friggin' hours." As expected, he was furious. He didn't end with a shout, however, but rather with a snarl, which was much more menacing.

She backed a step away from him. "They questioned you based on what I told them?"

He put his hands on his hips and closed the distance she'd created. "Ya think?"

"Trapper—"

"You suspect me of trying to kill my own father?"

"No."

"That's what it sounds like. I know I didn't make a very good first impression on you, Miss Louis Vuitton, but Jesus!" He raked his fingers through his damp hair. "You changed the sequence of events in your story—"

"I didn't *change* the sequence. I hadn't remembered it correctly."

"Until when, Kerra? Before or after you talked me through it last night?"

She avoided looking him in the eye.

"That's what I thought."

She defended herself against the accusation behind his droll remark. "I wasn't completely honest with you last night because you'd made me—"

"Afraid."

"All right, yes! You sneaked into my room after you'd left with the sheriff, which was frightening enough, but then you demanded to know if I'd seen the men who'd attempted to kill The Major. What was I supposed to think?"

"You were supposed to think that a son would want to know who'd tried to off his father."

"A son who hadn't spoken to that father in years, who emanated so much hostility you could cut it with a knife? *That* son?"

He glared at her then turned away, mumbling things she thought it just as well she didn't catch. She gave both of them a short timeout to cool down, then said quietly, "I had to tell the authorities, Trapper."

"You did what your conscience dictated and"—he snapped his fingers—"next thing I know, everybody puts me creeping around in the dark back rooms of The Major's house, jiggling doorknobs."

"I understand why you would take offense at the allegation, but it will go away as soon as you provide an alibi for Sunday night."

"Right. Right." He rubbed the back of his neck. "I'll think of something."

Her lips parted in shock.

He rolled his eyes. "That was a joke, for crissake."

"It wasn't funny."

"You're right. Not a damn thing's been funny since you knocked on my office door."

"Well, I'm sorry about that, but you haven't helped yourself, either. How did you get my bag?"

He spread his arms from his sides. "*I don't have your bag.* Glenn and those Rangers hammered me hard about that thing. I denied knowing anything about its missing status."

"Did they believe you?"

"Didn't stick around long enough to find out. I told them I wasn't saying another goddamn word without a lawyer, got up, walked out."

"They let you go?"

"They had to. They've got nothing on me. And, in case you're still wondering, I do have an alibi. I was in a sports bar where I'm a regular. I had a dinner of wings and cheese fries, watched a game that went into overtime, and didn't leave till the final buzzer. Bartender knows me. He can vouch. Plus I put the tab on a credit card, so the receipt will be time-stamped. Satisfied?"

"Did the sheriff check it out?"

"In the process when I left."

"What about the earring? How did you explain having it?"

"I spotted it on the floor under your hospital bed last night while I was waiting for you to come out of the bathroom." He paused, then added, "Smelling like bath powder."

"That isn't true."

"It absolutely is. Baby powder, I'm guessing."

"Not about that," she snapped. "About the earring."

"Oh. Yeah, that was a lie. That's how I *explained* having it. But the truth is that I found it out behind The Major's house."

Rendered speechless by that, she sat down on the edge of the bed and stared up at him.

He said, "When I left the hospital after seeing you Monday morning, I went out there to look around."

"Weren't crime scene investigators all over it?"

"Pretty much. But the sun hadn't come up, and, besides, the sky was overcast. It started to rain, which soon turned to freezing rain. Everybody was wearing winter gear up to their eyebrows. I blended in with the diehards poking around outside. I found the earring in a patch of dead grass twenty yards or so away from the house."

"How would it have gotten there?"

"You told Glenn you're positive it was in an inside pocket of your bag."

"That's right."

"Zipped in?"

"No. I put the earrings in a slot in the lining that doesn't have a zipper."

"And your bag doesn't close at the top. I remember that from when you came to my office. The earring could have shaken out when whoever took the bag was running away from the house." He tipped his head. "Conceivable?"

"Conceivable. But why didn't you turn it over to the authorities?"

"Until I watched the interview and saw that you were wearing it then, I didn't even know it belonged to you."

"That's flimsy, Trapper. You were at a crime scene and found something. You knew it wasn't The Major's earring. It should have been left where it was and brought to the attention of the investigators. You should've let them retrieve it."

"That would have been proper procedure."

"And we know what you think of that. You would also have had to account for yourself being there in the first place."

The more he explained, the more he baffled her. She didn't know what to believe and what not to. With seamless ease, he melded fact with fabrication and sarcasm with sincerity.

She had been with him enough times now to recognize the barriers he raised to hide a long-simmering anger and wounded pride. He also used his glibness and charm without shame. He could disarm with intimidation as well as with a wolfish grin, and she'd been susceptible to both.

"Did you discover any other evidence while poking around with the diehards?" she asked.

"No."

"Why should I believe you?"

"You shouldn't. But it's the truth. If I had found something I deemed important to the investigation, I would have handed it over to the authorities immediately. I swear."

She had to take him at his word. At least for the time being. "How do you think the culprits got away? Where did they go?"

"They believed The Major was dead. You had escaped, and they ran out of time to look for you, probably because they saw the TV van returning. They went out the back and skedaddled. They had left a vehicle a safe distance away, with or without an accomplice waiting behind the wheel.

"While your crew was freaking out, calling 911, and so forth, the bad guys were driving away undetected. There are lots of back roads and old cattle trails out there. You can get lost if you know where you're going."

He smiled at his own irony, then continued. "It was lucky for them that the rain didn't come till after they were long gone, or there would've been footprints, tire tracks. Now an inch of sleet is covering any they might have left. If they're eventually found, they'll be so compromised, any punch they might have given a prosecutor's case will be diluted.

"Lucky for you the production people returned when they did. If the perps had had time, they would've searched till they found you. You would have made an easy target from the drop-off above the creek bed."

"I thought of that while I was lying there."

"Did you see them, Kerra?"

She had been absorbed in recollections of the harrowing experience, but his abrupt question brought her head up. "No."

"You were holding something back last night? What?"

"The fact that someone tried to open that door before the gunshot."

"So you do think there were three would-be assassins? Two came to the front door where The Major was shot. Another came in through the back and saw you go into the powder room? He knew you were in there, but his buddies didn't until after The Major was down? Is that what you think?"

"Honestly, I don't know what to think any more."

They lapsed into silence, but as he looked her over, his grim expression relaxed. "Well, honestly, what I think is that before going on TV you may want to change that outfit."

Gracie had purchased the fleece tracksuit and sneakers for her to wear as she left the hospital. She looked down at herself. "Good advice. It's ugly."

He didn't echo her self-deprecating laugh. All seriousness, he said, "Better yet, Kerra, change your mind. Don't do the interview."

"No one in law enforcement is keen on the idea, so the interview could be scrubbed. If it is, all your ranting over it will have been for nothing. You didn't give me an opportunity to tell you that before blazing in here and drinking my beer."

"I was pissed."

"I gathered that."

"I'm also a real jerk for not even asking how you're feeling."

"I told you. Weary, achy, dizzy. But I was exaggerating a little bit," she admitted with a sheepish smile. She stood up and walked toward him. "I am sorry that you were taken in for questioning. But I don't regret telling them about the earring. I had to, and I know you understand that, Trapper."

"I do. Of course I do. I admire you for it. It's just that I have issues with authority."

"I've gathered that, too."

They exchanged smiles. He moved to the door, but stopped and turned back before opening it. "Say, I've been catching up on my Kerra Bailey–watching and—"

"You have?"

"On my laptop. Helps kill time in the waiting room."

"I hope I'm at least as engrossing as white-tail deer."

"I don't know," he said, giving her a lazy grin. "Tell me about your mating rituals." At her look, he shrugged. "Worth a try. Anyway, I saw an interview you did with Thomas Wilcox."

"It was one of the first feature stories I did here in Texas."

"Why'd you choose him to focus on?"

"He's mega successful."

"That's the only reason?"

"Why do you ask? Do you know him?"

"By reputation only. Everything I've read about him says he's secretive. Keeps his business private. Shuns media attention."

"All true. I had to finagle him."

His eyes narrowed to slits. "That sounds like really dirty foreplay."

She laughed, but stopped laughing when he slid his hand under her hair at the nape of her neck and turned them until her back was to the door. Leaning in, his lips skimmed her beauty mark on their way to her ear, where he whispered, "I'd like for you to finagle me."

She didn't speak a word, didn't move, didn't do anything except give herself over to his body heat and largeness and maleness and sexiness, the blend of which seeped into her like a potent restorative. He had made her fearful, had bullied her, lied to her, tricked her. But now, all she wanted was to be against his skin. She arched her throat, giving access to his nibbling lips.

"I bother you?"

She responded with a sound that could have gone either way, but he took it as a yes.

"Good," he said in a near growl as he used his knee to nudge hers apart. "'Cause you sure as hell have kept me bothered."

His inner thigh rubbed against hers, creating a different kind of achiness that made her forget all her other twinges and pains. This ache was a feverish yearning that felt good, that made pleasure points throb.

He moved his hand up from her nape to cup the back of her head and held it in place while their mouths opened to each other. During the deep and greedy kiss he worked his free hand under her top and into the elastic waistband of the baggy pants. He lightly ground the heel of his hand against her hipbone while his fingers curved around the slope below her waist. He drew her hips forward. She gladly went along with his subtle invitation, and their parts fit together perfectly on the first attempted connection.

He groaned, "Christ, Kerra. Please tell me I'm gonna get to fuck you."

The knock sounded loudly directly behind her head.

Her body, bowing tautly against his, went slack. Trapper blistered the wall paint with his raspy swearing as he dropped his hand from the back of her head and pulled the other from her waistband.

She smoothed her hair, turned, and opened the door.

Sheriff Addison was standing just the other side of the threshold, scowling, not at her but looking above her head at Trapper.

Trapper scowled back. "What now? You're missing a spoon from the family silver chest?"

"It's The Major."

Chapter 12

Major Franklin Trapper listened to them discussing his condition.

He couldn't have picked the doctor out of a crowd, because he'd never actually seen him, but he recognized his voice from having heard him talking to the nurses earlier. He was saying, "He's been responding to commands. Wiggle your toes. Raise your index finger. I realize that doesn't sound like much, but believe me, it is."

John asked, "Can he hear us now?"

"Major Trapper," the doctor said, raising his volume a notch. "If you can hear us, open your eyes."

The Major did as commanded, and you would have thought he'd summited Everest without supplemental oxygen. The doctor was a blur in a white lab coat, his face a smudge of flesh with nostrils and eyeholes, but The Major made out his wide smile. He even chuckled. "Welcome back. Your son is here and anxious to see you."

He stepped aside, and John moved into view. He dwarfed the doctor by half a foot. He was wearing a shearling coat that added breadth to his shoulders and blocked everything else from The Major's field of vision.

"Hey. It's good to see you awake. You had everybody worried sick."

The Major didn't so much note what John had said as the way he'd said it: like he meant it. His usual insolence was missing.

"You've had a rough go," he continued, then turned his head aside to address the doctor. "Will he have any memory of it?"

"With head injuries, the patient rarely remembers the event itself. He may be able to tell you what he ate for breakfast that morning, but—"

"Oatmeal," The Major croaked.

That was the first time he'd spoken. It surprised John and the doctor, who shuttled John aside and asked, "You ate oatmeal that morning?"

"Every morning."

"Oh, I see," the doctor said. "What year is it?"

He answered.

"Can you tell me your birthday?"

He mumbled the date. The doctor looked to John for verification, and when he gave a curt nod, the doctor beamed again. "Excellent."

John asked, "How's he doing with the chest wound?"

"No complications from the surgery. He's breathing on his own, so we were able to take out the tube. It's remarkable, really."

"We're lucky you were on call in the ER that night," John said. "If it'd been someone without your experience and know-how, he wouldn't have made it. You saved his life." John extended his hand to the doctor, and they shook.

"Thank you, but I believe your dad had something to do with it. He has an indomitable life force. Good karma. A guardian angel, maybe."

"He bleeds like everybody else," John said in his blunt manner of speaking. "And he almost bled out."

"All I know is, in his lifetime he's had two close calls and survived both. He'll be even more of a legend now than before, and it'll start as soon as I address them downstairs."

"Address who?"

"Media. I've been holding them off until I had something to report, good or bad. A hospital spokesperson alerted them that there'd been a development. They're assembling in a conference room, waiting for me. You're welcome to join me. In fact, it would be quite special to have you there."

"No thanks," John replied, seeming not to have to think twice. "It's your show."

The doctor returned his attention to The Major, gave him an encouraging smile, told him that he would be checking on him later, then said to John, "Take a minute or two, but don't pressure him to answer questions. His anxiety level should be kept to a minimum."

"Of course. Thanks again."

The doctor went out, leaving him and his son looking at each other. The moment stretched out until it became awkward, especially for John, who slid off his coat and folded it over his arm. "We're in the thick of an ice storm."

The Major didn't want to talk about the weather. "How long have I...?"

"Been here? Going on forty-eight hours. It's been touch and go. Glenn and Linda, Hank and Emma, they're out in the waiting room. Rushed here as soon as word got around that you'd regained consciousness."

"What happened?"

"You don't remember?"

"Vaguely. Kerra..."

"Escaped the men who shot you. She fell into the

creek bed and suffered some injuries. None too serious. She's already out of the hospital. Doing okay."
The Major exhaled a long breath as he processed
that.

John shifted his weight, moved his coat from one
arm to the other, glanced at the row of blipping,
blinking machines, and finally came back to him. "I
should go and let you rest. You had a close call. Hang
in there, all right?"

But even after having said that, he stayed where he
was, looking down on him with his all too familiar
cut-you-to-the-quick eyes and expression of consternation. His son pretended to approach each of life's
roadblocks with a blasé attitude, indifferent as to
whether or not he would clear the hurdle.

His feigned apathy fooled many. But in truth, even
as a boy, John never could leave something unfinished,
incomplete, or unanswered. If an article got lost, he
searched until he found it. He couldn't put away a broken toy until he'd repaired it. He would stick with a
puzzle until he'd solved it. He would push a boulder
up a mountainside with his nose if that was the only
way he could get it there.

Now, he leaned down until their faces were only
inches apart and whispered, "I warned you, didn't
I? Because you didn't listen, you almost got yourself
killed, and Kerra along with you."

He had just surfaced from a coma, and John wanted

to play "I told you so"? How like him. But he had neither the stamina nor the desire to wrangle with John's stubborn streak just now. He shut him out by closing his eyes.

"Major?" John repeated his name until he gave in and opened his eyes. John looked madder and meaner than he'd ever seen him. "Did you see the sons o' bitches? Could you identify them?"

He mouthed, *No*, then held his son's unwavering stare for several seconds until closing his eyes again, and this time resolutely kept them shut until John stalked out.

———◆———

Trapper pushed the large red button on the wall, and the pneumatic double doors opened. As expected, the moment he cleared them, he was surrounded by at least two dozen people. Along with Glenn, Hank, and their wives, also there were the lady who cleaned house for The Major, and the crusty old rancher with whom he shared a property line.

The others were strangers to Trapper. He supposed several were from Hank's congregation, and some were acquaintances of The Major's that he'd never met. All were eager to hear the update.

"He's awake, he's moving on command, and he talked," he said up front, then recapped what the doctor had said about The Major's progress, omitting the part about good karma and guardian angels, neither of which Trapper believed in.

Following several outbursts of happy relief, a lady on the fringe of the group stated that The Major's recovery was nothing short of a miracle, and there were murmurs of agreement. Hank's wife, Emma, invited anyone who wished to pray to join her in the seating area. Several did. Others drifted toward the elevator bank but not before either hugging Trapper or shaking hands and asking him to pass along their regards to The Major, which he promised to do.

Soon only he, Hank, and Glenn remained huddled.

Hank eyed him with concern. "You okay? You look a little unsteady."

"Post-traumatic relief. I'm good."

"What would be good is if you left your goddamn cell phone on from now on," Glenn grumbled. "Instead of me having to drive all over town in a blizzard looking for you."

Trapper squared off with him. "I told you. I silenced my phone and slipped it into my coat pocket while you and those Texas Rangers were trying to decide between waterboarding or the rack. Kerra's room was like a frickin' greenhouse, so I took off my coat, which is why I didn't feel my phone vibrate." He raised his hands in surrender. "Are those hanging offenses?"

Hank divided a look between the two. "Am I missing something?"

"Tin Star here hauled me in for questioning."

Hank turned to his dad and looked at him with surprise and perplexity.

Glenn was quick to defend himself. "After Kerra told me about the earring, what was I supposed to think?" he demanded of Trapper.

"I've already been asked that question once tonight, and I'm not going to honor it again. Think whatever you damn well want to."

"What were you doing in Kerra's motel room?"

"Giving her a piece of my mind for going behind my back with incriminating allegations."

"Not what it looked like to me."

Trapper didn't respond to that.

Glenn continued. "She gave us relevant information, otherwise known as cooperating with a criminal investigation. Which is more than I can say for you."

"Ask me anything."

"Already did. You told me to screw off and walked out. It was all I could do to keep those Rangers from slapping you in lockup."

Trapper put his hands on his hips, looked over at Hank, then came back to Glenn. "The Major and I haven't spoken in years, and the animosity runs both ways, but do you seriously think I went out to his house, hid in the dark, and then shot him?"

"Of course not."

"Well then, why the third degree?"

In an attempt to mediate, Hank, who by now had caught the gist of what was going on, held up his hand. "Dad was only doing his job, Trapper."

"I know," he muttered. "It still sucked."

"I couldn't play favorites with you just 'cause we're friends," Glenn argued. "It had to be official."

"Agreed. But you could have called and asked me to come in. You didn't have to send deputies to fetch me."

Glenn, red-faced, cussed under his breath as he rhythmically tapped his cowboy hat against the outside of his thigh, but finally he took a breath and relaxed his stance. "I admit that it came off a little more official than I meant for it to."

Not quite ready to forgive, Trapper held his silence again.

Glenn asked, "When do you think they'll let me talk to The Major?"

"Not my department. Ask the doctor."

"Was he lucid?"

"In his right mind, but groggy."

"Did he see who shot him?"

"I asked; he said no. He asked about Kerra. Eased him to know that she was all right." He paused before asking, "Are you going to allow her to do that interview tomorrow evening?"

"I've mulled it over. Discussed it with key people.

We've decided it could actually be beneficial. Nervous suspects do stupid things. We'll have someone standing just outside camera range to signal Kerra not to answer any questions that could impede or compromise the investigation."

"What about her personal safety?"

"The place will be saturated with uniforms. Plainclothes, too. She's already got a guard on her, twenty-four–seven."

"Yeah, about that," Trapper said, "I blew right past him when I went into her motel room, ready to throttle her."

"That deputy knows you. Besides, he said she 'admitted' you into her room."

"But he didn't follow up. He didn't come to check on her. In the amount of time I was with her before you came banging on the door, I could've strangled her a dozen times over."

"You'd never do that. Not with a cop car out front and all those witnesses who saw you go in."

Glenn's tongue-in-cheek response to his serious observation frustrated Trapper and made him want to shake the older man until he saw sense. "Glenn—"

"Hold on." The sheriff reached for his cell phone, barked his name into it, listened, then said, "Be right down." As he clicked off, he said to Trapper and Hank, "Press conference. They're asking to hear directly from me about the crime scene. Hank, give your mother a lift home, please. Tell her I'll check in when I can. Trapper, keep your damn phone on and . . . Aw, hell."

He left them for the elevators, and one arrived just as he punched the down button, which was a good thing because he looked ready to boil over.

"I'm the one with the right to be pissed," Trapper said to Hank as they watched the elevator doors close. "His best friend is off the critical list. He ought to be dancing a jig. Why's he so steamed?"

"It's a culmination of things," Hank said. "The investigation is going nowhere. They don't have any solid leads. No suspects. The Rangers are flexing muscle. The FBI has offered their services should they be needed, implying that they are."

Sensing that Hank had stopped before he was through, Trapper said, "And?"

"And," Hank said, stretching out the word, "he's afraid that your intentions toward Ms. Bailey aren't exactly honorable."

"He thinks I want to, uh, in preacher speak, have carnal knowledge of her?"

Hank's expression formed a question mark.

"It's crossed my mind," Trapper said. *About a thousand times.* In his fantasies, he'd had carnal knowledge of her in every way it was to be had, and if Glenn hadn't interrupted them at the motel, they might be indulging in one of those ways right now.

"Well," Hank said, "please wait until she's safely back in Dallas and no longer in Dad's jurisdiction."

"What business is it of his?"

"He's scared something bad will happen to her on his watch, while the whole world is looking on."

"Something bad has already happened to her."

"Something worse."

"I'm worse than falling over a cliff while escaping would-be murderers?"

Hank winced. "Don't be mad."

"Mad, hell. I'm flattered."

Just then Trapper noticed that Emma's prayer group was breaking up and members of it were moving toward the elevators, giving him an ideal opportunity to split. He reached out and clasped Hank's right hand. "Thanks for being here. You and the flock grab the elevators. I'll take the stairs."

Before Hank could detain him, Trapper headed for the fire stairs, jogged down to the ground floor, and pushed open the door into the lobby just as Kerra came through the automatic doors at the main entrance.

She was wearing a coat over the unflattering tracksuit. There was sleet in her hair. Her cheeks and nose were red with cold. Spotting Trapper, she hurried over. "I was coming to look for you."

"I was coming to find you."

"The Major?"

"Against all odds, it looks like he's going to make it." Talking over the questions he saw forming on her lips, he said, "Your car's an icicle. How'd you get here?"

"I hitched a ride in the van with the crew. They were deployed to help cover the press conference. I had them drop me here in front, and they drove around."

"I thought you had a deputy guarding you."

"He followed us in his patrol car." She pointed through the glass doors. Parked at the curb was a sheriff's unit, engine running, lights flashing. "He's going to wait there. I told him I wouldn't be long."

Trapper hooked his hand around her elbow and steered her down a corridor. "You weren't invited to the press conference?"

"Another reporter is covering it. Besides, I have an exclusive with the son. How is The Major?"

"I told you."

She pulled up and brought him around to face her. "I want details."

He gave her the summary and answered a dozen questions. When she was satisfied that he'd told her everything he knew, she said in wonderment, "I can't believe it. It's a miracle."

"No miracle. Good trauma surgeon." Trapper took her arm again and propelled her to the end of the wide hall, where he shoved open a heavy metal door, an employee exit, and ushered her through.

"Where are we going?"

"I'll give you a ride back to the motel."

"I hoped to see The Major."

"They won't let you tonight."

"Just long enough to say hello and tell him—"

"They won't let you."

She conceded. "All right. I'll try again in the morning. But you don't have to give me a ride. I can wait till the press conference is over and go back with the crew or the deputy."

"I thought you wanted an exclusive with 'the son.'"

She looked back toward the building they'd just exited. "Can't we talk inside? Maybe over some hot chocolate?"

"If you're spotted in there, you'll be stampeded. I have been. We won't have any privacy."

After a few seconds of indecision, she took her phone from her coat pocket, tapped in a number, and told whoever answered that she had another ride back to the motel. During her brief conversation, Trapper steered her around patches of black ice on the parking lot. Nearing the SUV, he unlocked it with a key fob and hoisted her into the passenger seat.

As he did, he made brushing contact with her thigh. He wished his hand were still inside the ugly, baggy track pants, his palm on her hip, pulling her to him and securing her there. He thought something similar must've been going through her mind, because when their eyes met, it was like time rewound at warp speed and they were mouth to mouth, middle to middle again.

But she took a quick little breath, then looked away.

And he was getting pelted with sleet.

He shut her door and went around. As soon as he climbed in, he cranked the engine and switched on the windshield wipers. They scraped across the icy accumulation a few times, but with the defroster on high, the crusting of sleet began to break up well enough for him to see to drive. He backed out of the parking space, navigated through the lot, and then turned onto the street.

"Do you still have your phone handy?" he asked Kerra.

"Where's yours?"

"Battery's dead." He held out his right hand. She placed her phone in it. With his hands propped on top of the steering wheel, he opened the back of her phone, removed the battery, and dropped it into his left coat pocket.

"What are you doing?"

"Making it impossible for you to record anything I'm about to tell you."

"I had no intention of recording it!" Thrusting her hand toward him, she said, "Give me back my phone."

He laid the phone in her palm but kept the battery. "For the time being, anything I say is off the record. Okay?"

She gave a curt nod.

"I want to hear you say it."

"Fuck you."

He snickered. "Good enough." He let her stew for a moment, then said, "Several times you've asked what caused my split with The Major."

Still miffed over the phone, she answered stiffly, "A perfectly valid question."

"It was the Pegasus bombing."

Her vexation immediately changed to captured interest.

"You also wanted to know what caused my severance with the ATF."

"Yes."

He looked across at her. "Same thing."

He held her gaze for several seconds, then returned his attention to the icy roadway. The SUV was better equipped to drive on it than his car would have been. Carson was good for something.

They rode in silence for half a mile before Kerra said, "Well? Talk to me. You had a quarrel with the ATF and with The Major over the bombing."

"Yes."

"Can you elaborate?"

"I will."

"When?"

"Soon."

He drove past the motel without even slowing down. She turned her head to look at the neon sign that blurred and then disappeared in the freezing fog and mist behind them. "You passed the motel."

"Did I?"

"You know you did, Trapper. What's going on?"

"I'm concentrating. Trying to keep this thing from skidding off the road and still maintain some decent speed."

"We don't need to maintain a decent speed."

"We do if we don't want them to catch us."

"Catch us? What are you talking about? Who's after us?"

"Nobody yet. But there will be as soon as you're reported missing."

"I'm not missing."

He didn't say anything.

"Trapper, what are you doing? Turn around this instant. Take me back."

"No can do."

"You damn sure can!"

He kept driving, eyes on the road.

"What is this? A kidnapping? I'm your hostage?"

"No, not a hostage."

"If you're hauling me off to God knows where, without my consent and against my will, then what would you call me?"

He shot her a glance. "Bait."

Chapter 13

Gracie knocked three times. "Kerra? Kerra, are you in there?" She waited for fifteen seconds, then knocked again. When she didn't get a response, she turned to the young man whose plastic name tag read "Travis." Gracie had dragged him from the check-in office, explaining that her friend wasn't responding to attempts to rouse her. "Still not answering. Unlock the door."

"Maybe you ought to call her first."

"Gee, why didn't I think of that?" She glared at him. "I *have* called her. About a dozen times."

"There could be lots of reasons she's not answering."

"Yes, and one of them could be that she's unconscious."

He went over to the window, cupped his hands around his eyes, and peered through the crack in the drapery. "No lights on. She's probably just asleep. Maybe left her earbuds in."

"Unlock the door."

"If we walk in on something, uh, personal—"

"I hope to God we do."

"I'll get canned."

"I'll take full responsibility."

"The owner's number one rule is to protect the privacy of our guests."

"My number one rule is to make sure my friend is breathing! Open. The. Door."

"We're not supposed to—"

Gracie grabbed him by the front of his shirt and jerked him toward her. "The woman is recovering from a concussion, you moron! If you don't open that damn door, I'm going to smash the window with your head."

"Okay, okay." She let him go. He fumbled with the key but managed to unlock the door, then opened it no wider than half a foot and called softly through the crack. "Ms. Bailey?"

"Oh, for god's sake." Gracie pushed him out of her way, shoved the door open, and strode in, flipping on the light switch in the process. The room was empty.

The young man was relieved, but Gracie's distress increased tenfold. Two members of the production crew appeared in the open doorway. One, the lighting tech, had the temerity to ask, "She's not here?"

"Does it look like she's here?" Gracie screeched. "And it's your fault for coming back without her."

"She's a grown-up. What was I supposed to do? Besides, isn't that deputy guarding her? He followed us to the hospital in his police car. Maybe she's with him."

Gracie said, "Tell me again what she said when she called you."

"'I've got another ride.'"

"But she didn't say with who? She didn't specify the deputy?"

"No."

"Call the sheriff's office. Ask."

"You know, keeping tabs on Kerra isn't in my job description."

Gracie placed her hands on her hips. "Your next job description could be cleaning the crapper."

He slunk away to make the call.

His fellow crew member weighed in. "Maybe she's with that guy. The one with the sweet truck."

The possibility that Kerra was with John Trapper made Gracie uneasy. She remembered how irate he'd appeared when he practically mowed her down outside Kerra's room. "Did you see him at the hospital?"

"No. The doctor made his excuses for not being at the press conference."

"Uh..." Travis the desk clerk cleared his throat. "When you say the guy with the sweet truck, do you mean Mr. Trapper?"

Gracie turned to him. "Speak!"

He nervously wet his lips. "He's got a room here, too. It's in the other wing. I can't remember exactly which number, but if you come back to the office with me, we can call it."

After they trooped out, Harvey Jenks took the first deep breath he'd taken in minutes.

He had heard the harpy terrorize the kid into unlocking the door and then had stood motionless and breathless inside the closet of Kerra Bailey's room during the ensuing discussion, which seemed to have lasted forever.

Somebody, probably the skittish motel employee, had conscientiously turned out the light as they went, so the room was in darkness when Jenks moved soundlessly from his hiding place.

His plan had been to be waiting inside the room for Kerra Bailey when she returned.

His plan was now screwed.

The closet had been a tight fit for him, but he thanked his lucky stars that he hadn't been discovered. He crossed to the door, opened it a crack, and made certain that the coast was clear, that the TV people weren't yet making their way back from the motel office, then slipped out.

Although he wasn't too worried about anyone seeing him leave. The weather was keeping motorists off the roads. Even if he were spotted by a passerby, so what? He was a deputy sheriff. One would assume he was guarding Kerra Bailey.

Inside her room?

If challenged, he'd come up with a rambling explanation that would sound plausible to a civilian even if it was nonsense. But he returned to his car confident that his break-in and breakout of Kerra's room had gone unseen. He slid behind the steering wheel and pulled out his cell phone.

His call was answered with a brusque, "Done?"

"She didn't come back."

"What?"

"I was in place. All set. Except she didn't come back from the hospital with the TV crew." He related the rest of the story. "Narrows down to her being with the deputy. Or Trapper."

"Shit!"

"Her coworkers are checking it out."

Jenks had won favor by returning from Monday's predawn excursion alone, without Petey Moss. He had a story prepared to tell anyone inquiring after Petey: He'd had to hightail it to Tennessee to lay low with a cousin until his ex, who now lived in Wisconsin or someplace equally remote, stopped hassling him about delinquent child support checks.

Petey wasn't likely to be missed by many. His ex was long gone. He never saw his kids, never bothered to contact them. He had lived alone and had claimed few friends.

Jenks had twinges of remorse whenever he recalled how trustingly Petey had accompanied him out to The Pit. Too large to be called a pond, too small for a lake, The Pit was an abandoned gravel pit that years ago the county had filled with water to create a swimming hole. The first summer it was open, two fourteen-year-olds had gone out there in the middle of the night to smoke dope and have sex. While skinny-dipping, both had drowned.

Their parents, looking for somebody to blame, had sued the county and won. After taking that financial drubbing, county officials hadn't had the budget to reopen The Pit. The only thing out there now was a rusty eight-foot cyclone fence with rustier "Keep Out" signs posted every so often. It was a good place to do something you didn't want witnessed.

Jenks had lured Petey to it by suggesting they kill a six-pack of Bud while watching the sunrise and commiserating with each other over the ass-chewing they'd received for botching the job at The Major's place.

Of course that wasn't what had gone down when they got there. Petey hadn't been given time to drink even one beer. He didn't regret tricking Petey. If he hadn't acted first, Petey would have. In which case, his carcass would likely be decaying on the bottom of The Pit right now.

Anyhow, it was done, and now he was faced with new concerns, like the disappointment and anger he sensed coming at him through his phone from the man at the other end of the call.

"With Kerra wanting to go on TV again tomorrow evening and talk about the Pegasus, The Major's near miss, all that, tonight's timing was crucial."

Jenks thought it best not to try to defend himself against the subtle rebuke. Instead he said, "What do you want me to do now?"

"I'm thinking."

Oh, Christ. Rarely did anything good come of that.

Chapter 14

⸻◈⸻

Frigid as it was outside, Kerra was smoldering. *"Bait?"*

"Well, when you say it like that—"

She unbuckled her seat belt, launched herself across the console, and grabbed Trapper's arm. The SUV swerved, went into a three-sixty spin, then another, and when it stopped, its rear tires were in the ditch, and it was resting at an angle so steep its headlights were projecting up through the sleet and snow mix.

Trying to shake her off, Trapper shouted, "What the *hell*?"

"Turn this thing around and take me back to town."

He swatted her hands away and yanked his head from side to side to prevent her from slapping him. "You could have gotten us killed."

"I'm going to kill *you*!"

"Okay, you're furious."

"That doesn't come close."

She went for him again. This time her palm connected with his cheek, and it smarted. "Dammit, Kerra, stop it! I don't want to hurt you."

He finally managed to get hold of both her wrists and trapped her hands inside his coat against his chest, then took a moment to catch his breath. He said, "That was a dumb thing to do."

"I lost my head. Can you blame me?"

"Maybe my tactic wasn't the best." She seethed, but that was all the apology she was going to get. "Ready to listen?"

Her eyes were still murderous. "Is this your scheme to prevent me from doing that interview tomorrow night?"

"This is about something a hell of a lot bigger than that."

She continued to breathe heavily and angrily, but at least he had her attention. She had calmed to a simmer. "I want my hands back."

"Are you going to pound at me like a crazy woman?"

"Maybe."

He released her, but she didn't go manic again. She settled into her seat. "All right, I'm listening."

He opened the driver's window a crack so he could safely leave the engine running, but he switched off the headlights. He organized his thoughts and decided to simply lay it out there.

"Kerra, twice in your life, you've narrowly escaped being killed. And both times you were with The Major. Now, you can lie to yourself, talk around it, rationalize, theorize about fickle fate, karma, and whatever other crap you want to throw into the mix, but you know, *I* know, there's only one explanation. The two of you survived the bombing, and somebody is scared of what will come of you and The Major putting your heads together and comparing notes on what you saw and heard that day."

"A generally speaking somebody?"

"A particular somebody. Which is why I kept going back to it."

She shook her head in confusion and stroked the bruise above her brow.

The reflexive motion concerned him. "Kerra, are you dizzy? Feeling sick? Does your head hurt?"

"Yes. No. I'm fine."

"You shouldn't have been flailing around like that."

"You shouldn't have kidnapped me."

"Do you want me to take you back?"

"Not until I've heard this. I'm all right. Tell me

what you meant when you said you kept going back to 'it.' The bombing?"

"I studied it from the inside out."

"While you were with the ATF?"

"In my spare time."

"To what end? The case was solved."

"'Solved' isn't the word I would use," he said. "There was never a mystery as to who'd done it or why. The guy confessed, said that he and two other men carried the bombs into the Pegasus Hotel and set them to detonate because they held a grudge against the hotel's parent company."

"The petroleum company."

"Yes. Everything he confessed to was substantiated by the FBI and ATF's investigations. The blasts were devastating in terms of casualties and destruction of property. But as far as bombs go, they were nothing fancy, and nothing fancy was needed for a building only sixteen stories tall. C-4, a high explosive. Blasting caps. Timers. One of them, swear to God, was an egg timer.

"The blast radius of each wasn't that large, but it didn't have to be. What made the Pegasus bombs effective was that they were strategically placed. You know like when an old building is imploded, the explosives are set near support beams, either around the perimeter or in the center? Same principle. Collapse the infrastructure, building crashes down."

"That sounds scarily simple."

"It doesn't take a genius. Nowadays we're conditioned to be on the alert for stray backpacks and the like. But two decades ago, three men dressed as businessmen carrying briefcases and rollaboards into a hotel wouldn't have been given a moment's notice.

"The confessor was an architect. He'd acquired a set of plans, all the schematics of the building, knew how to access the areas they needed to get to, and he had his escape route mapped out."

"Remember, I've studied the bombing, too," Kerra said. "One of the things I found incomprehensible was that he was the one who set the timers, then lied to the other two about how much time they had to get clear before detonation."

"Exactly," Trapper said quietly. "He planned it so he would be the sole surviving bomber. But only so he could confess? Does that make sense to you?"

"That's what bothered you, what got you interested?"

"It was one of the things," he said. "When I first got into the ATF, I was merely curious to learn more about the event that had dominated my life since age eleven. I wanted to tackle it, like a foe, and now I had access to files, reports, information that the general public is never exposed to because it's either too technical or too graphic, horrific, gruesome. I was like a scholar deprived of books who suddenly finds himself locked inside the Library of Congress. But for all the access I had, the deeper I dug, the more curious I became."

"Why?"

"It takes years for specialists to recreate a catastrophic event like that. They do it bit by minuscule bit, but even when they've fit together all the pieces available, it's common for questions to remain. The laws of physics apply to explosions, but anomalies occur that defy logic and/or science. How did that human ear wind up a quarter mile away while its mate was discovered six blocks in the opposite direction? Why didn't that one window blow out like all the others on that side of the building? Why did that can of Coke remain intact when everything around it was blown to smithereens?

"But with the Pegasus, everything was neatly wrapped up. No ambiguities. Every *t* crossed, every *i* dotted. No loose ends. Not even the culprits. The guy who confessed didn't make it to his sentencing trial. He died of stomach cancer, which had been diagnosed months before he carried those bombs into the Pegasus."

"Leading you to conclude what?"

"He didn't bomb the place to settle a score with the petroleum company that had gouged him at the gas pump."

"He claimed that he and his friends were making a statement."

"That's what he claimed, but what was the statement? I've read the transcripts, watched the videos of his sessions with the investigating agents. He rambled, he groused, but he never gave a clear-cut explanation of their gripe. He had the world's attention, but didn't step up on the soapbox?" He shook his head, negating the reasonableness of that.

"There was no indication of religious fanaticism, no white supremacy or anti-establishment leanings. No saber wielding, no screamed threats of annihilation, no swastikas. All the same," he said, lowering his voice, "three men who, on the surface, were perfectly ordinary, were indoctrinated into committing mass murder."

"Indoctrinated? That connotes the opposite of what you just said. They didn't have a cause."

"They had one. I just don't know what it was. I was stopped before I could find out."

"Is this where the aforementioned 'somebody' comes in?"

"He's the indoctrinator. I was close. This close," he said, holding his thumb and finger an inch apart, "to nailing him. But before I had all the evidence I needed, the plug got pulled. I was making a nuisance of myself, so I got called on the carpet and was reminded that the Pegasus Hotel was a closed case.

Sure, my interest in it was understandable; it was deeply personal."

"You'd almost lost your father that day."

Trapper was thinking that he *had* lost his father that day, but he didn't say so.

"Why was he in the hotel?" Kerra asked. "We didn't cover that in the interview."

"After retiring from the army, he went to work for a software developer. A lot of their clients were government agencies, so his military background was useful. The day of the bombing, he and other middle management were courting a potential client. They decided to break for pie and coffee in the Pegasus's dining room. It was a two-block walk from their office.

"When Mom saw the news bulletin on TV, heard that nearby buildings had been damaged by the explosion, she called him, concerned that his workplace was so close to the hotel. She had no idea that he was in the Pegasus until two policemen showed up to tell her that he'd been taken to the hospital."

"She must have been frantic."

"I missed that. I was at school. She was still shaking and crying when the three of us were reunited in his hospital room that evening. He had bumps and bruises, but kept asking the medical staff about the fate of the others in his group, and when he heard, he and Mom both had breakdowns. It was a bad scene."

"None of them survived?"

"Only two besides The Major. One lost a leg. Never really recovered. Died within a couple of years. The other didn't suffer any serious injuries but succumbed to survivor's guilt. He killed himself."

"Lord." She took the time to clear her mind of that, then asked, "What put you and The Major on the outs?"

"Several things, but all relating to the Pegasus. At work, I was being reminded that the perps were dead and buried, so what was behind all this poking around, nosing in where I didn't belong? I was ordered to drop 'that nonsense,' move on, and work only on assigned cases."

"That's when you quit."

"Before they could fire me," he admitted with a rueful smile. "Seconds before." He checked the road in both directions. It was still dark, no vehicles in sight. Sleet pecked against the windshield. Snow swirled.

"Around the same time," he continued, "The Major was approached about writing a book, followed by a movie based on it. He'd had similar offers many times over, but this one had serious money behind it and sounded like more than just hype by a Hollywood asshole.

"When it looked like it was actually going to happen, I panicked. I sat down with him, confided my theory, told him I'd become convinced that the individual responsible for the bombing was still out there, and, I was damn sure, monitoring survivors to make sure none ever questioned the outcome of the investigation.

"I told him to scratch the book and movie idea. In fact, I urged him to shut the hell up about that bombing altogether, stop going on TV and talking about it, or the real culprit might get the idea that The Major saw and heard more that day than he even realized, that he might wind up with a bullet in his head to guarantee he wouldn't reveal an incriminating detail while waxing eloquent at a Rotary Club luncheon."

"He denounced your theory?"

"In spades. He said I made the whole thing up because I was jealous of his fame. Nobody was after me to write a book, were they? Nobody wanted to make a movie based on my life, did they? Unless it was a porn flick. Furthermore, I was 'trashing my career' as well as making a laughingstock of myself with this ridiculous fantasy. No wonder the ATF had fired me. The family could boast only one hero, and he was it."

"Trapper." Her expression turned sorrowful, almost pitying, and he couldn't countenance that.

"Doesn't matter," he said with terse emphasis. "He said what he thought, and it was ugly, but I didn't want to see him dead. Since he refused to listen to reason, I resorted to another means of shutting him up."

"What?"

"Blackmail."

She flinched.

"I'm not proud of it," he said.

"What did you blackmail him with?"

"Mom's journal." Kerra blinked but didn't say anything, so he went on. "He denied she kept one. I asked how he would know, since on every page she wrote about the other side of Major Franklin Trapper, the one who neglected his wife and son while he went off heroing for weeks at a time. I told him that if he signed this book deal, I'd make a deal of my own with the tabloids and shatter the myth of how fucking fabulous 'The Major' was."

"Would you really have done that? I think he loved your mother."

"I know he did. But that didn't keep him from making her a distant second to his celebrity." He stared into middle distance for several seconds, then said, "Anyway, he took the threat to heart. He stopped. Cold."

"Until I came calling," she said softly.

"You dangled the carrot. He didn't have to take it."

"It's clear to me now why you tried so hard to get rid of me. You're still protecting him."

"Yes. Whether or not he ever speaks to me again,

I'd prefer him to die of natural causes at a ripe old age, still a hero in everyone's eyes. But he's not the only one who needs protection, Kerra. You showed up out of nowhere and announced your intentions, and my gut dropped to my boots."

He reached across the console and brushed his thumb over her beauty mark. "You had a jewel of a secret and couldn't wait to show it off. But you were setting a deathtrap for yourself. This somebody never worried about that little girl in the photo. Didn't even know her name until Sunday night. She turns out to be not just a grown woman with a memory, she's famous. A newscaster, no less. A reporter who gets to the bottom of things.

"When he learned that, he wasted no time, did he? You and The Major were on TV talking about your shared experience, then hours later two gunmen showed up to silence him forever. They failed. Worse, they squandered an unexpected opportunity to kill you, too."

"I've told you, I'm no threat to anyone."

"He won't see it that way. He's got to be nervous about what you and The Major discussed when the cameras weren't rolling. What did you two talk about? Will you make another startling revelation during tomorrow night's interview? If not tomorrow night, when?"

He reached for her hand. "Kerra, do you get what

I'm telling you? You're like that egg timer to him. He's not going to let it blow up in his face."

Her eyes were wide and still. They gazed into his as though she'd been hypnotized. Before either of them spoke again, his phone rang, causing her to flinch.

"That's probably Glenn calling to ask if I've seen you." He pulled his phone from his coat pocket. It was Carson. Trapper clicked on. "Is this important? I'm busy."

"Two things. First. Did you know about Thomas Wilcox's kid?"

Trapper shot a glance over at Kerra, whose ears perked up when she heard the familiar name. "His kid?" Trapper said. "No, what about him?"

"Her. Died a year and a half ago."

"How old was she?"

"Sixteen. Light of his life. Apple of his eye. Pride and joy."

"Died how?"

"That's the interesting part. Nobody's really saying."

"What's that mean?"

"I don't know. I'm not the investigator, you are. But her manner of death was murky, and it was kept very hush-hush, which is why you didn't know about it."

Carson was right. That was interesting. "Send me what info you have. Dare I ask how you came by it?"

"Better not. If you're ever put on the witness stand—"

"Understood. What's the second thing?"

"It's about the SUV."

Trapper didn't want to tell him that its rear end was presently in a ditch. "Sorry to be keeping it so long. Did you tell the guy I'll pay him a rental fee?"

"That's not the problem."

"Then what's the problem?"

"The vehicle is sort of, uh..."

"Sort of what?"

"Sort of stolen."

Just then Trapper's attention was drawn to the horizon, where he saw one, possibly two, police units braving the icy conditions, running hot, and coming in their direction.

Chapter 15

As he did most nights after his wife, Greta, had gone to bed, liberally dosed with vodka and Xanax, Thomas Wilcox sat on the edge of his late daughter's bed. He was anchored there by guilt.

Tiffany's room had been preserved like the tomb of a pharaoh. Everything she had loved and valued remained where she had last placed it. Their housekeeper had been given strict instructions not to touch or move anything, to dust around every item: a snow globe with a carousel; the picture of the high school dance squad, of which Tiffany had been captain; the trophies and ribbons from the riding academy where she had excelled at dressage. Her goal had been to make the U.S. Olympic team.

The room and every tangible thing in it was a heart-wrenching reminder of her, but Thomas noticed that the remnants of her vital spirit diminished a little bit each day like a slow leak from a stoppered bottle of perfume. At first, the room had contained a strong essence of her soul, but its evaporation was inexorable. Soon it would disappear altogether, and she truly would be gone.

Believing himself to be untouchable, Thomas had called another man's bluff. Tiffany had been the price he'd paid for his misjudgment.

He took a final look around, ending on her pillow where lay the teddy bear she'd slept with every night since infancy. "Night-night, sweetheart," he whispered. Then he pushed himself to his feet, switched out the lamp, and left the room, gently closing the door behind him.

He glanced down the hallway toward another closed door, that of the bedroom now occupied by his wife.

Initially Greta had used bereavement as her excuse for leaving the master suite to sleep in the guest room. But now, eighteen months after the death of their only child, she was still there, permanently installed.

Neither he nor Greta acknowledged this estrangement. Their interactions these days were reserved and formal. They didn't love, nor did they fight.

Any emotion required too much of them. From Tiffany's birth until the day she died, she had been the sun around which their lives orbited. When her life blinked out, the two of them had been left in a vacuum, devoid of light, warmth, and energy.

Thomas descended the sweeping staircase to the ground floor and headed for his study. He'd just reached it when the intercom panel buzzed. The blinking dot of red light was labeled "Front Gate." He depressed the speaker button. "Yes?"

"It's Jenks."

Thomas's melancholia vanished. His body language, tread, and facial expression reflected this automatic shifting of gears from that of grieving parent to that of a man who protected his interests. At all costs.

He crossed to the window and, being mindful to stay behind the adjacent wall, flipped open one panel of the louvered shutters. His sprawling lawn was frosted with sleet. The fountain in the center of the circular driveway had become an ice sculpture. From the distance of thirty yards, twin headlight beams shone through an aura created by the frozen precipitation, making it impossible to identify the vehicle or the driver.

Thomas returned to the control panel. "What are you doing here at this time of night, during an ice storm?"

"I was sent to tell you that we have a problem."

"I already know. The ten o'clock news covered the press conference from the hospital. The Major is going to make it."

The deputy snuffled. "Actually, that's the good news."

Thomas deliberated then punched the button to open the gate.

Going to his desk, he took a pistol from the lap drawer and checked the cylinder to see that every chamber held a bullet. The revolver was nickel-plated and had a mother-of-pearl-inlaid hand grip. But for all its fanciness, it was essentially a six-shot cannon. He held it at his side against his thigh while waiting at the front door as the deputy alighted from the sheriff's unit and stamped up the stone steps.

Jenks removed his leather gloves and slapped them against his palm. "Cold as the very dickens." He tugged off his wet boots and placed them just inside the front door. He also removed his hat, but held on to it.

Thomas tipped his head in the direction of the study. Having been here before, Jenks knew the way. As they entered the room, Jenks looked toward the wet bar. "What I'd give for a whiskey."

Thomas didn't offer to pour him one. Jenks would have declined, not because he had a conscience about drinking and driving, but because he wouldn't leave a fingerprint on a drinking glass, or on anything inside this room, this house.

Thomas sat down behind his desk and placed his hand, still holding the pistol, on the leather desk pad. He was certain the deputy had noticed the revolver the moment he'd entered the house, although he hadn't remarked on it.

Jenks glanced at the framed portrait of Tiffany that hung above the mantel. She had posed for it dressed in her equestrian habit. Red coat, shiny black boots, small derby atop the platinum blond braid that draped over one shoulder. Her enchanting smile was forever preserved in oil paint.

It was likely that the man looking up at her had had a hand in her murder, and to Thomas that was obscene. He wanted to raise the pistol and blow Jenks's head off where he stood in his stocking feet. The only reason he didn't was because he knew that Jenks and the man who'd sent him on this errand would have liked nothing better than for him to attempt it and provide them with a valid reason to kill him.

They hadn't up till now only because he had something they desperately wanted. As long as it remained in his possession and inaccessible, he was safe from assassination.

However, they had ways of reminding him that he

was vulnerable. He'd tested them; two days later his daughter was dead.

Keeping his hatred under control, his expression vacant, he said, "Why risk the long drive here on a night like this? Why not just call and tell me the bad news?"

"He wanted you to hear it in person. Wanted me to gauge your reaction."

"Well?"

"Kerra Bailey has gone missing."

Thomas just stared at him, unable to contain his bafflement. "She ran off?"

"She's presumed kidnapped."

"What? As of when?"

"Couple of hours ago. And it gets worse," Jenks continued in a way that was almost snarky. "The person who took her? John Trapper."

Jesus Christ. On the inside, Thomas deflated. "The proverbial bad penny."

"Ain't he just?" Jenks said. "How come you haven't taken him out of circulation?" He raised his index finger and tapped it against his temple. "Bet I can guess. I figure it's because you don't know what all Trapper's got on you or where it's stashed."

Although his thoughts were in turmoil, Thomas resumed his usual stone face. "Is that what you figure?"

Jenks grinned. "Am I warm?"

He was precisely right, but Thomas wouldn't credit it. "Doesn't it stand to reason that if Trapper had anything incriminating, I would be in prison already?"

"Just because the feds didn't run with it doesn't mean it isn't there. With The Major being shot and all—"

"Perhaps you shouldn't have shot him."

"I didn't. Petey did."

"Same difference."

"Not hardly. Anyway, as I was saying, whatever it is Trapper's got on you, he may take it out, dust it off, try again, and this time get somebody to give a listen. Think how bad things would get if Trapper has more goods on you than you're aware of."

"He doesn't."

"You hope."

Thomas frowned with annoyance. "No one takes him seriously."

"Kerra Bailey might."

"She won't. All Trapper has are his wild speculations."

"And pretty blue eyes."

"Ms. Bailey is ambitious. She's smart. She won't risk her career breaking a story, especially one of this magnitude, on a pair of blue eyes. She would insist on seeing proof. None exists."

"All that noise Trapper made three years ago—"

"He was spinning his wheels, and got nowhere."

Jenks settled back on his heels. "That's what I came to hear, and I'm glad of it. Otherwise, things might've got...messy."

"Haven't we had enough messiness this week?"

Jenks ignored that. "So, you don't see Trapper as a serious threat."

"Not at all. You can comfortably convey that message."

"I wouldn't say *comfortably*."

"What would you say?"

"I'd say it's Trapper we're talking about. At the very least, he stirs things up and makes people nervous."

"I'm not in the least bit nervous. Nor should anyone else be, or they risk doing something foolish." Thomas stood and motioned toward the door. "You can convey that message, too."

Chapter 16

———◦◉◦———

Trapper growled into his phone, "I'm going to kill you, Carson." He clicked off and immediately punched in a number on his speed dial. With his free hand, he turned on the truck engine.

"Did he say *stolen*?" Kerra asked.

"That's what he said."

"What are you going to do?"

"Turn myself in." As he said that, a voice barked his name through the phone loud enough for Kerra to hear.

"Listen, Glenn," Trapper said, interrupting the sheriff's tirade. "Call off your hounds. Swear to God I didn't know about this souped-up truck."

"Souped-up truck? What souped-up truck?"

"Oh. Never mind."

"I'm calling about *Kerra*. Is she with you?"

"You're breaking up, Glenn. Say again? Shit! Are you still there? I can't hear you." Although he could, because Kerra could. The sheriff was shouting epithets and demanding that Trapper explain himself.

Trapper let him rant while he switched back and forth between drive and reverse, trying to gain enough purchase to get the SUV out of the ditch and up onto the roadway. Finally the vehicle gave a lurch up the incline and skidded onto the icy pavement. Trapper spun the wheel sharply to the right, heading them in the direction they'd been going before they'd spun out of control.

Trapper shouted into his phone, "Glenn? Glenn? Can you hear me? Damn!" Then to Kerra's astonishment, he lowered the driver's window and pitched the phone overhand out into the blizzard. As he raised the window, he accelerated. The SUV fishtailed, but he brought it under control, and they sped forward into utter darkness.

Clumsily, Kerra fastened her seat belt. "You forgot to turn on the headlights."

"No I didn't."

"Can you see where you're going?"

"No, but neither can they."

She turned to look out the rear window. Lights

flashed in tri-color blurs through the mist and precipitation, but Trapper was rapidly increasing the
distance between them and their pursuers.

She said, "Do you mind explaining why you're doing this?"

"Remember when I told you that you could get lost
out here if you knew where you were going?"

"Yes."

"I'm testing that theory. Glenn's department will
have been tracking my phone. The guys after us will
find it in a minute or two, get out to investigate, and
by the time they remove their thumbs from up their
asses, we'll be several miles away. Hard to find us in
this," he said with a gesture toward the weather.

"Tire tracks."

"They're a worry, but I don't have a choice."

"The choice is to stop. Go back."

"Not a *good* choice."

"You're fleeing the police, Trapper. In a stolen
truck."

"I didn't steal it."

"But it's stolen property."

"I doubt they'll quibble over that."

"In light of kidnapping, probably not."

"I didn't kidnap you."

"What would you call it?"

"We're adults. We left together. Simple as that."

The truck swerved when he made a left turn. She

grabbed the handhold above the window. "It's not at all simple, Trapper."

"It's believable. We were only one door-knock away from getting nekkid, and Glenn knows it. He thinks my intentions are impure. His son, Hank, told me he's worried because any involvement with me would be the worst thing that could happen to you."

"I tend to agree."

"Only because you haven't been nekkid with me yet."

"Trapper, this is serious."

He dropped his crocodile grin. "I know."

Taking his foot off the accelerator, he slowed down gradually until the vehicle rolled to a stop. He pushed the gear into park and turned to her. "Say the word and I'll take you back to town. No argument. You can tell them the tension of the past couple days caught up with us and we needed a breath of fresh air, or that we were so relieved over The Major's improvement, we went for a joyride. Tell them I dragged you off by the hair, but you talked me out of ravishing you. Whatever you tell them, I'll back you up. Carson will confirm that I didn't know I was driving a stolen vehicle."

She thought it over and asked, "Then what?"

He raised his shoulder in a semi-shrug. "The dust settles, you do your scheduled interview tomorrow evening. You wait and see what happens."

"I don't believe anyone is going to make an attempt on my life while I'm on live national television."

"Me either. But what about next week? Two weeks from now? A month? Are you willing to live with that ongoing threat?"

"The Major has."

"He was oblivious to it until I made him aware. Then he accused me of being addled by envy. He pooh-poohed the notion, leaving *me* the one who's had to live with the dread of somebody capping him, and, believe me, living in constant fear of impending peril sucks. It makes you drink too much, work too little, trash friendships, fuck anything, and crack cynical jokes, all in order to get through just one more day. You don't want to become like me, do you?"

She bent her head down and rubbed her temple.

He put his hand on her knee. "Sorry about the wild ride. Are you dizzy?"

"No."

"Does your head hurt?"

"Only when I think this hard."

"Then stop thinking. Tell me to carry on."

She raised her head and looked at him. "Carry on? Carry on with this escapade in a stolen SUV? People call Clyde the psychopath, but in my opinion, it was Bonnie who was crazy."

"Do you want the story behind the bombing or not?"

"Of course I want the story. But this..." She raised her hands helplessly. "This... is insane."

It wasn't that she doubted his conviction or the feasibility of his theory. But she had lived a structured, planned life. Each step had been charted. The single timetable not devised by her had been that of her father's death. Only that had been left to fate—her father's, not hers.

Kerra Bailey set goals and stuck to the program to achieve them. She didn't go chasing off into the night with a man of dubious reputation, who acted on impulse, whom she knew to be a trickster and liar, whom she'd met barely a week ago when he'd been too hung over to stand upright.

So just what the hell was she doing here? "I could get the story without becoming a fugitive in the process."

"You could. Possibly. With or without me, you'll become more famous than you already are."

"Does that gall you? That I'll get credit for research you've done?"

"No," he said, peeved. "I was just thinking that it's too bad your mother isn't alive to bask in your success."

She recoiled. "That was a heartless thing to say."

"Damn straight, it was, Kerra," he said with

anger. "Even more heartless is the bastard behind her murder. Don't you want to see him held accountable? The three you know as the Pegasus bombers were errand boys. They were sent to do the dirty work of a man who conspired to kill your mother and one hundred ninety-six others. And I'm certain he sent those two to kill The Major on Sunday night."

"They could have been burglars who overreacted when he went to the door."

"They were puppets. Dispensable, and, since they failed, probably already dispensed with."

"You're guessing, Trapper. You don't *know*. Maybe they were vagrants. Two . . . two . . . addicts looking for drug money. Or . . ."

She searched but couldn't think of a plausible alternative to his explanation, and, in her heart, knew the men on the other side of that door hadn't been wanderers or crackheads. Trapper was watching her as though following her thoughts. "You truly believe I was a pop-up that the individual behind the Pegasus bombing didn't expect."

"Yes, Kerra. If you were any ol' reporter who'd finally coaxed an interview out of The Major, we wouldn't be here having this conversation. But you were inside the Pegasus Hotel when it was bombed."

"I was a child."

"Not anymore. You're a smart, savvy woman who

has a great big spotlight shining on her. As long as you're alive, you represent a threat."

"Who is the puppeteer?"

"If I told you, you wouldn't believe me."

"Is he aware of your suspicion?"

"Maybe. I don't know."

"Then the threat to you is as real as it is to me and The Major. Even greater because you were a federal officer."

"Who blew it. I might have spooked him three years ago when I started digging, but nothing came of it except me getting fired. I went into a downward spiral and hit rock bottom. Even my own father has wanted nothing to do with me. I'm a joke. A burnout. This guy isn't scared of me. At least he hasn't been."

Suddenly, she understood why he had referred to her as bait. "But now you have me."

"Now I have you," he said solemnly. "You plus me equals double jeopardy for him. When he learns that you and I are together, he'll make a move. I'll be waiting."

"To do what?"

He was about to answer, hedged, and said, "Understand this, Kerra. If you stick with me, you're taking a huge risk. But we've already concluded that your life has been at risk ever since you came out as the little girl in the picture. Sunday night was an indication that he is not fooling around. He'll go to great lengths to shut you up, and he has the resources to act with the speed of light."

"You're trying to frighten me."

"I am, yeah. If I'm wrong, you can still be laughing at me in your old age. But I believe you're on borrowed time."

"If I'm in that much danger, we should go to the FBI, Homeland Security, the—"

"I tried that, remember? They'll say that the Pegasus bombers are dead, that the case was closed twenty-five years ago, that Sunday night had nothing to do with it. They'll venture that a pair of whack-jobs wanted to make a name for themselves by gunning down a hero. Or they were a duo of anti-Americans who hated what The Major represented. Or animal rights activists who opposed seeing the hunting trophies on his walls. Something like that.

"You start linking Sunday night's boys to a mastermind who got away with blowing up the Pegasus, and they'll start snickering behind their hands. I know. Been there." He gave her a hard look. "Maybe you think I'm the whack-job."

"No. But I wish you'd share more with me. Tell me the basis of your theory."

"Not until I know where you stand."

"What is Thomas Wilcox's connection? Why does his name keep cropping up?" He just looked at her, and when it became apparent that he wasn't going to answer, she said, "Not until you know where I stand."

"Right. And your time to decide just ran out. Do I drive back to town and drop you at the motel?"

"As opposed to what?"

"I make some arrangements for tonight. Tomorrow I start sharing more."

She didn't think he was crazy. Undisciplined and unpredictable, yes. But not insane. However, she might very well be, because she heard herself saying, "All right, Trapper. I'll be your bait. On one condition."

"Shoot."

"Actually two conditions."

"The first?"

"If at any point along the way you ask me to do something illegal, I'm out."

"Agreed. But I have a condition, too. Starting now, everything said or done is off the record. You don't go public with anything till I give you the okay with a capital *O*. When I do, you can have at it. You can have at me. No matter how it turns out, the story is yours. But not until it's over."

That was a tough condition to concede. She thought of Gracie, the station's news director, the network executives in New York who were eager for her to go back on camera as soon as tomorrow evening. If she withheld a story of this magnitude because of a promise given to John Trapper—possibly delusional John Trapper—she could lose all credibility and be banished from television journalism forever.

But she balanced that against the promise of rich rewards if the story panned out to be as monumental as Trapper suggested it would.

"Agreed," she said.

"Shake on it?" He extended his hand across the console.

"You haven't heard my second condition."

"Oh, right. What?"

"We don't get nekkid."

He snatched his hand back.

"I mean it, Trapper," she said. "This is a professional agreement between a private investigator and a journalist. I need your input for the story that, when told, will be astonishing. You need me to tell it so you'll be validated and the mastermind of the Pegasus bombing exposed. We're working partners. I guarantee you my confidence until I receive a capitalized okay from you, but no—"

"Getting nekkid."

"Right."

"Well, damn."

"You still have the option of taking me back to town."

He looked out across the dark, barren landscape, made even more forbidding by the swirling snowfall. He cussed under his breath but then came back around. "I'm tempted to wish you luck and part ways. But I'd never forgive myself if anything happened to you. So..." He thrust his hand toward her. They shook on it. Then he reached beneath the driver's seat and produced a cell phone.

"You have two?" she asked in surprise.

Distracted by punching in a number, he said, "Several. All with disposable SIM cards and blocked numbers." Then he held his index finger vertically against his lips. She heard a man answer with a hello. "Hank?"

"Trapper? Where are you? Dad is about to stroke out, and I kid you not."

"Are you with him now?"

"No, I'm at home." In the background the sound track of a TV show could be heard, along with children's laughter. "What are you up to?"

"It's complicated."

"With you, it always is."

"I need you to do something for me."

"Trapper—"

"Hank. You're a minister. Isn't this your calling? To help people in need? Or is that just hype?"

After a pause, Hank asked, "What do you want me to do?"

"First of all, has there been any further word about The Major's condition?"

"Last report Dad got, he was holding steady. Even talking a little more."

Trapper exhaled slowly, revealing to Kerra that he cared far more deeply about his father than he let on.

"Do you have Kerra Bailey with you?" Hank asked.

"Yes."

"Is she all right?"

"Give me a break, Hank. You think I'd hurt a woman? Or take her by force?"

"I want to hear it from her."

Trapper held the phone out to her and she said hello.

"Are you all right?"

"Perfectly fine."

"Did he take you against your will?"

Maybe she was becoming hysterical over the madcap chain of events, because his phraseology almost caused her to laugh. "No. I came with Trapper willingly."

Trapper took the phone back. "Satisfied? You're off the hook. If you help me, no one can ever accuse you of aiding and abetting a kidnapper."

"What about aiding a car thief?"

"Oh, so Glenn followed up on that. That'll teach me to keep my big mouth shut."

"What the hell, Trapper? You stole a truck?"

"No! I'll explain everything, but later. Listen, you know the place we took the two girls that time? They had a bottle of homemade peach brandy?"

"The old line shack?"

"Right. Your condom broke. Hard to say who freaked out more, you or the girl."

"That was before I started dating Emma."

His self-righteous tone caused Trapper to look across at Kerra and roll his eyes. He asked, "Do you remember how to get there?"

"To the line shack? I think so."

"Kerra and I need to drop out of sight for a couple of days. We'll need supplies. Packaged food. Bottled water. Extra blankets. I'll text you a list."

"Are you nuts? The roads are frozen over. I'm not getting out in this tonight."

Trapper swore, then said grudgingly, "Okay, wait till daylight."

"I can't do it at any time. First of all, Dad would go ballistic, if he didn't put me in jail, which he probably would."

"Only if you're caught. Or blab."

"Secondly, it just doesn't feel right."

"I haven't broken any laws, Hank. Neither God's nor man's. Well, a few of God's."

"I don't believe you've done anything illegal, per se."

"I haven't. So you'll help?"

"Trapper, please don't drag me into this."

"Okay. Forget I asked. And, look, about the condom malfunction. It could happen to anybody. Especially in the heat of the moment. Lust fueled by peach brandy. I'm sure Emma and your congregation would understand."

This time it was the pastor who swore. Then he sighed with resignation. "Text me your list. Will you be all right tonight?"

"It won't be the Ritz, but we'll manage. See you in the morning."

"I can't give you a time. A lot depends on the weather."

"Whenever you can make it." He paused. "And, Hank, I realize this is asking a lot. I owe you big time."

He clicked off, then went into messages and began making a list of basic necessities. "Any special requests?"

"Toilet paper. Can Hank be trusted?"

He chuckled. "He can now."

"You're ruthless, Trapper."

"You're right," he said and sent his text.

Around three a.m. the precipitation began to taper off. By dawn, it had stopped altogether. The sun came up behind an overcast eastern horizon, but the skies began to clear from the west, making the day brighter, the icy surfaces reflective.

Hank squinted against the harsh light as he braked his car at a distance from the shack.

Nobody knew who'd built it, somebody in the last century, possibly in the one before that. It had been used for shelter by cowboys checking herds and rounding up strays, or riding the miles of barbed wire fences checking for breaches, manmade or otherwise.

Most cattlemen now kept tabs on their herds and graze land from the cockpit of a helicopter, so nobody used the shack except for the occasional drifter who veered off the beaten path, or hunters caught in storms, or randy teenagers who upheld the tradition that Trapper had initiated.

After a quail hunt, during which The Major and Glenn had acquainted their two sons with the existence of the rough-hewn cabin, Trapper had claimed it as his personal pleasure palace, an ideal place to sneak away with a girl whenever he visited Lodal. One time Trapper had invited him to go on a double date. That was the last misadventure he'd had in Trapper's corruptive company.

It was impossible not to like Trapper. He had charisma. Charm was effortless, as much a part of him as his fingerprint. He walked into a room, and the atmosphere became charged with vitality. He was the devil whispering in one's ear of the delights to be found in sin if only one dared.

Throughout their boyhood, Trapper had mocked Hank's conscience. He'd resented being the object of Trapper's ridicule, but he'd also harbored a deep-seated jealousy of Trapper's flagrant disregard for rules and often wished he could be that cavalier.

But bad behavior that could be forgiven in an adolescent was unacceptable in a grown-up. Trapper's unconcealed scorn for high ideals and morality had left him a lonely, bitter man. He was liked, but not admired.

What mystified Hank was that Trapper seemed unaffected by the opinion of others. Indeed, he seemed indifferent to anything that truly mattered, including his own self-destruction.

Hank eased his foot off the brake and drove at a snail's pace toward the squat, weathered structure. It was somewhat protected from the elements by the rocky hill that rose behind it. The rusty tin roof had barely a dusting of last night's snow, while the black SUV parked outside had an inch of accumulation on its level surfaces. The tall off-road tires were caked with frozen mud.

How like Trapper to defy a blizzard.

Hank pulled up beside the SUV. He got out of his car and retrieved two bags of goods from his backseat. When he reached the door of the shack, he tapped it with the toe of his shoe. "Hey, Trapper, it's me." He hunched his shoulders in order to raise the collar of his coat up around his ears to protect them from the wind. "Hurry up. It's freezing out here."

When nothing happened, he set down the bags and tried the door. It swung open, was caught by the wind, and blew wide, banging against the interior wall.

The shack was empty. From the looks of it, it had been vacant for a long time. Cobwebs clinging to the doorjamb fluttered against Hank's face.

His breath escaped through his teeth in an angry whistle that matched the wind curling down the rocky face of the hill. He took his phone from the breast pocket of his coat and used speed dial. His call was answered on the first ring. "They're not here."

"*What!* Are you sure he meant this shack?"

"Yes, Dad. The SUV is here, but Trapper and Kerra Bailey aren't. You can come on up."

In a matter of seconds the sheriff's unit, which had kept just out of sight, appeared on the horizon. Glenn sped toward the shack and, when he reached it, got out of his car, stormed past Hank and through the open door.

Immediately, he came back out, hands on hips,

breathing fire. "How could they've left while that SUV is still here?"

"Well," Hank said, "I don't believe Trapper was raptured."

"Son of a bitch." Glenn's angry gaze swept the open landscape. "Where the hell is he?"

Chapter 17

The seedy motel was on the frontage road of eastbound I-20.

Trapper was lying on his side in bed next to Kerra, watching her sleep. He was outside the covers, she was underneath, a stipulation she had insisted on after Carson had brought them here in the wee hours and checked them in. He'd used fake names and paid in cash. The desk clerk was one of his clients, currently on parole. He asked no questions.

Kerra had demanded separate rooms. Trapper had told her to forget it. She capitulated, Trapper figuring because she'd been too exhausted to argue further. But when they entered the room and saw its one bed, she'd made him swear that he would behave himself. He solemnly swore that he would.

Minutes after Carson left, she had removed only her shoes before climbing in and pulling the covers up to her chin. She fell fast asleep. Trapper had checked the bathroom window and determined that it was too small for an adult to get through. He tested the door lock, slid the chain into place, and wished for sturdier of both. He switched off the light. Then for half an hour, through the pair of ratty curtains, he watched the parking lot to make certain that, by some miracle, no one had followed them.

Finally satisfied that he'd thrown Glenn off track—because surely Hank would have informed him that, come morning, he was meeting Trapper at the line shack—he'd removed his pistol from the holster at the small of his back and set both on the nightstand, pulled off his boots, and lay down as close to Kerra as he could get. He fell asleep immediately.

Now, six hours later, she must have sensed that he was awake, because she stirred, then opened her eyes and looked at him drowsily. His cock went from semi-hard to battering ram, decimating his vow to behave himself. He leaned over her.

"Trapper, we had an agreement."

"We're not nekkid."

"You promised to behave."

"I'm not doing anything."

"You're crowding me."

"You've got all the covers. I'm cold."

"You're a furnace." Suddenly she tensed against him. "Where'd that come from?"

At first he thought she was referring to his erection, but seeing that she was looking beyond him, he glanced over his shoulder at the nightstand. "I don't think the Tooth Fairy left it."

"You've had a gun all along?"

"All along."

"Oh."

"I told you I had one."

"I thought you were just being a jerk."

"I was. But it was also the truth." He ran his finger between her eyebrows to smooth out the worry line and pushed aside a strand of hair lying across her left cheek. "You never asked what I was thinking."

"When?"

"In my office while you were sitting across the desk from me looking all prissy and disapproving. Did you ever figure out what was going through my mind?"

Sounding prissy and disapproving, she said, "I didn't want to know."

He grinned. "I was thinking about your beauty mark."

"That's it?"

"Disappointed?"

"Surprised. I thought it would be something crude."

"No. I was focused on your beauty mark, thinking it looked like a speck of dark chocolate and wondering if it would melt against my tongue." He dabbed his tongue against it now, then a second time. "Hmm. Still there. Guess I'll just have to keep testing it." He did once again, then moved his mouth down to hers.

The kiss was long and languid, openmouthed and evocative, and ended only when he closed his hand around her breast. But whatever her protest would have been, it was replaced by a whimper when his fingers caressed her nipple. Even through layers of cloth it hadn't been difficult to find.

"I might've been thinking about more than just your beauty mark," he whispered. He shifted closer, covering half of her, and used his nose to nudge aside the collar of the tracksuit jacket so he could nibble her neck, then lowered his head and nuzzled her breast, rubbing his open mouth against the hard tip, taking love bites of it through her t-shirt, pushing at it with his tongue.

"You'd blush to know all the places my wandering mind has taken me. I've touched you, tasted you..." He wedged his hand down between them and cupped her sex. "...everywhere."

Urged by gentle pressure, her thighs parted. She adjusted her hips to his advantage. He removed his hand only long enough to slide it into her waistband, over smooth skin and lace panties, then inside them where the hair was damp, and beneath it his fingers found her pliant and wet, more honeyed than she'd been in all his daydreams.

He slipped his thumb inside her. She arched up, inviting another stroke, and he obliged her, then he withdrew and with the slippery pad of his thumb traced small, teasing circles over the sensitive target. He kept that up, and sent two fingers deep, and God, she felt too incredible to be believed, so he tested just how good she felt by withdrawing his fingers before sliding them in again.

Her breath caught. His thumb added pressure. Another catchy breath, another clench around his fingers. She gasped his name.

"Wait. Don't come yet." He levered up and began working open the buttons of his fly.

To his utter shock, Kerra shoved him off her, kicked away the covers, and got up. She stood beside the bed, he lay sprawled on it on his back, and for the next several seconds, they just gaped at each other, breath rushing through open mouths, she looking as startled as he by her action.

Then he shouted, "What the *fuck*?"

Kerra yanked the sides of her jacket together and zipped it over her t-shirt so the damp spot molded to her nipple wouldn't show. "I won't be one of your 'fuck anythings.'"

His eyes were blank, but when he realized what she was referring to, he got up and faced off with her. "That's what this *interruptus* is about?" He flung his arm out to his side. "I only said that to make a point."

"Oh, so it's not true?"

He opened his mouth, but nothing came out. His arm dropped to his side.

She laughed softly, but there was no humor behind it.

He pushed his fingers up through his hair and walked a tight circle of frustration. He looked down at the bed. He looked at her breasts as though he could see the damp spot through the jacket. When his eyes lifted to hers, he said, "It's not like that."

"No?"

"No, dammit."

"What sets me apart, Trapper? What makes me special?"

He copped an attitude. "I don't know. Let's see. Could it be your face? The silky hair I want to feel sliding across my belly? The hot body I want to finger paint? The way you move? Your voice? Name something. All I know is, ever since I laid eyes on you I've been one big boner." He took a step toward her. "And forgive me for pointing out that you—"

"Don't." She held up her hand, palm out. "Please don't say something vulgar that's going to make me angrier."

"Hold on. *You're* angry at *me?*"

"No, at myself."

He smoldered, all six feet four of him rocking slightly, as he waited for her to elaborate.

"I saw how women react to you," she said. "Furthermore, I saw how you *know* how they react to you. You're everything bad-boy wrong, which makes you everything desirable, and, yes, even knowing better than to fall for the sexy charm, I did." She gestured toward the bed. "But it wasn't fair to you to let it go that far. I'm sorry."

He folded his arms over his chest and cocked his hip, which was risky since his jeans remained unbuttoned and low-slung. He squinted one eye as he looked at her. "In addition to being bad-boy wrong, etcetera, know what else I am? Smart. And I have a built-in, fool-proof manure detector, and everything you just said is pure bullshit."

She was about to deny it, but he overrode her.

"You wanted me moving inside you just as much as I wanted to be. You didn't call it off because your better judgment suddenly asserted itself or you got turned off by my alley cat ways.

"No, you called it off because you still don't trust me. You're scared. You think I'm either a paranoid

lunatic who dreams up conspiracy theories or an em-
bittered son with so much pent-up rage against my
famous father that I tried to kill him."

"That's not true!" she exclaimed.

"No?"

"If I didn't trust you, if I was still afraid of you,
would I be here?"

"Then what is it, Kerra?"

Matching him in angry volume, she said, "I don't
know how this is going to end."

"This what? This quarrel? This—"

"This whole thing. The way you laid it out last
night, we're in a precarious situation. If it's as dangerous as you indicate, the outcome could be that we
both wind up dead."

He dropped some of the attitude. "A valid concern.
But you knew that last night. Before you made the
choice to stick with me, I made it clear that if you
did, you'd be taking a huge risk."

With my life, yes, but not with my heart.

Those were the words in her mind, but she didn't
say them out loud.

Simply looking at him now in his dishevelment
made her mouth water. She wanted badly to put her
hands on him, pull him to her, feel him inside her
and appease this craving that was as wonderful as it
was terrible. If she thought that having sex would fix
the problem, she would do it, and happily.

But along with the sexual yearning, she was also emotionally drawn to the man who'd had to live in the large shadow of his father.

Trapper didn't whine about it. He didn't tell a sob story to elicit pity. In fact, he rebuffed anything that smacked of compassion and sadness for him. Nor did he seem jealous of The Major. Trapper didn't vie for his father's celebrity. He did everything he could to avoid it.

So while he thumbed his nose at propriety and rebelled against authority, Kerra sensed that underneath the charm, and flippancy, and screw-you attitude, was a boy who'd been abandoned at age eleven. Young John Trapper had been unable to compete with the allure of fame, which his father had chosen over him.

She knew better than to open this up to discussion, of course. Wounded animals bit the tender hand extended to them. He would hate her for perceiving and exposing the anguish he suffered day after day.

He was in mourning, not over the loss of a dead parent, but a living one.

If she were foolish enough to let her heart get entangled with Trapper, he would break it. That's what she didn't want to risk.

They both reacted to the sudden knock on the door, but in different ways. Trapper lunged across the bed, grabbed his pistol, and made it to the window in the same wink of time that Kerra took a startled breath and slapped her hand over her jumping heart.

"It's Carson." Trapper let the curtain fall back into place, slid the chain free, and unlocked the door.

The lawyer, whom Kerra had met the night before, came in carrying two sacks from a fast food chain in one hand. In the other he had a grip on a pair of plastic shopping bags. He took in the rumpled bed, Trapper's open jeans, and her dishabille.

"Is my arrival untimely?" He turned to Trapper and scowled. "I hope. I owe you about five more interruptions."

With no discernible self-consciousness, Trapper buttoned up his fly. "You bring us a car?"

"Isn't that what you ordered?"

"What kind?"

"You have the audacity to be particular?"

"Well, I'd rather this one not be hot."

"It isn't." Carson turned to Kerra. "I told him I was sorry about the SUV. Ungrateful bastard never accepts an apology."

Her eyes met Trapper's. "No, he doesn't."

Their gazes held until the tense silence became awkward. Carson chuckled. "I believe I did walk in on a scene. I love it." He placed the carryout food sacks on the table beneath the window and tossed the shopping bags onto the bed. "There's everything on the list you texted me. I took a stab at your size," he said to Kerra. "Hard to tell in that baggy get-up you're wearing."

"I'm sure that whatever you got will be fine. Thank you."

He motioned toward the table. "Y'all eat while it's hot. I'll sit here." He sat down on the end of the bed. "I gotta make this quick. The missus followed so she could drive me back to Fort Worth. She's waiting in the car."

"She's welcome to come in," Trapper said as he divided the food.

"No way," Carson said. "She doesn't like you. Says you're rude, and bad news, and you didn't call her bridesmaid like you promised to."

Kerra looked across the table at Trapper. He avoided looking back, biting into his breakfast sandwich instead.

Carson raised both hands in front of his chest, palms out, as though warding off something. "Really, truly, Trapper, don't go out of your way to thank me for doing your shopping. Or for the breakfast. Or for driving out across the prairie last night during a snowstorm to rescue your ass. I mean, what are friends for?"

"Thank you. I'll overlook that you arrived at the shack an hour and a half later than you said you would."

"It was *snow-ing*." Carson paused, then asked,

"Do you think the preacher showed up there this morning?"

Trapper nodded. "Yep. With a posse."

When they'd reached the line shack and Trapper had explained to Kerra how he planned to ditch the stolen vehicle and throw Sheriff Addison off their trail, she'd been flabbergasted.

"You manipulated Hank so well, even I believed you," she'd told him. "How do you know he'll tattle?"

"Because he always comes clean. He'll have been on the phone with Glenn in a matter of seconds."

He'd explained that Glenn and Hank would judiciously wait till morning to come to the shack and that by that time he and Kerra would be long gone. Through the windshield there had been absolutely nothing to see except for the darkness, dervishes of snow, and the vague outline of an inhospitable looking structure. "Long gone to where?" she'd asked.

That's when he'd told her the second half of his plan, and they'd begun the seemingly interminable wait for Carson Rime, who'd had to rely on GPS coordinates to locate them. Trapper had kept the SUV's engine running so they could use the heater. He had urged her to recline her seat and sleep while he kept vigil.

She had leaned her seat back as far as it would go, but she never went to sleep. She had been chilled and tired and plagued with the fear that she was engaging in something doomed to end in disaster.

The lawyer had finally found them. On the way back, he'd talked nonstop, telling anecdotes about his clients, until they'd reached the motel, which he'd designated as "perfect for their purposes."

Now, Trapper polished off his sandwich, took a sip of coffee, and said to Carson, "Tell me about Thomas Wilcox's daughter."

"Name, Tiffany. She came along late in the marriage. He and his wife, Greta, doted on the kid. Which you'd think would make her a spoiled rich brat. But looks like she was everything a parent could hope for. Straight A student. Lots of friends." He enumerated her achievements and told them she'd excelled at horseback riding. "The English kind. Little saddles, funny hats, fences to jump."

"Boyfriends?"

"You know how those private all-girl schools get together with all-boy schools for dances? Like that. But no one steady, nobody unsavory, nobody her daddy would disapprove."

"So no sex scandals, abortions, nothing like that?"

"If there was such, my research assistant didn't find it."

Trapper gave him an arch look. "Did your research assistant learn if Tiffany Wilcox was ever in trouble with the police?"

"Un-huh. Not even a traffic ticket."

"Drugs?"

"Not unless you count the overdose that killed her."

Trapper exchanged a look with Kerra before he went back to Carson. The attorney shrugged. "The obituary said she died of respiratory 'complications,' when it was actually respiratory *arrest*. Basically she stopped breathing and died of asphyxiation. And she stopped breathing after ingesting a massive amount of heroin. Official ruling was accidental intravenous overdose."

"Self-administered?"

"That could be what the Wilcoxes wanted hushed up."

"Could be? Or...?"

"You're the investigator, Trapper, not me. It's all foggy."

"Is this research assistant reliable?"

"Reliably criminal. But I trust the information because he owes me a favor." Looking at Kerra, he added, "I got his last sentence reduced to time served."

Trapper ran his hand over his bristly jaw. "Where was she?"

"The Wilcox girl? When she died? Don't know. My assistant didn't get that."

"Who found her?"

"Didn't get that, either. She was pronounced DOA at Presbyterian Hospital in Dallas. After the autopsy her body was cremated. No funeral. No nothing. Her horse was donated to a ranch that has riding programs for autistic kids, and this is no nag, it's a fancy horse.

"The music room at her school has been named after her, but, at the Wilcoxes' request, there was no big to-do made over it. It's like Tiffany..." He made a fluttering motion with his fingers to indicate that she'd been dispersed into the air.

A car horn sounded. "My signal." Carson stood up and divided a look of worry between them, chewing the inside of his cheek. "Wilcox walks in tall cotton. Y'all know what you're doing?"

Neither answered.

"What *are* you doing?"

Neither answered.

"Well, if you ever need a lawyer..." He moved toward the door.

Trapper asked him if he'd seen anybody who didn't belong lurking around their office building.

"Nobody. Guess everybody knew you'd be up in Lodal with your daddy."

Another horn honk sounded. Trapper opened the door and, despite Mrs. Rime's dislike, gave her a friendly wave, in response to which she laid down on the horn. Trapper merely laughed.

On his way out, Carson handed him a set of car keys. "Not pretty to look at, but my new brother-in-law swears it runs like a Swiss watch."

Trapper glanced out at the car and grimaced. "Well, he wasn't lying about its looks." Then, "Really and truly, Carson, thanks for all this."

"I don't do anything out of the goodness of my heart. You ever heard of billable hours? I'm chalking 'em up." He blew Kerra a kiss and left to join his impatient bride.

Trapper shut the door and went through the locking process. He checked the contents of the shopping bags Carson had left on the bed and lifted one in each hand. "Boxers or briefs?"

"Briefs."

He passed her one of the bags. "Briefs and other girl stuff. You can shower first, but save me a towel."

"We didn't finish our conversation."

"Yeah, we did. Message received. You're morally superior and don't want to screw the likes of me. Fine. Occasionally I ask, but I never, ever beg."

"Trapper—"

"I got a call to make." He turned away from her, picked up his coat, and took from an inside pocket one of the several cell phones he'd retrieved from under the seat of the SUV.

He placed his call. "Hi, this John Trapper. How's The Major this morning?" He listened for several moments, then said, "Really? He's up to it? That's a good sign, right? Sure. Hold the phone to his ear." Then, "Hey. You're doing even better. The nurse said—"

As he listened, Kerra watched his smile gradually turn into a thin, stern line. "Yeah, I guess you could call it a wild goose chase." More listening, then, "No matter what I say in my own defense, you've already judged me." Several seconds later, he gave Kerra a sharp look. "She's standing right here."

He walked over and ungently thrust the phone at her. "The Major wants to talk to you."

Chapter 18

Trapper brushed past her and went into the bathroom, slamming the door behind him.

She said into the phone, "Major?"

"Kerra. I've been beside myself ever since I was told you got hurt. Are you fully recovered?"

His voice was faint and scratchy, but she smiled at the sound of it. "Almost. Soon you will be. I'm so grateful."

"You might have been killed."

"I survived. *We* survived. Don't think about what could have been." She laughed shakily. "Of course, I've had to tell myself the same thing numerous times."

After a brief lapse, he said, "Lucky for me, the nurse

John schmoozed was right here in my room when he called her."

"That was lucky."

"I'm surprised he called to ask after me."

"Why would that surprise you? He's terribly worried about you."

"Then why isn't he here with me instead of out doing . . . what he's doing?"

During her hesitation to answer, The Major muffled the phone and asked the nurse to give him a moment's privacy. Then he asked Kerra if she was alone. "Can we talk candidly?"

She could hear the shower running through the closed bathroom door. "Yes."

"I know some of what's going on because Glenn stopped by earlier," The Major said, still speaking in a rasp. "He was fit to be tied. Told me how John had tricked Hank."

"He went to the line shack this morning?"

"Glenn with him. As John knew would happen. Hank's always been gullible, but Glenn was also made a fool of."

"That wasn't Trapper's intention. He only needed to buy some time."

The Major pulled in a ragged breath. "Kerra, is he chasing that notion of his about the Pegasus?"

She didn't say anything, which was answer enough.

The Major sighed. "When he was here last night,

I was barely conscious, but he launched right into it. Said I hadn't listened when he warned me, and as a result you and I nearly got killed."

Not wanting to be argumentative, as Trapper would be, she chose her words carefully. "If Sunday's incident had nothing to do with our reunion and the Pegasus bombing, the timing *is* uncanny."

"I agree, but it's not up to us or to John to decide that. If he thinks the two are connected, he should take it up with the authorities. Federal authorities."

"He tried," she reminded him.

"Yes," he said with discernible regret. "I got frustrated with him over that, and I was wrong. But John is his own worst enemy. A superior calls his methods into question, he shoots off his mouth, gets into trouble, causes grief for himself and everyone around him."

Kerra knew that to be true, but The Major's labored breathing concerned her. "We shouldn't be talking about this right now. It's upsetting you."

"I've been upset for three years. John was a bright and shining star at the ATF until his obsession with the Pegasus took hold. He stopped at nothing to try and prove that he was right and everyone else wrong. He disobeyed orders to drop it, and that cost him his career. Cost Marianne hers, too, and destroyed their future together."

The last statement struck Kerra like a blow to the

chest. She took several steps back and dropped down onto the edge of the bed.

Oblivious to his unwitting revelation, The Major continued. "He took his failure hard. We had a vicious quarrel. Issues that had been brewing between us came pouring out and... Did he tell you about Debra's diary?"

Marianne had obviously been someone important to Trapper. That didn't trouble her as much as the fact that he'd never even mentioned her name. However, he'd spoken freely about his mother's diary and how he had used it as a weapon against his father, but it would be a betrayal of his confidence to admit she knew about that.

When she didn't respond to his question, The Major wheezed, "Well, no matter. Each of us said things that damaged our relationship."

"That saddens me."

"Me too. Can't speak for John."

"I believe he regrets the rift. Deeply."

"If he does, he sure hasn't shown it."

"I don't believe it's irreparable."

"Because you don't know John. He gives no quarter. He can be unmerciful. Harsh. Cruel, even."

Kerra's throat grew tight. "Why are you telling me this?"

"According to Glenn, you've 'taken up with him.' You're adults. It's not my business except that—I suppose because I saved you once before—I feel a certain responsibility toward you, Kerra."

"What about Trapper? Don't you feel a responsibility toward him?"

"Of course I do. I love my son, but he rejects it," he said, his voice cracking. "He's discarded everything and everyone who cares about him. He's chosen a destructive path and is determined to stay on it. If only to spite me," he added in an undertone.

She disagreed. Trapper wasn't motivated by spite, or jealousy, or the pettiness The Major attributed to him. But she wasn't going to get in the middle of the conflict between them, which was already complicated enough.

She said, "Trapper believes he's right."

"If he is, that makes him a target. Don't you see? Like I was Sunday night. Like you were and still are. Take my warning to heart, Kerra. John is reckless and won't listen to anybody, and as long as you're with him—" He broke off. "The nurse is back and reclaiming her phone. I have to go." He heaved a rattling breath. "For god's sake, be careful."

"I will. Now please rest."

They exchanged subdued goodbyes. For minutes after they disconnected, Kerra remained seated on the bed, her posture slumped with despondency over everything The Major had told her.

She didn't realize the shower had stopped running

until Trapper opened the bathroom door and came out, a cloud of steam escaping with him. "I hope I didn't use all the hot water."

He was wearing only a towel around his hips, his hair still soaked and dripping onto his shoulders. His torso was lean, skin tightly molded to muscle and rib cage. The wedge of damp, softly curled hair over his pecs tapered to form a sleek, yummy trail. The landscape beneath the towel was so well defined it was decadent.

He would have looked delicious if not for the hostile glint in his eyes as he walked over to the bed and held out his hand. "Give me the phone."

She laid it in his palm. He took the back off and removed the battery. In a dull voice she said, "I thought the number was untraceable."

"Not worth chancing. You and The Major have a nice chat?"

"Not really."

It wasn't the reply he'd expected. He stopped fiddling with the phone and focused the cold blue eyes on her.

"He said that I should take warning."

"Against?"

"You."

"Figures."

"He called you reckless, and said that you can be harsh, cruel, and that you've chosen a destructive path."

He assimilated all that, then smirked. "You know where the door is."

He moved away and took a pair of Levis from one of the shopping bags Carson had brought. Turning his back to her, he dropped the towel and pulled on the jeans sans boxers or briefs.

Kerra stood up. "Who's Marianne?"

He froze for a five-count, then hiked the jeans over his butt and did them up before coming back around. "I hate new jeans," he muttered and began rummaging in the shopping bag.

"Trapper?"

"Hmm?" He snapped the price tag off a long-sleeved black t-shirt and pulled it on over his head, seeming to have forgotten that his hair was wet. After pushing his arms through the sleeves and working the shirt over his chest, he bent down and scooped the towel off the floor, then vigorously rubbed it over his head.

"Are you going to answer me?"

"Obviously, if the old man is that talkative, he's recovering. I should stop wasting good worry on him."

"Answer me!"

He dropped the wet towel back onto the floor, then placed his hands on his hips and glared at her from the opposite side of the bed.

She didn't cower.

He raised his hands at his sides in a *no big deal*

gesture. "Marianne Collins. She was another ATF agent."

Kerra held her ground but didn't say anything.

He stayed as he was for a few seconds, then picked up the shopping bag and dumped the contents onto the bed. He found a pair of socks among the items. He ripped open the packaging with his teeth and sat down in one of the chairs at the table to pull them on.

As he reached for his boot, he glanced at Kerra, who hadn't moved from her spot. He cursed under his breath as he pulled the boot on. "If he brought up her name, the least he could have done was give you the nitty-gritty. Or did he?"

"He said your obsession with the Pegasus cost Marianne her job, too."

"It did. She defended me and supported my hypothesis about an instigator. The bureau decided that if her loyalty to me outweighed her loyalty to it, she should go when I did. The difference was . . . " he said, taking up his other boot and shoving his foot into it, " . . . she gave a fuck." He stood up and tested the feel of his boots and the stiff new jeans before looking across at her. "The hot water's probably been replaced by now."

"Marianne wasn't just a colleague, was she, Trapper?"

"Too bad none of this was covered in all those

Internet articles you read about me. You could be taking a nice, hot shower, and I could be *left the hell alone*!"

"You were together?"

He hissed an expletive, but then took a breath and flatly stated, "We were engaged."

"She broke the engagement after she was fired?"

"No, I did."

"Why?"

"Because she was learning what life with me would be like. How reckless, harsh, cruel, and ... What was the other thing?" He snapped his fingers several times in rapid succession. "Destructive."

Suddenly, his head dropped forward. He pressed his thumb and middle finger into his eye sockets. When he lowered his hand, he walked over to the window and parted the curtains to look out. Kerra knew he wasn't taking in the scenery. There was nothing to it except a potholed asphalt parking lot and tumbleweeds trapped against a leaning, snaggle-toothed fence.

He was quiet for so long, she thought he was done talking about it. Then he began in a monotone.

"I came home one day. Middle of the day. Marianne was in bed, crying. Like, sobbing. Wracking sobs. Inconsolable. She cried for a long time." A beat later, he said, "While I cleaned up the blood on the bathroom floor."

Kerra felt as though she'd swallowed a stone. She stood as unmoving as one.

"Marianne hadn't told me she was pregnant, not wanting to add to the pressure I'd been under at work. But that only compounded the pressure she was under. All that stress and bitterness and uncertainty about the future didn't make for a healthy environment for an embryo."

A full minute ticked by. When he turned around to her, his impenetrable mask was firmly fixed. "So, yeah, definitely destructive. I was afraid that if I stayed, I would only cause Marianne more grief, more heartbreak, and from the reproachful way she was looking at me, I knew she was afraid of the same. So I packed my things and left that night. Which is what you should do. Heed The Major's warning. Leave."

He went to the closet and got the components of her cell phone from one of his coat pockets. He restored it and checked to make sure it had a signal, then pitched it onto the bed directly in front of her.

"Call a car service," he said. "Call that woman with the wild hair and orange glasses and ask her to come get you. Or, if you'd rather, take that ugly car Carson borrowed from his brother-in-law. Keys are there on the table. You can let Carson know when and where to reclaim it."

SANDRA BROWN

Kerra searched his eyes for a flicker of the passion and heat that had been in them earlier when he was wooing her. But there was no emotion whatsoever in the implacable eyes that stared back at her now.

She picked up her phone.

Gracie answered on the first ring. "Kerra?"

"Yes, it's me."

"Thank God! Are you all right? Do you know how frantic I've been? This is about the fourth heart attack you've caused me this week. Where are you?"

"I apologize for not calling sooner. I didn't mean to bring on a heart attack."

"Just tell me you're all right."

"I'm all right."

In an undertone, Gracie asked, "Are you saying that under duress?"

"Duress? No."

"It's been rumored that John Trapper abducted you from the hospital parking lot."

"That's ridiculous. I bumped into him at the hospital. It was getting a little claustrophobic. Guards on me. Media clamoring for a sound bite from him. We each felt the need for some space."

"He had better get used to small spaces. The truck he was driving was stolen."

"He didn't know that. There was some confusion."

"I'll say. The cops who tried to chase him down were damn sure confused. Where did you go?"

Kerra sighed. "It's a long story, Gracie, and I'm too weary to tell it. The upshot is that we got waylaid by the storm and wound up at a motel on the interstate. I don't even know the name of it."

Gracie realized she was getting a heavily edited version. "I can read between the lines. I hope you had fun with the hunk. In your place, I would have been all over him."

"It wasn't much fun, actually. I ... He and I parted company. I'm at home."

"You're at *home?* That's great! I can leave Podunk Town and hurry back. We'll do tonight's interview from the studio."

"I'm not going to do the interview."

Gracie sputtered, "But the police, or sheriffs, or whatever they are up here, have given their permission."

"I'm still uncomfortable with it."

"Not to worry. I'll call the station. We'll have plenty of protection for you, a whole lot better than—"

"I'm not concerned for my safety. It's ... it's everything, Gracie."

"What's that mean? Everything such as what?"

Kerra took a deep breath. "That's all I'm going to say right now except that I won't be appearing on tonight's newscast. From the start I had reservations about it."

"But there's good news. The Major is off the critical list. He's improving by the hour."

"I know. I talked to him earlier today."

"You did?"

"By phone. Each of us had been worried about the other. Talking alleviated some of our concerns."

"Fantastic! The sensitivity issue no longer applies."

"It applies to me. The Major is no longer critical, but he sounds weak. He's fretful. Worried about my safety because the suspects who tried to kill us are still at large."

"Regarding that," Gracie said, "you're not helping to capture them. You're impeding the investigation. Or so the sheriff said."

"He did? When?"

"Little while ago. Came pounding on my motel room door, demanding to know if I'd heard from you. Glowering. Red in the face and using *Law and Order* jargon about you being a hostile material witness."

"I cooperated fully and told him everything I know."

"The FBI will probably want to question you, though."

"FBI?"

"Addison—is that his name?—said that the feds have taken over center ring, and he's chalking that up to your disappearing act. He's pissed, and that's putting it mildly."

Kerra said nothing for a moment, then, "If I'm questioned again, I'm going to have a lawyer with me. But for right now, I'm going to unplug. I've already emailed the news director telling him that I need to use some sick days."

"This story is still hot, Kerra. He'll have a conniption."

"Too bad."

"Where is John Trapper?"

"I don't know. As I said, we parted ways. I'm going to hang up now. I'm exhausted."

"Kerra, wait! You can take sick days after tonight's broadcast. Whatever you need to perk you up, I'll provide. Massage. Martini. A shot of vitamin B-twelve. You name it."

"That's generous, but no thank you."

"For all the reasons we've discussed, I implore you to reconsider."

"Sorry, Gracie. My decision is final."

Shifting away from her cajoling tone, she said, "Well, your decision doesn't affect just you, you know. Have you thought of that? It's my career, too. Think of the crew."

"Their careers will survive, and so will yours."

"What about *yours*?"

"Goodbye."

The line went dead.

Gracie huffed out a breath and clicked off. "I kept her on for as long as I could."

Sheriff Glenn Addison was standing over her. "Why would she want to have a lawyer?"

"Because she's no fool," Gracie retorted. "You, on the other hand..."

"You could have pressed her harder about Trapper's whereabouts."

"Isn't that your job, sheriff? You lost track of your key witness, so you hauled me down here and coerced me into sitting all day in this swell office of yours, waiting for her to call, so you could find her." With scorn, she added, "No wonder the FBI has taken over your investigation."

"It's a coordinated effort involving several agencies."

Gracie harrumphed. "Good sound bite, and, like most sound bites, it's ass-covering." She enjoyed watching him turn livid.

"We appreciate your cooperation, Ms. Lambert," he said stiffly. "You're free to go."

She picked up her handbag and walked toward the door. "I hated what I just did. It felt wrong and deceptive, but at least I know that Kerra is safe at home."

"*If* she is." The sheriff turned to address the phone techie sitting at a desk across the room. "Get it?"

"Got it. She's in downtown Dallas."

He recited the address that Gracie knew to be Kerra's condo. She gave Glenn Addison a smug smile as she went out.

———◆———

When Kerra exited her building, Trapper flashed the car's headlights so she could see where he was parallel parked a block away. She jogged down the sidewalk and got into the passenger seat. He asked if anybody had seen her leaving her building.

"The concierge—not your concierge, a male one— was on the phone. We didn't acknowledge each other. If he saw me, it wouldn't be anything out of the ordinary. I frequently walk to work and back."

"Go okay?" he asked.

"I told the truth."

"That rarely gets me anywhere." He wheeled out onto the street. "Could you tell if anyone was listening in?"

"No."

"Doesn't mean they weren't. You forwarded your calls to this blocked number?"

"As instructed, and left my phone on the kitchen island."

"Okay. Tell me everything she said."

She recounted her conversation with Gracie, and

when she finished he looked over at her. "You didn't tell the truth about knowing where I was."

"Technically, I did. We did part company when you dropped me off at the entrance, and I didn't know where you were while I was inside."

He grinned. "You're getting better at this. With more practice—"

"I don't want to get better at it. I didn't lie in a literal sense, but it was definitely duplicitous."

Several good comebacks sprang to mind, all relating to Kerra's moral compass and his lack thereof, but he kept those remarks to himself. He'd been walking on eggshells since she had declined to split after he had all but shoved her out the door.

"Regardless of The Major's warning and my own misgivings," she'd said, "I'm going to see this through."

To which he'd said, "Suit yourself."

At the time, he'd been mired in the self-loathing always induced by memories of Marianne and the loss of the baby. Nevertheless, he'd been relieved and glad of Kerra's decision to stay with him. He wasn't ready to see the last of her. Not by a long shot.

But for once, he'd been prudent enough to keep his mouth shut and not jinx it. He'd curbed his natural impulse to either lash out or make a sarcastic wisecrack. He hadn't pressed her to explain why she'd decided in his favor. When she'd headed for the bathroom to shower, he withheld an innuendo, and when she complained that Carson had bought her jeans a size too small, he'd refrained from telling her how smokin' her rear end looked in them.

It had been midafternoon before they left the motel. As they departed it, Kerra told him that she must notify Gracie. "If I don't, I may not have a job to go back to."

He'd understood the necessity but prevailed on her to wait until they reached Dallas.

"I thought we'd be going to Fort Worth."

"Not yet," he'd told her. "Call Gracie on your phone from your apartment. That way, if Glenn is tracking us via your phone, it'll place you there."

Now, as Trapper navigated the streets of downtown Dallas toward the westbound freeway, Kerra asked what he thought about the FBI's involvement.

"Unsurprising," he said. "It was a matter of time, and I couldn't be happier. While they're poking into the case in Lodal, they might uncover something that would support what I have."

"What do you have?"

"No proof. Just a preponderance of evidence filed away."

"Where is it? Your office? We're going there now?"

"We are, although it requires backtracking."

The thirty miles between the cities took them an hour to drive because of a multi-car accident. But the delay worked well into Trapper's plan. He wanted it to be full-on dark when they arrived at his office. He killed even more time by picking up drive-through burgers and eating them in the car.

By the time he drove onto the street where his office was located, nightfall was complete, and in this seedier section on the fringe of downtown, darkness was either sought or avoided, depending on one's purpose.

One exterior light illuminated the building's address formed by block tiles above the entrance, but the office windows on every floor were unlit. Trapper took the precaution of driving around the block, then pulled into a parking space on the opposite side of the street.

"Let's sit tight for a while," he said as he cut the car's engine.

"Why?"

"To see what happens. If nothing does, then the coast is clear."

An occasional car drove past, but none slowed down as though surveilling the area. He watched surrounding buildings for movement behind windows, watched alleyways for signs that someone was lurking in them, but in half an hour, he didn't see anything to arouse suspicion.

"Okay."

They got out of the car. He hustled Kerra across the street, bypassed the lighted entrance, and went to one on the side of the building. He punched in the code on the keypad to unlock the heavy metal door. They slipped through. He made certain that it locked behind them.

He chose the fire stairs over the elevator. The stairwell was illuminated only by red exit signs, but they had no difficulty climbing to the third floor. The moment they stepped out into the hallway, he saw the broken glass that had been the upper half of his office door.

He motioned for Kerra to freeze and slipped his pistol from the holster at the small of his back. For a full two minutes they stood motionless, his ears straining to hear the smallest sound.

Eventually he reached for Kerra's hand, afraid to leave her out of his sight, and pulled her behind him as he approached his office. The door was ajar. Pistol extended, he eased it open with the toe of his boot.

Enough light was coming through the partially open window blinds that he could see that the place had been ransacked. His file drawers had been pulled from the cabinet and emptied, their contents strewn everywhere. The cushions on the couch had been slashed and disemboweled. Chairs and lamps had been overturned.

Only his desk remained as he'd left it. Seated in the chair behind it, holding a nickel-plated revolver, was Thomas Wilcox.

Chapter 19

———◆———

Trapper recognized Wilcox, although he'd never met him face-to-face. With a casualness that belied the life-threatening situation, he said, "Hey, Wilcox. I think you know Kerra Bailey."

Wilcox smiled. "You would be John Trapper."

"I would."

"Set your gun on the floor and come up slowly."

"Better idea," Trapper said. "You drop yours before I kill you."

Beside him, Kerra whispered, "Please, Trapper."

Wilcox shifted his gaze from Trapper to her, then back to Trapper. "We're making the lady nervous. Why don't we end this ludicrous standoff, conduct ourselves in a civilized manner, and set our weapons down simultaneously?"

"Because I'm barely civilized. Ask anybody. And on behalf of everyone who was injured or died in the Pegasus bombing, I would enjoy nothing better than to blow you straight to hell."

Wilcox took his measure and must have determined that he'd meant every word. He lowered his revolver to the desk and raised his hands.

Trapper kicked aside the files and paperwork in his path as he walked to the desk. He grabbed Wilcox's pistol, released the cylinder, and emptied the chambers. One by one the six bullets pinged onto the hardwood floor.

Wilcox looked beyond him and addressed Kerra by name. "Sunday night was a fiasco. Are you well?"

"I'm all right, but I've been better."

During their exchange Trapper had halfway been expecting an attack to come from behind them. He kept his senses attuned to any sound or motion that would have signaled it. But no one sneaked up on them. It appeared that Wilcox was acting alone. Wilcox indicated the mess that had been made of the office and said, "I didn't do this. It was this way when I got here."

"Why'd you come?"

"It was imperative that I see you, because I fear you'll soon be assassinated. It's assumed by some that I will take the honor upon myself."

Trapper chuffed. "You're mulling it over?"

"I believe I have a better idea, yes. Better for both of us. Why don't you sit? We'll talk about it."

Trapper considered telling him to kiss his ass and then shooting the bastard. But Kerra came forward and gave him a cautionary look.

He righted one of the straight chairs that faced his desk and motioned her into it. He remained standing and hefted Wilcox's pistol in his palm as he studied the pearl-inlaid grip and elaborate scrolling on the barrel.

"During Prohibition, the madam of a whorehouse here in Fort Worth owned a pistol like this. She shot and killed one thieving whore, a cheating blackjack dealer, and three double-crossing bootleggers."

Wilcox smiled. "I acquired the pistol at her estate auction. Anonymous bid."

"Ever kill anybody with it?"

Wilcox said, "You would've been my first."

"Wow. I could've been tacked on to the legend."

"As I said, I have a preferable option to killing you."

"You held us at gunpoint for the hell of it?"

"No, to protect myself from you. You have a reputation for being a hothead, and, so far, you're living up to it."

"Well, it tickles me not to disappoint."

"I had hoped to open a dialogue with you, Mr.

Trapper. I'm afraid the rifled office got us off on the wrong foot."

Trapper cut a glance toward the wall socket just above the baseboard behind his desk chair where Wilcox sat. The outlet plate had been unscrewed and pulled from the wall. Wiring curled from the jagged hole in the Sheetrock.

Wilcox noticed Trapper's consternation, and his knowing smile made Trapper see red. "Dialogue? You and me?"

Wilcox nodded. "I want to propose a deal."

Trapper scoffed. "Not likely. Not even remotely. Instead, let's talk about Sunday night's fiasco. Did you order the hit on The Major?"

"I wouldn't be that stupid."

"It was stupid. A hit botched by two jerk-offs sent by someone a whole lot smarter. I'm guessing"— Trapper aimed his nine-millimeter at the center of the man's forehead—"you. Just like the Pegasus."

"You're getting way ahead of yourself, Mr. Trapper."

"No, you are. By thinking there's going to be any dialogue, much less a deal, between us." Trapper took a cell phone from the front pocket of his jeans and tapped in 911.

The millionaire said, "You're not going to call the police."

"You don't think so?"

"You won't because you know the legend of the notorious madam." Looking at Kerra, he explained. "She was never charged for the killings."

"Why not?"

"Because several judges, the district attorney, the chief of police, and half the force were frequent customers of her establishment."

Trapper said, "Kerra, that's his way of telling me that he's above the law because he's got well-positioned people in his pocket."

And the smooth-talking son of a bitch was right. Trapper didn't want to call the cops and have Wilcox hauled in for a B & E when he was accountable for a minimum of one hundred ninety-seven murders.

As though reading his thoughts, Wilcox said, "Why don't you sit down?"

"Why don't you go fuck yourself?"

"Trapper." Kerra touched his left sleeve. "Sit down."

He wasn't good at parleying, didn't believe in bargaining with the bad guys, but in spite of himself, he was curious to hear more about this deal Wilcox had in mind. Without taking either his aim or his eyes off the man, he righted the other chair, straddled the seat backward, and propped his gun hand on the top slat. "Okay, I'm sitting."

Wilcox looked at Kerra. "This is off the record."

"Of course. I assumed that."

Going back to Trapper, he said, "The people who vandalized your office want you dead. When not an outright threat, you've been a pest. Once and for all, they'd like to see you squashed."

"Thanks for the warning."

"The only thing these people want more than to see you dead is to know how much information you gleaned during your investigation into me and how incriminating it is."

Again Trapper glanced at the hole where the electrical outlet had been.

Wilcox swiveled the desk chair to follow Trapper's gaze, and when he came back around, he said, "They found your hiding place."

Trapper gnawed his inner cheek but didn't say anything.

Kerra murmured with anguished disappointment.

"What was inside that wall?" Wilcox asked.

"Electrical wiring and lousy insulation."

Undeterred by Trapper's quip, the millionaire said, "It couldn't have been anything very large. A file or two? Strongbox? Or something as small as a flash drive, perhaps?"

Trapper shifted in his seat but didn't say anything.

Again Wilcox smiled with smugness. "And all this?" He indicated the contents of Trapper's file cabinet scattered across the floor.

"Trash."

"I believe you. You wouldn't keep your files on the Pegasus that accessible." He motioned behind him. "But it appears they got what they came for. The question is, will they be able to make heads or tails of it? Is it in code?"

Trapper narrowed his eyes. "Worried, Tom? Can I call you Tom?"

"I am worried, but not in the way you think." Wilcox leaned forward and rested his forearms on the desk.

The shift in body language made Trapper chuckle. "Getting down to business, huh? Is this where you lay out the terms of the deal? If so, you can save your breath. I have no authority to make a deal with you. I'm out, remember? Expelled. Disenfranchised. Professionally speaking, my dick was cut off."

"You have friends in—"

"*Former* friends."

"Surely not all your former associates thought you were wrong." When Trapper didn't either deny or confirm that, Wilcox continued. "Tell me what you have. I won't admit to anything. But I'll steer you along if you begin to stray."

"I saw that movie, too," Trapper said. "Me Bernstein, you Deep Throat."

Wilcox looked annoyed. "If you don't want to do this, I'll leave."

"Hell you will. You'd have to get past me and this pistol."

"Shooting me wouldn't accomplish anything."

"Yeah, it would. It would make me feel better. Great, in fact."

"Not for long. You'd be snuffed in a matter of days. You probably will be anyway."

"I'll take my chances."

"With Kerra's life, too?"

That silenced Trapper's wisecracking. Much as it galled him to play Wilcox's game, he asked, "What are you offering?"

"I equip you to get reinstated and to reopen your Pegasus bombing case. I can make sure you're listened to this time."

Trapper hadn't expected that, but he tried to conceal his shock. "You'd do that for me?"

"I would."

"Even though you know I'd be coming after you first, and coming full throttle."

"Yes."

"Okay, I'll bite. You cooperate with me in exchange for what? Life rather than the death penalty?"

"Full immunity."

Trapper barked a laugh. "Hilarious."

Wilcox leaned back in his chair. "We need each other, Mr. Trapper. Think about it. Take the deal. Play it smart."

"Oh, smart like you? Coming here alone? Waving around a flashy pistol?"

Wilcox said nothing for several seconds, then softly, "I had hoped you'd see reason, and it wouldn't come to this."

"Come to what?"

"I didn't come alone."

Trapper kept his facial expression as blank as possible, but every muscle in his body tensed.

Wilcox said, "There are five men outside—"

"Bullshit."

"—waiting to escort me safely out of here after you and I have concluded our business. If we don't reach a conclusion that's satisfactory to me, they're to make certain that you die. I really didn't need the madam's pistol. I was only showing it off." He smiled.

If the man was bluffing, he was damn good at it.

"I can see you're unconvinced, Mr. Trapper. Give Kerra the phone." Trapper hesitated. Wilcox said, "I strongly advise that you do as I ask."

Trapper held on to the cell phone for only a couple of seconds more, then passed it to Kerra.

"Call this number." Wilcox gave her a ten-digit number, which she tapped in. "After one ring, hang up immediately."

She did as told.

"Now go to the window."

She looked at Trapper for instruction. He didn't

take his eyes off Wilcox. "If you're setting her up to be hurt, your gray matter is gonna be dripping down that wall behind you." Again, he took a bead on the space between the man's eyes.

Kerra got up and walked to the window that overlooked the street.

Within a few seconds, she said, "Two men are coming from the corner. A third from the other direction."

Wilcox didn't blink. Trapper could hear his wristwatch ticking in the silence. Fifteen seconds elapsed. Then ten more before Kerra said, "There's a fourth, Trapper."

"The fifth is inside the building across the street," Wilcox said. "I suggest Kerra not move because she's in the crosshairs of his scope."

Trapper sprang to his feet.

"Sit down or she dies," Wilcox ordered.

"I'm going to blow your brains out." Trapper jabbed the barrel of his pistol between Wilcox's eyebrows.

"If you pull the trigger, Kerra will die within a second of me."

"How do I know there's a fifth guy?"

"You don't. But will you gamble with Kerra's life that there isn't?"

"Trapper, I'm okay," she said.

Trapper stayed as he was. Wilcox said, "Those men

have been instructed to wait for a second call, a second hang-up. If it doesn't come within ten minutes, they've been given orders to rush the building and kill you, Mr. Trapper. After which, I go home. I haven't touched anything. Not even the arms of this chair. No one will know I've been here, and the people who wish you dead will be thrilled to learn that you're no longer a bother."

Trapper risked a glance toward the window. Kerra remained with her back to them, frozen in place.

Wilcox said, "You're reckless with your own life, but you won't risk Kerra's. And you're too principled to shoot an unarmed man."

"For you, I would make an exception."

"You're wasting valuable time, Mr. Trapper."

Shit! Trapper retracted the pistol and sat back down. "Quite a setup. How did you even know we would be coming here tonight?"

"Deductive reasoning. I heard about your madcap getaway from Lodal last night. When were you last at your apartment?"

"Sunday night, when I was notified that The Major had been shot."

"I sought you there first." Wilcox indicated the mess. "This looks good by comparison. When your home didn't yield anything, my...associates...must have reasoned, as I did, that whatever goods you have on me, and by extension on them, would be discovered here."

He glanced at his gold Rolex. "You're down to seven and a half minutes. Why don't you start telling me what's on that flash drive. What am I up against?"

Trapper thought about that scope fixed on Kerra and began talking fast. "You were thirty-two years, fifty-eight days old when the Pegasus Hotel was bombed. You were Dallas's real estate whiz kid. You had it all goin' on.

"But you stayed under the radar. You weren't into party girls, cars, private jets, yachts, none of the trappings of a man who was making money hand over fist. You didn't mix with society, you dodged publicity, you didn't have any close friends.

"Then one day I got an anonymous tip that you did. Have friends, that is. Or at least the occasional *visitor*. Your guests crossed ethnic lines, age groups, came from different socioeconomic levels. No common denominator. *Except* that you met with them individually and under guard, and every one of them went in to see you looking mildly curious and came out looking like he'd been poleaxed."

"Six minutes," Wilcox intoned.

"The tipster went on to say that after such meetings with you, things happened. 'What things?' I asked. 'Bad things,' he said. 'Like what?' 'Like the Pegasus Hotel bombing.' Tongue in cheek I said, 'Are you telling me that Thomas Wilcox was behind the Pegasus Hotel bombing?' He said yes, and, to my everlasting regret, I laughed at him. Out loud and hard."

Wilcox's expression didn't change.

"Kerra, anything moving outside?"

"No. But the four are still on the street."

Trapper continued. "I wrote my tipster off as a kook who had singled me out because of my relationship to The Major. I recommended he have his meds better regulated and told him not to bother me again.

"Weeks went by, and I'd almost forgotten about him. Then one day he called again. Frantic. He told me that a family-owned factory was squatting on acreage where a group of investors wanted to put a new sports arena. Heading that conglomerate was Thomas Wilcox. He forecast that the factory was as good as history.

"No way, I thought. The guy had to be either misinformed, misguided, vengeful, drugged to the gills, or outright crazy." He stopped and waited several beats. "I was proved wrong."

With remarkable calm, Wilcox said, "The site of the sports arena was previously home to a clothing factory that was tragically destroyed by fire. That's common knowledge."

Trapper squeezed the grip of his pistol. "Two night watchmen died in that blaze. Their bodies had to be identified by their teeth, which was all that was left of them."

Kerra made a small sound of dismay, but Wilcox was unfazed by it, and Trapper didn't let himself be distracted. He was racing the clock. In under six minutes, absolutely nothing might happen. But something might. And if it came down to a shootout, Kerra would be the first to die.

He continued. "I told my superiors about the tip I'd gotten on the factory fire, but I didn't want to give up your name yet. Not until I'd checked it out. It took me weeks to identify my anonymous caller. His name was Berkley Johnson. He drove you and acted as bodyguard. He'd pledged an oath of secrecy and silence.

"But he'd found Jesus and could no longer live with himself for not reporting conversations he was privy to. He and I had several clandestine meetings. He gave me a lot of stuff but was skittish about talking to anyone but me until I could arrange for witness protection for him and his family."

"What happened to him?" Kerra asked.

"Ask Mr. Wilcox here," Trapper said.

"Berkley Johnson died while in my employ."

"He didn't *die*," Trapper said. "He was shot in the head during a carjacking. His family lost their livelihood, and I lost my witness who would've put you away. I also lost credibility with my bosses, who said

I'd been led down the primrose path by a disgruntled employee. I was asked if I genuinely believed that Thomas Wilcox had committed a carjacking. To which I said, hell, no. He hasn't got the balls to do his own dirty work."

"Was that insult worth the precious seconds it cost you?" Wilcox asked.

"You had Berkley Johnson executed. How close or far off am I, Tom?"

"Keep going."

From her place in front of the window, Kerra gasped. "This is all true?"

Wilcox said only, "It's a captivating story," which could have meant anything and validated nothing.

"No one was ever arrested for that factory fire," Trapper said. "I asked permission to reopen an investigation into the Pegasus, and I had to justify it by explaining how it could be traced back to you. My superiors told me to back off that, that it was preposterous. But, being me, I did some digging anyway. And guess what it yielded. Thomas Wilcox. Just like Berkley Johnson said it would."

"Two minutes," the millionaire said.

"What was Wilcox's connection to the Pegasus?" Kerra asked. "Why wasn't it found before?"

Trapper replied, "The authorities had a confessor. Why dig deeper? Without Berkley Johnson I wouldn't have."

"Exactly what did you discover?"

As he answered Kerra's question, Trapper kept his eyes trained on Wilcox. "He wanted the Pegasus to be the hub of an entertainment complex he wished to develop. But the oil company who owned the hotel wouldn't sell. They thumbed their noses at his repeated offers. This bargaining went on for a year or two. Eventually he realized that it was the plot of ground he really coveted. The Pegasus could be replaced with a newer, flashier hotel. So he obliterated it. Never mind all the people inside."

Trapper made a scornful sound. "You peaked early, Tom. You never topped the Pegasus. It was your opus, your Super Bowl ring. In the process of obtaining it, you killed Elizabeth Cunningham, and made her husband, James, a quadriplegic, effectively robbing their little girl of both her parents."

In a voice vibrating with grief and wrath, Kerra said, "My mother was crushed to death."

Wilcox looked over and spoke to her back. "I didn't detonate those explosives. I wouldn't have the slightest idea how to go about making a bomb. A man confessed. Those are facts." Coming back to Trapper, he said, "Isn't that so?"

His unflappability made Trapper seethe. "I've changed my mind. I don't want to shoot you. I want to tear out your throat just to see if your blood will run warm like all the blood spilled that day. Or does your blood always flow cold?"

For the first time, Trapper got an involuntary reaction. Wilcox's right eye twitched. "It's always cold. But it turns icy whenever I think about the men who murdered my daughter."

Chapter 20

Kerra had listened with increasing dismay as Trapper outlined what he believed to be Thomas Wilcox's egregious crimes. There must have been some truth to the allegations. Surely an innocent man would have been sputtering outraged protests. She also trusted that Trapper wouldn't make such claims if they were completely unfounded. Unproven, perhaps. But not without basis.

"Time's up," Wilcox said from behind her. "Kerra should make that second call or the men outside will come in blazing. What's it to be, Mr. Trapper? I want a deal with you, and you want Kerra to live. Decide. Now."

Kerra's heart was in her throat. She knew how

difficult it was for Trapper to give an inch of ground to anyone, but especially to the man who was responsible for the loss of so many lives.

However, he must have seen the wisdom in keeping Wilcox talking. He said, "Kerra, redial the number."

"Move slowly," Wilcox said. "Once it rings, hold the phone so I can be heard."

She placed the call. She saw one of the men below raise a cell phone to his ear, but he didn't say anything into it.

Speaking loudly, Wilcox said, "For the time being, stand down."

The call was immediately disconnected. She watched the man lower the phone.

"What are they doing?" Trapper asked.

"Just standing there."

"See?" Wilcox said. "All well. You can come back now, Kerra."

When she turned, her gaze immediately went to Trapper, who still held his pistol aimed at the millionaire. But as she returned to her chair, he asked, "You okay?"

"Fine." She sat down, and, needing badly to make physical contact, pressed her thigh against his.

She looked at Wilcox and marveled over how unmoved he appeared to be by Trapper's numerous accusations. His composure was disgusting and infuriating. Her impulse was to lash out and remind him that Trapper had alleged *murder*—her *mother's* murder. But she held her peace because she, as much as Trapper, wanted to hear what Wilcox had to say.

He addressed Trapper. "Over the course of the past ten minutes, you've come to realize that you need me in order to get yourself reinstated. Especially now that your hidey-hole has been discovered and raided. Without my testimony, you've got nothing."

"And what do you want from me, except your Fantasyland wish for immunity?"

"Justice for my daughter."

"What makes you think she was murdered?" Trapper asked.

"I don't think it. I know it." He drew in a breath. "Do you know the circumstances of Tiffany's death?"

"I didn't know anything about it at all until last night," Trapper said.

"That doesn't surprise me. We swept it under the rug."

"She died not long before I did the interview with you," Kerra said. "Like Trapper, I was unaware of your loss. You must have thought I was awfully brash even to approach you so soon after."

"At that point in time, the grieving was still very raw."

"Then why did you agree to the interview?" she asked.

"To make Tiffany's killers nervous. They didn't know what track the interview would take, whether or not you would ask me something about Tiffany's death. For all they knew, that was to be the context of it. I wanted to make them squirm, even if just a little."

Kerra looked to Trapper, whose subtle nod prompted her to continue. She sat forward and spoke to Wilcox with the delicacy the subject required. "Trapper and I were told that Tiffany died of an overdose of heroin."

"True. The needle was still in her arm when she was found."

"Who found her?"

"A policeman on patrol. Her car was parked alongside the road at the edge of a municipal park, not more than a mile from the riding academy where she'd spent the afternoon practicing her jumps and then had stayed to groom her horse.

"She'd called to say she would be a few minutes late for dinner, for us to start without her. I told her we would wait. 'Okay, I'll be there in a few. Love ya.' That was the last time I heard her voice."

This man had robbed Kerra of her mother, but his bereavement was genuine, and it was difficult for her not to feel some empathy for him.

The same might also be said of Trapper, who'd lost a child to miscarriage. His hand was cupped over his mouth and chin as though to keep his compassion from showing.

Wilcox cleared his throat before continuing. "Tiffany was found sitting in the driver's seat, but slumped over. Given the amount and strength of the heroin, and the toxins in the substances it had been mixed with, the ME told us that she probably died within five to ten minutes of ingestion. It's believed, *hoped*, that she would have been unconscious for much of that time."

Nobody said anything until Kerra broke the silence in a voice that had gone hoarse. "She'd never done drugs?"

"No. And I'm not an oblivious parent now in denial. Even if she had decided to experiment, it wouldn't have been that way. She was terrified of needles. Paraphernalia was found in her car, in her lockers at school, and at the equestrian center, but I know with absolute certainty that all of it was planted."

"No clues ever led to a suspect?" Kerra asked.

"No. Joggers and bicyclers who'd been on the park trails that day were interviewed and dismissed. None claimed to have seen either her car or anyone sinister. There's a dog run in the park within walking distance of where she was found. I surmise, although I don't know, that someone looking like the frantic owner of a runaway dog flagged Tiffany down. She was the kind of person who would have stopped to help. Whoever killed her was quick, thorough, gone within minutes."

"Who was it?" Trapper demanded.

"I don't know."

"Who was behind it?"

"I'm not ready to name names."

Whatever sympathy Trapper had been feeling toward the man vanished. He now looked ready to strangle him. "Look, Wilcox, I can still call the police. They'll arrest you and your musketeers for vandalism if for nothing else, and I could persuade them to throw in assault with a deadly weapon."

"None of it would stick."

"Of course not. You'd have a highly paid lawyer at the jailhouse within an hour. But Kerra and I would make damn sure the media was alerted. It would be on the front page of tomorrow's newspaper and reported on every local TV station. Being camera shy like you are, I don't think you want that kind of publicity.

"And you sure as hell don't want to raise the ire of your... 'associates'... by being put in the slammer even for a short time. Who knows what kind of deal you'd try to cut? Wondering might make them edgy. Now, goddammit, give me something to keep me from making that 911 call." He'd pushed the last few words between his clenched teeth.

Wilcox eased back, putting more distance between him and Trapper, as though realizing that he'd come to the end of a short and unraveling rope. "All right. Let's pretend that I did entertain an occasional visitor—"

"Who left the meeting looking poleaxed."

"That was your word."

"Berkley Johnson's, actually. What word would you use to describe your new recruit?"

"I wouldn't use any word," Wilcox said. "You're the one who maintains that such meetings took place. I haven't conceded that they did. Nor have I said anything about recruits."

"Come on, Tom. Let's be straight. You were piecing together, one member at a time, your personal feudal army. You were assembling a clan. No pointy hats or silly costumes, no rallies around bonfires, no chanting, although I wouldn't rule out a blood oath. But whatever was at the heart of this conclave, you were the high priest, the head honcho who could get men to do your bidding.

"What did you indoctrinate them to? No offbeat religion like Koresh's. No Aryan nation. What was it? Hmm? Tell me. Confide. Just between us. Kerra's off the record. The office isn't bugged."

"I know. I swept it with a detector."

"So talk. And let's leave off with the double-talk and euphemisms. Plain English."

Wilcox shook his head. "It stays metaphorical."

"Until after you've made your deal with the feds."

"Which is where you come in."

"And if I tell you no soap?"

"You'll forever remain a hero's son who couldn't hack it."

The two men eyed each other, warring silently but with palpable hostility.

Kerra spoke Trapper's name softly. He turned his head to look at her. "Let him tell it his way," she said.

Grudgingly he motioned for Wilcox to continue. "But it had better be good."

Wilcox said, "After years of holding the leadership role in this so-called clan, let's say the high priest senses grumbling in the ranks and confronts the loudest grumblers. They're bold in their criticism of him. They accuse him of going soft, of passing up opportunities that should have been seized, of calling for caution and patience when muscle should be flexed."

Trapper said, "Rumblings of an overthrow of power? I doubt the high priest would stand for that kind of saber rattling. How does he react to this threat of mutiny?"

"He calls their bluff."

"They call his. They flex muscle." Kerra could tell the moment it clicked with Trapper. He said, "They kill his pride and joy."

Wilcox acknowledged it with a nod, then turned to her. "Kerra, about the tragedy that befell your parents, I was glib before. I apologize. I know the excruciating pain of loss."

She didn't address that but asked a question. "Does your wife believe that Tiffany was experimenting with drugs?"

"Greta accepted the medical examiner's ruling that she died of respiratory arrest due to an accidental overdose. But, to this point, it's been too painful a subject for us to discuss, even privately. She's been shattered."

Trapper said, "Like the people who lost loved ones to the Pegasus bombs." He was eyeing Wilcox with unmitigated contempt. "Kerra may forgive you for the agony you brought about that day. That's her prerogative. But don't expect me to."

"I don't."

"You tell a sad story, Wilcox. And I'm *not* being glib. I mean it. I hope the bastards who did that to your girl are captured, castrated, and then drawn and quartered. It would still be too easy on them. But am I supposed to be so moved by your personal tragedy that I'll go to the FBI, or whoever, and advocate that they let you off the hook?"

"No, I don't expect you to do anything for my sake."

"Then what's to motivate me?"

"These are the same men who tried their best to kill your father, tried to kill Kerra."

Trapper and Kerra exchanged another glance, then both of them went back to Wilcox and simultaneously asked, "Who are they?"

But it was Trapper who, when Wilcox didn't answer, lunged out of his seat, braced his hands on the desk, and shouted into the other man's face. "*Who?* Tell me, damn you."

"No." Wilcox rolled the desk chair backward and stood up. "You can't beat it out of me, either. Nor would you try. Because you still need me."

"Let me get this straight," Trapper said. "Bottom line. Your bargaining chip for immunity in the case of the Pegasus is to finger the men who tried to kill the hero of it?"

"There's symmetry in that, don't you think?"

"What I think is that you're a piece of shit."

Before Trapper took a swing at Wilcox, which he seemed on the verge of doing, Kerra nudged him aside and faced Wilcox across the desk. "Why was the attempt made on our lives so soon after the interview?"

"I think you've figured that out," he said, dividing a look between them.

"They're afraid of my memory?" she asked.

"Should they be?"

Trapper said, "Don't answer that."

"He's right, Kerra," Wilcox said. "Until these men are arrested, whatever you remember of that day, you should keep to yourself." He looked between them again, but landed on Trapper. "I want to see the people who killed my daughter brought to justice."

"Then why didn't you sic the police on them when it happened? Why sweep it under the rug? Oh, wait. I know. You couldn't expose them without your own crimes coming to light."

"Not entirely."

"Then enlighten me."

"If I'd implicated them, the backlash would have been unmerciful."

"You would have been knocked off next? Or your wife?"

"Oh, no. They would've punished me on a much grander scale. A school bus full of children would've been disintegrated. A nursing home's heating system would've malfunctioned, and everyone in it would've been asphyxiated. Those were only two of the possibilities suggested to me."

"Jesus."

"Are you serious?"

Kerra and Trapper had spoken at the same time. Wilcox said, "That's what I've been trying to tell you. They're ruthless. They'll stop at nothing."

"They learned from a damn good high priest," Trapper said.

The other man lowered his head for a moment and exhaled, but he didn't own up to it.

Trapper tilted his head in puzzlement. "One thing I don't get. Why haven't they just popped you?"

Wilcox's smile didn't reach his eyes. "Because I have an assassination-proof life insurance policy."

"Bulletproof vest?" Trapper said. "Life preserver? Food taster?"

"Something much surer."

"What?"

Wilcox smiled. "Not until we've made our deal, Mr. Trapper." Wilcox checked his wristwatch again and stood. "This has gone on too long. You don't have to give me an answer tonight. But until you do, your life is in jeopardy, along with Kerra's and The Major's. You've made clear what you think of me. But balance their lives against your enmity toward me, and your decision should become clear. The sooner we strike our deal, the better for all concerned." He extended his hand. "May I have my pistol back, please? You may keep the bullets, but the gun is a valuable artifact."

Trapper regarded him closely, then reached around to the small of his back, pulled the revolver from his waistband, and handed it over. Wilcox thanked him and dropped the pistol into the pocket of his overcoat.

"I'll leave first," he told them. As he moved past

Kerra, he paused and looked at her as though he would say something more, then he went out without further comment, the broken door glass crunching beneath his shoes.

They heard the whirr of the elevator. "Isn't the entrance kept locked?" Kerra asked. "How will he get out?"

"If he managed to get in..." Trapper said. He went over to the window and peered through the blinds.

"Is he leaving?"

"With the musketeers flanking him." He continued watching for a time, then whispered, "Son of a bitch."

"What?"

"There was a fifth. He just came out of the building across the street, carrying a rifle case. They're going, him and his armed escorts." When he came back around to her, he said, "Or those guys could be his Tuesday night poker group, and he's just telling us bogeyman stories to throw us off."

"He might have lied about everything else, but I don't believe he lied about his daughter and how she died."

"Me either."

"And the rest of it?"

"I tend to believe that, too," Trapper said grimly. "He's spooked, or he wouldn't have been here. And those guys were too good to be poker buddies. I didn't know they were there."

"Will you intercede on his behalf?"

"With the feds, you mean?" He huffed a laugh. "He's got a whole lot more faith in my influence than I do."

She looked down at the wall outlet. "What was hidden in there?"

"Wilcox made a lucky guess."

"You'd put everything on a flash drive?"

"Yep. Copies of every scrap of information, names, dates, transcripts of interviews with people who survived the Pegasus, and a recording of Berkley Johnson spilling his guts to me."

"On video?"

"Yeah. I didn't want Wilcox to know about that. Not yet."

"Did you ever show it to anyone?"

"My immediate supervisor. He debunked it, believed it to be an elaborate lie Johnson concocted because of a grudge against his employer. He was a recovered alcoholic and in his youth had served time for committing a series of burglaries. They were penny-ante crimes, but his record brought his credibility into question.

"I suggested we depose him, where he'd be under oath—plus under pain of death from me if he was lying. But before that came about, he was killed." He moved behind the desk, crouched in front of the hole in the wall, and stuck his arm inside up to his elbow, feeling around. When he stood up, he dusted his hands.

Kerra deflated. "They got it?"

"They got one of them."

"One of them?"

A slow smile spread across Trapper's face.

———❦———

"Where'd you find it?"

Jenks replied, "Behind a wall outlet. Last place I looked."

The other man pushed the flash drive into the computer port. "Where you find something is always the last place you look."

The deputy chuckled. "Before I got to that outlet, I had the pleasure of turning the place inside out. Trapper won't recognize it. Or his apartment, either." He raised his glass of whiskey and saluted his own success.

"Let's see what we have."

Jenks scooted his chair closer so that he could see the computer monitor. The files on the drive were numbered, but not named. "May as well start at the top," Jenks said.

The file opened onto a video screen. The play arrow

was clicked on. For several seconds the screen remained black, but audio began playing. It was a
percussion beat.

Then the video fade-in showed three naked people
on an unmade bed, two women and a man, *in fla-
grante delicto*. A *ménage à trois* to the accompaniment
of a monotonous *thump, thump, thump*.

Chapter 21

Kerra sputtered and then laughed out loud when Trapper told her what the vandal would find on the flash drive. "How many such videos did you put on there?"

"Ten or twelve. But after the first file is opened, he'll know he's been had."

They'd left his office within minutes of Wilcox's departure and were back in the ugly car borrowed from Carson's brother-in-law. Trapper was driving.

"I knew it was only a matter of time before someone came searching to see what I had on the bombing and determine whether or not it was cause for concern. In light of this week's events, it was almost a sure thing. I'd even asked Carson to keep his eyes peeled."

"The file cabinet?"

"All for show. Trash, just like I told Wilcox. It wouldn't have taken the intruder long to figure that out. I hid that flash drive behind the outlet so he'd think he'd found the mother lode."

"Genius."

"Not so genius. I still don't know who he is, who *they* are, if there was more than one. Remains to be seen how many members there are in Wilcox's fucked-up band of brothers."

"Berkley Johnson didn't specify?"

"He 'couldn't say for sure,' and he might have been telling the truth. He could have lost count over the years. Or he was afraid to tell too much until he got into witness protection, which I think is more likely. I know he was scared of reprisal."

"Rightfully."

Trapper sighed. "Yeah. I live with that every day. I should've kept much better watch over him."

"Blame the people responsible, Trapper. Not yourself."

"Easier said." He'd failed Berkley Johnson by not doing enough, soon enough, to protect him, which was why he was determined to keep Kerra in his sight. Not that having her within touch was hardship duty.

Trapper took a circuitous route from downtown, driving through residential neighborhoods, entering parking lots on one side and exiting on the other. Where traffic was heavier, he wove in and out of lanes, shot through yellow lights, made sharp turns at the last possible moment, constantly checking the rearview and side mirrors for a tail.

When he was certain they weren't being followed, he backtracked in the same zigzagging way and now pulled to the curb in front of a neat, cottage-style house in one of Fort Worth's established but recently refurbished neighborhoods.

Looking at the house, Kerra said, "This isn't where I envisioned you living."

"I don't."

"Then whose house is it?"

Disregarding the question, he said, "Come on."

He got out on the driver's side and went around. He ushered her up the front walk to the small, square porch where matching pots with narrow evergreen shrubs flanked a brick-red front door. An iron light fixture hung above it, but it was off.

Ignoring Kerra's stare, which was demanding an explanation, he pressed the doorbell. It could be heard chiming inside. He continued to look straight ahead at the glossy surface of the door until the light fixture came on, the door was pulled open, and he was looking into the face of his former fiancée.

Marianne was as pretty and sweet-looking as ever. Her eyes were still guileless. But there were noticeable differences in her appearance. She was wearing her hair shorter, and, always trim before, her belly was now distended with advanced pregnancy.

She spoke his name softly.

"Hey, Marianne."

Her smile was as wobbly as his felt. She said, "It's good to see you."

"You too. You look great." Awkwardly, he motioned toward her midsection. "Congratulations."

"Thank you."

"When?"

"April."

"Not long, then."

She laughed in her self-deprecating way. "By the due date, believe me, I'll be ready."

"I'm glad for you," he said, meaning it to his marrow.

"Thank you. I'm glad, too." She continued looking into his eyes for several seconds more before shifting to Kerra.

"I'm sorry," he said. "Marianne, this is—"

"No introduction necessary. Welcome, Kerra."

"Thank you." Kerra reached across the threshold, and the two shook hands.

Marianne stood aside and motioned them in. Just as she closed the door behind them, a man stepped into the central hallway from one of the rooms opening off it. "Marianne, who—"

Upon seeing Trapper, he stopped as though he'd run into a glass wall, and, if hostility had a sound, he would have crackled. His bearing indicated that he'd like nothing better than to drop his book and reading glasses where he stood and lay into him.

In her quiet and unassuming way, Marianne tried to defuse the situation. "My husband, David. David, this is John Trapper."

"What's he doing here?"

Trapper said, "I won't be here long."

"Damn right, you won't. In fact, you're on your way out."

"David, please," Marianne whispered.

Her husband hesitated as though he might yet whale into Trapper, but he responded to the tension in Marianne's face and the pleading in her eyes by saying nothing more. He did, however, remain standing in the middle of the hallway with the rigidity of a palace guard and the territorial menace of a junkyard dog.

Marianne broke the tense silence by introducing him to Kerra. They exchanged how-do-you-dos and she congratulated him on the pending arrival. "Do you know what you're having?"

"A girl," the couple chorused.

"We're very happy," David said, and shot a look

toward Trapper that dared him to question his and Marianne's marital bliss and delight over the baby.

Marianne offered them something to drink. They declined. Then no one said anything for an interminable length of time, until Trapper cleared his throat and gave Marianne a meaningful look.

She turned to her husband. "Trapper's visit isn't entirely unexpected, David. I didn't tell you because, well...I just didn't. He came to pick up something."

"What?"

"Honestly, I don't know."

David came back to Trapper looking even more murderous than before. "I don't know what you're up to. Still playing government agent, I guess. But whatever your game is, if you've put my wife and our baby in any danger—"

"I haven't. I won't."

"You have just by showing up on our doorstep. You're a nightmare, and I want you to get the hell out of my house."

Up till now, Trapper had tolerated the man's animosity because, in David's place, he would have felt the same. But the chest beating was wearing thin. "Look, I don't want to make trouble."

"You are trouble."

"Once I get what I came for, you'll never see me again."

"Which will be too soon."

They might have continued interminably, but Marianne saw an opening and seized it. "It's in the kitchen."

David looked like he wanted to object, but he was simply too well bred to make a scene that would no doubt upset his pregnant wife. Kerra's presence also might have had something to do with his backing down.

He moved out of the way so Trapper could follow Marianne. David's drop-dead look was mollified only slightly when Trapper linked his fingers with Kerra's and pulled her along as they filed down the hall toward the back of the house. Trapper tried his best not to swagger.

Kerra couldn't help but compare Marianne's cluttered and homey kitchen to her own. This one smelled like the chocolate cake cooling on the counter. Hers smelled like cake only when she burned a certain candle. There were dishes in the sink that hadn't yet been loaded into the dishwasher. Kerra's kitchen needed cleaning only when the dust began to show.

She felt terribly outshone.

"Would you like some cake?"

She and Trapper declined, and Marianne seemed to have anticipated they would. She went to a desk built into the cabinetry, opened a lower drawer, and took out a padded envelope bearing a label that had required her signature. As she handed it to Trapper, she said, "I opened it because it was addressed to me."

"That's okay." He shook the envelope, and an article wrapped in newspaper and cellophane tape dropped into his hand. He ripped open the crude packaging. Kerra wasn't surprised to see that it contained a flash drive.

Marianne said to Trapper, "Even though there was no return address, I knew it had to be from you."

"How'd you know?"

"Because it looked like your gift wrapping. And this is exactly like something you would do."

"I had to send it to somebody who would get that, somebody I could trust to hold on to it until I came to get it."

They smiled at each other in the way of a pair who are able to communicate without words.

Kerra felt terribly excluded.

She felt terrible, period.

Marianne took the empty envelope and wad of newspaper from Trapper and stuffed them into the wastepaper basket in the knee space under the desk. "Does this have to do with what happened at The Major's house on Sunday night?"

Trapper made a noncommittal motion with his shoulder. "Better that you don't know."

"At least tell me how he's doing. I've been worried."

"He's come a long way since Sunday. Looks like he'll be all right."

She looked over at Kerra. "What a terrifying experience that must have been for you. Have you recovered from your injuries?"

"If you look closely, you can still see some bruising that makeup doesn't cover. But I got off light compared to The Major's injuries."

"The TV station publicized that you were going to be interviewed tonight on the news, but then had to retract and say that you weren't feeling up to it." She looked Kerra over, a question in her kind eyes.

"I had planned to do it, then..." She glanced at Trapper. "I changed my mind."

Marianne smiled as though she understood how rapidly plans could change when Trapper was involved. She looked at him. "What about you? How are you? Are you taking care of yourself?"

"Aw, you know me. Nothing touches me."

Her rueful smile said she knew better.

"Excuse me." They all turned toward the open doorway where David stood. "You may want to see this."

Kerra was the first to fall in behind him. She followed him back down the hallway and into a den with comfortable furnishings, a well-lived-in ambiance, and a flat-screen TV mounted on the wall above a low mantel.

"News bulletin," David said, reaching for the remote and pumping up the volume. Looking over his shoulder at the three of them, he said, "They caught the guy who shot The Major."

Chapter 22

—◆—

Who's this?"

"Trapper." He was driving with one hand, holding a cell phone to his ear with the other.

Glenn growled. "Aka Unknown Caller."

"I'm on a burner."

"Since your phone is busted all to hell."

"I was trying to get a better signal by holding it out the car window. It slipped out of my hand."

"Sure it did. That was also a cute trick you pulled on Hank. How'd you leave the line shack? Sprout wings? Or have somebody come pick you up?"

"It was a spur-of-the-moment thing. Came about too late to notify Hank of the switch in plans."

"Like hell."

"I'll apologize and buy him a beer."

"He doesn't drink."

"A new Bible, then," Trapper said with mounting impatience. "I'll make it up to him, all right? Now what about this guy you have in custody?"

"I figured when you got wind of that, you'd reappear."

"What's the skinny?"

"Leslie Doyle Duncan. New to us, but no stranger to the law in Oklahoma, where he's from. He was stopped this afternoon for blazing through a school zone, and when his license was run, come to find out he was being sought for several parole violations, the worst of which is possession of a handgun. One was found under the driver's seat of his pickup."

"So far, just another day at the office."

"Except that the pistol is a nine-millimeter, one bullet missing from the clip, which synced with the number that blew a hole in The Major's lung."

"Huh."

"Feds are with him now, putting on the pressure. 'We can't help you if you don't help us, Mr. Duncan. Talk to us.' Meanwhile, the pistol's on its way to have ballistics run."

"What song is Duncan singing?"

"Denial. He never saw the pistol before the traffic cop pulled it out from under his seat."

"Who's it registered to?"

"Number's been filed off."

"What was he serving time for?"

"It's been a revolving door, but his most recent stint was for armed robbery. He was also indicted for assault but made a plea bargain."

"Where's he say he was Sunday night?"

"Home in the trailer park with his old lady."

"What's his old lady say?"

"We're trying to run her down. He said she went to Ardmore yesterday to visit her mama."

"Where's he work?"

"Nowhere. His last job was at one of the Choctaw casinos. But when it was discovered that he'd lied on his job application and was a parolee, they fired him. He crossed the Red and, lucky us, moved to Lodal."

"How long ago?"

"Few months."

"Why'd he choose Lodal?"

"He threw a dart at the map."

"Why would he want to pop The Major?"

"According to him, he wouldn't. Said he knew who The Major was because of the picture, and knew he'd been shot because it's been all over everywhere." Glenn took a breath. "That's the latest. Agents are still grilling him."

"He lawyer up?"

"Not yet."

"I want a crack at him."

Glenn laughed.

"You could deputize me."

"I could also take a winter vacation to Siberia, but it ain't gonna happen. I'm trying to keep the Rangers and feds from arresting you for making off with their material witness. Where'd you stash Kerra? Because I know she's not at her condo in Dallas."

"Why would you think she was? Unless...Glenn, you devil. You browbeat Gracie into telling, didn't you?"

Without acknowledging that, Glenn continued. "When Kerra failed to answer her phone the many times I called, I spoke to the condo concierge. He said Kerra had been there, stopped at the desk to borrow the master spare key to her apartment because hers had been lost.

"But less than fifteen minutes later he saw her leave on foot, carrying what looked like a gym bag. Funny thing is, her phone is still signaling from the apartment. And all that bears your stamp, Trapper. Where are you now?"

"On my way back. But before I cross into your county, I want assurance I won't be arrested for grand theft auto."

"That two-bit lawyer friend of yours called," Glenn grumbled. "He explained the situation and apologized profusely."

"So we're good."

"Not quite. Kerra with you?"

"How about I deliver her to your office in the morning?"

"How about you deliver her now?"

"Because you have your hands full applying pressure to the Okie. You already have Kerra's signed statement and recorded interview, and anything she might possibly add can wait till tomorrow. And by the way, I didn't kidnap her. She came willingly. We cool?"

"That time you substituted raw Easter eggs for boiled ones?"

"Yeah?"

"I shouldn't have talked The Major out of paddling you."

Trapper laughed. "See you in the morning."

"Wait. Where are you—"

"Bright and early," Trapper said, and then clicked off.

Kerra, who'd remained silent but had been following the conversation, asked, "Will we be there?"

"You bet. I really do want a crack at that guy."

"Even if you twist the sheriff's arm, the FBI will never permit it."

"You're right, they won't. But I have an ace to play."

"The flash drive?"

"Flash drive?" He looked across at her and asked innocently, "What flash drive?" Her expression made him chuckle. "No, I've got another ace."

———◆———

"Goddammit!" Glenn swore when Trapper hung up on him.

He swiveled his desk chair around to the credenza. The carafe of the outdated coffeemaker had been made cloudy by oceans of bad coffee, and the dregs in it now smelled burned and looked as thick as tar, but he emptied it into his mug anyway. The stronger the brew, the better it masked the aroma of the whiskey he laced it with.

He was pouring from the bottle he kept in his bottom desk drawer when one knock landed hard on his office door before it was pushed open and Jenks strode in.

Glenn expelled a gust of breath and sucked sloshed whiskey off the back of his hand. "You almost gave me heart failure." He recapped the bottle and returned it to the drawer.

"You ought to be more careful," the deputy said. "I could've been anybody."

"That's what scared the bejesus out of me." Glenn took a drink and sighed appreciation. "What's up?" He nodded at the form Jenks had brought in with him. "No, don't tell me. That's Leslie Doyle Duncan's signed confession."

The deputy snorted. "Missing person report."

"She's with Trapper."

"Huh?"

"Kerra Bailey."

"This isn't about her."

Glenn reached across the desk to take the sheet from the deputy and read the typed-in name. "Petey Moss." He looked up at Jenks and frowned.

"His neighbor went over Monday evening to collect a ballpeen hammer Petey had borrowed from him," Jenks said. "Petey wasn't there. Neighbor's been keeping an eye out for him ever since. He really wants his hammer back.

"There's been no sign of Petey. Neighbor called his workplace today. His boss hasn't seen him all week, either. The neighbor, who's also his landlord, went over to his house again this evening, and when he got no answer, let himself in. Said Petey's mailbox is overflowing, his goldfish are belly up, and everything in the fridge has gone bad.

"I told him the last time I saw Petey he was talking about cooling his heels in Tennessee for a while, but I agreed that it wasn't like him to leave town without giving his boss notice and settling his lease." He motioned at the report. "I thought you oughta know."

"I'll put somebody on it right away," Glenn said. But he didn't. He slid the form into a stack of other unattended-to paperwork and sipped from his mug of coffee. "Now to the real problem."

Without even having to think about it, Jenks said, "Trapper."

"They won't let us see The Major at this hour," Kerra said as she and Trapper stepped off the elevator on the ICU floor of the hospital.

"I won't ask permission. If necessary, I'll beg forgiveness."

He had to do neither. They waited until someone exited the pneumatic doors and slipped through before they closed. The corridor was empty. Unobserved, they went into The Major's room. It was lighted only by the glow of the various machines to which he was still attached. He was sleeping.

"This is the first time I've seen him since it happened," Kerra whispered. "It comes as a shock. The last time I saw him, he was his robust self."

"Stunned me to see him like this, too," Trapper said. "The white whiskers really threw me."

"I talked to him this morning—"

"It was yesterday morning."

At the sound of his voice, both she and Trapper

reacted with surprise and moved closer to the bed.
The Major opened his eyes. She smiled down at him.
"I stand corrected. It *was* yesterday. I've lost all track
of time."

He seesawed a look between them. "What have you
been up to since we talked?"

Rather than address the question, Trapper asked
how he was feeling.

"Fair to middling."

"You'd look better if you'd lose the scraggly beard."

"You could stand a shave yourself."

Kerra interceded. "Are you eating yet?"

"Tomorrow. Broth and applesauce. I can hardly
wait."

"It's progress," Trapper said.

"Too slow."

He told them he'd been tested on mobility, dexter-
ity, and coordination, language retention and memory, and had passed all. "They did another brain scan
today, looking for bleeders. None were found."

"That all sounds good," Trapper said. "How's the
breathing?"

"Better at times than at others. I'm still so damn
weak."

Hearing the discouragement in his tone, and
knowing how the former soldier had prided himself
on staying fit and strong, Kerra patted his shoulder.
"Don't rush it."

"I don't have a choice." He looked her over carefully. "You seem to have come through it without any noticeable damage."

"Yes, most of my scratches—"

"I wasn't referring to Sunday. I was talking about the time you've spent with John."

Although she wasn't sure whether he'd meant that as a joke, she treated it as one. "Granted. He can be a real pain in the butt."

But The Major was no longer looking at her. He was looking at Trapper. "Back to my original question, what have you been up to?"

"What do you know about Thomas Wilcox?"

Kerra hadn't expected Trapper to bring up Wilcox so soon, and The Major seemed as struck by his blunt question as she. His eyebrows drew together above the bridge of his nose. "Dallas real estate? That Thomas Wilcox?"

"Do you know him?"

"I met him once. He attended a banquet where I delivered the after-dinner speech. He came up afterward and introduced himself."

"Hmm. That's interesting."

"Why?"

"How'd he act?"

"Act? As I recall, he was very pleasant."

"Did he mention the Pegasus?"

"Only in the context of complimenting me on my

talk." The Major looked over at Kerra before going back to Trapper. "Why bring him up?"

"You ever hear any dirt on him?"

"No. But he and I hardly run in the same circles."

"Shady business practices? Winner take all? Hear anything like that?"

"I wouldn't have had occasion to."

"Did you know he coveted the plot of ground under the Pegasus Hotel?"

Kerra watched The Major's expression grow increasingly stern as he began to grasp Trapper's meaning. "What are you driving at, John?"

"Go back a year or two before the bombing and scan through the business sections of the *Dallas Morning News*. It's well documented how Wilcox tried like hell to acquire that property. No dice. Oil company didn't want to sell." He paused before adding, "But Wilcox wound up with it after all."

The Major stared at his son for a moment, then put his middle finger and thumb to his eye sockets in a manner that reminded Kerra of Trapper when he was forced to think about something he'd rather not.

"Three years ago," The Major said, "when you came to me with your theory of a mastermind behind the bombing, you refused to give me a name. Please don't tell me that Thomas Wilcox, a millionaire—"

"A millionaire many times over. Partially because of the hotel and entertainment complex in the heart of downtown that he developed on the tract where the Pegasus had been."

"You think Thomas Wilcox instigated the bombing?"

"Let's just say he had his nerve even attending a banquet where a survivor of it was speaking, much less coming up to you afterward and being pleasant and complimentary."

The Major shook his head sorrowfully. "If this is the speculation you took to the ATF, it's no wonder they fired you."

Had The Major slapped him, Trapper's hardened expression couldn't have been more telling. He turned on his heel and headed for the door. "I'm glad you're feeling better."

The Major tried to call him back. "John."

"Eat your applesauce," Trapper said over his shoulder, "you'll be out of here in no time."

"Damn it, come back. I apologize."

Trapper stopped and turned around but stayed where he was.

The Major made a placating gesture. "What I said was uncalled for."

Unmoved, Trapper said, "But what? You think I'm delusional?"

"No, I think you're pigheaded and can't stand to leave anything alone. You want answers about the Pegasus and—"

"I got answers. Everybody got answers. The problem with those answers is that they're crap."

"And you can prove that? I asked you three years ago if you had proof that the one who confessed was acting on someone else's orders. You admitted then that you didn't have enough. Do you now?"

"Working on it."

"Working on it," The Major repeated in a woeful mutter. "For how long, John? At what point will you give this up and take on a life?"

"I *had* given it up. Then you went back on TV and got yourself shot."

The Major sighed and said quietly, "Glenn has a suspect in custody for Sunday night's attack."

"Hate to spoil your news flash, but I already know that."

"Well? This man Duncan is far too young to have had any connection to the Pegasus. Meaning that it and Sunday night's episode are unrelated. He and his buddy, whose identity is yet unknown, probably heard about my gun collection and came to the house to rob me."

Trapper scoffed. "If it eases your mind, stick with that. But you know in your gut that's not the case. This all goes back to the Pegasus."

"All right, for the sake of argument, let's say it does. The character that Glenn described to me isn't a fifty-something bigwig millionaire."

"I'm not saying that Wilcox himself was sneaking around your house."

His frustration mounting, The Major looked up at Kerra, who had remained silent throughout their contentious exchange. Looking at it from The Major's standpoint, without knowing what had occurred with Wilcox in Trapper's office, without knowing about Berkley Johnson or the factory fire that had initiated Trapper's covert investigation, the allegations against a wealthy and influential man would appear completely irrational.

"You're a smart young woman, Kerra," he said. "You deal in facts. Truth. Are you buying into this cockamamie theory?"

She looked across at Trapper before answering. "I went to Trapper's office as a total stranger. I caught him...not in prime form. I showed him the photograph that has been seen by millions of people over the course of two and a half decades. In a matter of hours, he puzzled it through and figured out who I was. So, Major, in answer to your question, I think his pigheadedness works for, not against him, and I wouldn't dismiss any of his theories as being cockamamie."

Kerra came out of the bathroom to find Trapper just as he'd been when she'd gone in.

He was lying on his back on the bed nearest the door, but he didn't look relaxed. His body was as taut as a piano wire. His jaw was locked and barely moved when he said, "I didn't need you to defend me."

"Well, at least now I know why you're angry and have barely spoken to me since we left the hospital."

"Don't come to my rescue, Kerra. With anybody, but especially not him. I didn't need—"

"I heard you the first time."

After leaving the hospital, he'd checked them into a motel—not the same one they'd stayed in before. She'd remained in the car but witnessed his transaction with the clerk through the dusty glass windows of the office. Trapper had paid with cash. The registration process was conducted with such efficiency and detachment by the attendant that, when Trapper returned to the car, she'd asked if he'd bribed the man to see nothing, hear nothing, remember nothing.

"Not necessary. He caters to a clientele desiring anonymity and privacy. For twenty minutes at a time." That was followed by a snide "But you can relax. The room's got two beds."

Almost as soon as they had cleared the door to the room, he'd shed his coat, pulled off his boots, and flopped down onto the bed, all without acknowledging her. She'd gone into the bathroom, taking with her the bag she'd brought from her condo, having stuffed into it a couple changes of clothes, a t-shirt and pajama pants, and some toiletries. She'd cleaned her face, brushed her teeth, and swapped the tight jeans for the much roomier and more comfortable PJs.

Now, after their brief but antagonistic exchange, she pulled back the covers on the second bed. The sheets were dingy, but they smelled of laundry detergent, which was reassuring. She climbed in, rolled onto her side, and looked across the narrow space separating the beds.

She defied his dark mood by saying, "She still loves you."

He didn't move, except for his jaw, which clenched tighter.

"Marianne. She still loves you."

He punched his pillow and resituated it beneath his head, mumbling, "She's where she belongs."

"Yes, and she knows that. But—"

"But nothing. Hearth and home were what she wanted."

"She has that with David. All the same, she still loves you. I could see it in her eyes."

"Affection. Sentimental fondness. That's what you saw. Like I feel for her. I want Marianne to be happy. She feels the same toward me. But don't read more into it than that. Now go to sleep." He reached up and snapped off the lamp on the nightstand between the beds.

Several moments passed, then Kerra said into the darkness, "Why do men avoid conversations like this?"

"Because they're pointless."

"What did you think of him?"

"Who?"

"You know who, Trapper. Marianne's husband."

"A prince among men."

"Who is resentful of you. What if he tells someone about the mysterious package you mailed to yourself?"

"He won't."

"You're that sure of him?"

"No, I'm that sure of Marianne. She knew that envelope had come from me. She knew if I'd gone to those lengths, it was no trivial matter. Despite her sweet demeanor, she was a federal agent, don't forget. She'll impress on her husband how important that package was and then tell him to erase it from memory. As far as he's concerned, we were never there."

"You're probably right. He wouldn't place her in jeopardy. He seemed very protective. He loves her."

Trapper mumbled something.

"What?"

"Nothing."

"*What?*"

He exhaled with annoyance. "He does love her, that was plain. But I'll tell you something. In his position, if my wife's former lover showed up at my house, a man I knew had caused her to lose her job, lose her baby, and had left her with a broken heart, I'd have flattened him as soon as I saw him, warned him not to even think about putting his hands on her, and then I'd've ripped his goddamn head off.

"Which is why Marianne is where she belongs, with a nice man who controls his primal impulses, instead of with a *nightmare* like me who's on a destructive path and a hazard to everybody around him, and that brings us right back to where we started, which is why I said that conversations like this are pointless."

His alpha male outburst caused an excited hitch in her breathing. "Maybe if Marianne had known you felt that possessive of her—"

"I didn't. Wasn't her I was thinking about."

She sensed the sudden motion, and then he was there, on his knees straddling her, pulling her into a sitting position. He took a fistful of hair at the back of her head and held it in place while he kissed her with unleashed hunger. His lips slanted across hers. He thrust his tongue into her mouth with insistence.

But then it gentled and moved slowly in and out between her lips with gliding strokes. When he finally broke away, she was left panting for breath and trying to balance. Her heart was pumping fast, but her bones seemed to have liquefied.

"I want to take you like that," he whispered as he dragged his open mouth down her neck to her collarbone, then lowered his head and rubbed his face against her breasts.

"I haven't forgotten how you feel inside. I want to be there. In you deep." His voice was rough and low, his lips aggressive against her raised nipple under her t-shirt. "It may never happen, but the mere thought of any other man being on you, in you...I'd want to kill him."

He pressed his face against her, breathing hard and hot. Then he came up straight and, clasping her face between his hands, stamped a kiss on her lips. "Now go to sleep."

Chapter 23

⇒=◉=⇐

Glenn looked down with distaste at The Major's hospital breakfast. "I wouldn't want to eat it, either."

"I'll choke it down only because I want to get my strength back."

"You've had a shock to your system. Most bet good money you'd never recover. You've beaten the odds so far. Don't rush it."

The Major smiled. "That's exactly what Kerra advised."

"Kerra advised? When was this?"

"Sometime in the wee hours. She and John sneaked in."

"They did, huh?" The sheriff propped one buttock on the end corner of the bed and recounted for his friend the telephone conversation he'd had with Trapper the night before. "He was coming back because he'd heard about our suspect. He didn't say outright that Kerra was with him, but he promised to produce her this morning. Bright and early." He arched an eyebrow.

The Major took his meaning. "They're sleeping together."

"You know John."

"All too well."

"They got off to a rocky start," Glenn told him. "Trapper was mad as hell at her over the earring business, but late that evening, when I went looking for him to tell him you'd regained consciousness, I interrupted a tender moment in her motel room."

"Back up, Glenn. What earring business?"

"I keep forgetting how much drama you missed that first couple of days." Glenn told him about Kerra's missing shoulder bag and the reappearance of one earring. "Though it seems highly unlikely Trapper discovered it under her hospital bed. If her bag didn't make it to that room, how'd her earring get there?"

"John lied to you?"

"Also to a pair of Texas Rangers."

"Why would he have taken Kerra's bag? And when?"

"All of the above remains a mystery. But looks to

me like Kerra believed his explanation, no matter how improbable, and he forgave her for suspecting him."

"Suspecting him of what? Why was he talking to Texas Rangers?"

The sheriff scratched his eyebrow with his thumbnail. "Don't make me play the tattletale on the boy."

"He's not a boy. He's a man."

Ill at ease, Glenn fiddled with the leather hatband around his Stetson. "From the get-go Trapper's been poking into the investigation, hovering around Kerra, wanting to know what she saw, who she saw, if she saw anything. I called him on it, but..."

"He responded to correction in his customary fashion."

"Basically. But his interest in what happened out at your place drew attention. It seemed more *intense* than a family member's wish to catch the bad guys who shot their kin. After the earring thing, the Rangers were ready to put him in lockup and hold him as a possible suspect."

"For shooting me?"

"I told the Rangers it was horseshit. But, let's face it, in view of your falling out, which everybody is aware of, he had to be given a hard look."

"John would never have done it."

"What I told the Rangers, and I don't think they really suspected him so much as they disliked his smart-aleck attitude. Anyhow, we had nothing to justify holding him. His alibi for Sunday night checked out. Since then, though, he hasn't curried any favor by running away with our material witness and keeping her under wraps.

"So either he and Kerra are screwing like bunnies and barely coming up for air, or he's keeping her in his hip pocket for some other reason, and, knowing Trapper as I do, I'm scared even to speculate on what that might be."

As he listened to all this, The Major's features had become increasingly knit with worry and indecision. He asked Glenn to close the door.

Glenn did as requested, then returned to his perch at the foot of the bed. "This looks and feels serious."

"It is," The Major said. "I'm afraid John is creating a dreadful situation for himself."

"What kind of situation? With Kerra?"

"No, this has nothing to do with her, except that he's drawn her into it."

He stopped with that, but it was clear to Glenn that his friend was still wrestling with indecision, so he kept quiet and gave him time to collect and arrange his thoughts. Then The Major began to talk and did so in a steady stream without interruption. It was ten minutes before he finished, and by then he was spent, his respiration wheezy.

Glenn ran his palm across his forehead, unsurprised

to find that it had turned damp. "Jesus. It's almost too much to take in."

"You only just heard it. In three years, I haven't taken it all in."

"Well, now I know how the rift between you and Trapper came about. Did he ever hand over Debra's diary?"

"No. But there's no doubt in my mind that he would have used it against me if I'd taken that book deal. He didn't want me out there talking about the bombing."

"For your own protection."

"That's what he believed and still does. I was hoping that he had let go of it while the rest of his life was going down the drain. Then Sunday night got him all fired up again. He's more certain than ever."

"That this Thomas Wilcox was behind the Pegasus?"

The Major nodded.

"And that now, twenty-five years later, he made an attempt on your life?"

"Because of Kerra's unexpected emergence and what the two of us might recall during the rehashing of the experience we shared. I know it sounds outlandish. But John is... is... John."

Seeking to reassure his old friend, Glenn addressed him by his real name. "Frank, listen to me. Trapper is as sly as a fox, impulsive, cocky as hell. About half the time, I'd like to whack him up alongside the head. The other half of the time, I wish my own son were more like him.

"But for all his brass, Trapper is also one damn good detective. He has an instinct for it that, honestly, I envy. What I'm getting to is, he wouldn't base a hunch on an influential millionaire unless he had *something* on the guy."

"He did tell me one thing. After the Pegasus was bombed, Wilcox acquired the site. He'd been coveting it for years."

Glenn tugged on his lower lip. "That's all Trapper's got?"

"Slim, right?"

"Very. Not enough to hang a conspiracy theory on. Did he advance this hypothesis to the ATF?"

"They dismissed it. He bucked them. It cost him his career and his fiancée but did nothing to sway his conviction. What happened to Kerra and me was the clincher. He's always been headstrong and rash, but now—"

"You're afraid he might actually be crazy."

The Major met his friend's gaze. "No, Glenn," he said softly. "I'm afraid he might actually be *right*."

On the other side of the car's console, Kerra sat hugging herself. Trapper asked, "What's the matter?"

"Nothing."

"Body language screams otherwise."

"I'm cold, that's all."

After two days of sunshine and milder temperatures, this morning's sky was overcast. The wind was from the south, but it was brisk and made it feel colder than the actual temperature. The real chill, however, was between him and Kerra.

She hadn't slept well, and he knew that because he hadn't, either. It was difficult to fall asleep with a woody the length and density of a baseball bat. They'd eventually gotten up and taken their turns in the bathroom. They had avoided eye contact and gave each other wide berth as they moved about in the confined space. Except for giving curt answers to direct questions, she'd been uncommunicative.

Now, as he sped through a yellow light, he said, "Would you rather I'd've gone against your express no-no and had my wicked way with you?"

She turned her head toward him. If looks could kill.

"Well, sorry," he said. "I'm confused. Yesterday morning, when on the brink of getting off, *you* called a sudden halt. You were mad at me then. Now you're mad because last night *I* called a halt before getting you off."

"Don't flatter yourself."

"I just wish you'd make up your mind."

"I have," she said with angry emphasis. "When we finish at the sheriff's office, I'm meeting with a locksmith to make me a key for my car. I'm going home. You go your way, I'll go mine. You do your thing, I'll do mine, which is to report the news, not be at the center of it, outrunning the police, and forwarding my calls to untraceable phones, and . . . such. I'm returning to my life."

He didn't say anything.

In a vexed tone, she asked, "Did you hear me?"

"Loud and clear."

He wheeled into a parking slot reserved for the Deputy of the Month, cut the engine, and got out before she said anything more. He came around, but she rebuffed his attempt to lend her a hand as she alighted. She went ahead of him as they approached the main entrance to the sheriff's headquarters, which was an annex of the courthouse.

He was glad to see the county hadn't yet sprung for a metal detector. He'd have hated having to relinquish his pistol. The only screening required was for one to stop at a window and announce his business.

But before Trapper even introduced himself, the female deputy behind the glass said, "Good morning, Ms. Bailey, Mr. Trapper. I'll call up and let Sheriff Addison know you're here. Second floor."

Trapper used Kerra's unfamiliarity with the

building as an opportunity to cup her elbow and guide her around a corner to the elevators. They boarded, and as soon as the doors closed, he said to her, "Stop flinching every time I touch you. First of all, it's pissing me off. Secondly, it doesn't lend credibility to our arrangement."

"What arrangement?"

Ignoring her question, he leaned down and spoke directly into her face. "To avoid future confusion over the other matter, *if* we ever get that hot again, we finish." Leaning down even closer, he whispered, "With me inside you."

The doors slid open and the sheriff was standing there to greet them, looking relieved but also cranky.

Trapper said, "What's the matter, Glenn? Not getting enough fiber?"

"I was afraid you wouldn't show."

"Well, here she is. Delivered as promised." It pleased him to see that Kerra looked a bit dazed by what he'd said. He had to nudge her before she stepped out of the elevator.

"I didn't expect you this soon," Glenn said. "The FBI agents haven't come in yet."

"I told you bright and early."

"When have you ever done anything you were supposed to?" The sheriff turned to Kerra. "Excuse me. I apologize for my grumpy mood. It's been that kind of morning."

"I know the feeling." She cast Trapper a sour look.

Glenn drew her attention back to him. "Trapper fill you in on the suspect?"

"The name Leslie Duncan means nothing to me," she said.

"He's used aliases. Give this a look." Glenn had Duncan's rap sheet with him and showed it to Kerra. "It's a current photo, taken just last night when he was booked."

She gave the attached mug shot the consideration it warranted, then shook her head. "I don't recognize him. I couldn't identify him as being one of the men at The Major's house. I never saw them. I've told you that."

"Maybe when you see Duncan in person—"

"Face to face?"

"He won't know you're there. They just brought him from lockup in the basement and put him in an interrogation room. All you have to do is look through the window."

"It's a waste of time, but lead the way."

Glenn turned to Trapper. "If you want to wait for her, do it down in the lobby. I'll alert you when she's done. But since you keep switching phones, I'll need a number to text."

"I stay with Kerra."

Glenn exhaled with exasperation. "Trapper, you've got no official reason to be here. Even if

I was okay with it, the agents conducting these interrogations—"

"I'm her bodyguard." He looked at Kerra and tipped his head toward Glenn. "Tell him." He held his breath, hoping she would realize that this was the "arrangement" he'd referred to.

She held his gaze for no longer than two heartbeats before turning back to Glenn. "It's, uh, one of the services offered by his ... firm."

"You can check the website," Trapper said, having no idea whatsoever if "bodyguard" was listed as one of his services. "Daily rate plus expenses. Kerra put me on retainer."

Clearly not buying it, Glenn scowled. "As of when?"

"As of the night your deputy was delinquent in his duty and stayed in his car while she went into the hospital alone. As of then, and until further notice, she doesn't get out of my sight."

"This is a sheriff's office, for crissake. City police department is in the other wing. What could happen to her in here?"

"Nothing." Trapper flashed a grin. "So long as I'm standing next to her."

Glenn gave up on Trapper and looked at Kerra. "It should ease your mind to know that we got the guy. One of them, anyway."

"How sure are you of him?" Trapper asked.

Before Glenn could respond, the elevator returned and the doors slid open. Carson Rime was the only person on it. He stepped out, his arm weighted down by a briefcase made of stamped saddle leather.

"Morning, all." Smiling at Trapper and Kerra, he shrugged off a tweed overcoat and, as he draped it over his arm, leaned forward to shake Glenn's hand. "Sheriff Addison? Carson Rime. We spoke on the phone yesterday. A pleasure."

Glenn didn't look like he shared the sentiment. "I thought we'd cleared up the stolen vehicle matter."

"Oh, we did. That's not why I'm here." Carson removed a business card from the breast pocket of his suit and handed it to Glenn. "I went to the basement first. The deputy down there said that my client, Leslie Doyle Duncan, had already been brought up here for an interrogation. The *first* interrogation that will ever be mentioned in court, should this comedy ever go to trial, because Mr. Duncan was denied legal counsel during his initial questioning."

Glenn rocked back on his heels. "He wasn't denied counsel. He had a court-appointed attorney who was unavoidably detained last night, but who should be here any minute now."

"He *had* a court-appointed attorney," Carson said. "He now has me, and I demand a consultation with my client. Please take me to him."

Carson's suit was shiny with wear. The points of his

collar flared up and out like a pair of white wings. Between them was a chunk of turquoise the size of a walnut that secured his black leather bolo tie. This morning, his comb-over had an extra layer of goo holding it in place.

But Trapper wanted to hug him. With only a token amount of whining and a vow to double bill, he had agreed to drop everything and haul ass to Lodal to represent Duncan. A lawyer, reputable or corrupt, first in his law school class or dead last, would be given access to the suspect that Trapper would be denied.

Glenn hitched up his gun belt as though to reassert that he was still in charge and motioned down the hallway. "Last room on the left."

"Kerra had just as well take a look at Duncan now," Trapper said. "Why make her hang around and wait?"

"All right."

Trapper could tell she was burning to ask questions, but when Carson made an after-you gesture, she started down the hall, the lawyer chatting at her side.

Glenn and Trapper fell into step behind them. "Clever," Glenn said under his breath. "But I don't get why you did it. Why are you so keen on defending the guy who shot your own father?"

"Why are you so keen on this being the guy? A

newbie in town that few people know. Criminal record. Parole jumper. Stopped for speeding in a school zone, and a weapon matching the kind used in the shooting found under the seat of his pickup?" Trapper winced with skepticism. "Seems way too slick and easy, and smacks of a frame-up. I thought an attorney might come in handy."

"Well, it won't matter if you reassemble O. J.'s dream team for him."

Trapper slowed his pace and looked at Glenn.

"Ballistics came back on the pistol, Trapper. No question. The match was so good, it gave our DA a hard-on."

"Your DA is a woman."

"Figure of speech."

The meaning of which didn't escape Trapper, but he didn't say anything more as they continued down the hall till they reached the specified room. Glenn stepped forward and opened the door. "Mr. Duncan, your lawyer is here."

"Yeah, well, you and him can go fuck each other."

Glenn turned back to Trapper. "He has an attitude. Thinks he's smarter than everybody else."

"Maybe he is."

"Different circumstances, y'all could be friends."

Carson passed his overcoat to Trapper, sidestepped Glenn, and entered the room. "Are the shackles really necessary?"

Glenn only harrumphed and pulled the door closed. "Kerra?"

She stepped up to the door and looked through the wired glass window. Trapper looked in from over her shoulder. Duncan appeared to be in his early thirties, although his eyes had the mistrustful, lupine quality of one who'd already endured a lifetime of hard knocks. He didn't look relieved or show any particular interest when Carson introduced himself. His indolent posture didn't change, although his surly lips moved, so he'd said something.

"I've never seen him before," Kerra said and was about to move away from the window.

"Give it a minute," Glenn said. "Maybe he'll do something that'll jog a memory."

Trapper held Carson's coat in the crook of his elbow and placed his hands on Kerra's shoulders. "He's right. Give it a minute."

"But—"

He gave her shoulders a slight squeeze. The private signal worked. She stayed where she was, sandwiched between him and the door. Trapper asked Glenn, "Did you locate his wife?"

"Girlfriend. If she's visiting her mama in Ardmore, she's gone to the cemetery."

"He lied about his old lady?"

"Worries us, because there's been no sign of her."

They couldn't hear what Carson was asking or what

the suspect was saying in reply, but occasionally Duncan would emphasize a point by stabbing his forefinger into the tabletop. Other times Trapper could tell even in pantomime that he'd given a flip response.

After several minutes, Carson took sheets of paper from his briefcase, spread them out on the table where Leslie Duncan could see what they consisted of, and went over the content of each sheet with him point by point.

"What's all that?" Glenn asked Trapper. "His rate chart?"

"I wouldn't be surprised. Mercenary son of a bitch."

Carson asked Duncan something. He hesitated then nodded. Carson beamed, gathered up the papers and replaced them in his briefcase, latched it, and shook hands with Duncan as facilely as could be done with the manacles. Kerra stood aside, and Glenn opened the door for Carson.

As he was passing through, Leslie Duncan called from the table, "How do you like being dead so far?"

Trapper, anticipating that, had stepped around Kerra in order to gauge her reaction. Her lips separated in shock over hearing the familiar words, but when she realized that Trapper was watching her, she looked up at him and shook her head. "The voice is wrong."

Glenn's face was mottled with fury. "Now I get it.

That's what he was about," he said, flinging out a hand toward Carson.

Carson retrieved his overcoat from Trapper. "Excuse me. I've got forms to file." Juggling coat and briefcase, he hurried down the hallway, almost running into a deputy as he stepped purposefully off the elevator.

Trapper was in a standoff with Glenn. "If I had asked nice, would you have given me access to him?"

"No," Glenn thundered.

"All Kerra needed to hear were those few words."

"The voice is wrong," she repeated, addressing the statement to Glenn. "Believe me, I get goose bumps when I think back to hearing those words and realizing what they implied. I'll never forget the voice."

"In your statement, you said that only one of the men spoke. Duncan here could be the one who stayed silent."

"He could. But I'm positive that's not the voice I overheard."

Trapper was listening to her and Glenn and following their thread, but he was also observing Leslie Duncan through the window. He was bobbing his head back and forth and playing imaginary drums on the table as though keeping time to an earworm.

"Sheriff?"

All of them turned to the deputy who had nearly collided with Carson at the elevator. "We got the search warrant about an hour ago," he reported. "Found this in Duncan's trailer. Isn't it the one that's been missing?"

He held up an evidence bag. Sealed inside it was Kerra's Louis Vuitton.

Chapter 24

When they returned to the motel room, Kerra remarked, "I'm surprised housekeeping has been here already."

"I'm surprised there's housekeeping."

Trapper's statement had been spoken in an absent mutter. He was preoccupied with checking one of his various cell phones for missed calls or texts.

"Nothing from The Major?" she asked.

"No." He tossed his coat onto the bed. "If he calls at all, it'll probably be to notify me that he's having me certified."

"He thinks you're pigheaded, not insane."

"Doesn't matter. I was over what he thought about me a long time ago."

She knew that wasn't the case at all, but she let it go. Things were already strained between Trapper and her. They'd driven back from the sheriff's office in silence. She supposed that he was mulling over how much significance the discovery of her missing bag would have on the investigation.

Pursuant to that, she asked, "What do you think?"

Trapper had his back to the room, staring through the window, hands turned palms out in the rear pockets of his jeans—the new ones he disliked.

"That you'd be wasting your money."

Because she'd been envisioning his bare backside inside the jeans, his statement didn't register. "Sorry?"

He turned to face her. "You'd be wasting your money on a locksmith. I'll break into your car and hot-wire it. You'll have to get it fixed when you get back to Dallas, but the repair will probably cost you less than a locksmith.

"Better still, ask Carson to set you up with his discount body shop guy. Just be sure that if he gives you a loaner car it isn't hot." He motioned to her small duffel bag on the floor in the corner. "Start gathering up your things. When you're ready, I'll take you to your car."

The drama in the sheriff's office had obscured her resolve to go home, but apparently it was still fresh in Trapper's mind, and he wasn't trying to talk her out of it. Quite the opposite. Before she had time to respond to this turnabout, there was a knock.

Trapper checked the peephole before opening the door.

Carson bustled in, rubbing his hands together. "How'd I do?"

"You did okay," Trapper replied.

"*Okay?*" he repeated with affront. "I was brilliant."

"Where is Duncan's old lady? Did you ask him?"

"Yes, but anything Mr. Duncan told me is privileged, Trapper. You know that."

"I need to know what he said."

"He's my client."

"And I'm financing his fee. Now tell me what he said."

"That's grounds for disbarment."

"Oh, for crissake. You choose *now* to turn ethical? Kerra's not gonna tell on you. Are you?" Trapper looked at her, and she shook her head. "See? And I'm not gonna tell on you. So talk."

Carson only assumed a more obstinate stance.

Trapper bore down on him. "I'm not gonna tell anybody that you violated attorney-client privilege … but I might let it slip that your law degree is counterfeit."

Carson started. "How'd you know?"

Trapper just looked at him and smiled, and when Carson realized that he'd been had, he swore.

"Now that we've got those pesky ethics out of the way," Trapper said, "what about Duncan's old lady?"

Carson sighed with resignation. "She's been passing bad checks. They thought it would be advisable for her to clear town for a while."

"When did she go? Was she with Duncan Sunday night?"

"Definitely. They were going at it all night long, he said, and had a sad parting Monday morning."

"Where was she off to?"

"Galveston."

"Duncan may need her to provide an alibi. If you know anybody in south Texas who could track her down and bring her back—"

"Already on it."

"Good."

"Except..." Carson grimaced.

"What?"

"He may not want to bring her into the picture even if it means sacrificing his alibi."

"The bad checks?"

"That, but there could also be an issue regarding her age. But he's fairly sure she's turned seventeen."

Trapper looked pained. "Does this guy have any redeeming qualities?"

"He has a heart tattoo with 'Mom' scrolled across it."

"That's something," Kerra said.

"With a dagger through the heart."

She couldn't tell if Carson was joking or not, but she thought probably not.

Trapper asked, "What about the pistol?"

"He swears to God he had never laid eyes on it."

"Until a traffic cop pulled it from under the seat of his truck."

"Noooo," Carson said, dragging out the word. "Until he found it in a trash can."

"You gotta be kidding me."

"Wish I was," Carson said. "He contends that when he went to put his garbage in the can, there was the pistol. Clip was full except for one bullet. Serial number scratched out."

"His lucky day."

"His words exactly."

"When did this miracle find occur?"

"Monday night. He remembers because the trash is picked up at the mobile home park on Tuesday morning."

"When questioned about the gun, why did he lie?"

"Wouldn't you?"

Trapper ran his hand around the back of his neck. "If I was in sexual congress with a minor, yeah, I probably would. Did you ask him about The Major?"

"Knows he's famous. Knows he got shot. Never

heard of you." Carson tacked that on with perceptible glee.

"What about Kerra?"

"He's only seen her once or twice, on account of his neighbor discovered that he'd tapped into his cable and cut him off."

"Did you ask if he knew Thomas Wilcox?"

"I did. He said, 'Sure.'"

Kerra and Trapper exchanged a fleeting look before going back to Carson. "Swear to God, when he said that, my heart nearly stopped. I asked him how he knew Thomas Wilcox, and he said, 'Hero of mine.' I asked why he considered Wilcox hero material, and he said, 'On account of his three-pointers, asshole.' I would have taken exception, but that kind of verbal abuse goes with the territory of being a criminal defense attorney, and since you're footing the bill—"

"Get on with it, Carson."

"I asked my client if it was possible we were referencing two different Thomas Wilcoxes. And he said, 'I'm talkin' about the all-star basketball player for OU. Black dude. Six nine. Went on to play for the Thunder till they started suckin', then moved to the Nuggets. Who the fuck are you talkin' about?' I think that's a quote," he said, giving Kerra an apologetic glance. "Anyhow, the basketball player is the only Thomas Wilcox he ever heard of."

After the buildup, the finale was a letdown. Kerra

could tell that Trapper felt it, too. Nobody said anything. Then, in a much more subdued manner, Carson said, "Your office got trashed."

Trapper played dumb. "You don't say?"

"Broke through the window in the door. The building custodian discovered it when he got to work this morning. Said the place had been torn apart. He tried your cell number; it went straight to voice mail. Didn't know how else to reach you, so he called me. I authorized him to get your window replaced and your lock changed."

"Thanks."

"I'll add the charges to your bill." Carson divided a worried look between them. "You know, Trapper, some people you're just better off not messing with. I ask again, do y'all know what you're doing?" His law degree may have been fake, but his concern seemed genuine.

Trapper pretended not to have noticed. He asked Carson how Duncan had responded to the request that he shout out the question.

Kerra said, "I assume that's what all the paper shuffling on the table was about?"

Carson nodded. "I'd typed it out and told Duncan it was important that he ask the question exactly as it was written and that he speak loud enough to be heard by anyone standing outside the door, including one of the victims, Kerra Bailey.

"He asked, 'What the eff for?' All I told him was that it would be in his best interest to do me this one tiny favor. After dropping a few more f-bombs, he said, 'Whatever, dude.'" Carson looked at them in turn. "You could've fried an egg on the sheriff's ass. What happened after I left?"

Trapper told him about the discovery of Kerra's bag. "The deputy said it was found in a corner under the bed in Duncan's trailer."

"Anything missing from it?"

"A modest amount of cash and my credit cards," Kerra told him. "Other than that, no."

"Good to know," Carson said. "At least I won't be blindsided about it at Duncan's arraignment. It's scheduled for three o'clock this afternoon."

"Plead not guilty," Trapper said.

"There's another way to plead?" Carson blinked several times as though astonished. Then, "Given the circumstances, the notoriety of his alleged victims, and Duncan's record, the judge will set his bail a mile high. He's gonna stay in jail."

"He'll be better off," Trapper said. "If he were released, he probably wouldn't live long."

Carson's brows shot up. "That statement begs elaboration."

Trapper gave it some thought. "If you'd just shot and left for dead an American icon, would you hang on to the weapon? Duncan had all of north Texas to lose it in. Even if he wanted to keep it as a souvenir to sell on eBay at some future date, would he safeguard it under the seat of his truck?"

He gave them each a look before continuing. "He takes the money and credit cards from Kerra's bag but stashes it where it could easily be found. Do you know a thief who holds onto a purse after he's emptied it of valuables?"

He directed the question to Carson, who replied, "I'm not acquainted with any thieves. All my clients are innocent."

"I was asking rhetorically."

"My answer stands."

"Back to what I was saying: Duncan is a cesspool, but I don't think he's stupid. If he was involved last Sunday, he wouldn't still have the evidence in his possession. He's hostile and pugnacious, but not the least bit nervous. Because he knows that even if the pistol and bag can be placed in that house last Sunday night, he can't be. Not by the sheriff's office, or the Rangers, or the big, bad FBI. And the reason he knows they can't place him there is because—"

"He wasn't there," Kerra said.

"He wasn't there," Trapper repeated. "He was in his mobile home all night shagging his underage girlfriend. Which is a felony. But it's not attempted murder."

"My client was obviously set up."

"He made a perfect candidate for it," Trapper said.

"Set up by whom? Why?" Kerra asked.

"By whom, I don't know," Trapper said. "As to why, to cool down the situation. You can hear it talked about over dinner tables across the country. 'They nailed one of The Major's assailants, the other is as good as got.'

"The media will move on to the next sensational story and so will the public's interest." He thought on it for a moment, then said grimly, "It also makes me look even more like a crackpot for exploring other possibilities."

Kerra frowned. "I follow your logic, but why are you so sure that Duncan wasn't man number two, the one who didn't speak?"

"Man number two would never have repeated that question knowing you were just beyond the door."

"Even if he wasn't the one to ask it in The Major's house?"

"At the very least he would have balked, fidgeted, altered his voice. I kept my eyes glued to Duncan. He had a 'whatever, dude,' attitude, but he asked the question without a qualm because it held no significance to him."

"I could tell that when I first showed it to him," Carson said. "Not rattled in the least."

"Plead him not guilty on the attempted murder charge," Trapper said, "but leave the lowlife behind bars. Fall guys often have short life spans. Not only will Duncan be safer in jail, if he's shacked up with a juvenile, he belongs there. I'm sure Oklahoma would like to have him back, too."

In a none too subtle invitation for Carson to leave, Trapper opened the door, took Carson's hand, and slapped a set of car keys into his palm.

"Oh, right. Almost forgot." Carson dug into his trousers pocket, produced a key fob and gave it to Trapper. "Around the north corner of the building. Last in the row. Maroonish sedan."

"Thanks." Trapper pocketed the key fob. "And thanks again for rushing up here on short notice. Let me know when I can return the favor."

"You can start by paying me the eight-fifty you owe me just for today."

"Dream on."

"Okay, three-fifty."

"I could mention to the Texas Bar Association that—"

"Two-fifty."

"Goodbye, Carson."

Trapper closed the door on him and leaned back against it as though to barricade it should Carson try to return. Kerra asked, "Why did you swap keys?"

"He's taking his brother-in-law's car back. He left me the one he drove up here from Fort Worth."

"Why?"

"Because I wouldn't put it past Glenn to have had a tracking device put on that ugly car while we were inside the sheriff's office. If I need to get lost again, he'll be tracking Carson, not me."

"You think of everything."

"No. I don't." With those three words, his tone became weighty and solemn, and so did his demeanor. "That's what has kept me up nights for the past three years. And since Sunday, it's only gotten worse, not better."

He looked at her pensively for several moments, then gave one shake of his head as though having reached a tough decision. "It's expected of me to go off half-cocked, but this chasing around isn't for you. I was wrong to make you part of it. Go back to Dallas and, as you said, do your thing. I'll do mine." He gestured toward her bag again. "You left some things in the bathroom."

Rather than moving to collect her belongings as he'd indicated, she sat down on the edge of the bed. "Why are you still chasing around?"

"I want justice."

"Of course that. But if that's all you wanted, you could go to the authorities right now with what you have on Wilcox."

"And give them another belly laugh? No thanks."

"This time you have Wilcox himself."

"He would deny that meeting in my office ever took place."

"I would bear witness to it."

"True. But you can't prove what we talked about."

"Yes, I can."

Not expecting that, he gave her a sharp look.

"Get the phone you had when you threatened to call 911."

He walked over to the bed and rummaged in the pockets of his coat until he found that particular phone, took the back off, and placed a battery in it.

Kerra said, "I carried the phone with me when I went to the window. My back was turned for ten minutes. I went to voice memos on the home page and pressed record. I was scared to death Wilcox would notice. Or the guy in the window across the street. I guess his sights were set on the center of my forehead, not my hands."

By now the phone was powered up. Trapper went to the voice memos icon and tapped play.

The recording began with Kerra's voice "... *coming from the corner. A third, from the other direction.*" After a lengthy silence, "*There's a fourth, Trapper.*"

Then Wilcox. "*They've been instructed to wait for a second call, a second hang-up. If it doesn't come within ten minutes...*"

Trapper tapped pause and stared down at her. "How much is on here?"

"I had to stop recording when I made the second call. You took back the phone immediately after."

"Pretty smart trick."

"Thanks."

He dashed her perky comeback with anger. "A trick that could've gotten you killed. *Us* killed. Why didn't you tell me about this before now?"

"Well, you've kept me rather occupied. First there was the unannounced visit to Marianne's house. Then our drive back here in the middle of the night. The tense conversation between you and The Major in the hospital. This morning—"

"That's all bullshit, Kerra. You didn't tell me because you knew I'd be mad as hell. Think what would have happened if you'd gotten caught."

"But I didn't! And now you have the recording."

"A recording of me spinning what Wilcox called a captivating story."

"He talked about wanting to avenge his daughter's murder. He talked about the four men outside standing by to rush the building and kill you. It's *something*. At least it's enough to get the authorities to listen to you without laughing." His lack of excitement dismayed and confused her. "I thought you'd be pleased."

"I'm glad to have the recording. And it is *something* on that son of a bitch. But it makes my point, Kerra. If not for me, you wouldn't have been there in that life-threatening situation, taking risks."

He paced a few feet away from her, and when he turned back, he said, "Your involvement in this should've ended the night I took you those damn flowers." He held her gaze for a moment, then looked down at his boots and, in a mumble, added, "I just couldn't stay away from you."

The admission made her heart flutter. But it turned to a thud of dread with his next statement. "Your involvement ends now."

"I've changed my mind from what I said earlier."

He gave a negative shake of his head. "You're going back to your life. Or not. But in any case you're going away from me."

"But I don't want to drop this."

"I don't want another Berkley Johnson on my conscience. Only with you, it would be worse. I never kissed him." The words shimmered between them, then he said, "Besides, this is something I've got to do alone."

That statement had a different ring to it. "You've got to do it alone? That's an odd thing to say."

"What's odd about it?"

"It doesn't sound like someone who's only seeking justice. It sounds like you have a hidden agenda."

"And that sounds like psychobabble."

If she hadn't hit on something, he wouldn't be responding so defensively. Determined to get to the bottom of it, she searched his face and asked again, "Why must you do this alone?"

"I just do, okay?"

"Not okay. That's not an explanation."

"That's all you're getting."

"Why alone, Trapper?"

"Kerra."

"To restore your pride?"

He drew himself up to full height. "Yeah. That's it. I'm a peacock whose tail feathers got plucked by the ATF. Save that quote. Put it in your story."

"Don't do that," she said, coming to her feet. "Don't slam the door on me or cop that smart-ass attitude."

"Then stop asking questions. I don't give interviews, remember?"

"Aren't we beyond that?"

"Well, I thought so, but obviously not."

"We're just two people talking, Trapper."

"Wrong. Only one person is talking. *You.* I'm not listening anymore."

He went around her, scooped her bag from off the floor, and carried it with him into the bathroom, where he began tossing in grooming articles and the sleepwear she'd left hanging on the hook on the back of the door.

She followed him as far as the threshold between the two rooms. "You're really sending me packing?"

He didn't say anything, just raided the shower of her shampoo and razor and added them to the bag.

"Me plus you equals jeopardy for the bad guys, isn't that what you said? Well, it's worked. Someone got nervous enough about our being together to ransack your apartment and office. Thomas Wilcox came to you wanting to make a deal for immunity. How likely was that to happen if he hadn't feared what you have on him? Someone went to a lot of trouble to set up Leslie Duncan for Sunday night's crimes."

She had to move aside or get mowed down as he came through the bathroom door. "We've stirred live coals, Trapper. Isn't that what you had in mind when you abducted me?"

"What I had in mind was banging you."

"That's very romantic," she said, "but it wasn't your primary motivation."

He lowered his eyelids to half mast. "Wanna bet?"

"Please follow along, ladies and gentlemen, as we move from scare tactic number one to scare tactic number two. Lewd and lascivious innuendo." She paused for a beat. "Save it, Trapper. I'm not going to have the vapors or run screaming in fear of my virtue."

"Don't be so sure. I can get really lewd and... whatever that other thing was."

She huffed out a breath. "Let me see what's on the flash drive."

He dropped all degree of suggestiveness and reverted to anger. "You're just after the story."

"Damn right, I am. But I can't turn my back on this injustice and then blithely go on with my life."

"It's your *life* I'm trying to save."

"Which is why I have a bodyguard."

"You haven't advanced me a penny of my retainer."

"How much?"

"You can't afford me."

"Try me."

"And anyway, I'm not for hire."

"Where's the flash drive?"

"Fuck!" Looking ready to throttle her, he stood there, breathing hard and angrily, then sliced the air with his hands. "Fine. I have transportation." He dug into his jeans pocket for the key Carson had given him. "I'll go. The room is paid up through today. You can stay here and figure out how to get back to Dallas on your own."

He pulled on his coat and went over to the door. "The offer's still good to take you to your car, but it expires in thirty seconds."

She continued staring into eyes that could be as hard as blue diamonds or as hot as blue flame. They were in the former mode, giving back nothing as she looked deeply into them.

Yielding was her only option.

She pulled on her coat, zipped the duffel bag and shouldered the strap, then got her purse. He took a wire coat hanger from the closet. They met at the door; Trapper held it open for her. Remembering Carson's instructions to Trapper, she turned toward the north end of the building.

A maroon sedan was one of only three vehicles parked on the rear lot. Trapper unlocked it. He set her bag on the backseat while she got in the front. It wasn't far to the motel in which she had originally stayed. They reached it before the car motor had warmed up sufficiently for the heater to work.

Trapper pulled up beside her car. "Wait here till I get it started. It may need some coaxing since it's been out in the cold for so long."

He left the sedan's engine running as he got out, taking the coat hanger with him. She thought car manufacturers had redesigned door locks so they were no longer susceptible to this kind of break-in, but they were susceptible to Trapper, who had it open within seconds.

Out the corner of her eye, she noticed another vehicle pulling into the parking lot. When it got even with the sedan, the driver slowed down to look at her, then past her toward her car where Trapper was bent down, only one leg visible where it hung out the open driver's door.

The man stopped his minivan and got out. He shot Kerra another glance, then strode past, shouting, "Trapper!"

Trapper sat up and, when he saw the man, scooted out and took a few steps toward him. "Hey, Hank. What are you doing here?"

The minister charged up to him and slugged him as hard as he could right in the jaw.

Chapter 25

Trapper fell back against the side of Kerra's car. "What the—"

Before he could get the rest of it out of his mouth, Hank slugged him again, this time catching him just beneath his eye. Reacting instinctively, Trapper rammed his fist as hard as he could into Hank's solar plexus. Hank doubled over and staggered back.

Trapper touched the heel of his hand to his cheekbone, and it came away red with fresh blood. He took a moment to clear his vision. Hank was no longer a threat. He was standing bent at a ninety-degree angle, gasping and gagging.

Kerra scrambled out of the maroon car and came running toward Trapper.

He held up a hand like a traffic cop, stopping her midstride. This was between him and Hank. He left the support of the car and walked toward him. "Okay, I had that coming. But bloody hell!" He dabbed his cheekbone again, felt a bump already rising. "Whatever happened to turning the other cheek?"

Hank sucked in hard to draw breath. "The only... cheek...I'll turn to you will be a butt cheek." He wheezed, coughed, wiped spittle off his lips. "So you can kiss my ass."

Trapper pushed up the sleeve of his coat and blotted blood off his face with the cuff of his shirt. "I shouldn't have sent you out to the line shack. I'm sorry. I just needed to throw people off track for a few hours. But which is the worse sin, manipulation or betraying a confidence? Which is what you did. So don't go all holier than thou with me."

Hank struggled to bring himself upright, though he continued to hold one forearm across his middle. He wiped his nose with the back of his hand. "This isn't about that. It's about what you're doing to Dad."

"Glenn? I'm not doing anything to him."

"No? He suffered some kind of...episode." Hank wiped more snot. "Shortness of breath. Chest pains. Red in the face. A deputy rushed him to the ER. His cardiologist met him there. Mom's hysterical."

He aimed an accusing finger at Trapper. "This is on you."

Trapper exhaled through his mouth and shoved his fingers through his hair. "I'll go right now—"

"You'll stay the hell away from him!" Hank shouted. Or tried to. It came out a croak, but with wrath behind it.

Kerra walked over to Hank and placed a hand on his arm. "I'm sorry to hear that your father is ill. I'm Kerra Bailey."

He looked at her with abashment. "Hank Addison. I'm sorry you saw that. Ordinarily I don't fly off the handle." He shot a glare toward Trapper. "I'm not that short-tempered."

"Trapper has that effect on people," she said. "How did you know where to find him?"

"Last I heard, you were both staying here."

She looked beyond Hank toward the café that shared the parking lot with the motel. "It would be warmer inside, and I think you probably shouldn't drive just yet. Can we continue in there?"

Hank nodded dumbly and let himself be guided toward the café. Kerra looked over her shoulder at Trapper. "Coming?"

He was on the verge of saying something caustic or profane about her turning into Mother Teresa, but she had a look in her eye that warned him not to press his luck.

He secured her car and the maroon sedan. He closed the driver's door of Hank's minivan, which had been left standing open when Hank launched his assault. He caught up with Hank and Kerra inside the café. Other than a couple of old-timers sitting at the counter and arguing the merits of Fords and Chevys, they had the place to themselves.

They claimed a booth. Hank practically fell into one side of it. Kerra slid in across from him and Trapper moved in beside her.

In an undertone, she said, "Your cheek is still bleeding."

He blotted it again with his shirt cuff. "Hurts like a son of a bitch."

He and Hank remained locked in a mutually antagonistic stare until the waitress came with menus. "We're only ordering drinks," Kerra said to her.

"Not me," Trapper said. "I'm starving. Cheeseburger, fries, coffee, please." Looking at Kerra, he said, "Long as we're here, eat. You haven't had anything."

She ordered a grilled cheese sandwich.

Hank told the waitress he would have only a Coke.

"Come on, let me buy your lunch," Trapper said. "Peace offering."

"Thanks all the same, but I can't stay. I'm needed out at the site."

"Want anything for that face, honey?"

Trapper, who'd been about to ask Hank what site

he was talking about, realized that the waitress was still there and addressing the question to him. He smiled up at her. "No thanks. I'm fine. My new kitten scratched me."

She gave him an arch look. "He must be a bobcat."

Kerra leaned across Trapper. "A paper towel soaked in cold water would help."

"Sure, honey. I'll be right back with that."

She left. Trapper asked Hank, "Site of what?"

"The new tabernacle. Foundation has been poured. They're putting up the I-beams today, and there's a problem with placement. The plans have one right in the middle of the choir loft."

"I didn't know you were building a new tabernacle."

"No, I'm sure you didn't," Hank said with testiness. "Furthermore, you didn't care. You don't care about anything except—"

Hank broke off when the waitress returned with the makeshift compress. Trapper thanked her and gingerly laid it against his throbbing cheekbone. "You were saying?"

Hank propped his elbows on the table and covered his face with both hands. Trapper wondered if he was praying. Eventually Hank lowered his hands and noticed the smear of Trapper's blood across his right knuckles. He pulled a napkin from the dispenser on the table and wiped at it. "Never mind."

"No," Trapper said. "You'd built up a full head of steam. Don't stop there. Let's hear it."

"Why? Anything said wouldn't make a dent, Trapper. You don't care about anything except yourself and whatever it is that's eating you. I just wish you'd have left Dad out of it."

"Glenn is in it because his best friend was nearly killed. Oh, and, by the way, he's also sheriff of this county."

"Yes, but you haven't made his job any easier. You've pulled one shenanigan after another. He's been more focused on keeping you in line than he has been on capturing the men who attacked The Major. Whatever the stunt was that you pulled this morning—"

"I retained a lawyer to represent the suspect."

Hank gave Kerra a knowing look before returning his accusing gaze to Trapper.

He removed the compress from his face and wadded it into a ball. "All right. It was a little bit of a stunt."

"Whatever you did," Hank said, "coming so soon after Dad's troubling talk with The Major, sent his blood pressure—"

"Wait. Troubling talk with The Major? When was this?"

"Early. He went to the hospital before breakfast. Came back to the house to eat before going to work. According to Mom, he was upset."

Kerra said, "He apologized to me for his mood, said it had been that kind of morning."

Trapper remembered Glenn being particularly choleric when he'd greeted them at the elevator. "Why would a visit with The Major have upset him? He's doing so much better."

"I'm surprised you've noticed his improvement," Hank said. "When did you work in time to see your ailing father, when you've been so busy wreaking havoc and making people miserable?"

"Okay, look, I'm maggot shit, and you're a saint. That's well known. But bring yourself down to my level long enough for us to talk about Glenn instead of my character flaws."

"That's what I'm trying to tell you. He hasn't been...right...since you showed up."

Trapper was having a hard time holding down his own temper. He didn't raise his voice, but he leaned forward and spoke with emphasis. "Don't lay all this on me, Hank. The night I walked in on Glenn unannounced and told him about Kerra's upcoming interview with The Major, he was guzzling Jack straight from the bottle. While I may have been an additional aggravation to him this week, I'm not the source of his problem. It was in place before the events of this week."

Trapper knew he'd struck a nerve when Hank glanced at Kerra, clearly uneasy.

"What's going on with him, Hank?" Trapper asked.

He hesitated, then, "I don't know. Something."

Trapper settled back against the booth, concern over Glenn replacing his anger with Hank. "Maybe he's sick, real sick, and is keeping it to himself."

Hank dismissed that. "Mom would know. She monitors everything from his daily baby aspirin to his bowel movements. The past few years he's had some health issues. High blood pressure, high cholesterol. Normal for a man his age, more nuisances than illnesses. Until today."

"Pressures of the job getting to him?" Trapper asked. "He told me he needed a man in his CAP department who was younger and smarter than him."

"He may be resisting aging in general," Kerra said. "It works on the minds of some people more than on others."

"All those could be factors," Hank said. "I think there's more to it than that, though. But I don't know. That's the bottom line: *I don't know.*" He struck the tabletop with his blood-stained fist to underscore the words.

"He doesn't confide in me. Won't. Whenever I urge him to, he says something cutting like 'when I need a priest, I'll turn Catholic.' Stuff like that. But whatever is bugging him, he didn't need any more stress." The last was addressed to Trapper.

"It wasn't my fault that The Major got shot."

"No, but have you made a terrible situation better or worse?"

"You've already made that point."

Trapper's quietly spoken concession took some of the starch out of Hank. He shook his head with frustration. "Trapper, I know you're fond of Dad. And I don't believe you do anything with malicious intent. You're just being you." He leaned forward. "But you make trouble. You always have. I can't help but think that the chaos you've generated this week is at least partially responsible for Dad being in the ER as we speak."

It upset Trapper to hear that. It bothered him more than he let on. He couldn't raise a single defense against a charge that was most probably true, so he said nothing.

Kerra breached the taut silence by asking Hank if he had any idea of how serious Glenn's condition was.

"The ER nurse who admitted him didn't think he was having a heart attack because he didn't have all the symptoms. We're hoping it was just an acute anxiety attack. Bad enough, certainly scary, but not deadly. Mom's supposed to call me after they've run all the tests."

The waitress arrived with their order. Hank took one sip from the straw in his soft drink, then scooted to the end of the booth. "I need to go and get things sorted out at the site. Whether or not Dad is hospitalized, I need to be available to him and Mom later today."

"I'll check in with you," Trapper said.

Kerra wrote down her cell number on a paper napkin and passed it to Hank. "Call me if there's an emergency."

"Will do." Hank pocketed the napkin. Then, looking at Trapper, he said, "Sorry about that," and motioned toward Trapper's face.

"Like hell you are."

Hank gave a soft laugh. "Like hell I am. It actually felt really good." He bobbed his head in a goodbye to Kerra, then left them.

The bell above the door jingled as he went through. The two old men had moved from auto makers to football teams but were still arguing. Seated on a stool behind the cash register, the waitress was flipping through a tabloid magazine.

Trapper picked up a french fry and studied it as he twirled it between his thumb and index finger, then dropped it back onto his plate.

"No longer starving?" Kerra asked.

"No." He noticed that her food had also gone untouched. "What's spoiled your appetite? Sitting next to me?"

"Trapper—"

Before she could say anything more, he got out

of the booth, pulled a twenty-dollar bill from his pocket, and placed it on the table. "That should cover it." He set a key fob on top of the bill. "Keys to the maroon car. Your bag is already in it. I doubt you know how to hot-wire, so I'll use your car. I'll get it fixed for you. In a day or two, we'll figure out where and when to make the switch. Phone."

From a coat pocket, he produced a cell phone and battery. While he was inserting it, he said, "This is the number yours has been forwarded to. You can undo it when you reunite with your phone. Be careful driving back."

"Wait a sec. You're just leaving? Like this?"

He paused to take her in. Eyes, beauty mark, mouth. She was everything desirable, and he wanted her.

But he made trouble. He wreaked havoc and made people miserable.

Like Marianne.

Like Glenn.

Like his father.

He was poison.

"I didn't want this to be my life, you know," he said. "It just is."

———

As Trapper drove through the gate, the wind whipped up a dust devil between him and the horizon. He braked and watched as it cut a swath across the ground. For a minute or more, it spun with furious energy, kicking up everything in its path.

Then, as though exhausted by its own futility, it disintegrated.

Except for the damage left in its wake, no one would have known it had been there, raging but aimless.

Trapper continued up the drive toward the house. One end of a strip of crime scene tape had come loose. The yellow ribbon snapped in the wind, whisking the windshield as he brought Kerra's car to a stop just short of the porch.

He left the engine running when he got out. The front door was locked, but he knew where The Major had always kept the spare key, and it was there, resting on the third support to the left under the eaves.

The crime scene techs had been thorough. There were markings on the floor where measurements had been taken. Tiny plastic tents in varying colors showed where pieces of evidence had been collected. Black dust coated articles from which fingerprints had been lifted.

He avoided touching anything as he made his way first into the kitchen. He gave it a cursory glance, seeing nothing in it to indicate that it had been an area of interest to the investigators.

Leaving it, he crossed the main room and entered

the hallway. The door to the powder room was missing, taken as evidence, battered latch and all. The window through which Kerra had escaped was intact, the upper and lower sections locked together. He marveled that she could have squeezed through a space so small, but then panic and adrenaline enabled people to accomplish amazing feats.

He continued down the hall. He'd never lived in this house, but when The Major and his mother had moved to Lodal from Dallas, she'd designated a guest bedroom as Trapper's room, making it homey and personal to encourage frequent visits. The wall opposite the bed served as a photo gallery, with all the pictures framed identically and attractively arranged.

Trapper stood before it now and studied the collection that more or less chronicled his life. He could have marked the year of the Pegasus Hotel bombing just by looking at the photographs.

In the pictures taken before it, his dad was beside him, hand on his shoulder, grinning proudly into the camera as they held between them a fishing pole sporting a catch, an athletic trophy won at summer camp, a Boy Scout sash with badges attached. Snapshots captured other such milestone markers up to age eleven.

In the pictures taken after that, Trapper was alone. The bedroom had been left undisturbed by the investigators. Trapper touched nothing in it now. Although the room had been prepared for him, he was never homesick for it. The things in it belonged to him, but he felt no emotional connection to anything, no compulsion to claim ownership. They were stage props.

He went out and closed the door behind him, then continued down the hall to The Major's bedroom. The door was standing ajar. He opened it the rest of the way and was embraced by familiar scents.

The room smelled like Old Spice. Leather. The wool coat hanging on the wall rack.

It smelled like Dad, like the man in the photographs.

This room, much like the front room, attested to the thoroughness of the investigation. It had been determined that the two intruders had gone out through a window in this room because it was on the back side of the house. That window, the wall surrounding it, the floor beneath, had evidence tags attached and a coating of fingerprint dust.

Trapper went over to the window and looked through it to gauge the distance to ground. Because of the grade, it was a more severe drop than the one outside the powder room, which Kerra had braved. A man with reasonable physicality could get out this way.

It would be much more challenging to get in.

As he made his way back down the hall, Trapper was so lost in thought, he didn't realize that anyone else was there until he reentered the living area and saw the silhouette of a large man filling the front doorway.

Chapter 26

Trapper dropped into a crouch and went for his pistol.

"Hell, man, easy there."

Trapper then identified the man by his cowboy hat and uniform. "Jenks?"

"Didn't expect you. Isn't that Ms. Bailey's car?"

Trapper eased up to standing. "Yeah. How'd you know?"

"It's been parked at the motel for almost a week. We've been keeping an eye on it, afraid somebody would strip it."

"She and I picked it up earlier today. Since her key is still in her shoulder bag, and it's in evidence, I had to break into her car and hot-wire it."

Jenks advanced into the room and took a look around. "She with you?"

"No, she's on her way back to Dallas."

"Without her wheels?"

"It's a long story."

"Sounds like it. Looks like it, too." Jenks motioned toward Trapper's cheek. "She do that?"

"No. That's courtesy of a preacher man."

Jenks guffawed. "Hank Addison threw a punch?"

"Hmm."

"I didn't think he had it in him."

Trapper touched the sore spot and winced. "He was riled over Glenn. I guess you know he's in the ER."

The deputy nodded. "I wasn't in the office when it happened, but everybody was in a flap. Word got around fast."

"Hank blames me for bringing it on."

"I heard about the scene this morning with the suspect. He's been arraigned. Bail denied."

Carson had already texted Trapper. He didn't pursue it with the deputy. "What's the latest on Glenn?"

"Wasn't cardiac, except that his heart was beating a mile a minute. Bad panic attack. They're going to monitor him for a couple more hours to make sure he's okay, but it's expected he'll go home."

Trapper exhaled a long breath of relief. "Good to hear."

Jenks nodded agreement, and for a moment nothing was said, then, "Officially, nobody's supposed to be in here, Trapper."

"Officially, I know that. But The Major asked me to fetch him a bathrobe. They're getting him up more, moving him around. He's tired of mooning the nurses."

Jenks chuckled, but he looked down at Trapper's empty hands. "Couldn't find his robe?"

"I did, but it was pretty sad, and you know how The Major prides himself on his appearance. I decided to buy him a new one."

"Good plan. I'll walk you out."

The deputy moved aside. Trapper realized the choice of whether or not to leave wasn't his to make. He headed for the front door, Jenks a few steps behind him. Close behind him.

As they moved onto the porch, Trapper asked, "Is this part of the county your regular patrol?"

"No. But when The Major comes home, sheriff wants the house to be intact. He asked me to drive out at least once a day, keep an eye out for intruders, souvenir seekers, like that."

"You going to write me up?"

"Naw. You own the place, right?"

"Only half."

"Did you stay on your half?"

Trapper gave him the expected laugh.

"Besides," Jenks said, "the sheriff's got enough on his plate. Had to bother him last night with a missing person report."

"She was with me."

Jenks threw back his head and laughed. "That's just what Glenn said, but it wasn't for Ms. Bailey. You know a guy named Petey Moss?"

Trapper shook his head.

"Well, doesn't matter. Landlord filed, but I think Moss is trying to outrun his ex. Left the landlord with dead goldfish and unpaid months on his lease."

Trapper replaced the spare door key where he'd found it, cleared the steps, and walked toward Kerra's car, which was still purring. "Thanks for keeping a watch on the house."

"You bet." The deputy brushed the brim of his hat with his finger and climbed into his unit.

He followed Trapper down the drive and gave two friendly honks of his horn as he turned in the opposite direction out of the gate.

A couple of miles down the road, Trapper spotted an old cattle auction barn, which now stood vacant and derelict. He pulled off the highway and drove around behind the structure where he couldn't be seen.

He got out of the car and began searching the wheel wells and undercarriage. In no time at all, he spied the transmitter. "Souvenir seekers, my ass."

"What happened to your face?"

"Hello to you, too." Trapper dropped a plastic Walmart bag onto the bed and sat down in the chair at The Major's bedside. "I went to the ICU floor. They told me where to find you. Not that I needed directions once I reached this floor. The hallway is so crowded with goodie baskets and flowers, the staff is having to run an obstacle course to get to their other patients. When did they move you?"

"Couple of hours ago."

"Means you're on the mend." He gave a casual look around. "Nice room. Open the blinds, you'll have a view of the sunset. And I can bring some of those flowers in if you want. I spotted some chocolates that look good."

"I asked you a question, John."

Trapper sighed, propped his forearms on his thighs, and stared down at his boots. They were covered with dust from the old auction barn. From there, he'd made a quick stop at the store before coming to the hospital. There were several things he wanted to discuss with The Major, all of them touchy subjects.

He said, "Hank is what happened to my face."

"Hank?"

"Right before he went to correct an I-beam

misplacement for the tabernacle that's under construction. Did you know about that?"

"Couldn't live here and not know about it. Hank says it will be the fulfilment of God's plan for his church."

"Well, God may want to anoint a new architect. This one fucked up the I-beams."

"Did Hank slug you for making a crack like that? Or did it have to do with Glenn's anxiety attack?"

"So you know?"

"Hospital grapevine. I'm told it was alarming but not life-threatening."

"I'm grateful it wasn't worse." He pointed to his injured cheek. "Hank blames me for maxing out Glenn's stress level. I contributed to it, I'm sure. But I'm told you two had a visit this morning, and that Glenn was upset after it. How come?"

The Major hesitated.

"Well?"

"I told him everything, John. Beginning with Debra's diary and how you used it to persuade—"

"Force."

"To force me to retreat from the public eye. I told him about the conclusions you'd drawn about the bombing and your certainty that there's a correlation between it and the attempt on my life."

"You mention Thomas Wilcox?"

"I told Glenn you suspected him of some involvement."

"What did he say to that?"

"I got no indication that he'd ever heard of Wilcox, but he said you must have something on the man or you wouldn't make such serious allegations."

"Nice of him to say. What did you come back with? Did you tell him you think I'm delusional?"

"No, I told him I think you're right."

That being the last thing he'd expected to hear, Trapper's heart bumped hard against his ribs. He was at a loss for words.

With tight-lipped reluctance, The Major continued. "I don't know if all your hypotheses are correct, but, along with your stubborn streak, you also have integrity that's equally ironclad. You wouldn't condemn a man on a whim, or for self-gain, or for any reason other than your conviction of his guilt."

Trapper was relieved of having to respond when a nurse entered the room to exchange bags on The Major's IV drip. Trapper left the chair and went over to the window, where he stared unseeing across the hospital parking lot and tried to come to terms with receiving even a backhanded compliment from his father.

Call him a cynic, but he couldn't help but wonder why the stroking was coming now.

He could validate his father's flattery by telling him about Wilcox's visit to his office, his willingness to make a deal with prosecutors, his admission that he needed Trapper in order to do that.

But Trapper was reluctant to share that just yet. Not yet.

He stayed at the window for as long as it took the nurse to go through her routine, then turned his back on the splendid sunset and faced The Major. "I went out to your house this afternoon."

"What for?"

"Ostensibly to get your bathrobe."

"But you didn't."

"No, that was my lie to cover why I was there." He motioned toward the Walmart bag. "You have a new flannel robe, and I bought myself a shirt. One with snaps, not a pullover." He pinched up the stretchy fabric of the black t-shirt Carson had bought for him. "This is a little too Euro to suit me."

"You're stalling, John. Who'd you lie to?"

"Deputy Jenks. Know him?"

"Only through Glenn. He says he's one of the best deputies in the department."

"Well, he's certainly been on the ball this week. He pulled a graveyard shift guarding Kerra's hospital room. Then today, he caught me at your house. Said he'd been asked to keep an eye out for intruders."

"Glenn told me he would see to it that the house wasn't looted in my absence."

Trapper supposed that was a valid explanation. But

he couldn't shake the feeling that there was something off about Deputy Jenks. He recalled him being exceptionally curious about Kerra's and his conversation in her hospital room. He'd specifically asked if she had recounted to him what had happened.

"Why did you go to the house today, John?"

Trapper returned to the chair and sat down. He assumed the same hunched position as before, looking down at the floor between his spread knees. "I went looking for something."

"What?"

"A way for someone to get in undetected."

"Into the house?"

"Kerra swears that someone tried to open the powder room door *before* she heard the gunshot." He raised his head to gauge The Major's reaction. He appeared to be thinking hard.

"The man who shot me and his accomplice were on either side of the front door. Are you saying there was a third?"

"*Kerra* says it. Her mind is clear on the point. So unless it was you—"

"Me?"

"Well, you were there."

"Why would I try to open the bathroom door, knowing full well Kerra was in there?"

"Then someone else was in the back of the house, and it had to be someone familiar with it, or they could easily break their neck trying to get inside. Especially on the north side at the back, and especially in the dark."

"Glenn hasn't mentioned a third suspect to me."

"Which is curious in itself. He's not convinced there was a third party. He thinks Kerra got confused, the concussion and all."

He gave The Major time to contemplate all that before continuing. "The day I delivered Kerra to meet you, I drove directly from your house to the Addisons' and informed Glenn of the upcoming interview."

"He called me soon after you left him. He wanted to confirm with me that the interview was actually going to take place. He was grousing about the commotion that having a TV crew in town would create, part-time deputies put on the payroll, the overtime it would cost."

"Soon everyone in his department would have been aware of when and where the interview was to take place."

"Soon everyone in the whole world knew, John."

But not everyone in the whole world knew about the sharply varying grade around The Major's house or the steep ravine where Kerra might have died. It would take someone familiar with the place to know the pitfalls to watch for if sneaking in through a rear window.

Trapper didn't believe that Jenks just happened to be passing by on that rural road and noticed Kerra's car at The Major's house. Finding the tracking device reinforced his suspicions of the deputy.

But he didn't air those with The Major, either. He was beginning to sound paranoid even to himself.

"You're frowning, John."

"Am I?"

"Just like you did as a boy when a riddle had you stumped."

He wasn't so much stumped by the things that weren't adding up as he was deeply disturbed by the things that were.

"Why all the questions about Glenn?" The Major asked.

"I'm worried about him."

"In what context?"

In the context of Glenn taking him to ball games when his own father was off making speeches. Glenn giving him advice on women, which he hadn't taken, and on where to buy the best boots, which he had. Glenn sparing him a paddling over an Easter egg prank. Glenn with an unspecified problem that was causing him to drink too much and giving him anxiety attacks.

Suddenly Trapper didn't want to talk any more. Or think any more. He stood up. "I gotta go."

"John—"

"You look tired. I think changing rooms must've worn you out."

"We didn't finish earlier."

"Finish what?"

"You know damn well what," The Major snapped. "I told you I thought you were right."

"Thanks."

"But—"

"See? This is why I avoided a finish. I didn't want to hear the 'but.'"

"*But* I don't want your obsession, as noble as it is, to destroy you. Taking on somebody like a Thomas Wilcox—"

"Believe me, I'm aware of the risks involved. Look at what happened to you."

"Then for god's sake ask yourself if persisting is worth it. Can't you just drop it?"

Trapper placed his hands on his hips. "Even though you think I'm right, I have ironclad integrity, conviction, etcetera, you're advising that I drop it."

"Yes."

"Why?"

"Why?"

"*Why should I drop it?* Tell me. Give me a reason."

"Because I want you to have a life."

"I do. This is it." He stabbed his finger toward the floor. "And this is the second time today I've had to tell somebody that."

"Kerra?"

"You'll be glad to know that she's safely off my destructive path. She's gone back to Dallas."

"By choice? Or did you drive her away?"

He didn't reply to that. Instead he said, "I'm not dropping it."

"No matter what?"

Trapper held his father's stare. "No matter what." He turned and walked out.

"Hello, it's Hank Addison."

"I saw your name on the ID," Kerra said. "I hope you're not calling with bad news."

"No, it's good. You were kind enough to ask me to call you if things went south, but I thought you'd like to know that my dad was released. We just got him home. He's irritable, but okay."

She smiled into the phone. "Irritable is a good sign, I think. I know you're all relieved."

"I tried to reach Trapper to let him know, but Dad says he's changed his phone number."

"I'll pass along the news. He'll be glad to hear it."

"I'm ashamed of myself for hitting him."

"Even he admitted that he had it coming."

"Still." He paused, then, "Well, I won't keep you."

"Actually I'm glad you called. I went online and

found the website for your church. The architectural renderings of the new tabernacle are most impressive. My schedule is in flux right now, but after I return to work and things settle down, would you agree to my doing a feature story on the church? If the stats on the website are true—"

"God would hold us accountable if we fudged on the stats."

She laughed. "Would you agree to letting me do a story?"

"Absolutely."

"Not so much from a proselytizing standpoint, but as an aspect of area growth. That kind of thing."

"I'll figure a way to work in the proselytizing without anybody noticing."

"Great, then. I'll be in touch, but in the meantime, please notify me if something of special interest occurs, and I'll try to—" She broke off when she heard footsteps approaching the door. "Sorry, Hank. I need to run. I'm glad your father is doing well. Thank you for letting me know."

She disconnected just as the lock clicked and Trapper pushed open the door. Seeing her, he stopped short of clearing the threshold. He looked around the room, taking in her bag on the floor in the corner, her laptop open on the table where she sat, her handbag on the dresser with a few articles scattered around it.

When he came back to her, his eyes were glittering with anger, his jaw set.

She stood up and faced off with him. "I forgot my toothbrush and had to come back for it."

He remained immutable.

"I bribed the manager into giving me an extra key. It cost me a ten-dollar bill and my autograph. Once I was here, I saw no reason to rush off."

He didn't even blink.

"You should have gotten stitches to close that cut." She motioned to the Walmart sack clutched in his right hand. "I hope you at least bought Band-Aids."

Nothing.

"All right, I know you're angry to find me here after trying to get rid of me, but I'm here, and I'm not leaving." In a gesture of defiance, she flicked a strand of hair over her shoulder. "What are you going to do about it?"

"Remember you asked." He came in and slammed the door shut.

Chapter 27

As he stalked toward Kerra, he dropped the Walmart bag and shrugged off his coat. Reaching behind his back, he unclipped his holster. It was still in his right hand when he took her by the shoulders and propelled her backward toward the bed.

Either she was too shocked to protest or she was ready for this, too, because she didn't resist as he, in one coordinated motion, set his holstered pistol on the nightstand and lowered her onto the bed. She grabbed a handful of his shirt as she lay back. He followed her down, maneuvering as he went so that when she was reclined, he was between her legs, the important body parts perfectly aligned.

Taking her face between his hands, he fused his

mouth to hers, pressing his tongue deep, thrilling to the way she hummed her pleasure. He might have gone on forever just kissing her if not for a greater hunger that he must gratify or die.

He worked her top up over her breasts. Her bra was lacy and sheer and only half there to start with. The cups were easily lowered. He took a moment to cradle a breast in each hand. "I freakin' love that," he murmured.

"What?"

That they get so hard so fast.

The words were in his mind, but he didn't say them aloud because by the time he thought them through he was already taking one nipple into his mouth and toying with the other, deriving pleasure from the pleasure he was giving her. With every wet tug of his mouth or sweep of his tongue or gentle pinch, she gripped his hair a little tighter and rubbed her body against his with matching maddening urgency.

He might die yet if he didn't get inside her.

He pushed up on his knees and yanked open the buttons of his fly. As he worked his jeans down, a drop of escaped semen slicked his thumb. He was that close.

Kerra, her gaze fixed on his erection, angled her hips up, grappled with button and zipper, then lowered her jeans and panties as far down her legs as she could reach. He pulled them down and off and threw them aside.

She was too many erotic images for him to register right now, so he concentrated only on the cleft between her thighs. He slid his hand between the swollen lips of her sex, tested her readiness, then spread his fingers to open her.

She gave a little gasp of feminine modesty, and he would enjoy reliving that purely feminine reaction. Later.

But now he took hold of his penis and planted the head of it against her opening. It was tight, but it was wet, and with a subtle push he stretched it, breached it, and secured his smooth tip inside.

It was ecstasy. But still not enough.

Looking into her eyes, he continued to press into her until he was completely sheathed. He could see in her face that the sense of wonder wasn't only his. Her lips silently formed his name.

He made a vow to himself to languish in her clenching heat, but later. Later. In the here and now he had to move. He began by pulling back ever so slightly. She clamped her lower lip between her teeth and held it until he sank into her again. When she released her lip, he ran his tongue across that incredible, turn-on pout. He kissed her beauty mark.

Responding to her restless motions beneath him, he shifted the angle of his hips and increased friction where she most wanted it, and he got it right. God, did he. Her throat arched into an offering made to him. He rubbed his open mouth along the smooth column. He nuzzled her ear and groaned the choicest of naughty words. He dipped his head and sucked her nipples in turn, causing her to whimper.

Even during this love play, he didn't stop pumping into her. He probably had been this hard before, probably as strained and blood-infused and lust-mad and unable to command the instinctual mating movement of his hips.

But if so, he didn't recall it, because this was the only time that mattered. He wanted this time to be an exorcism and possession at once. Doom and salvation. He wanted it to be both carnal and sacred.

He wanted this to be the fuck Kerra would remember for the rest of her life.

Her hands, which had been on his back, had moved to his butt, and now her fingers were digging in deep, holding him to her. Her head went back and her breathing turned choppy. Knowing she was about to come, he pushed deep and held, moving only to grind against that most sensitive spot. She made a sobbing sound an instant before he felt the clutch of her orgasm all along his cock.

She came long and lusciously. Just before the last rippling aftershock, he held her hips between his hands, gave a few quick thrusts, and then had the most wrenching climax of his life, expanding and pulsing until he gave a hoarse cry of helplessness and fell into her embrace.

Through the moments of subsiding, she held him close and continued to hug him to her until it was over. Only then did her body relax and settle. He lay motionless and heavy on top of her. His skin and hair were damp with sweat, his limbs deliciously heavy, his penis still snugly imbedded inside her.

He nestled his face in the curve of her neck and felt the first heartbeat of contentment he'd known in years.

"Kerra?"

"Hmm?"

Trapper stirred, then raised his head, lifted a strand of hair off her neck, and twined it around his finger. "Why is it that every room you occupy feels like a tropical rain forest?"

She laughed. "Because I'm cold-natured."

"Not all parts are cold," he growled, and she felt his teasing nudge inside.

She swatted his backside, then ran her hand over the taut muscle and squeezed it until he grunted a pleasured sound. "We generated a lot of heat," she said, "and you've got all your clothes on. What happened to getting nekkid?"

"I think we did just fine with clothes on."

"Better than fine." She gave an exaggerated purr.

"That sound alone makes me want to lose the threads." He withdrew from her, levered himself up, then left the bed and began pulling off his boots.

Kerra stacked her hands beneath her head and watched as he undressed, admiring each part of him as it was revealed. The yummy trail that she had admired from the towel up thickened and flared around his sex, of which he could be justifiably proud. She reached out and brushed her fingers across him. The hair and flesh were wet. She gave him a meaningful look.

"About that . . ." He exhaled through his lips. "It was safe sex. I swear. Just unprotected."

As she lay back, she trailed her fingertip along his hard thigh from crotch to knee. "I knew what I was doing."

They looked deeply into each other's eyes. Seconds ticked past. It was an ideal time to acknowledge that something important had happened.

His voice low, Trapper said, "It felt good, Kerra."

"It did," she whispered back.

It was simple, but, in its way, profound. He wasn't one to make romantic declarations, and if she said anything now, it would be more than he would want to hear.

She was perilously close to letting this evolve into

something that would leave her heartbroken. She was perilously close to becoming like Marianne. But she wouldn't take back having made love to him. Not for the world.

They continued to hold each other's gaze for a few moments longer, then Trapper changed the mood by crawling back onto the bed and leering at the provocative display of her bared breasts. "I don't know whether to strip you or not. I kinda like you the way you are."

"I look shameless and slutty."

"That's what I meant."

"I know," she said, laughing. "But it's a little uncomfortable."

"Then I'll strip you." He pulled her top over her head and reached behind her to unhook her bra. When he came away with it, he held it up against the lamplight and looked through the sheer fabric. "Why bother? This thing is useless."

"Not my choice. Carson picked it."

He looked at her, then at the bra, then back at her. "*Carson* picked it?"

"When he did that shopping for us."

"That settles it. I'm gonna kill him. Fucking pervert." He flung the bra away, then leaned over her, wrapped his hand around her breast with the finesse of a caveman, and fastened his mouth to her nipple.

Her laughter ended on a sigh when the lashing of his tongue turned lazy. "You love this?"

"Hmm?"

"What do you love? Specifically."

"Hmm?"

"Trapper?" She pulled his head up by his hair. "Are you listening?"

"No."

He raised up and kissed her thoroughly but without the fervency of before. This was a tender and leisurely after-sex kiss. But it stirred her no less. And him. In the midst of it, he took her hand and moved it down, pressing her palm over his penis and rubbing the back of it until she took up the massage. She felt the heat spread through him, signifying a reawakening of the passion that had consumed them only minutes ago.

"Yes, I was listening," he said when he ended the kiss but continued whisking his lips across hers. "Specifically, I love that your nipples stay hard."

"They do not!"

"Most of the time."

"You're imagining that."

"Maybe," he admitted. She felt his smile against her lips before he leaned back in order to look at her. "But it wasn't my imagination that night I came to see you in the hospital." He stroked her as he talked, following the path of his hand with his eyes. She felt their touch as keenly as that of his fingertips.

"I was chilled," she said.

"You were scared. But you would have been really scared if you'd known what was going through my mind."

She raised her head high enough to kiss his scruffy chin.

He smoothed his thumb over a red spot on the slope of her breast. "Maybe I should do a clean shave."

"Don't you dare. What was going through your mind?"

"That night in the hospital? How to get my hands on you without you screaming the place down. Besides those prim white socks, the only stitch you had on was that flimsy gown. Knowing there was nothing but you underneath, wanting to see it all, touch you everywhere, it was killing me."

"Was it?" she asked in a sexy voice.

His breath caught suddenly, and as he released it, he moaned, "What you're doing now is killing me."

She made another tantalizing pass across his glans with her thumb. "Want me to stop?"

"Hell no. I've done it so many times to myself while thinking of you doing it just like that, wishing it was you doing it."

He wet the tip of her breast with his tongue, then pressed it between his fingers before laying the backs of them in the hollow between her rib cage and drawing them slowly down the center of her body. They drifted across the sensitive span of skin below her navel, then back and forth over her mound.

"When you sat down on the hospital bed, that gown molded perfectly to this." His finger traced the V, following the grooves that formed it on both sides, then down the seam between her thighs, before sliding back up and coming to rest at the point where the three met.

"I mean, it couldn't have been more perfectly delineated for my viewing pleasure. And, I thought, God help me." He met her gaze and added drolly, "Then you pulled that sheet up over your lap."

He'd entranced her with his touch, his words. She cupped the back of his head and pulled him down to her for another kiss. When they pulled apart, she gingerly kissed the cut on his cheek. "Hurt?"

"Wouldn't know. I've been distracted by other physical sensations brought on by your talented hand."

"I offered to stop."

"Don't. You're better at it than I am."

She smiled. "What makes me better?"

"I tend to be more...uh, efficient."

"I can be more efficient."

"Please, no. Take your time. In fact, you've got more area to cover now than when you started."

She laughed softly as her fist moved up the full length of his erection and rode it down again.

He asked, "How come you didn't live with that guy in Minneapolis?"

Her hand stilled. "How did you know—"

"I checked you out, remember. Or Carson did for me." She gave him a reproving look, but he seemed not the least bit repentant as he reached down and started her hand moving again. "You two weren't that serious?"

"I thought we were, but then I was offered the job in Dallas, and when I accepted, without hesitation, he wished me luck, without hesitation. It had been a convenient and uncomplicated relationship, and that's how it ended."

"He was a loser."

"I wouldn't call him a loser. He developed software for the medical industry that he then sold for millions."

"Medical software sounds dull as dirt."

"That's true. With him I never outran the police in a stolen vehicle during an ice storm. Nothing near that exciting."

"That excited you?"

"Very much."

He hooked his hand behind her knee and propped it on his hip. As boldly as before, he opened her with stroking fingers. "Anything else excited you lately?"

She rocked against his caressing hand. "The way you looked at me."

"When?"

"When you came into the room and slammed the door."

"How'd I look at you?"

"Exactly the way you're looking at me now."

"Thomas?"

He hovered on the threshold of the bedroom. Having heard the door opening, Greta had sat up in bed, her pale nightgown making her look like a wraith in the dim room.

"Did I wake you? I'm sorry. I was just checking on you before turning in myself."

In a voice as unsubstantial as her body, she said, "I wasn't asleep yet."

A bottle of vodka was on the bedside table in addition to an array of prescription medications for depression and insomnia. Greta moved from doctor to doctor, cleverly juggling refills so she would never be without an anesthetic.

When Thomas had become aware of her abuse, he had started monitoring the prescriptions and alerted the doctors to her machinations. But despite his precautions, she seemed never to be in need of her next pill, and the supply seemed limitless. Eventually he had stopped interfering.

He was twelve years older than she. At age forty, he'd decided it was time to marry. Dallas was a hothouse of cultivated beauties. He had his pick of many, but he chose Greta because she'd best filled his list of requirements. She was pretty, scandal-free, the reigning princess of Dallas society, and the only child and heir of parents with old wealth and prestige from both families.

He won Greta over with his ardent pursuit. "I won't take no for an answer." She had thought his insistence terribly romantic. Never would she have guessed how literally he had meant it.

His father-in-law admired and respected his business acumen, and was perhaps a bit intimidated by it, which Thomas used to his advantage. His mother-in-law considered him to be a "divine catch." All Greta's friends said it was a match made in heaven.

They were wrong.

Divine intervention had nothing to do with it. Thomas had made it happen, and he was the antithesis of godly.

Although he'd married Greta for practical reasons, he actually formed a strong affection for her. She could be enchanting and entertaining. By nature, he wasn't given to frequent laughter, but she could coax it out of him. She was a generous and attentive bedmate.

To compensate for the weeks he worked nonstop,

he treated her to lavish vacations. He bought her the mansion she'd long admired. The house and grounds took three years to renovate, and that kept Greta occupied and happy. He discovered that he enjoyed indulging her.

Two things he refused her. He wouldn't attend every charity event and fund-raising ball and black-tie gala to which they were invited. He insisted on living a private life, out of the mainstream and certainly out of the limelight.

The second refusal regarded her infertility. He refused to participate in any humiliating testing or biological engineering.

Not to be denied her heart's desire for a child, Greta scheduled monthly sexual marathons until one resulted in pregnancy. Her joy was complete. To Thomas's staggering surprise, he'd shared it. From the day of her conception, Tiffany had been the golden fabric that had enwrapped them.

Now here they were tonight, as estranged as two people could possibly be.

"You didn't eat much dinner," he said. "Can't I get you anything?"

"No, thank you."

He never failed to offer; she never failed to decline. "Well, I hope you can get to sleep soon. Good night."

He was backing away when she stopped him.

"Thomas, who was that who came to the house a few nights ago?"

Rarely was he taken completely off guard. It took him seconds to recover. "What?"

"The night of the ice storm. Someone buzzed from the gate. You let him in."

"Oh, that. Yes. It was one of our neighborhood security officers. He was checking to see that none of our lines were down and that we still had power."

"No, it wasn't."

The contradiction was another turnabout. He covered his surprise with an abrupt laugh. "I beg your pardon?"

"He wasn't wearing the uniform of our neighborhood patrolmen."

A trickle of cold sweat slid down Thomas's spine. "You saw him?"

"I looked over the balcony as he was leaving. Was he...Did it have something to do with Tiffany?"

He gave an exaggerated sigh of impatience. "There was a break-in at one of the office buildings I own. The alarm went off and scared the intruders away. The officer came to report the incident to me personally. Nothing to it at all."

"Then why did you lie about who he was?"

"Because I never want to burden you with trivial matters. I'd forgotten all about it." She said nothing. As they stared across the room at each other, Thomas imagined the chasm between them widening. "Try to sleep," he said. "Good night."

Almost as soon as he pulled the door shut and headed down the hall toward his bedroom, his cell phone rang. Greta's uncharacteristic curiosity had unsettled him. He answered with a brusque "Yes?"

Jenks said, "Bad time?"

Thomas went into his bedroom and closed the door. "What do you want?"

"I caught John Trapper snooping around The Major's house."

"When?"

"This afternoon. Our man in common thought you should know."

Thomas had expected that by now Trapper would have followed up on their meeting in his office. He had anticipated hearing *something* from him today, and it was perturbing, and a little disquieting, that he hadn't.

"Did he say what was he doing there?"

Jenks told him how Trapper had explained himself. "But I didn't buy it, so I circled back and checked the house, inside and out. I didn't notice anything missing or disturbed. But just Trapper's being there is disturbing enough."

"I'm sure it is to you."

"Should disturb you, too."

"Why? I didn't flub the attempt on his father's

life." He could imagine Jenks gnashing his teeth over the insult. "Anything else?"

"This morning Trapper created a ruckus in the sheriff's office over the suspect."

"Who anyone with half a brain can see is being set up. It does sound as though Trapper has had a busy day, but I haven't heard anything that warrants this call at this time of night."

That was a lead-in for Jenks to tell him about finding the flash drive in Trapper's wall and to share with Thomas what was on it.

But Jenks said, "That's it for now."

No mention of the flash drive? Thomas couldn't ask outright about it without revealing that he knew of its existence, and the only way he could know was through Trapper.

Either the men in Lodal didn't have it, or had it but couldn't crack it, or were purposefully keeping from Thomas that it existed and what was on it. Each of those eventualities was worrisome.

With feigned nonchalance, Thomas said, "If that's it, please tell our *man in common* to stop whining to me about his own failures, and Trapper."

Before Jenks could offer a comeback, Thomas disconnected. He crossed to the bar, poured a scotch, tossed it back, and poured another, something he rarely did. More than he wanted to admit, even to himself, Jenks's call had upset him.

If the men in Lodal were in possession of Trapper's flash drive, they wouldn't be overly concerned about his snooping around the crime scene or creating ruckuses.

But if they hadn't raided Trapper's office and taken the flash drive, who had? Who had it now, and just how incriminating was the evidence on it?

Thomas had gambled on making a preemptive move, but possibly, in his eagerness to get justice for Tiffany, he had left himself vulnerable. Trapper might yet go to the authorities with no intention whatsoever of negotiating a deal for Thomas, with or without his flash drive, with or without anything substantive.

Thomas didn't believe he would. He was still smarting too badly from the humiliation he'd suffered three years ago. He wouldn't risk ridicule again by making unprovable claims.

But Trapper was unpredictable. He might surprise him.

Fortunately, Thomas had safeguarded against surprises and unpredictability.

He still had his insurance policy, and it was brass-bound. Even to Trapper.

Chapter 28

Trapper didn't know what Kerra saw in his "look."

Whatever it was, it aroused her. The second time was as intense as the first, the only difference being that he pulled out just before he came. Now they lay belly to belly, idly stroking, nibbling kisses.

"Your skin tastes salty," she said.

"Price you pay for keeping this room like a sauna. My sweat's drying." He rolled off her. "Let's shower."

She complained as he took her hand and pulled her off the bed and into the bathroom. "That shower stall isn't big enough for both of us, and, besides, I like salty."

"I'm not showering to get clean." He bobbed his

eyebrows. "I do some of my dirtiest play with soapy hands."

She laughed, and, although he enjoyed that husky sound, he loved the sighs and moans and whimpers she made when he proved it wasn't an empty boast. He examined her with the precision of a diamond cutter.

Her body still bore bruises and scratches from her fall. Those he could reach within the confines of the minuscule shower stall, he kissed. Those he couldn't touch with his mouth, he gently caressed with fingertips and palms, being especially careful with the two stitches on her thigh. Facing each other as warm water sluiced over them, they kissed endlessly, the notch between her thighs nestling him, her nipples small and hard against his chest.

He washed her hair and turned her away from him as he rinsed it just so he could watch the shampoo suds slide down her back and funnel into the cleft of her amazing ass. She didn't quite believe him when he told her it was necessary for his hands to be there to ensure that all the soap had been rinsed away.

Nuzzling her ear through her wet hair, he whispered, "However, the only truly reliable way to know for sure is by tasting." Reaching around her, he turned off the taps, one with each hand, then stayed that way, holding the levers. Drops of water plunked from the showerhead. The drain gurgled its last swallow.

Kerra turned within the circle of his arms and
looked into his eyes in that slumberous way that
made his cock rigid and his knees weak.

He pushed open the shower door and assisted her
out. Maintaining eye contact, he dragged the two
towels from the bar. With them in one hand and
taking Kerra's with the other, he pulled her back to
the bed.

———◦———

Trapper guided her down onto the two towels, which
he'd spread end to end on the bed before going to
his knees. She lay with her hands palms up at shoulder level, thighs together. With his index finger, he
again traced the V, ending at the point. Just that was
enough to spread a fever upward from beneath his
fingertip. She became full and achy, yearning.

He curved a hand around each of her thighs and,
as he drew them apart, bent down and kissed her
between them. His lips were closed and soft and, after that first contact, unmoving. They remained like
that until she thought she would die from wanting to
squirm, move, indicate in some subtle way that she
craved more.

When she didn't think she could stand the antic-
ipation for one more heartbeat, his lips parted and
she felt the first touch of his tongue. It was a swirl of

caresses, a thrusting invasion as though staking her as his, followed by a succession of French kisses, the last one deep and searching and ending with a slow withdrawal that left her melting.

She bowed up, seeking—

But he knew. He slid one hand under her and tilted her up, his strong fingers kneading her bottom. The other hand he splayed wide between her hipbones, his thumb perfectly placed to gently pull back the softest of skin. Then his mouth was on her again, hotter, wetter. His tongue was in turns fervid and barely there, still and firm, then fanning and feather-light.

She sank her fingers into his hair, a silent plea.

He increased the pressure and the tempo. He laved her, loved her, until she was shattered by her orgasm. He held her, drew on her with tenderness but also unquestioned mastery, and didn't stop until her body went limp.

When she opened her eyes, he was standing at the side of the bed, one knee planted on the edge of it between her open thighs. He was looking down at her with a slight frown, and suddenly she realized why. There were tears on her cheeks.

When she'd climaxed, not only had her senses become untethered, her emotions had as well. She had expected Trapper to be skilled. She hadn't expected him to be so unselfish, so sweet.

"You okay?"

"Yes." She sniffed and wiped away the tears as she came up on her elbows. "Yes."

"Tears of joy?"

"Something like that."

His features relaxed. "It was good for me, too."

"So I see." His erection couldn't possibly have escaped her notice. A bead of semen was clinging to the tip.

"Could I impose on you to do that thing with your thumb again?"

"Absolutely not." She came up the rest of the way, and reached around him to place her hands on his butt. Leaning into him, instead of her thumb, she applied her tongue.

———— ◆ ————

"I fantasized about that," Trapper said in a drowsy voice.

He had already told her that her hair felt as silky against his belly as he'd imagined it would. Now he was sifting his fingers through it although it wasn't completely dry. They had pulled back the covers and had gotten into bed. They were half lying, half propped against the headboard, legs braided together under the sheet, her head on his chest.

Idly she explored its contours. "You seem to have an extraordinary number of fantasies."

"Guilty."

"All of them erotic."

"Got me again. But my fantasy women never had a face before."

She stopped her play and tilted her head back to look at him.

"Recently," he said, sweeping his thumb over her cheek, "the rock star of my fantasies has this bewitching beauty mark."

She swallowed. "Does she?"

"Hmm. Eyes the color of a Hershey bar. And lips..." He rubbed the lower one. His voice dropped in pitch. "Two minutes after you knocked on the door of my office, I was fantasizing your mouth taking me." He pressed her lower lip with his thumb. "I thought it was sexy then. Now...Damn." He continued staring at her lips, gliding his thumb back and forth across the lower one.

Eventually, though, he withdrew his hand. His forehead furrowed. He cleared his throat. "Kerra—"

"You won't respect me in the morning."

He smiled, but his eyes remained serious. Realizing that he was done teasing, she moved off his chest and onto her own pillow.

"It's about Marianne."

"That's none of my business, Trapper. I should have kept my observations to myself. You don't owe me an explanation."

"But I want to explain, without losing my temper the way I did before."

"Bad timing on my part. You were already mad at me."

He acknowledged that with a nod, but she could tell that he wished to stay on track. He'd given thought to what he wanted to say, and he wanted, perhaps needed, to say it.

"Usually I don't give a shit what anybody thinks about me, or what I do, or how I conduct myself. But since you've met Marianne, seen the kind of person she is, I want you to know how much I hate that she got hurt. No," he said sternly. "That's too lenient. I hate that *I hurt her.*"

He paused as though waiting for her to comment, but, when she didn't, he continued. "But the way it turned out really was for the best. If she hadn't miscarried, and we'd gotten married, it wouldn't have changed the outcome, except that there would be another kid in the world growing up without a live-in daddy. Because eventually Marianne would have gotten sick of me and run me off, or I'd have left.

"Hank accused me of not caring about anything except myself and what's eating me. I know that's how it looks. To him. To everybody. But he's wrong. I cared enough about Marianne to leave her. I knew if I didn't, I'd make her miserable, and she deserved better."

He inhaled deeply. "Sometimes I think about the baby we lost. Wonder if it was a boy or girl, if it would've looked like me. It haunts me some. But I believe it worked out the way it was supposed to. I'm not glad it happened. God, no, nothing like that. And I'm not rationalizing, I swear. I'm—"

"I know," Kerra said, interrupting him. "I know you regret the temporary unhappiness you caused her. But you were right to leave. Marianne knew it was right, too."

"How do you figure?"

"If she had believed you belonged together, she wouldn't have let you leave. Did she go after you, ever reach out, try to contact you?"

He shook his head.

"If she'd really wanted you, *you*, warts and all, she would have fought like hell to keep you."

She could tell by his expression that he'd never thought of it that way before. Relief flickered in his eyes. Then, in typical Trapper fashion, he dodged the seriousness of the subject with a quip. "I don't have any warts."

Kerra didn't let him get away with it this time. "Come here." She clasped his head between her hands and pulled it to her chest, then wrapped her arms around it. His arm closed around her waist and hugged tightly. Though his cheek rested on her breast, it was with intimacy of a different sort.

She studied the growth pattern of his hair on the crown of his head and kissed it. "Did The Major ever know about the miscarriage?"

"No." He worked free of her embrace, making her wish she hadn't asked. Back on his own pillow, he said, "My 'skipping out on Marianne,' as he put it, was one of the hot spots of our quarrel. The miscarriage would have confirmed his belief that I was throwing my life away on a fantasy. And *not* the erotic kind."

"Have you checked on him today?"

"He's been moved to a private room. I stopped by the hospital after I went to the house."

She shook her head in confusion. "The Major's house? Catch me up. Is that where you went after dumping me at the café?"

"I didn't *dump* you. And, anyway, it was for your own good."

"Well, I decided against it."

"Yeah, and look where it landed you."

She shifted her legs to rub against his.

"Not that I'm complaining," he growled. Then he turned serious again. "The Major asked about you. I told him you were safely back in Dallas, which at the time I thought you were. He accused me of driving you away. As usual, we got into it."

"I hate that you got into it over me."

"Wasn't over you." He smiled without humor. "He

started out by telling me he thought my conspiracy theory had legs and that he admired my integrity."

She leaned up, at attention. "That's good."

"For a few minutes there, I thought so. I'd been waiting a long time to hear him say he thought I was right about something. Anything. Any fucking thing. The weather forecast. So you can imagine my astonishment when he commended me for having integrity. But *then* he told me I should let go of my obsession, drop it, and get a life."

"That's contradictory."

"Damn sure is."

She waited for him to add whatever it was that had caused his brows to pull together in a frown, but he didn't. She rolled onto her stomach and came up on her elbows so they could talk face-to-face.

"Was there anyone in your division of the ATF, or an FBI agent, anyone who believed in you and your suspicions about Wilcox?"

"There were a handful who didn't laugh out loud."

"You could take what you have on that flash drive, plus the cell phone recording I made of Wilcox, go to someone you trust, and lay it all out."

He was shaking his head before she finished. "The number one rule of bureaucracy is CYA. If they even saw me coming, any of my former associates would use both hands to cover their asses. They remember what happened to Marianne."

"I'll go with you. They wouldn't laugh at you with me there. They'd fear a media smear campaign."

He took her hand and kissed the palm. "I appreciate the gesture. But—"

"You have to do this alone."

"Not out of vanity, Kerra. It's not that, I swear. It's that I've got to be *right*. There's no guarantee that I'll get even one more shot. But if I do, it has to count. I must have Wilcox's balls in one hand and his goddamn insurance policy, whatever that is, in the other."

"Wilcox said he wouldn't give up anything until you can guarantee him immunity."

"I know." He sighed. "It's called an impasse."

"How are you going to break it?"

"Hell if I know."

They were quiet for a time, but she could practically hear the gears grinding in his mind. She reached up to smooth out his brow. "You could let the dust settle for a while, Trapper."

"That's what I've been doing for three years, and I'm choking on it." He gave a small shake of his head. "I gotta get this off me, Kerra. Not that my life counts for much, but yours does. Now it's not just The Major I'm worried about. If I turned my back on you, on this, and one day you were found—"

He didn't go on, but she filled in the blank,

and it was troubling to acknowledge that she was vulnerable.

Speaking softly, but with ferocity, he said, "It's gotta be now."

She leaned over and bit him gently on the shoulder. "I knew you'd say that. And if The Major expects you to drop it, he doesn't know you at all." She wished to say more. Emotions were welling up in her throat, her heart, but she kept them to herself for now. "Why did you go out to his house?"

"I have an itch I can't scratch."

"Pardon?"

"Hear me out."

"I'm listening."

"They've got Leslie Duncan behind bars, which is a frame. They say they're looking for his accomplice, who doesn't exist."

"You could be wrong, Trapper."

"Okay, say I am. Let's say Duncan is guilty as hell. He and his unsub did the deed."

"Maybe the unsub was his girlfriend."

He arched an eyebrow with skepticism, but said, "All right, let's go with that. Who was the third person?"

"The one who tried to open the bathroom door? Maybe *that* was the girlfriend, and the unsub was the man who asked the question."

"We won't know until he's apprehended. And that's

my itch. His apprehension. To my knowledge, nobody is even looking for a third person. When's the last time you even heard it mentioned?"

"Not since I was last questioned."

"See what I mean? Glenn hadn't even told The Major there was a third suspect."

"The house didn't turn up any clues? Were you looking for something specific?"

"Point of entry. I didn't find it, but it wasn't a wasted trip." He told her about his encounter with the deputy.

"Jenks?" she repeated when he told her his name.

"Met him?"

"I don't think so. I'm not matching a face to that name."

"He was guarding your hospital room the night I brought you the flowers. Today he pops up at The Major's house, while I just happen to be there, except I don't think it was happenstance at all. I'm almost positive he's been tracking you."

"*Me?*"

He told her about discovering the transmitter on the undercarriage of her car. "Remember, I told you I wouldn't put it past Glenn to try and keep tabs on me that way. I didn't think he'd pull the same with you."

"Did you leave it on the car?"

"No I dropped it in a Portacan on the hospital

parking lot. I guess they can find us if they really want to, but I didn't want to make it easy for them."

"Another headache for Sheriff Addison," she said. "He's home now. Hank called me just before you came in. He'd tried to reach you. I told him I would pass along the update."

"I hate to admit that Hank is right about anything. But it's true that Glenn's had a hard time of it since I hit town. The Major said that when Glenn called to confirm the interview, he was already griping about all the overtime he would have to pay."

"He was still griping about it the afternoon I met him. He stopped by The Major's house during our first pre-interview session. He made me feel that I should apologize for all the inconvenience I was causing him. He was a little more mellow about it when he came by my motel room."

Trapper gave a start. "First I've heard of this."

"It was on Friday evening."

"Courtesy call?"

"In a manner of speaking. He was following up to see if his department was doing a good job of keeping autograph hounds at bay." She smiled. "Actually I took advantage of his being there to run past him the list of questions I was preparing. The Major had insisted on seeing them in advance of the interview.

"I asked the sheriff's opinion on whether I should omit any mention of you. He told me that would be his recommendation, that the interview would cause enough fireworks after I sprang my big surprise, that adding you to the mix would—"

Trapper sat bolt upright and held out his hand to stop her from saying anything more. "He mentioned the big surprise?"

"Honestly, I was miffed that you'd told him."

"I didn't."

She sat up so she could see his face, which was taut with concentration.

"I warned Glenn of the interview, but I didn't give away your secret." For a time, he sat so still that he startled her when he abruptly threw off the covers and lurched off the bed.

He grabbed his jeans from where he'd slung them onto the floor, stepped into them, then shook a shirt from the Walmart sack, ripped off the tags, and pulled it on. Responding to his urgency, she came off the bed and began dressing as hurriedly as he.

"In the wee hours of Monday morning," he said, "when you regained consciousness, Glenn and I were in your room."

"Yes, yes." She crammed her feet into her shoes. "I woke up to the two of you talking. He was describing the crime scene."

"Right. He asked if I knew prior to the telecast who you were. I confessed I did. He acted pissed off that I hadn't told him, acted like he'd learned it along with everybody else in the TV viewing audience. Yet you say he knew on Friday night."

"The Major could have—"

"If The Major had told him, why not just say so? Why did he pretend to me that he didn't know?"

She processed that, but couldn't come up with a logical answer.

"Glenn knew before Sunday night, but he didn't want me to know that he did." Trapper checked the clip in his pistol, then replaced it in the holster and attached that to his waistband.

Kerra grabbed her handbag. "If neither you nor I told him, and if it wasn't The Major, then who?"

Trapper pulled her coat off a hanger in the closet, tossed it to her, then picked up his own. "Good question."

Chapter 29

Hank answered the mudroom door to Trapper's knock.

Peering at them through the screened door, he said, "We aren't exactly up to having company tonight."

"We're not company." To include Kerra in that, Trapper placed his arm across her shoulders.

He hadn't even considered leaving her behind. Not after discovering the tracking device on her car, and not after having Jenks show up *coincidentally* at The Major's house, and not after learning that there was something hinky about the timing of when Glenn became aware of her connection to the Pegasus Hotel bombing.

He wanted Glenn's explanation for all these

peculiarities, and he didn't care if he had been rushed to the ER today, he wanted to hear what the sheriff had to say now, even if he had to drag him from his bed.

Hank still didn't invite them in. "How's your cheek?"

"It's not terminal."

"You probably should have had it stitched."

"Is Glenn still up?"

Hank sighed. "Trapper, the last thing Dad needs—"

"I need to talk to him."

"What for?"

"That's for him to know."

"Can't it wait till morning?"

"If it could wait till morning, I wouldn't be here now."

Hank looked from him to Kerra as though seeking her support, which she didn't lend. Going back to Trapper, he said, "Don't you have a filter, any sense of propriety?"

"You have to ask?"

"He's not going to go away." The gruff voice reached them from beyond Hank in the direction of the kitchen. "You had just as well let him in."

With unconcealed reluctance and dissension, Hank flipped the latch on the door, pushed it open, and stepped aside. Kerra went in first. Trapper followed, and, when he walked past Hank, said under his breath, "You ever hit me again, you'll be preaching through extensive dental work."

When Trapper entered the kitchen, Glenn was holding one of the dining chairs for Kerra. The kitchen smelled like the baking dish of lasagna that had been left on the stovetop. And of the whiskey in the glass on the table in front of the chair Glenn dropped back into.

Trapper was shocked by his appearance. He was disheveled and seemed to have aged twenty years since this morning during the questioning of Leslie Duncan. Trapper wondered if Glenn hadn't suffered something more serious than an anxiety attack. It must have been one hell of one. It was also obvious that the drink in front of him wasn't his first. Or even his second.

"Kerra, something to drink?" Glenn asked. "Soft or hard? Coffee?"

"Nothing, thank you."

"Trapper?"

"Believe I will." He excused himself to step around Hank, got a glass from the cabinet, and returned with it to the table. He sat down across from Glenn and adjacent to Kerra. Hank took the fourth chair.

Trapper asked where Linda was. Hank said, "She was exhausted. I made her go to bed with the promise that I would stay here overnight in case Dad needed anything or took a turn."

"I'm not going to take a turn," Glenn muttered.

Trapper poured himself a whiskey, shot it, then set the empty glass on the table and clasped his hands. Addressing Glenn, he said, "The next ten minutes or so aren't going to be any fun for me. I want you to know that."

Glenn topped off his glass and took a drink.

Trapper didn't waste any more words. "Who told you that Kerra was the little girl in the picture?"

"Thomas Wilcox."

Trapper thought his heart might stop. He hadn't expected Glenn to come forth with an answer so readily. And although Trapper had had a premonition that this would eventually lead to Wilcox, it was a jolt to hear his name right off the bat.

As upsetting as it was to learn that Glenn had an association with the man, it was even more alarming to learn that Wilcox had known in advance of Kerra's interview with The Major that she was a survivor of the Pegasus bombing. For all they'd talked about in Trapper's office, he hadn't mentioned knowing that when he and Kerra had first met.

Why not? Trapper wondered.

He could tell by Kerra's expression that this disclosure troubled her, too.

"Who's Thomas Wilcox?" Hank asked.

Trapper ignored him and focused on Glenn. "When did Wilcox tell you who Kerra was?"

"The night you told me about the upcoming interview. Soon as you left, I alerted Wilcox to it."

Trapper leaned forward across the table. "Why would you do that, Glenn?"

"What is going on?" Hank said.

Glenn turned to him. "Hank, stop asking questions and let me talk. You had just as well hear this, too."

"This what? *What?*"

Glenn went for his glass of whiskey, but Trapper moved it and the bottle out of his reach. "Start at the beginning, Glenn, and tell me everything. What's your link to Wilcox?"

"It goes back several years."

"I've got all night."

"You wearing a wire?"

"I don't work in law enforcement."

Glenn held his gaze. "You wearing a wire?"

Trapper shrugged off his coat and raised his shirt. "Neither is Kerra."

Glenn looked at her. She said, "I'm not recording this." She took the cell phone she'd been using from her handbag. "It's not even on, but you can check." She set it on the table.

As she was about to pull back her hand, Glenn reached out and covered it with his own. "I'm sorry. Jesus, I'm sorry." His eyes turned watery. "I didn't know. I swear to God." He glanced at Hank. "I'd swear on your Bible. I didn't know that Wilcox would try to kill you and The Major. I didn't think he'd go that far."

"Talk to me, Glenn," Trapper said. "And it has to be more than 'I'm sorry.'"

Glenn gazed longingly at the whiskey, then dragged his hands down his face. "I'm ready to unload. I've been hauling around this guilt since Sunday night. Finally got to me today. Sent me to the hospital. I don't want to live with it anymore."

The word "guilt" had brought Hank to attention. He placed his hand on Glenn's shoulder. "Dad, maybe you shouldn't say anything. I mean if this is some kind of legal matter...Should I call a lawyer?"

Glenn shook his head. "Not yet. I want to get this off my chest. Trapper needs to know." Looking across the table at him, he said, "You're a target, too, I'm sure."

"Talk to me," he repeated, this time softly but with urgency. "When did you meet Wilcox?"

"What year did your folks move back here from Dallas?"

The question seemed out of context, but he answered. "Soon after I graduated high school and left for college. Ninety-eight, ninety-nine."

Glenn nodded. "One evening shortly after they'd gotten settled, I was approached by a man as I was leaving the office. I don't remember his name. He was only a messenger. He told me that I was going to win the upcoming election. Hands down, he said. A landslide."

He scratched his cheek. "I was facing stiff competition for the first time. Secretly I was worried my opponent would beat me, narrowly maybe, but, if I lost, it wouldn't matter by how much.

"I figured this guy was one of those campaign gurus who was soliciting me to use his services for a heap of money." He shook his head. "Nope, he said 'you're going to win,' and 'remember I told you.' Walked off into the dark. I didn't know what to make of it. Just thought he was a loony tune."

"You won."

"By a landslide." He stopped, looked Trapper hard in the eye and said, "Not another goddamn word until I get my drink back."

Trapper pushed the glass across to him, and he drank from it before resuming. "A week goes by. I get this voice mail on my phone. Said to come to an address in Dallas and told me to be there at the appointed time if I wanted to remain sheriff. Voice had threat behind it. Creeped me out. I was thinking maybe my opponent had demanded a recount, something like that.

"I went. The address was an ordinary office building, except that it didn't have room numbers, no names on any of the doors. I had to check my weapon, was frisked, and was put through a series of security checks. I was beginning to think it was some kind of covert government organization. Eventually I was shown into a room. Only one person in it, a neatly dressed man of average height and weight. Good looking enough, but nobody to swoon over."

"Wilcox."

Glenn nodded. "He looked ordinary, but I gotta tell you, first time I looked into his eyes, a chill went down my spine."

"Did you know who he was?"

"No. He introduced himself by name, but it didn't mean squat to me. So when he began asking questions about my friend The Major, I was still under the impression that he might be an agent of some sort conducting an investigation for a government outfit."

"What kind of questions was he asking?"

"About the bombing. Had The Major ever told me anything about it that wasn't public knowledge? Had he seen something quirky, something that didn't quite add up? Did he ever specifically refer to the three bombers?

"I got real uneasy real quick and asked him point blank if he was implicating The Major. When he smiled, I got another chill. 'No,' he said. 'I blew up the Pegasus Hotel.' Just like that. I nearly messed myself. What the hell had I been dragged into? Who was this guy? Was he joking?"

"No," Trapper said.

"I soon got that. He was as serious as death." When Glenn reached for his glass again, Trapper noticed that his hand was trembling. "I played dumb when The Major told me that you've been on to Wilcox for years, have a whole dossier on him, so no need for me to elaborate about the Pegasus, the confessor, all that." Looking at Kerra, he said, "I assume Trapper has shared with you."

She nodded.

Hank said, "Well, I'm glad somebody has been clued in, because I'm still in the dark here."

"The three men who detonated the bombs in the Pegasus did so at the bidding of a man named Thomas Wilcox." As Trapper laid it out for Hank, he was watching Glenn, so he saw the pain in Glenn's eyes when his son confronted him.

"Dad? Is that true?"

Glenn's lips moved, but no sound came out.

"*Dad?* Answer me."

"Yes. It's true."

Hank stared at him with bafflement and disbelief. "You knew? Since...since...whatever year that was. You knew, but you never reported him? Why? Why didn't you turn him in?"

Glenn looked miserable. He rubbed his hand across his eyes. "That's not the end of the story, Hank."

"You're damn right it's not," he said, popping up

out of his chair, his voice going shrill. "Call the FBI. If you don't, I will."

"Let him finish first," Trapper said.

"And you, you worthless prick." Hank looked down at him and sneered. "You've known, too, and haven't done anything about it?"

Trapper glared at him. "You don't have any idea what we're dealing with here. You blow the whistle on Thomas Wilcox without a shred of evidence, and you had just as well throw Glenn under the next freight train that comes by, because he'll be dead just about that soon. Now, if you want to stay and hear the rest, come down off your judgmental podium, sit down on your self-righteous ass, and shut the fuck up."

As before, Kerra stabilized a situation rapidly spinning out of control. "Let's hear the rest of the story before we jump to conclusions or make any rash decisions."

Hank smoldered as he looked at each of them in turn, but he sat. He looked at Glenn. "What? You took a bribe?"

"In a sense, I already had. I'd won the election that many predicted I wouldn't, that *I* had predicted I wouldn't. Wilcox went on to tell me that I would get to keep the office for as long as I wanted it. Each time I came up for reelection, no contest."

"In exchange for what?" Trapper asked.

"Keeping Wilcox apprised of The Major's comings and goings. Who he saw, who came to see him. Government types like I'd mistaken Wilcox for. I was to tell him anything The Major said about the bombing when we were in private, especially if he ever questioned the findings of the investigation or the three men who were credited with the crime."

Hank was gaping at him, incredulous. "You *spied* on The Major."

"On my best friend," Glenn said, his voice gravelly with emotion. He took another drink.

"How could you do that? Why didn't you just tell this Wilcox no? Or pretend to agree, and then go straight to the FBI and turn him in?"

"Tell him, Trapper."

"No evidence," Trapper said. "Wilcox wasn't at the Pegasus. He wasn't at the factory that burned to the ground. And there would've been no evidence of his having tampered with the election. I could go on, but you get the point."

"You've got to understand, Hank," Glenn said, virtually pleading. "That's how this guy operates. If he tells you to do something, you're already indebted. You're already in. At least I was. The only option is to say yes, unless you want the sky to fall, not just on you, but on someone you care about."

"Admit it, Dad, you were a coward."

"Goddamn right," Glenn fired back, no longer

imploring him for understanding. "Wilcox had me sign a pledge, but not before covering all the signatures above mine. You don't know who he's got watching you. He says it keeps everybody honest. There was no one—*no one*—I could trust with this. First person I confided in could be the one watching *me*, and, like Trapper said, I'd be found looking like a sausage patty under a freight train. Or you. Or your mother."

Hank looked both frustrated and fearful, but he stayed silent.

Trapper let Glenn catch his breath, then said, "You upheld your end of the bargain."

"Wasn't really a bargain, but, yeah, I began conveying information on The Major, but it didn't feel like spying, because nothing he did or said aroused suspicion. There was never anything noteworthy to report. Months would go by when I'd forget about Wilcox. But he didn't forget about me. The first time my loyalty was tested was when you joined the ATF."

"Wilcox was keeping tabs on me?"

"Not until he learned you were with the bureau. Then he was on me for months. 'What's this about John Trapper going into the ATF? What does The Major say about it?'"

"You came to see me," Trapper said. "You brought a bottle of cheap champagne to celebrate my being inducted."

"I'm ashamed to say that I was fishing. I reported back to Wilcox that your interest in bombs and such was natural, seeing as the Pegasus had so impacted your life. That didn't pacify him, though. Periodically he would ask me to find out what you were working on. I held my breath, fearing you'd start looking into the Pegasus."

"Then I did."

"Then you did," he said with unnatural huskiness. "I didn't know for certain, but I had an inkling that was what was causing you trouble inside the bureau. The best day of my life was when you were fired."

"Yeah, that was a real party."

Glenn had the grace to look remorseful. "Forgive me, Trapper. It got Wilcox off my back. When The Major retired and went into reclusion, I thought, 'Thank Christ. I'm reprieved.'"

"Until I appeared on the scene," Kerra said quietly.

Glenn sighed and gave her a rueful smile. "You didn't know it, but when you entered the picture, so to speak, you might just as well have put a bullet in my head. It ended my life as I knew it."

Chapter 30

The more Glenn talked, the deeper Trapper felt the cut.

Maybe he'd never professed it out loud, but he loved the guy. To hear all this hurt. He wished he could be someplace different, doing something different. If he could *be* someone different, maybe the laceration wouldn't be so painful.

His heart was bleeding.

But he had to keep at it. Glenn had betrayed not only their close relationship, he'd betrayed his oath of office and the law he was duty-bound to enforce. Trapper wouldn't let him make excuses for that.

"Sooner or later, Glenn, one way or another, you

would have been found out. Don't put it off on Kerra."

"I don't." When he reached for his glass, Hank said a cautionary "Dad," but Glenn ignored him and took a drink. To Trapper, "When you told me The Major was going back on TV, I was surprised but not panicked. Dutifully I called Wilcox to let him know. He wasn't overjoyed, but, like me, he didn't think it was cause for alarm.

"But when I told him that Kerra Bailey was doing the interview, it was like I'd launched a rocket up his butt." He turned to her. "That's when he told me who you were and why he didn't want you and The Major comparing notes, especially on live television."

"I interviewed Wilcox barely a year ago," she said. "He never let on that he knew I was the girl in the picture."

"I don't know when or how he made the discovery," Glenn said. "But he knew, and it made him paranoid as hell that you'd be one-on-one with The Major."

"But why?"

"He feared that if you began swapping experiences about that day, one or the other of you would realize something was out of joint."

She looked over at Trapper. He said, "That's why I tried to warn you off doing it, remember?"

Glenn said, "Wilcox really got nervous when I told him it was Trapper who'd alerted me."

"That explains why you were so upset the night of the Bible study, Dad." Hank looked at Trapper. "You sent Tracy in to tell me that he was hitting the bottle pretty hard."

"I asked her to be discreet."

"She was. She whispered it to me while someone else was talking. The study concluded about ten minutes later." Going back to Glenn, he said, "I asked Emma to head off Mom so she wouldn't catch you drinking. When I came here to the kitchen, you nearly bit my head off. I figured Trapper..." He looked over at Trapper, his implication clear.

"It had to be my fault that Glenn was getting drunk," he said. "This should be enlightening to you, Hank. Now do you understand what's been 'eating me' and burdening your dad?" He turned back to Glenn. "What was it like for you, plotting with Wilcox to kill The Major and Kerra?"

Glenn made a choked sound that was half belch, half sob. "I swear to God, I didn't. I told Wilcox to keep his cool, told him I would check into the situation and get back to him. I went out to The Major's house the following day. You were there," he said to Kerra. "The Major didn't introduce you to me as the girl in the picture, just as Kerra Bailey, 'I'm sure you've seen her on TV.' That kind of thing.

"I reported back to Wilcox that we didn't have a problem. Y'all didn't know. Kerra wanted to score an exclusive interview with The Major and had somehow sweet-talked him into it. That's basically what Trapper had told me, too. But Wilcox was still antsy."

"That's why you came to my room at the motel," she said.

"I wanted to see how you would react when I mentioned the big surprise you had planned for Sunday night's audience. You didn't ask me what big surprise, you only acted miffed that I knew about it."

"I had expressly asked Trapper and The Major not to tell anyone else."

"In any case, I had my answer, and I had to tell that snake-eyed son of a bitch," Glenn said. "The Major might not know who you were, maybe the surprise would be on him, too, but we could expect the big reveal come Sunday night."

Glenn covered a dry cough with his fist. He shifted in his seat. He reached for his whiskey but let his hand drop before picking up the glass. "Wilcox told me to take preventative measures to be sure that didn't happen."

His admission dumbfounded Kerra.

Hank's head dropped forward, and he clasped his fingers together on the back of his neck.

Trapper got out of his chair, rounded it, and gripped the top rung, tempted to pick it up and bash it over Glenn's head.

"One thing I don't get," Trapper said tightly.

"Why didn't you attack before the interview instead of after? How did you even know that Kerra would still be in the house?"

"I didn't attack anybody."

"You just said—"

"You didn't let me finish."

Trapper spoke over him. "Oh, wait. You wouldn't have done it yourself. You sent those three flunkies out there to do it."

"No, I didn't."

"Jenks and who else?"

"I didn't send anybody."

"Ever at the ready, Deputy Jenks—"

"Be quiet, John!" Glenn banged his fist on the table hard enough to rattle the glassware, then took a deep breath. "For once, will you shut up and listen? I talked Wilcox out of doing anything. Or I thought I had." When Trapper would have interrupted again, Glenn held up a hand. "Let me talk."

Trapper was seething, but he made a grand, sweeping go-ahead gesture.

Glenn turned to Kerra. "I told Wilcox that you'd shown me the questions you intended to ask. I gave him a run-down of what they entailed, told him they were chatty, innocent, nothing mysterious. They wouldn't raise eyebrows or red flags or pose a threat to anybody. I urged him to let the interview proceed as scheduled.

"By contrast, if tragedy were to strike you and The Major within days of you going on TV together, it would be like ringing a fire bell, and the FBI would come running. A data analyst couldn't ignore a coincidence like that, and the feds wouldn't depend on a department as small as mine to investigate the double murder of two celebrities. They would take over, and that would create a media frenzy like none other."

"Which is exactly what's happened," Trapper said. "Obviously Wilcox didn't heed your caution."

"Obviously. But he *led* me to believe that he agreed with my reasoning. He threatened me with dire consequences if I was wrong, but said he would trust my judgment. We hung up, and I took a huge breath of relief. Crisis averted and no one was the wiser."

Still addressing her, he raised his right hand. "On my solemn oath, I had nothing to do with what happened to you. I knew nothing about it until after the fact."

She looked up at Trapper, and he knew that she was remembering, as he was, that Wilcox had denied ordering the attempted assassination. Were both Glenn and Wilcox telling the truth about that? Or were both lying?

Trapper leaned down and placed both palms on the tabletop. "Why didn't you warn The Major, Glenn? You could have told him you had a gut feeling. Or a nutcase had called the SO and issued a threat. *Something*."

"I did caution him. Roundaboutly. I suggested he keep a pistol handy in case he had to ward off any paparazzi. Made a joke of it, but advised him to be vigilant till the interview was behind him.

"I kept several units out there patrolling for hours before the telecast and until the crew left in the van. I thought it was over and done. Nothing had happened. I called everybody in. That must've been what they were waiting for."

"They," Trapper said. "Who?"

"Whoever Wilcox sent," Glenn said. "He pretended to go along with my recommendation, but he doubled down. Even if I had told him I would do it, he knew I wouldn't."

Trapper snickered. "You suddenly grew a conscience?"

"No. I gave up my conscience a long time ago. But kill my best friend? And a woman?" He looked at Trapper with imploring eyes. "How could you think I would do that?"

"I wouldn't think you could make a pledge to Wilcox, either. Or wasn't it as sacred as your solemn oath?" Mimicking him, Trapper raised his right hand.

"The pledge extended to spying, not killing."

Trapper's initial reaction was to verbally lash out

at that, but arm-wrestling his temper into submission, he rounded the chair and sat back down. "Do you think Leslie Duncan was one of the three at the house?"

"We're not firm on there being three."

"There were three," Kerra said.

"Answer the question, Glenn," Trapper snapped. "What about Duncan?"

Glenn hesitated just long enough for Trapper to jump on it. "Did you set him up?"

"No."

"He was caught with the pistol all but smoking."

"Wasn't me."

"And my bag," Kerra said.

"Wasn't me."

"This morning—"

"Look," Glenn said, dividing a look between him and Kerra. "I'm still wearing the badge, so I have to go through the motions. But that guy is too obvious. And Kerra said his voice was wrong. Do I think he's being framed? Yes. Am I doing it? No."

"Someone in your department?"

"Must be."

"A Wilcox puppet?"

"Must be."

"But you don't know who?"

"No."

Trapper didn't quite believe that, but he let it pass

for the time being and moved on. "Why've you been bloodhounding Kerra and me?"

"Because I'm afraid for you! For Kerra because they missed her the first time. For you because you came charging into town, breathing fire, making scenes, second-guessing every-goddamn-body, but especially me, and absconding with our only material witness."

Glenn aimed a finger at him. "Don't think for a minute I believe that cock-and-bull story about you finding Kerra's earring under her hospital bed. You went to the crime scene, didn't you? Don't bother lying. I know you did. And you were out there again today."

"Jenks told?"

"He did."

"I hope he found the transmitter, and that he was up to his neck in sewage when he did."

"Transmitter?"

"The tracking device you put on Kerra's car."

Glenn looked over at her with puzzlement, then came back to Trapper and raised his shoulders. "Don't know what you're talking about, but I wish I had thought of it. Because all you've been doing is making a bright red target of yourselves."

Glenn had worked himself into a lather. Suddenly he flattened his hand against his heart. Trapper sat forward. Hank exclaimed, "Dad?" Kerra reached toward Glenn with apparent concern, but he waved her off. "I'm fine, I'm fine. They've got me on anti-anxiety pills."

She said, "You shouldn't be combining those with alcohol."

"Maybe he'll listen to you, Kerra," Hank said. "He won't listen to me."

Trapper noticed that the angry archangel who'd slugged him this morning now looked defeated, but he doubted Hank's dejection was solely for his father's sake. Glenn's treachery was going to be bad for Hank's business. The offering plate yield might be lighter.

After Glenn regained his breath and fortified himself with another belt of whiskey, he continued, speaking directly to Trapper. "This morning, in my talk with The Major, he told me you're still trying to build a case against Wilcox. That true? What have you got?"

When it became apparent that he wasn't about to respond to that, Glenn sat back in his chair, and his expression turned ineffably sad. "I don't blame you for not confiding that. I wouldn't trust me, either."

Trapper didn't let himself be emotionally moved. "Where does it stand between you and Wilcox now? When was the last time you spoke to him?"

"As I was speeding out to the crime scene. I called from my unit, demanding to know what the hell he'd done, what was I going to find when I got out there? I was furious, heartsick. I was screaming, bawling, cursing him to perdition."

"What did he say?"

"He claimed not to know what I was talking about. He hung up on me and hasn't answered his phone to me since."

Trapper thought on that, then asked Glenn if he and Wilcox had ever met face-to-face other than that first time.

"No. I hope I never have to look into those eyes again. Made me shiver."

Trapper glanced at Kerra, then said to Glenn, "You may find him changed since the death of his daughter. What do you know about that?"

"Only that she died," Glenn said. "Never knew the details, and I didn't send flowers."

Trapper pushed his chair back, pulled on his coat, and motioned for Kerra to do the same.

Glenn looked up at him with bleary-eyed apprehension. "What happens now?"

"You resign, Sheriff Addison."

"Will I face criminal charges? Will I go to prison?"

"I don't know. Won't be up to me."

"How much do you have on Wilcox?" he asked again. "*What* do you have? How incriminating is it?"

Trapper didn't answer him.

"The reason I'm asking is..." Glenn wet his lips.

"Maybe I could help you, John. We could work together. Partner."

"Until tonight I thought we were."

The brutal but truthful words seemed to crush him. His chest caved in. "Tomorrow, I'll put together everything I can remember about Wilcox, everything I know. If I help you make your case, and you deliver Wilcox hogtied to the authorities, maybe they'll let me plead out."

There were tears in his eyes. He was all but begging, and Trapper wouldn't be human if he weren't affected by his mentor's humility. "Whatever else happens, Glenn, you resign tomorrow. You're not entitled to wear a badge a single day more."

"What'll I give as a reason?"

"Health. You had a close call today. It woke you up to priorities."

Glenn nodded. "The other? My turning state's evidence?"

Trapper kept his expression neutral. "I've got to deliver Wilcox first. I do . . ." He shrugged. "What they do to you or to anyone else who signed his fucking pledge won't be up to me."

"I love your dad," Glenn said, his voice cracking. "I love you like a second son. I would never have let anybody harm either of you."

Glenn waited to see if Trapper was going to say or do anything in response to that. But anything he said would come out laced with either anger, sarcasm, or heartbreak. He didn't trust himself to speak at all.

"Well." Glenn pushed himself out of his chair. "I'm going to bed. Tomorrow's going to be an eventful day." He took the bottle of whiskey with him as he shuffled out of the room.

Hank set his elbow on the table and rested his forehead in his palm. "So much for my tabernacle."

Trapper took a step toward him and would have leveled the self-absorbed son of a bitch if Kerra hadn't stepped between them.

"It's time we left, Trapper," she said.

Trapper looked down at Hank with contempt. "Couldn't agree more." He guided her through the mudroom and outside.

Chapter 31

———◦◦◦———

Trapper had driven them in the maroon sedan, choosing it over Kerra's car, which still had to be hot-wired.

From the Addisons' back door, they walked to the car in silence, and neither of them spoke until several minutes later, when Trapper pulled into a gas station and Kerra remarked that it was closed.

"I'm not here to get gas." He switched on the flashlight app of one of his several cell phones, got out, and searched the underside of the car. When he got back in, Kerra asked if he'd found anything.

"No, and I didn't really expect to. When I mentioned the transmitter, Glenn's puzzled reaction was genuine. I don't believe he knew anything about it. Which means that somebody else put it there."

"Jenks?"

"My money's on him. But was he acting on his own authority or someone else's?" He pinched the bridge of his nose. "Jesus, Kerra, I don't know who or what to believe anymore. It's tough to hear, much less accept, that Glenn has been in cahoots with Wilcox for years. No wonder he insisted I stay far removed from his investigation. He was afraid I would discover his collusion."

"Is he framing Leslie Duncan?"

"I'm not sure about anything, but I'm inclined to say no to that, too. He owned up to doing much worse than planting evidence, so why not admit to that?"

He restarted the car and steered it back onto the highway. "I can't believe I'm even talking about Glenn Addison in criminal terms."

"You went there tonight knowing that at the very least he'd been disingenuous," she said. "You started out by saying it wasn't going to be fun."

"I know, but it really, *really* sucked. I have a lifetime of good memories with that man. Tainted now. Gone. Because Glenn made a bargain with the devil. That breaks my heart. But—"

"But?"

"It also pisses me off," he said in a lower, deadlier tone. "It's time Wilcox was stopped from destroying lives. Especially mine."

To punctuate his hatred of the man as well as his new resolve, he floorboarded the accelerator. "We probably won't be coming back to the motel, so we'll make a quick stop there and get our things."

"Where are we going?"

"Dallas."

"Now?"

"You can nap on the way. I'll drop you at your condo, then I'm going to pay a call on Mr. Thomas Wilcox."

"By the time you get there, it'll be . . ." She tried to estimate the time. "One o'clock in the morning."

"All the better. He won't be expecting me."

"His estate is a fortress, Trapper. There's a gate. He'll never let you in. He'll call the police."

"No, he won't. For the same reason I didn't call them when he ambushed us in my office. I was curious to hear what he had to say. Tonight he'll be more than curious, he'll be itching to know if I've started negotiations with the feds on his behalf."

"You said you wouldn't until you had his balls in one hand—"

"Tonight I do." He held up his fist.

"But you don't have his insurance policy in the other."

"No, but at least now I know what it is."

"The pledge he has everyone sign."

"Right. Just my knowing about it, plus the phone

recording you made of our conversation, which he's unaware of, plus Berkley Johnson's video, which he's unaware of, plus—"

"Everything Glenn told us."

"That may come in useful later, but I won't bring Glenn into it tonight. I won't need to. Everything else we have adds up to a lot of leverage. But the real kicker? I'm betting that a small-town sheriff is chicken feed compared to the other power players who've signed Wilcox's pledge. One or a cadre of them want him dead, and he knows they're not squeamish about committing a murder here or there because they've already killed his daughter. Hammering that home will be my thumbscrews. He'll start rethinking his terms and give me that goddamn list."

"It may work."

"I'll make it work."

"There's only one glitch in your plan."

"What?"

"You're not going to drop me anywhere."

"I wouldn't drop you *anywhere*, Kerra. You'll be safe inside your condo, especially after I threaten to emasculate the doorman if anybody except the people who live there are allowed in."

"I'm going with you to see Wilcox."

"Like hell you are. I don't want you near him again. I didn't want you near him in the first place, and that was before I knew that he knew that The Major carried you out of the Pegasus. You're a danger he can't afford."

"So are you!"

"Yeah." He jerked the car to a halt only a few feet from their motel room door. Reaching around to the small of his back, he drew his pistol, flourishing it. "But I've got a gun."

She produced a cell phone. "I've got the recording."

He snatched the phone from her hand. "Now I've got the phone."

"But not the code."

"It doesn't have one."

"It didn't when you gave it to me." She shot him a cheeky grin and pushed open the car door. "It won't take me but a sec to get my stuff."

"Dad?" Hank had been lying on the sofa but sat up when he heard Glenn's tread on the stairs.

"That fourth step has always squeaked," Glenn complained.

"What are you doing up? And in uniform?"

"Just got a call from Jenks. I've got to go meet him out at The Pit."

"The Pit? All the way out there? *Now?*"

"Jenks thinks he's found a missing person. What's left of him."

Hank got up, and, in stocking feet, followed his father into the kitchen, where Glenn went to the cupboard and retrieved his gun belt from the top shelf. "Surely somebody else can handle this," Hank said.

"Surely somebody else can. But I want to. Until tomorrow, I'm still sheriff." Glenn buckled on the belt, adjusted it to his hips, and took his hat from the hook near the door.

"Does Mom know you're going?"

"I don't ask her permission to perform my duties." He looked at Hank sourly. "Give me at least a five-minute head start before you go tattle."

"You shouldn't go, and you certainly shouldn't be driving. You drank a lot, you're on medication, and in addition to what Trapper did to you—"

Glenn turned to face him and tapped the center of Hank's chest for emphasis. "Listen to me, Hank. Trapper didn't do anything to me. I did it all to myself." He bobbed his head for emphasis, then put his hat on.

Hank watched through the screened door as his father climbed into his sheriff's unit and backed down the drive. He didn't turn on the light bar until he reached the road. Hank continued to watch until the flashing lights disappeared behind a rise.

As he returned to the living room, he took his cell phone from his pants pocket and placed a call. Jenks answered on the first ring.

Hank said, "Whatever you told him, he fell for. He's on his way."

"I'm here, ready and waiting."

"I can send somebody to help if you feel like you need it."

"I'm good."

"I don't want another debacle like Sunday."

"Neither do I," Jenks said. "I got this."

Hank clicked off and lay back down on the sofa. He needed to catch some shut-eye before his mother woke up, discovered that Glenn wasn't in bed with her, and came downstairs looking for him.

Chapter 32

Thomas reached for his cell phone on the bedside table before realizing that the chime was coming not from it but from the intercom panel. He threw off the covers and went over to the keypad on the wall. The blinking red light was labeled "Front Gate." Parting the window drapes, he saw a pair of headlights shining through the iron pickets. Swearing under his breath, he returned to the keypad and pressed the button. "Jenks?"

"Wrong. But that's an interesting guess."

Trapper.

"What do you want?"

"Well, for one thing I want to know why you would assume I was Deputy Sheriff Jenks, dropping by in the middle of the night, when this isn't even his county." He waited, then taunted, "Nothing? Not even a plausible lie? We can't be friends if you don't open up to me, Tom."

"I hope you have good news."

"Matter of fact, I do. I've got such a tight grip on your balls they're turning blue. Oh, you meant good news for *you*? No, sorry." Changing his tone to one of no nonsense, he said, "Open the gate."

Thomas pressed the button.

He pulled on the cashmere sweat suit he'd been lounging in before going to bed, slid his feet into leather slippers, and left his bedroom. He'd reached the top of the staircase before he thought to go back. He tiptoed to the closed door of Greta's room and put his ear to it. He didn't hear a sound, and no light shone beneath the door.

Stepping quickly but as quietly as possible, he retraced his steps, descended the stairs, disengaged the security alarm, and pulled open the front door just as Trapper was reaching for the bell.

"Please don't. My wife's asleep."

Trapper said, "I was beginning to wonder if you'd rolled back over."

Kerra Bailey was with him. Both looked untidy and tired, but Thomas was discomfited by the way Kerra was staring at him, with perplexed concentration, as though trying to discern what was behind his eyes.

"Did you know when I interviewed you last year that I was the girl in the Pegasus Hotel picture?"

Her question caught him off guard. Unprepared to answer just yet, he opened the door wider. "Come in." The pair stepped into the foyer. Thomas reset the alarm system, then motioned them toward his study.

"I'm surprised you don't have guards," Trapper remarked. "Or do you, and they're hiding in the bushes? Snipers on the roof? Dobermans on sentry?"

Thomas steeled himself against Trapper's wisecracking. He wasn't going to let it get to him tonight. "After Tiffany's murder, although there hadn't been a breach of our property, we did employ security guards for a time. But rather than giving Greta peace of mind, their 'lurking,' as she called it, only made her more nervous."

"Security cameras?" Trapper asked.

"No."

"Right. You wouldn't. They could catch a corrupt cop paying you a call at an ungodly hour."

As they entered the study, Kerra went directly to the fireplace and looked up at the portrait above it. "Your daughter was beautiful."

"Inside and out." Thomas gestured to the bar in the corner. "Can I get you something to drink?" They declined. "You don't mind if I do?"

"It's your liquor," Trapper replied.

Thomas poured himself a neat scotch from the Baccarat decanter. When he turned back around, Trapper was twirling the madam's pearl-handled pistol around his index finger like a gunslinger.

"Look what I found in your desk drawer, Tom. I'll hold on to it for the time being. Not that there's any mistrust between us."

Thomas indicated an armchair to Kerra. She sat. He calmly walked over to the leather love seat and sat down. Trapper remained with his rear end propped against the edge of Thomas's desk. He had put the pistol down but within his reach.

Thomas took a sip of single-malt. "Why would I shoot you when I've admitted to needing you?"

"About that." Trapper crossed his arms and his ankles. "That's why I'm here. Time to renegotiate, Tom. The power has shifted."

"How can that be, when you were robbed of that flash drive?"

"I was robbed of *a* flash drive. The one taken out of the wall had porn on it."

Well, that explained why Jenks hadn't mentioned finding the buried treasure. The deputy had been made a fool of. More galling, Thomas had fallen for Trapper's bluff as well. "Your inflection indicates that there's another flash drive."

"Sure is," Trapper said. "And its contents are even juicier than the nasty movies."

"What's on it?"

"For starters, a video of Berkley Johnson, telling

all. The time burn-in is dated two days before he was killed."

"If I'm not mistaken, the authorities dismissed his allegations as sour grapes."

"But his soul-searing video, plus this audio recording..." Trapper gave Kerra a silent signal. She took a cell phone from her handbag and went through the appropriate steps to engage it. Thomas's voice came through the speaker.

Thomas listened to half a minute of the recording and then quietly asked Kerra to turn it off. "You would never use that," he said. "It would violate your integrity as a journalist. You had agreed that we were off the record."

"I don't intend to publish or broadcast it," she said coolly. "Besides, it was a unique circumstance. I was in fear of my life."

"Are you recording this conversation?"

"No."

"I'm to believe that?"

"Same as we're to believe that you didn't have Jenks put a tracking device on Kerra's car," Trapper said.

Wilcox turned back to him. "I didn't."

"See? Some things we just gotta take each other's word for. Now answer Kerra's question."

"About knowing if she was the girl in the picture?" He looked her straight in the eye. "Of course I knew.

Within a few weeks of the bombing, I knew your name and that you'd been shuttled off to Virginia by an aunt and uncle."

Her lips parted.

"How can you be surprised?" he asked. "I had to know everything about every single survivor, where they were inside the building when the bombs were detonated, who or what they might have seen."

"Even a child of five years old?"

"I don't take chances. Since your identity had been so scrupulously protected, it took some ingenuity and money, but a wily individual on my payroll, the likes of Mr. Trapper here, identified and located you.

"I kept track. Years passed. You grew up, a normal little girl in every respect. Neither you nor your relatives ever referenced the bombing or drew the connection between it and yourself, not even as you pursued your profession when that level of notoriety would have been a boon to it. I believed I had nothing to fear from you. Until you moved to Dallas."

"The wily likes of me would have sat up and taken notice," Trapper said.

"Shortly after your arrival," Thomas said, still speaking to Kerra, "you began requesting to do an interview with me."

"Panicksville."

Again Thomas ignored Trapper. "I agreed to the

interview to test you, Kerra, to see if, while profiling me, you had somehow linked me to the Pegasus."

Trapper said, "You told us you did the interview to make those who killed your daughter nervous."

"That's true, in part. Definitely. But I had to know if Kerra posed a threat." Going back to her, he said, "You didn't touch on anything remotely connected to the bombing or the complex I developed on the hotel's former spot. Again, I relaxed."

"Then you learned that I was going to interview The Major," she said.

He took a sip of scotch. "That was one coincidence too many."

"You decided he and I had to be killed."

"Initially." He could tell the admission stunned them, Kerra in particular. He rolled the highball glass back and forth between his palms. "However, I was advised to reconsider the fallout that a double murder would generate, the subsequent investigation, etcetera. I agreed that perhaps I had overreacted."

"You called off our execution."

"I postponed it," he said with bald honesty. "I would wait to see what repercussions, if any, came from the interview and then make a decision. I watched the broadcast, but nothing about it unnerved me." He paused before adding, "Obviously someone was of a differing opinion."

Trapper raised his index finger. "I've just figured out why the attack occurred after, not before, the interview. Unlike you, these someones didn't know Kerra's significance until she announced it Sunday night."

"When she made the public disclosure—"

"The shit hit the fan."

"They acted with remarkable speed."

"Jenks and who else?"

Thomas didn't say anything to that.

"Come on, Tom. Cough him up, and I'll take it from there. The G-men might listen more attentively if I deliver a crooked deputy sheriff to them."

Thomas tipped his head toward the cell phone in Kerra's hand and said to Trapper, "That audio recording is of little consequence. You did most of the talking. I responded with nothing incriminating or even affirming, except to say that you told a captivating *story*."

"You said you would direct me. In my summation, tell me where I went wrong."

Thomas didn't say anything.

Trapper said softly, "You've got to give me more, Tom, or I am *not*—and you can record this your ownself, spray paint it on the field of the Cotton Bowl, skywrite it over downtown, carve it into your skin, whatever—I am *not* going to the feds and sticking my neck out for you.

"If you continue to hold out, I've a good mind to call your buddy Jenks and tell him you've ratted him out. That'll guarantee that I won't have to waste another minute of my life obsessing over you because you will be O. V. E. R. Talk to me, *now*, or all bets are off."

Thomas assessed his situation and, although it rankled, acknowledged that Trapper did hold the advantage. Thomas had only one chance to see justice done for Tiffany. The tradeoff was admitting to Trapper his own wrongdoing.

He swirled the liquid in his glass as he carefully chose his words. "Where you went wrong was overthinking it. You envisioned a conclave of like-minded men, a *clan*. You imagined it being founded on a doctrine, because you couldn't conceive of it of being so incredibly simple. There is no higher cause. Never was. No philosophy or creed or anything like what you surmised. Nothing idealistic or anarchist or radically inspired."

"Then how did you get your converts?"

"When something needed doing, I looked for a candidate or candidates to do it, singled them out, discovered what their heart's desire was—"

"And provided it."

Thomas didn't admit it out loud but gave a slight nod. "A public office, a piece of real estate, a seat on the board of a lending company, a national championship. The object of desire could be something as highflown as that, or as plebeian as a married woman's sudden availability."

Trapper said, "She would become widowed."

"Accidents occur," he said, "and the results are often fatal."

"You're contemptible," Kerra whispered.

Thomas smiled blandly. "Not in the opinion of the frustrated suitor who was so grateful, he threw a playoff hockey game."

She averted her gaze as though unable to stand looking at him.

Trapper was wearing a thoughtful scowl. "A man recently diagnosed with terminal stomach cancer..."

Picking up on the lead-in, Thomas said, "Who had inadequate health and life insurance, would welcome a lifetime income for his wife and children."

"All he had to do was carry a time bomb into a hotel and confess to mass murder."

Thomas raised his hands up shoulder high but, again, didn't admit anything aloud.

"Still," Trapper said, "that would have taken some convincing. It's not like you promised him paradise and an inexhaustible supply of virgins."

Trapper had hit on an essential element of Thomas's success. "Often the favor was done *prior to* the recipient's knowledge of it."

"Ah-ha! Of course. So when you tell him to do

something, he's already obligated. How can he refuse? The noose is already around his neck. Either he signs your pledge or you open the trap door."

Thomas blinked.

Trapper saw his surprised reaction and smiled. "Yeah, we know about your pledge. That's your insurance policy, right? A list of everybody you've corrupted. How many are we talking, Tom?"

"It would keep the FBI busy for years."

"A lot of cold cases would go hot again. Including the Pegasus."

"And my daughter's murder. That's why I came to you. We want the same individual. I'll give him to you, but I want your word that he'll be punished to the fullest extent of the law, along with whoever he got to push the plunger on that syringe."

Trapper placed his hands on his knees and leaned forward. "I understand that. But you need to understand this. You can hand-deliver that individual, hell, you can waltz Jack the Ripper in there. Uncle Sam's boys aren't going to let you walk for the Pegasus. Maybe for a Berkley Johnson, or the two who burned to death in the factory fire. But not for one hundred ninety-seven souls."

"I'm betting otherwise. You don't know the caliber of the names on my list. Federal prosecutors will be falling all over themselves, thanking me for turning them over."

"Like who? Give me a hint."

"I'll hand over the list after you've struck my deal."

"No list, no deal."

"Then we're in limbo."

"I've been in limbo," Trapper said. "And you know what? It ain't that bad being known as a hero's son who couldn't hack it. The lower people's expectations are of me, the fewer responsibilities I have. We stay in limbo?" He shrugged. "I'm used to it. I can live with it.

"The question is, can you? Do you want to see the people who murdered your daughter brought to justice, or not? They seriously wounded The Major, but he's alive. Tiffany's dead. They wanted your attention so they pumped enough heroin into her vein to bring down a bull elephant. They're walking around free. Can you continue living with that?"

"I don't believe you can," Kerra said. "Give Trapper what he needs, and he'll see to it that her murderers are punished."

Thomas wavered.

"Where do you keep the list?" Trapper asked. "Here?"

"No. Everyone who signs realizes it's completely inaccessible. Otherwise someone would have killed me a long time ago, then excavated this house searching for it."

"How do they know it's inaccessible?" Before

Thomas had time to give Trapper the answer, light dawned in his eyes. "You don't bring it to them, you take them to it. Bowels of a bank vault? Or something more *Raiders of the Lost Ark*? A cave, a bunker reachable only through a maze of booby-trapped tunnels?"

"You have a vivid imagination."

"Right. I do. But here's the point. If some poor bastard signs your pledge, then changes his mind, he's doubly screwed. The document is inaccessible, and he can't trust anybody to tell because he doesn't know who else has signed. You've covered up the names of his predecessors."

Thomas wondered how Trapper knew all that but didn't ask. He suspected Glenn Addison.

"Nifty loophole there, Tom."

"It's kept me alive."

"So far. But your future isn't looking too bright. You've got a revolt on your hands. Killing your daughter didn't bring you around, so they've gotten bolder. They took matters into their own hands Sunday night. If they continue to override your decisions, and ineptly, eventually they're going to screw up real bad, get caught, and guess who they're going to finger as their mastermind? 'Thomas Wilcox? Isn't that the guy John Trapper keeps harping about?'" Trapper gave another shrug.

"Time is running out for you to act, Tom. Either

you're going to get double-crossed and arrested or double-crossed and killed. In the event of your untimely demise, if I don't have that list, your daughter's murderers go free. Forever."

Every word out of Trapper's mouth had been what Thomas had himself concluded. "I've prepared for that contingency."

"Smart move. What's the contingency?"

"Some of the signatures on the original document are unintelligible. In the event that I'm not around to decipher them, I typed all the names in alphabetical order. It required several sheets of paper."

"Very convenient. Thanks. I appreciate that. Where're these sheets?"

Thomas gestured toward the fireplace and the heap of cold ashes beneath the grate. "But I took a cell phone photograph of each page before burning it. I realize those pictures won't qualify as evidence, but they should be adequately persuasive until the original can be accessed."

"Where's the cell phone with the pictures?"

"In a safe place."

"A storm cellar is a safe place. The far side of the moon is a safe place. Where is it?" Trapper looked around the study, his eyes lighting on the painting. He strode toward it.

"No!"

But the admonishment came too late. Trapper had

discovered the concealed hinge running vertically down the side of the ornate frame. He swung it open, exposing a wall safe with a keypad. He turned back to Thomas, eyebrow cocked.

"No," Thomas said adamantly. "I will not open it tonight. Tomorrow—"

Trapper made a sound like a buzzer.

"You convene a meeting with federal agents. Senior agents," Thomas stressed. "I'll hand the phone over to them."

"The second you clear the door."

"After I'm guaranteed immunity."

"It'll never fly, Tom. They may hear me out tonight, say, 'Thanks for the tip, Trapper, now get lost,' and then drive over here and arrest you. If you don't deliver that list beforehand, you don't have a prayer of making any kind of deal."

Thomas thought it over and gave a reluctant nod. "All right. The photos on the cell phone should be sufficient to start a dialogue, but it's still only a long list of typewritten names. I'll hold the original with signatures in abeyance until I get my guarantee."

"Why not, as a sign of good faith—and the feds really get off on good faith—give me the phone now and let me use it to start the dialogue?"

"Because, as you just said, they may laugh at you yet. Given your reputation as a hot-headed crackpot, who could blame them?" It did Thomas's heart good to see how the words affected Trapper. He wasn't as cocksure as he pretended.

"Also," Thomas said, "even if you do manage to get me an audience, the outcome of that meeting is uncertain." He threw a glance up toward the second story. "Greta knows nothing of this. She's fragile. I need time to prepare her for what could be difficult days ahead."

Trapper thought on that, looked back at the safe, then returned the painting to its original position. He contemplated the portrait, then came around to Thomas. "Okay, here's how it's gonna be. I'll be on the phone for the rest of the night, hoping to persuade somebody that I'm not drunk dialing and that this is for real. If I can convince somebody to hear us out, I'll call you and tell you when and where to show up with the original signature list, and the cell phone with pictures of the typed names, and a good lawyer. Maybe you should bring a battery of good lawyers."

"Not the original list."

"The original," Trapper repeated in a tone that left no room for further compromise. "If you fail on any of these points, God help you. Because then your wad is shot. If I don't kill you myself, Jenks probably will. The feds may put you in protective custody, but you'll have lost any wiggle room for negotiation because you reneged on the preliminary bargaining points. Beyond all that, your secret life will be exposed. Right, Kerra?"

"I and a cameraman will set up outside your gate," she said. "I'll do the first of many reports on how you're refusing to address allegations that you planned the Pegasus Hotel bombing. After my recent interview with the man who saved me from dying in the blast, this will incite media coverage around the world."

"You wouldn't break a story like that without corroboration," Thomas said. "And Trapper is hardly a reliable source."

"The story would be the allegations themselves, not whether or not they're true," Kerra said. "In our society, once suspicion is cast, one is as good as guilty. You know I'm right."

Trapper said, "And pledge or no pledge, at the first hint of trouble, one or more of your signers may turn on you to save themselves prison time, disgrace, God knows what else." Trapper squared off with him. "Face it, Tom, you're kaput. You're out of play. Do we have a deal?"

Thomas hesitated, then gave a curt nod.

"Say it."

"We have a deal."

Trapper took a cell phone from his coat pocket. "What number should I call to tell you where to be and when to be there?" He tapped in the number

Thomas recited. "I'll be in touch." He returned the phone to his pocket, then went around the desk and replaced the pistol in the drawer.

"What if none of your former colleagues listens to you?" Thomas asked.

"Then you're screwed." Trapper shut the drawer soundly. "Which you deserve to be for all the people you've caused to die and all the lives you've made a living hell. Ready, Kerra?"

She directed Thomas a glower of pure loathing as she walked past him and out of the study. Trapper followed her, and Thomas fell into line. He disengaged the alarm and opened the front door for them.

No one said good night.

Kerra preceded Trapper out. But before reaching the front steps, he pivoted suddenly and came back. He reached across the threshold, grabbed Thomas by his zippered top, hauled him out onto the porch, and slammed him back against the brick exterior wall.

Shoving his face close to Thomas's, he said softly but with lethal intent, "The Pegasus bombing has governed my life, and I'm sick of it. Tomorrow, I'm putting my future on the line. If you fuck me over, I'll cut out your heart and eat it."

Trapper's electric blue eyes speared into his, then as quickly as Trapper had seized him, he let him go. Thomas slumped against the wall and remained there until they'd driven through the gate and it had closed behind them.

He pushed himself away from the wall, rearranged his clothing, and chuckled. "Ah, Trapper. You should have had a scotch."

He bolted the door and reset the security alarm before heading for the study to pour himself another. But as he entered the room, he stopped short. "Greta. You startled me. What are you doing up?"

She was standing beneath Tiffany's portrait, one hand braced on the brass andiron for support. "Is it true?"

"You should be in bed. You look faint."

"Is it true? My baby was killed because of *you*?"

"Greta, listen to me. I don't know what you overheard, but—"

"My beautiful baby." She looked up at the portrait, tears streaming from her eyes. "My baby."

His voice cracking, he said, "She was my baby, too."

Greta glared at him through tears of wrathful contempt. "You heartless bastard."

Chapter 33

———⊙———

As Trapper entered the kitchen of Kerra's condo, she turned away from the stove. "Did you find the bathroom?"

"Yeah. What's this?"

"Food." She spooned scrambled eggs from a skillet onto two plates. "Doesn't surprise me that you don't recognize it. When's the last time we had any?" She added slices of bacon and buttered toast to the plates and handed one to him. "Sit."

The aroma of hot food had caused his stomach to growl, which caused her to laugh. He carried his plate to the tiny table. She joined him and they began eating.

"Who will you call first?" she asked.

"In addition to Marianne, there were two or three who at least listened and didn't dismiss my notion out of hand. I'll start with them. Maybe one of them can recommend someone for me to talk to, either in our bureau or with the FBI.

"But, contrary to what I told Wilcox, I'll wait till morning. I remember calling former colleagues when I was falling-down drunk, especially soon after I got fired. I don't want them thinking this is just another of those times."

When they finished the meal, Trapper carried his empty plate to the sink and rinsed it under the faucet. "That was great."

Kerra moved up beside him. "I don't bake cakes, but I know how to scramble an egg."

"I can do without cake." He dried his hands and took hers. "I was against you going with me to confront Wilcox. But I'm glad I lost the argument. Thanks for being there."

He wanted to thank her for having faith in him, believing him, standing up for him and with him. But he couldn't think of a way to express all that without sounding like a sap, so he didn't say anything else.

Kerra smiled as though she knew all the things he'd left unsaid. "You're welcome." Still hand in hand, she towed him out of the kitchen and through the living room. One of its walls was solid glass, affording a spectacular view of the Dallas skyline.

They continued down the hallway, past the small bathroom he'd used when they arrived and into the master bedroom that was furnished as tastefully as the rest of the apartment.

"This place is amazing," he remarked.

"I'm glad you approve."

"But it shows how much you outclass me."

"Don't say that."

"It's true." He took her by the shoulders. "A classy guy would thank you for the eggs, give you a peck on the cheek, and leave." He lowered his head and nuzzled his way through her hair to the soft spot behind her ear. "Or at least lay you down on the bed first."

"First? Before what?"

He backed her into the wall. "Before taking your top off."

"The window shades are up."

"See? I've got no class. I don't care if somebody's watching."

Assuming he was joking, she laughed.

He pulled her top over her head, then threaded his fingers up through her hair and held her head between his hands as he plundered the hottest, sweetest, sexiest mouth he was ever going to miss.

Because, she didn't know it, but if things didn't work out for him tomorrow, he wasn't going to drag her down into the muck of failure with him. He wouldn't let her jeopardize her career by doing a story on Wilcox that nobody except him would or could corroborate. He'd tell her "so long" and mean it.

But for right now, he was with her, and she was kissing him back for all she was worth, and, by God, he'd earned at least this.

While holding her mouth with his, he popped the snaps on his shirt and pulled it off, then hooked his thumbs beneath the shoulder straps of her bra and pulled them down her arms until the cups fell away. He scooped a breast in each hand but only held them as he broke the kiss and looked into her eyes.

In a low voice, he said, "They've had a lot of rough play already tonight."

"Hours ago," she whispered. "It's okay."

"Thank God," he moaned and lowered his head.

She undid his fly, took him in hand, and began milking him from root to tip.

"Wait." He removed her hand, then unfastened her jeans and knelt to pull them down her legs. She steadied herself with one hand on his shoulder as she stepped out of them. He gently gnawed her through the lacy triangle of her panties, breathed her in, blew against her. She sighed his name.

He slid the underpants down and off, then stood and replaced her hand around his cock and guided it between her thighs. He kept his hand covering hers as he whispered in her ear.

She angled her head back and looked at him with surprise. "Use you to...?"

"One of my many fantasies," he said.

He withdrew his hand and let her take over. He was afraid she would demur, but she didn't. He watched what she did to herself with him, and in turn watched her face: the bite she gave her plush lower lip; the frown of intense feeling as the lips of her sex closed around his smooth tip.

The slippery friction she created against her sweet spot was almost his undoing, but he concentrated on her, on the escalation of her breathing, on the increasing tension in her neck and chest, the tightening of her clasp around him, the beading of her nipples. He brushed one with his tongue, and his timing was perfect to catch her gasp of ultimate pleasure with his mouth.

He maintained the kiss as his arms closed around her. He held her skin to skin until her orgasm subsided and continued to hold her until she slowly spiraled down, bumped her head back against the wall and opened her eyes.

She gave him a drowsy smile. "What about you?"

"We're getting to that."

He lifted her against him and carried her to the bed. As she lay down, he stripped off the rest of his clothes. He did a push-up above her and settled between her thighs. She tilted her hips up to accommodate him, and he delved into her in one long glide. She was incredibly wet, but still glove-tight. He luxuriated simply in being grafted to her and feeling her subtle contractions that became ever stronger and soon had his breath hitching.

He groaned, "You're killing me doing that."

"I'm trying my best."

"It's working."

He took her hands and stretched her arms above her head. Fitting her palms into his, he linked their fingers and began to stroke her inside. As before, he wanted her to remember this, because it would be engraved on his memory: the feel of her around him, the way she hugged his hips with her thighs, the sexy undulation of her belly against his, the sight of his chest hair dusting the hard tips of her breasts.

The kiss.

He kissed her, and, of all the other mind-blowing sensations, it was that of her mouth so greedily taking his tongue that caused his control to burst. When it did, she arched up and ground against his straining pelvis and brought on another soul-rending orgasm.

Later, he didn't remember separating from her. He thought that both of them might already have been in the twilight of sleep before they moved, but when he woke up a short time later, he and Kerra were spooned together, his sex dormant now, but intimately tucked into the furrow of hers, her heart beating against his palm. He removed his hand from her only long enough to pull the covers over them, then returned it to cover her breast. Sleepily she murmured his name and snuggled closer.

For the first time in years, Trapper fell asleep without anger, at peace.

The Major was in conversation with the doctor who'd been overseeing his care when Hank poked his head around the door. "I can come back later."

"No need, reverend," the doctor said. "We're finished."

The doctor left. Hank came in. His smile was anemic, his manner subdued, his expression telegraphing bad news. "I haven't seen you the whole while you've been here. You're looking remarkably well for—"

The Major interrupted him. "Thank you for coming, Hank, but you can skip the pastor part. What's the matter?"

"Nobody can locate Dad."

The Major tried but failed to wrap his mind around what that signified. "Can you elaborate?"

"I was the last person to see him, and that was after midnight."

"I haven't heard from him since early yesterday."

"Yesterday," Hank said, pressing his temples between his middle finger and thumb, "turned out to be a dreadful day."

"I know he had an anxiety attack," The Major said.

"That was the diagnosis, which was a relief, but he was depressed after." Hank described how Glenn had begun to completely unravel soon after getting released to go home. "Mom practically had to fork food into him to get him to eat. He was well into killing a bottle of Jack when Trapper showed up. Late. Uninvited. Kerra Bailey was with him. And before Trapper got done with Dad, he—"

"Got done with him?"

Hank expelled a sigh. "Trapper's latest wild hair is that this guy from Dallas was behind the Pegasus Hotel bombing, that the men who did the actual deed were pawns. Supposedly, he—Wilcox is his name—has a stranglehold on Dad and involved him, to some extent, in the attack on you."

"Glenn?"

"At first I thought this had to be just another of Trapper's pranks. But no, he was dead serious. And what I really couldn't believe is that Dad confessed to . . ." He gave a humorless laugh and shook his head. "In the light of day, it sounds crazy, or like I dreamed it."

"Tell me."

"Dad confessed to signing some kind of pledge

with this guy to spy on you, *you*, in exchange for winning reelection."

"The past election?"

"No. Back in the late nineties."

The Major registered shock.

"It gets even more bizarre," Hank said. "This week, Wilcox supposedly ordered Dad to kill you."

The Major was too shocked to speak.

Hank shook his head. "I told you it sounded crazy."

"Glenn sent those men to my house?"

"No! He thought he'd talked this Wilcox out of it. He swore to Kerra that he had nothing to do with it." He looked at The Major with helplessness. "The whole thing is preposterous, right?"

The Major lost focus and thoughtfully stared into near space.

"Major?" Hank spoke his name with irritation to snap him back. "Surely you don't believe any of this."

"I don't believe Glenn would do anything to hurt me, no. But Trapper has long contended that Thomas Wilcox was behind the bombing. How did last night's conversation end?"

"Trapper issued Dad an ultimatum to retire from office. Today. Dad went upstairs. Trapper and Kerra left. A couple hours later, Dad came downstairs, in uniform, told me Jenks had called him out to investigate a missing persons case."

"You were there?"

Hank told him why he'd planned to stay over. "I tried to talk him out of leaving the house in his condition, but he went anyway."

"What happened when he met Jenks?"

"That's just it," Hank exclaimed. "Jenks says he didn't call Dad last night about a missing persons case or anything else. He figured Dad was knocked out on meds, and he should have been." He raked his fingers through his hair. "I waited up for him for a while, then fell asleep on the sofa. Mom came down early, woke me up, asked where he was.

"I've been calling his cell, but it goes straight to voice mail. After I checked with Jenks and he told me he'd made no such call, he canvassed the whole sheriff's department. Nobody's seen Dad this morning. I thought maybe he'd come to see you and had failed to notify dispatch."

"Who's looking for him?"

"Everybody who wears a badge. DPS troopers. The whole SO. All the personnel are worried about him, especially after his collapse yesterday. But it's been coming on ever since Sunday night. Well, actually even before, ever since he was notified of your interview with Kerra." He paused, then added bitterly, "News also delivered by Trapper."

The Major's thoughts were pinging from one point to another like a pinball. "Maybe Glenn left to find John and try to reason with him."

"That's a possibility, I guess," Hank said. "Do you know where Trapper is?"

"I haven't seen or heard from him since he visited me yesterday afternoon."

"He's not at the motel. I already checked."

"What did you plan to do if you found him? Ask him if he knows where Glenn is? Or slug him again?"

"I'm not proud of that," Hank mumbled, "but I'd like to hit him again. He brought Dad down low last night." He fiddled with a loose cuticle on the side of his thumb. "Dad prefers Trapper to me. No, don't bother to contradict it. You know it as well as I do. Whether or not Dad is guilty of corruption, what hurt him most was Trapper being the one to accuse him of it. Did Trapper share his speculation with you?"

"About Glenn? No." Although something had been weighing on his mind, because during their visit yesterday John had brought up Glenn's name several times.

"What about Wilcox?" Hank asked.

"For several years, he's been of interest to John."

"It has to be all conjecture, though, or else Wilcox would be in prison."

"John's official investigation ended when he left the ATF."

"But unofficially?"

"He remains convinced of some collusion."

"Jesus," Hank whispered. "And I mean that as a prayer."

He sat down on the corner of the bed, not knowing that it was the same spot in which Glenn had sat twenty-four hours earlier, pretending never to have heard of Thomas Wilcox. It pained The Major to think of his lifelong friend lying to him, even by omission.

"I'm frightened," Hank was saying. "If Dad's honor is brought into question at this stage of his career, he might take an easier way out than retirement."

"Suicide?" The Major asked with horror. "Glenn wouldn't do that to himself, to you, or to Linda."

"But—"

"I've known him longer than you have, Hank. He wouldn't." Suddenly The Major was disgusted with Hank. "You whine over Glenn liking Trapper better? Why wouldn't he? If Trapper was frightened for Glenn, as you claim to be, he wouldn't be sitting here wringing his hands, he'd be out beating the bushes for him. What good are you doing Glenn in here?" The Major poked his index finger toward him. "Get out there and find him."

———◆———

Trapper had been sequestered in the spare bedroom Kerra used as a home office for the past hour while

she wandered the other rooms of the apartment, in-
venting ways to keep herself busy and her mind off
what was happening behind the closed door. Now,
as she heard Trapper emerge, she rushed to intercept
him in the hallway and looked at him expectantly.

He gave her a crooked grin. "It was easier than I
anticipated."

A gust of breath escaped her. "Trapper!" She nearly
bowled him over as she threw her arms around him.

He hugged her back. "Having Thomas Wilcox
made all the difference. I'm not just an agent who
went off the rails. That Wilcox wants to bargain,
and that he's bringing in lawyers, signals them that
he's guilty of *something*. And, unbeknownst to me,
someone who read my reports three years ago didn't
dismiss them altogether. The FBI has had a man
working the inside, so—"

Kerra's cell phone jangled, cutting him off. "I'll get
it later," she said. "Keep talking."

"Too much to tell right now, but bottom line, the
meeting is set for two o'clock this afternoon in the
federal building. That should give Wilcox time to
round up his legal team and retrieve his everlovin'
list. If he knows what's good for him, he'll show, because they're ready to listen."

"Do you have your flash drive?"

He tapped his jeans pocket. "Can I borrow your
shower? And a razor? And I probably should go out

and buy a pair of slacks and a dress shirt. I want to look respectable."

Her phone rang again.

"You grab that," he said. "I'll hit the shower."

"Razors are in the second drawer, right-hand side." She beamed another smile at him. "I'm so glad for you."

"Me too. The only thing they laughed at was when I told them Wilcox wanted full immunity. But I won't break that to him till he gets there."

He gave her a quick kiss and headed down the hall-way. Her lips were tingling from the kiss when she answered the phone.

Gracie blared into her ear. "Well, it's about time!"

"Hi, Gracie. I'm sorry I've been out of touch. The past couple days have been—"

"Never mind the apology. We have a hot-hot-hot story cooking."

"I'm on sick leave."

"Not anymore. It's all hands on deck."

"But—"

"Look, Kerra, I went to the mat for you when you bailed on the network interview. I took up for you because you were so shaky and feeble. Blah, blah. But I won't cover for you on this. Besides, you wouldn't want me to. I'm going to send a news van to pick you up outside your building in ten. Look sharp."

Kerra wasn't ready to plunge back in, but Trapper

was going to be busy, and if things went well for him today, he was going to be a lot busier for months to come. She couldn't be of any more help to him today, and, after all, she had a job to protect. Or salvage.

"All right. In ten. What's the hot-hot-hot story?"

A few minutes later, she went into the master bathroom. Trapper saw her through the shower stall door and leered. "You're just in time to wash my back. Or my front."

But he must have read her expression because the teasing glint in his eyes winked out. He shut off the taps and pushed open the glass door. "What?"

"Thomas Wilcox is dead."

Chapter 34

It appears to have been a murder-suicide," Kerra said. "His wife shot him, then herself."

Trapper reached for a towel and began drying off. "Where'd you hear it?"

"Gracie just called."

"Meaning the media is already on it."

"I've been commandeered to cover the story. Gracie's sending a news van to pick me up."

"I guess those federal officers I talked to half an hour ago will wonder how I plan to produce a dead man." He tossed aside the towel and eased around Kerra to get into the bedroom, where he began collecting his clothes.

"What are you going to do?"

"Get dressed."

"No, I mean about—"

"When's the van coming for you?"

She made a dismissive gesture. "In a few minutes."

"Bathroom's free. You'd better hurry. I'll be out of here in a jif."

"Where are you going?"

"Back to life as I knew it before you knocked on my office door."

"You can't just drop this, Trapper."

He clipped on his holster and tossed a set of keys toward her, which she made no effort to catch. They landed on the floor in front of her. "The keys to the maroon sedan. I'm sure Carson won't mind you keeping it until you can get your car back from Lodal."

"What will you do?"

"Call Uber."

"About *Wilcox*."

"What's to be done about him? I'm not an undertaker, and I doubt he'd have wanted me as a pall bearer."

"Keep your meeting, Trapper. Lay out your case. I can vouch—"

"No."

"You can tell them about the cell phone in the safe behind the painting."

"Pictures of a list of names. It could be Wilcox's Christmas card list."

"Sheriff Addison's name will be on there."

"Solid citizen Wilcox didn't neglect to thank regional officials."

"But Glenn Addison will—"

"Talk? Go on record with what he told us last night?" He negated that with a shake of his head. "He may surrender his badge and retire. But he'll cite declining health or wanting more leisure time. He won't undo forty years of law enforcement by admitting to... what? What malfeasance? Keeping a close eye on an American hero? He'll be admired, not indicted."

"Why are you being so obtuse?"

"Not obtuse, Kerra. Realistic."

"Well, here's a piece of reality for you. Somebody tried to kill me and The Major last Sunday."

"Whoever they are, they'll either be captured or not, but they'll never be connected to Wilcox."

"But the sheriff knew about the threat to us and did nothing."

"His word against mine on that. And, don't forget, I'm the spinner of tall tales and conspiracy theories."

"I was there, too. With everything I've heard this week, I can break this story wide open."

"Without corroboration?"

"You would corroborate it."

"Hell I would. I don't talk to the media."

"Fine. I don't need you. Hank Addison was witness to his father's confessions."

"Hank would love nothing better than to see me brought to heel and humiliated. He'll either develop amnesia or say that I bullied Glenn into making false confessions while he was drunk and stoned on antidepressants. Who knows? Maybe I did, and his confessions *were* false."

"You're going to let Leslie Duncan be convicted for a crime he didn't commit?"

"Maybe he did commit it. Maybe all my intuitions are just *wrong*. Anyway, he's a lowlife and not my problem."

After checking to see that he had all his belongings, he left the bedroom. Kerra caught up with him in the living room as he was pulling on his coat. She reached out for his arm, managed to catch only his sleeve but hung on tight.

"I know you, Trapper," she said. "You won't be able to let it go."

"Watch me."

"The people trying to overtake Wilcox—"

"Maybe there were none."

"Somebody killed his daughter."

"Or did she shoot up and die of an accidental overdose? Maybe Wilcox came to my office to see if he could find what I had on him, and everything he told us was pure fabrication for his own amusement."

"You don't believe that. I don't believe that. I think everything he told us was the truth."

"Prove it."

Her lips parted, but there were no words to speak.

"I couldn't have said it better myself." Trapper pulled his sleeve from her grip and opened the door.

"What am I supposed to do with this information?" she asked. "Forget I ever heard it?"

"Do whatever you want. I don't recommend that you run with it. If you reported it without any corroboration, you could lose all credibility, and then where would you be? Fucked. Like me." He looked her over. "Although that part of this misadventure wasn't too bad."

He went out and closed the door behind him.

Rather than wait for the elevator, he took the fire stairs. Midway down, on the landing of the eleventh floor, he fell back against the wall, squeezed his eyes closed, and tried to block out Kerra's wounded expression over his parting words.

The tactic didn't work.

He looked up through the switchbacks of the stairwell and considered racing back to apologize, pull her close, hold her. But a sweet embrace and fond farewell weren't going to change the situation. He had vowed to himself that if things didn't go well today, he wasn't going to drag her down with him. A clean break was best.

Besides, if he went back to say a proper goodbye, he didn't trust himself to walk out a second time.

Between Kerra's condo and Trapper's office building, not a word passed between him and the driver of the hired car.

After being dropped at the address, in order to get to the entrance, he had to step over the parking meter, which still lay flat against the sidewalk. It crossed his mind to wonder about the status of his car, but he couldn't work up any real interest or concern over it.

He entered the building, and immediately the door to the law office was jerked open. Carson took one look at him. "I guess you've heard."

"Who told you?"

"Kerra was on TV doing a standup outside Wilcox's gate."

"That didn't take long," Trapper muttered. Then to Carson, "I ought to strangle you with that brassiere you bought her."

"I didn't buy it for her, I bought it for you. Like it?"

Trapper gave him a scornful look and tried to go around him so he could get to the elevator, but Carson sidestepped and blocked him. "They cleaned up your office."

"Who?"

"I authorized the janitor only to change the lock and replace the glass, but I guess he saw a chance to make some extra coin. Couple of guys were banging around up there yesterday afternoon. I took a peek. Looks good. I settled the bill for you." He fished in his pants pocket for a key and handed it to Trapper. "It goes in with teeth side down."

"Thanks."

"Of course I'll have to tack those charges onto your bill."

"Whatever, Carson, just let me by, okay?"

Carson stopped him this time by placing his hand on Trapper's chest. "Wilcox getting iced sucks for you. Right?"

"Genius deduction."

"They're saying his old lady killed him with his own fancy six-shooter."

"Jesus." Trapper had replaced the revolver in the drawer, but apparently Mrs. Wilcox had known where to find it. "Have they estimated time of death?"

"Around two o'clock this morning."

Shortly after he and Kerra had left.

Carson said, "They got a sound bite from one of the wife's friends saying she'd suffered from severe depression since they lost their kid. So, you know, all things considered, Trapper, maybe this ending is for the best."

Trapper's eyes narrowed in anger. "Don't make me hit you, Carson." He pushed the lawyer's hand off his chest. Carson judiciously backed away. Trapper continued on to the elevator.

As soon as he stepped off on his floor, he smelled fresh paint. The frosted glass pane in the door had been replaced, but no stenciling had been done yet. Which was just as well. It would save the new tenant the hassle of having it redone.

Trapper planned to move out as soon as he had the wherewithal to go through the necessary motions. He didn't know what he was going to do or where he was going to go, but he knew he was finished here.

It wasn't the finish he'd hoped for. He had wanted it to end with clarity and absoluteness. He'd wanted vindication, yes, but, more than that, he'd wanted closure. Solid closure, which, either way, left no niggling ambiguity or debilitating doubt.

As it was, he would remain in limbo. Limbo for life.

And although he'd told Wilcox that he was fine with that, he wasn't. Especially after this week. After Kerra.

The floor of his office had been swept clean of broken glass. He checked the file cabinet. The meaningless paperwork that had been scattered about the office had been arranged into meaningless stacks inside the drawers. The sofa was a carcass, but the stuffing that had been pulled out of the cushions had been gathered and removed. All the furniture was upright.

He hung his coat on the rack behind the door,

walked over to his desk, and sat down behind it. The surface of it gleamed with polish, which was, to his knowledge, a first. He opened the drawers one by one. The bottom one contained basic office supplies. The middle held empty file folders and a roll of the plastic bags he used to preserve the photos he took of illicit rendezvous. The only thing remaining in the lap drawer was the magnifying glass.

He left it where it was and closed the drawer.

Swiveling his chair around, he noticed that the electrical outlet plate had been replaced, the Sheetrock patched and repainted.

He wondered who had watched the dirty videos on the flash drive. Jenks? Glenn? Wilcox himself? Wilcox had pretended not to know what the flash drive had on it, but Trapper trusted nothing anymore.

He stretched out his leg and dug in his jeans pocket for the other flash drive. He bounced it in his palm, thinking with self-deprecation how clever he'd believed himself to be, shipping it to Marianne and then pretending to Wilcox that his hidey-hole had been discovered and his own insurance policy heisted.

He'd played it up big, but just subtly enough to make the ruse convincing. Wilcox had been fooled. Even Kerra had fallen for the bluff.

Trapper bounced the flash drive one time more, then his hand fell still. He went still all over. He even stopped breathing.

Seconds later, he came out of his chair as though it had launched him. He left it spinning as he dashed from the office, barreled through the fire stairs door, and leaped the treads three at a time until he reached the first floor.

He barged into Carson's office, startling his former stripper-turned-receptionist. "He's with a client," she said.

But Trapper was already pushing through the door into Carson's private office. "What couple of guys?"

Carson's client had the reflexes of the guilty. He sprang from his chair, whipped a knife from his coat sleeve, and brandished it.

Carson stood up and patted the air. "Put the blade away. He's harmless."

"Long way from harmless," Trapper told the sneering miscreant. "Get that knife out of my face or I'll break your arm." The client obviously believed him. He did as told. Trapper went back to Carson. "The repair to my office. You said a couple of guys. Who were they?"

"I don't know. Guys. In coveralls. With tools and paint cans and shit."

"Whose name was on the invoice for the job?"

"No invoice. Cash got me a ten percent discount."

"Do you have a hammer?"

Carson looked at him like he'd asked for the tail of a mermaid.

"A hammer, a hammer."

"What would I need with a hammer?"

Trapper left three stunned people behind as he left as rapidly as he'd appeared and ran back up the stairs to his office. He gave his desk chair a shove that sent it rolling out of his way, then kicked the wall just above the outlet plate, striking it with his boot heel until it caved in.

But the hole he'd made wasn't large enough to get his hand through.

He opened his lap drawer, got the magnifying glass, and wielded it as he would have a hammer, beating the metal casing of it against the Sheetrock until chalky hunks of it were chipped away and he had an opening large enough to work his hand inside and up to his elbow.

The cell phone was duct-taped to one of the studs.

After pulling it out, he tapped it against his forehead in time to his whispered chant, *sonofabitch, sonofabitch, sonofabitch*. Wilcox's contingency.

He allowed himself about ten seconds to be overjoyed.

And thirty seconds to be terrified of how he would be impacted by what he held in his hand.

He had to know.

He turned on the phone and was relieved that it didn't require a code to open. He accessed photos. There were five in the folder.

Heart thudding, he opened the first. It required magnification before he could read the names. He scanned them. Some celebrity names jumped out at him. He recognized the names of politicians, living and dead. Names that had "Dr." in front, names with "The Honorable" before them, names with distinguishing ranks.

The list having been alphabetized, Glenn Addison's was near the top.

He went to the next photo, then the next. He had expected to find a few names there that weren't.

Heart near to bursting with dread, he ran down the list of names beginning with the letter T. Trapper wasn't there.

A dry, harsh cry of gladness escaped him. His knees gave way with relief, and he sank to the floor. He sighed an inarticulate prayer.

He sat there clutching the phone, giving his heart time to stop racing and his breathing to return to normal before going through the remainder of the list. The alphabet gave out in the center of the fourth photo.

Trapper tapped on the fifth and final. In the dead center of the page, there was only one name. Not typed. A signature.

Major Franklin Trapper.

There could be no mistake. The signature was too distinctive to have been forged. It was his father's.

Trapper fell back against the wall, his shoulder blades banging hard against it, but he didn't feel it. He raised his knees, bent his head over them, and heaved a series of dry sobs so wrenching they made his breastbone ache.

This was what he had lived in fear of finding at the end of his quest for truth. He wasn't shocked or disillusioned. He had suspected it. *Expected* it. What he hadn't anticipated was that it would hurt this bad to know for certain.

It was clear now why Wilcox had put the list into Trapper's hands. It hadn't been because he feared prosecution or assassination by one of his own, or because Trapper had intimidated him into surrendering it. It wasn't even to bring his daughter's murderers to justice, although if he were alive, Wilcox surely would have assigned Trapper to eliminate them.

The list was Trapper's heart's desire.

Wilcox had given Trapper what he most wanted, proof of his years of corruption and bloodletting, but Trapper couldn't use it to incriminate Wilcox without incriminating his own father.

He must drop the investigation, stop asking questions and making a pest of himself, tell the federal agents, "Just kidding," and bury any lingering suspicion of the Pegasus bombing. His conviction about a conspiracy would never be vindicated or validated. He would remain a burnout who couldn't hack it, and people would continue to roll their eyes whenever his name cropped up.

He could delete photo number five, but The Major's signature would still be on the original pledge. Even though the authorities didn't know of its existence, Trapper did. He would live each day knowing that he was breaking the law by obstructing justice. Wilcox had known how onerous that would be to him. How had he kept from laughing out loud?

It didn't even matter that Wilcox was dead. In order for The Major to remain a hero in the eyes of the world, Trapper would have to abandon his crusade.

Forever and ever. Amen.

He sat there on the floor, gripping the phone so tightly his fingers turned white, staring at his father's signature through a glossing of tears.

Then he wiped them from his eyes and stood up.

"Fuck you, Wilcox."

Chapter 35

The law secretary was only slightly less startled than before when Trapper strode in again and went straight into Carson's office. The client was still there, slumped and sullen, looking pessimistic about his future.

Trapper said, "I need to borrow—"

Carson pitched him a set of car keys. "You okay?"

"I'm fine."

Carson came to his feet. "You sure? 'Cause you look—"

"Which car do these keys go to?"

"Yours. Remember it? It's parked out back looking as good as new."

"Thanks. I owe you."

"Trapper?"

But he was already out the door.

In his car, he checked the console cubby and the glove box for his phone charger. Missing. Carson's shop guy must've helped himself to it. Trapper patted down his coat pockets until he found a phone that still had battery life and used it to call one of the ATF colleagues to whom he'd spoken earlier. "Meet me at the curb outside your office in three minutes."

It took him four, but when he arrived the agent was there. No doubt he'd heard the news about Wilcox, because he practically had steam coming out his ears.

Trapper lowered his driver's window and thrust a sealed plastic bag at him. "I know I let you down. I'm sorry I can't hand over Wilcox, but here's the cell phone I told you about. The photos of the list are on it, and it's a hell of a list. The flash drive has my stuff on it, the Johnson video, the phone-recorded conversation with Wilcox. The password to open it is 'RED,' all caps. Give it to the FBI."

Trapper sped away before the flustered agent got a word in edgewise.

Next, Trapper called Kerra. Her phone rang twice before going to voice mail. He didn't leave a message, but he called three more times in as many minutes with no success. At a stoplight, he asked Siri to dial the TV station's number. He went through the unending recorded list of options and finally reached a human being in the newsroom.

Trapper asked for Gracie and was put through. He identified himself. "I need to speak to Kerra."

"She's on location, about to do a live report."

"It's an emergency."

"Your emergencies have almost cost Kerra her job. I'd bet good money you're the reason she looks like her pet just died and her eyes are red and puffy."

"I need to talk to her. Get that message to her."

"She's *busy*. You'll have to ask forgiveness for whatever you did some other time."

"This isn't about that. About us. It's—"

"They're going live in sixty. I have to go."

"Tell her—"

"I will. Goodbye."

"Listen to me, goddammit!" He took a breath. "Granted, I'm a shit."

"John Trapper is a shit. I'm writing that down."

"Write this down. It's the number she needs to call." Twice he repeated the number of the phone he was using. "Got it?"

"Got it."

"Tell her that the cell phone wasn't behind the painting."

"Are you drunk?"

"It'll make sense to Kerra. Tell her it was a bluff. Like the wall outlet."

"Okay."

"Tell her I got the list."

"You got the list."

"Can you remember all that?"

"They're down to thirty. I have to go."

The producer clicked off.

"We'll bring you updates as they occur. This is Kerra Bailey reporting."

The cameraman signaled her when they were off the air. The microphone felt like a fifty-pound weight in her hand as she lowered it to her side.

The scene was familiar: she and colleagues jockeying for position at the site of a major news story; a row of vans with satellite dishes on top; cameramen practicing their panning shots; sound techs testing mike levels; reporters adjusting earpieces and checking their appearance in whatever reflective surface was available within seconds of being told to stand by.

This is what she thrived on. Today she felt removed from it. She was going through the motions, but her heart wasn't in it. She had threatened Thomas Wilcox that she would show up with a cameraman at his gate, but she hadn't expected to be reporting a murder-suicide. His pitiless disregard for the lives he'd taken was repugnant. But wouldn't she be as despicable if she weren't saddened by the desperate action that had ended his life?

Any of her colleagues would give an eyetooth to know that shortly before Wilcox's wife fatally shot him, Kerra had been face-to-face with him inside the barricaded mansion. It would be a scoop to top all scoops, but she wouldn't be the one to tell it. She wouldn't exploit the man's tragic death, no matter how evil he'd been, nor that of the pathetic Mrs. Wilcox.

She also wouldn't break her promise to Trapper that she wouldn't tell the whole story before getting his okay.

"Kerra, Gracie needs to talk to you."

Given her thoughts, Kerra wondered if Gracie had somehow learned of Trapper's and her visit with Wilcox last night. God, she hoped not. Gracie would fire her on the spot.

She thanked the production assistant who'd delivered the message and made her way back to the van. She climbed into the passenger seat, took her phone from her handbag, and hit speed dial.

Gracie answered on the first ring. "Your eyes still look red on camera."

"Allergies."

"Right. Well, the allergen called."

Kerra's heart bumped, but she didn't say anything.

"He was in a breathless rush, of course. Emphatic that he needs to talk to you, but not about 'us.' Said to tell you the cell phone wasn't behind the painting. It was a bluff like the wall outlet. He has the list."

"He has the list?"

"I accused him of being drunk. "

Kerra's lethargy had dissolved, and now she was charged. "Did he say where he is?"

"No, but he left a phone number."

"Text it to me. I'll call him right now."

"Hold on, I've got another assignment for you."

"Gracie, for the time being we've gotten all we're going to get out of the PD. The spokesperson will say nothing except that they're investigating. They've sequestered the housekeeper, so I can't even get near her. The lead homicide detective dodged me. All I'm doing is repeating myself."

"I'm sending Bill to take over there. I need you to get to Lodal."

"What for?"

"The Major's being released from the hospital."

"What? Today? That has to be a rumor."

"I have a reliable source. While up there, I bribed a hospital orderly to call me with any updates or hearsay. I just talked to him. That's still your story, Kerra, and if you hurry, it'll be an exclusive for the evening news."

After a short pause to take a breath, she continued. "Assuming you won't be an idiot and pass this up, if you could possibly, pretty please with sugar on top, get a shot of you and The Major together, that would be fantastic. A sound bite from him would give me an orgasm. And need I spell this out? You'd be the network's reigning princess."

Kerra had stopped listening after being told that The Major was leaving the hospital. She was flabbergasted. "You trust this source?"

"He loved my orange glasses. The crew has already left. They'll meet you there."

"My car—"

"Rent a limo. Hitchhike. I don't care. Just squirt some red-out in your eyes and get your ass up there."

Trapper wanted to notify Glenn that he was on his way to Lodal so he could tell him in person that the FBI now had the goods on Wilcox. Regardless of what he'd told Glenn last night, he thought he could swing a lenient plea deal for him if he agreed to testify against Wilcox.

Frustrated after repeatedly getting his voice mail, he called the SO's main number and asked to speak directly with Glenn. Rather than being put through, he was asked to identify himself.

"John Trapper."

"The sheriff didn't come in today."

"I'm a friend."

"Yes, I know, but he's not here."

"Do you know where I can reach him?"

"I'm sorry, I don't."

After disconnecting, Trapper had the uneasy feeling he'd been given a scripted answer that was intentionally evasive. He called the Addisons' home number. A woman answered. "Hey, Linda, it's Trapper."

"Mrs. Addison is on her cell phone and can't be interrupted."

"Who are you?"

She identified herself as a family friend. Why did Linda need family friends around her? "Is Glenn there?"

"No, and, I'm sorry, but that's all I'm at liberty to say."

"How come?"

"You may want to call Hank," she said before hanging up.

Maybe he was getting the runaround because Hank had spread the word that Trapper was persona non grata.

Or perhaps, after tendering his resignation, Glenn was ducking people in general to avoid having to answer questions.

Maybe he'd suffered another bad anxiety attack or something worse.

With that worry in mind, Trapper called the hospital, asked if Glenn Addison had been admitted as a patient, and was relieved to learn from the switchboard operator that he hadn't been.

"Good. Thank you." Uncertain how he was going to feel about talking to his father so soon after the discovery he'd made, he hesitated.

"Can I be of further assistance?" the operator asked.

"Yeah. Please ring Major Trapper's room."

"I can't do that."

"This is his son."

"I'm sorry, Mr. Trapper. I can't connect you because your father has been released."

"*What?*"

"He's checked out of the hospital."

"When? Why wasn't I notified?"

"I...I..."

"Never mind. Put me through to the senior nurse on his floor."

While his cell phone battery drained, the phone on the other end rang at least two dozen times. He had about decided to hang up and call the switchboard back when a man answered, sounding harried. As soon as Trapper said his name, the guy identified himself as the floor's supervising nurse and got defensive.

"We tried to contact you, Mr. Trapper. None of the numbers we had on your father's chart went through. We tried persuading him to stay until you could be reached, but he was insistent on leaving. His doctor strongly advised against it, but—"

"How long ago was this?"

"Half an hour. Maybe a bit longer."

"Was he taken home by ambulance?"

"No. Reverend Addison was here. He offered to drive him."

Chapter 36

A minivan Trapper recognized as Hank's was parked in front of The Major's house.

Trapper sped through the gate and kicked up dust on the drive. He braked so hard the car skidded before coming to a jarring stop. He was out of it in a blur and bounding up the steps to the porch.

The door was unlocked. Trapper rushed in. Then stopped dead in his tracks.

The Major was in his recliner but sitting upright. He looked pale and weak, shaky and shrunken, but also enraged.

Standing over him was Hank, who backed up a few steps and swung the barrel of the rifle he was holding away from The Major and toward Trapper, who said, "What the hell are you doing?"

Hank replied, "Isn't it obvious?"

"No Bible?"

"This gets attention faster."

"In anybody else's hands, maybe. You just look like a jackass."

Trapper was cracking wise, but his gut had drawn up as tight as a drum, and he was attuned to every nuance of Hank's tone and expression, because his finger was tapping against the trigger of the deer rifle.

But his father's labored breathing was Trapper's immediate concern. "I'm going to sue that hospital for letting you leave."

"He told me we were going to search for Glenn together." He raised his chin toward Hank. "Instead he drove me here. Took that rifle from the cabinet..."

"Save your breath," Trapper said. "I can figure out the rest." His thinking had snagged on the need to *search for Glenn*. He was desperate to have that explained, but first he had to disarm Hank. "Do you even know how to load that thing?"

"It was loaded for me."

"Huh. Let me guess. Jenks?"

"Handy guy."

"I'm sure. But come on, Hank. Put down the rifle before you hurt somebody."

"I'd love to start with you."

"You never could hit the broad side of a barn. You'd

miss me, and then I would have to kill you, and I don't want to. Not because I'd miss you or anything, but it would be hard on your family."

"Slowly, using one hand, remove your holster."

"Holster?"

"If you don't do it now, I'll shoot The Major."

"With the rifle my mom gave him? That's unsportsmanlike."

"Do it, Trapper."

The gleam in Hank's eyes made him look maniacal enough to turn this standoff bloody. Trapper couldn't risk that until he had a better grasp of what was going on. "In order to reach my holster with one hand, I have to take off my coat."

"Slowly."

Trapper shrugged the coat off his shoulders, then let the sleeves slide down his arms. It fell to the floor. Reaching behind him with one hand, he detached his holstered nine-millimeter from his waistband.

"Now pitch it over your shoulder."

"That's dangerous. I'm not sure the safety is on."

"Do it."

He tried to pinpoint the spot of the thud against hardwood when the holster landed.

"Keep your hands raised," Hank said.

Trapper held them at shoulder height. "Now what? We stand here until one of us caves? Your lifetime record for holding out is for shit, you know."

"Shut up!"

The Major's breathing whistled when he inhaled. "Hank, why are you doing this? Have you lost your mind?"

"His soul, I think," Trapper said. "What's this about having to search for Glenn?"

The Major said, "He hasn't been seen or heard from since last night."

"He was called away from the house," Hank said.

Trapper didn't like the sound of that, or the gloating expression on Hank's face. "Called away?"

"By Deputy Jenks."

"Department business?"

"Not exactly."

"What exactly?"

Hank said, "I notified Jenks that Dad had—as you put it—grown a conscience and spilled his guts. Which presented us with a problem. Jenks lured him out to The Pit. No more problem."

"He killed Glenn? Jesus Christ," The Major whispered. "Why?"

Trapper said, "Because the reverend here wanted to take over for Thomas Wilcox as chief bad guy." Trapper snickered. "But the thing is, Hank is so screwed and doesn't even know it."

"Whatever your con is this time, Trapper, I'm not falling for it."

"No con. Hadn't you heard? Wilcox is dead."

"Oh, I heard all the gory details. Your girlfriend reported them from outside the Wilcox mansion."

"What you don't know, but I think that maybe now is the time to enlighten you, is that Kerra and I were *inside* the mansion last night with Wilcox."

Hank guffawed.

"Cross my heart."

"You went to see Wilcox?"

"After leaving you."

"And he welcomed you with open arms?"

"I wouldn't go so far as to say that. But over the past few days, he and I had formed a mutually beneficial quasi-partnership." Trapper stopped and raised an eyebrow. "Oh, I see you're taken aback. You didn't know that." He sighed and ruefully shook his head. "Yeah, time was that Tom even had me at gunpoint but couldn't bring himself to kill me. Instead we talked through our differences—"

"Get back to last night."

"Or what? You're going to shoot me? I don't believe you will. Although you've already hurt my feelings. I know you're pissed at me for sending you out to that line shack, but isn't this taking your payback a little far?"

"Get on with it," Hank snapped.

"I forgot where I was. Oh, yeah. We three—Wilcox, Kerra, and I—had two interesting conversations, the most recent being around one o'clock this morning."

"Did you tell him that Dad had betrayed him?"

"No, I didn't."

"I don't believe that."

"I don't give a damn if you believe it or not. It's the truth."

"Then what was discussed during this meeting which I still don't believe ever took place?"

"Serious stuff, and I'm not joshing you. Wilcox had the one thing, shy of a signed confession, that would persuade the feds to reopen the Pegasus bombing case. He agreed to give it to me."

"Wilcox wouldn't give you the time of day, much less anything that would incriminate him."

"Ordinarily, no. At first he was coy, the dealmaker, the wheeler-dealer. You know how he was. He was holding out for a guarantee of full immunity. But those are details that probably don't interest you or anyone except federal prosecutors."

"Get on with it," Hank repeated, this time straining the words between his teeth.

"If you'd stop interrupting...Suffice to say only one thing would have compelled Wilcox to come to a burnout like me and ask me to negotiate a deal for him."

"Well?"

"Vengeance for his daughter's murder."

Hank blinked, always a giveaway.

"He made me promise to make that a priority."

Speaking softly, Trapper said, "Who'd you get to do it for you? Because I know you don't have the stomach or the balls to have done it yourself."

"Shut up, Trapper."

He smiled. "Fine. I'll shut up. Just one last thing. I repeat: You. Are. So. Screwed. You can kill me, you can kill The Major, but Kerra was with me last night. She knows all about Wilcox's pledge, signed by people who do dirty deeds for him. She'll make certain that everybody on it is exposed and made to answer for his crimes."

Hank laughed out loud. "Trapper, Trapper, Trapper. Always trying to hoodwink me. But it won't work this time, because I didn't sign that ridiculous pledge." He adopted a Count Dracula reverberation. "Down into the bank vault. Down long dark corridors to the inner chamber."

Returning to his normal voice, he said, "I was put through the wringer just like Dad described to you last night. Wilcox smoothly reminded me how much he had donated to the tabernacle building fund. With a single stroke of his Mont Blanc, he had saved my fledgling TV ministry. The bill was due, he said. Words to that effect. Sign on the dotted line.

"But, I said, 'Not so fast, Thomas.' See, the previous Sunday, I had shared the good news of his generosity from the pulpit. Hallelujah! All saints be praised!" He laughed again. "What was he going to do? Take the money back? Welsh on an offering made to God Almighty?"

"What did he want from you? Absolution?"

"Very little, actually. He was growing increasingly concerned that Dad would crack. He was getting older, more sentimental, maudlin when he drank too much, which was all the time. Wilcox wanted me to do to him what Dad had been doing to The Major."

"Spying."

The Major's succinct remark surprised Trapper. Sensing that, The Major looked up at him. "Hank told me about your visit with Glenn last night, his confessions."

"It wasn't an easy or pleasant hour for me."

"I believe that, John."

The Major looked dejected and resigned, but even more worrisome to Trapper was that he seemed to be physically diminishing with every passing moment. He wanted to hear everything Hank had to say about his adversarial relationship with Wilcox, but he needed to hurry him along.

"Okay, so you refused to sign Wilcox's pledge. He took umbrage with your audacity, got huffy, issued some threats. 'You don't have any idea who you're up against.' That kind of thing. But Wilcox had good game."

"You must admit," Hank said, "his method worked for decades."

"Centuries. It's Machiavellian. Not original but effective, and you took your cue. You showed him. You killed his daughter."

"Not I, of course."

"Right. We concluded that you're too chicken-livered. Who'd you send to do it?"

"I had shown the path of righteousness to a former drug user."

"Cost of redemption: one murder."

Hank's smile turned angelic. "God works in mysterious ways."

"So does the devil." Trapper's smile was more like the latter's. "Remember when I said you were screwed and didn't even know it? Well, you didn't sign Wilcox's pledge, so the feds don't have your signature. But they do have—because I handed it over to them—a list Wilcox conveniently typed and alphabetized. Now, take a wild guess whose name he added?"

Wilcox had done no such thing. Hank's name hadn't been on the roster, but maybe Hank would believe it was. It was very like something Wilcox would have done out of sheer spite.

"Sorry, Hank," Trapper said with feigned regret and took a step toward him.

Hank jabbed the rifle forward. "You're lying."

"You can kill me, but the FBI still has those names, and Kerra can testify as to how I came by them. She can attest to everything."

"Then I'm doubly glad she beat it up here to cover The Major's release from the hospital."

Trapper's stomach plunged. "What?"

"Oh, I see you're taken aback," he mocked. "You didn't know that." Then, "Kerra?"

She appeared in the doorway between the living room and the hall. Jenks's left hand was wrapped around her biceps. In his right was a revolver, the caliber of which you didn't argue with.

Kerra's lips were almost white with fear, but she was putting up a brave front. "Gracie gave me your message. I tried to reach you."

"The phone ran out of juice."

"They warned The Major and me that if we signaled you that I was here, we would all die."

"I think that's the plan anyway." Trapper gave her only a half smile, but he hoped she realized that it was brimming with apology and regret.

"Jenks, bring her over here," Hank said. Jenks propelled her forward, and when she was within reach, Hank took her arm and jerked her in front of him, facing Trapper. "Take hold of the rifle."

"Go to hell," she said and elbowed him in the stomach.

Acting instinctively, Trapper lurched forward.

Hank yelled, "Jenks! Shoot him!"

"Wait!" Trapper froze and raised his hands higher. "Leave Kerra alone, you can do with me whatever."

Hank, breathing with exertion—excitement?—said, "Well, that's real generous of you, Trapper, but you're in no position to dictate terms, seeing as how I have all the advantages here. Tell Kerra to take hold of the rifle."

Trapper glanced at Jenks, who had moved to stand at The Major's side. Any of them made an easy target for his revolver. Coming back to Kerra, he bobbed his head. "Do as he says."

Eyes locked on Trapper's, she allowed Hank to place her hands where he wanted them and secured them with his own. Her left supported the barrel, her right was wrapped around the trigger guard. Hank's finger remained crooked around the trigger itself.

Looking at Trapper from over Kerra's shoulder, Hank chuckled. "It was the darnedest stroke of luck. I was about to leave the hospital with The Major tucked into my van when she drove into the parking lot. I invited her to ride along with us and told her she could call her crew to meet us out here. Except—"

"Except that when I tried to make the call," Kerra said, "he backhanded me and took my phone."

Trapper settled an icy gaze on Hank. "I'm going to have to kill you after all." He glanced over his shoulder and spotted his holster on the floor two yards away. He knew a bullet was chambered, but how to get the pistol out of the holster...

Reading his thoughts, Jenks said, "I don't advise it."

"Better heed him, Trapper," Hank said. "Being a lawman, he's got lots of tricks up his sleeve."

"Tricks like planting evidence to frame a white-trash parole violator for attempted murder?"

"That's the least of Jenks's talents," Hank said. "He can make people disappear without a trace."

"The Pit."

"Your bodies will never be discovered."

"Like that of his partner Sunday night?"

"Petey Moss," Hank said.

"Who was the third?" Kerra asked.

"Wasn't a third." That from Jenks.

"Yes, there was." Trapper directed Kerra's attention to The Major.

She looked down at him, her lips parting with bewilderment. Wearily, he nodded. "He's right."

Trapper wished he could take satisfaction from his father's admission. He couldn't. He said to Kerra, "The day I came here, I figured out it had to have been him who tried to open that door before you heard the shot. But I couldn't reason why. No, let me rephrase." He looked down at his father. "I didn't *want* to reason why. I get it now."

"I don't think you do, John," he said. "I heard them coming toward the house and tried to warn Kerra. Ran out of time. That's all."

Trapper held his father's gaze. Breathed in,

breathed out. He thought his ribs would break from the pressure building behind them. His heart was already broken.

Hank said, "Ah. A pregnant pause."

Trapper ignored him and looked at the six-shooter in Jenks's large hand. "If The Major doesn't get back to the hospital soon, you'll be charged with murder."

"I didn't shoot him, Petey did. Excitable little bugger."

Hank said, "Language, Jenks, language."

Trapper was still holding the deputy's implacable stare. In his mind, he was reconstructing Sunday night's scenario, piecing it together, getting a fix on how it had played out from Jenks's point of view. "Petey was quick on the draw. You didn't expect that. Seconds after The Major was down, you noticed the powder room light go out."

"Didn't expect that, either," Jenks said.

"There wasn't supposed to be anybody else here."

"No. She," he said, glancing at Kerra, "was a mean surprise. Otherwise, I had it all worked out."

Looking into the man's rock-steady gaze, Trapper murmured, "But things didn't go as planned."

"You could say."

"That was then." Hank's impatience drew Trapper's attention back to him. The rifle barrel was still aimed at his chest. "This is now. And I've got *this* all worked out."

Trapper made brief eye contact with Kerra. Her face was stark with fear. His own heart was stuttering, but, trying to keep his tone casual, he drawled, "You do? Just out of curiosity, Hank, how do you plan on killing the three of us and getting away with it?"

"I'm not going to kill anybody." He forced Kerra's index finger around the trigger. "Kerra is."

"No!"

"I'll let her choose who goes first." Hank shifted the rifle's barrel fractionally so the bore was now aimed at The Major. "She can put The Major out of his misery. That would be rather poetic, wouldn't it? He saved her life, she ends his. The irony of it gives me cold chills. Or," he said, aiming again at Trapper, "she can shoot you."

"Not with that rifle she can't. It isn't loaded." Trapper lowered his raised hands.

"Keep them up," Hank shouted.

"No, no, no," Kerra was saying as she strained against Hank's increased pressure on her finger.

"Hank, for god's sake, stop this." The Major placed his hands on the arms of the recliner as though to lever himself up, but Jenks pulled him back and cocked his revolver.

Trapper kept his eyes trained on Kerra's. "Pull the trigger."

She gave a small but emphatic shake of her head.

"It's not loaded," Trapper said.

Hank laughed loudly in her ear, causing her to cringe. "Like I'd fall for that."

"Did you check it, Hank?" Trapper asked.

Hank hesitated, "I didn't need to."

"Jenks always does what you tell him to?"

"Always."

Trapper turned his head and looked at Jenks. No expression, solid as granite, nary a twitch, but keenly alert to every blink of an eye.

Trapper came back around to Hank. "If you're sure the rifle is loaded, then seconds from now I'll be dead, and you'll be happy."

"John, what are you doing?" The Major said, wheezing. "Stop provoking him."

Trapper said, "Kerra, pull the trigger."

"I can't." Her voice was mournful, barely audible.

"Nothing will happen."

Hank chortled. "You're bluffing, Trapper."

"Pull the trigger, Kerra."

"Trapper, please," she sobbed. "I can't."

"Do you trust me?" he whispered.

Her eyes probed his. She nodded.

"Then do it. Pull the trigger."

She hesitated for the length of one heartbeat, then jerked her finger against the trigger.

The rifle clicked but didn't fire.

In the instant of Hank's bafflement, Trapper

lunged toward Kerra and pushed her aside, then charged Hank. Hank swung the rifle like a club. The steel barrel caught Trapper on the side of his head, but he kept going, ramming into Hank's center and pushing him backward for several yards like a tackling dummy, before finally landing him on the floor.

Hank tried to scramble backward, but Trapper grabbed him by his shirt and jerked him upright.

"This is for whatever you did to Glenn." Trapper drew back his fist and hit him as hard as he could in the center of his face. Bones cracked, blood spurted, Hank screamed. His head flopped forward.

Trapper grabbed him by the hair and yanked his head up. "This is for The Major." He hit him again, harder, dislocating his jaw but maintaining a fistful of his hair. "You hypocritical cocksucker, I should kill you for what you did to Tiffany Wilcox, but I'd rather watch you rot for the rest of your miserable life." He drove his fist into Hank's gut, but by then Jenks was restraining him. He wrestled him up and away from Hank.

Trapper flung him off. "I'm done, I'm done." Woozy from the blow to his head, he swayed as he stood up and turned to Jenks. "You son of a bitch. You're FBI, right?"

"North Texas field office." He proffered his FBI ID.

"Would have been nice of you to clue me."

"Nice, maybe, but against orders."

"I nearly shot you that day."

Agent Jenks gave a wry grin. "No need to remind me. When did you guess?"

"About a minute ago. I couldn't figure why you were just standing there, taking it all in, instead of making quick work of me with that," he said, indicating the revolver Jenks still had in hand. "I hoped to God my hunch was right. You got backup coming?"

"On the way."

Trapper kicked Hank in the knee. "Read him his rights."

"Trapper!"

He turned toward Kerra's startled voice.

Chapter 37

She had reclined The Major's chair and was leaning over him. Trapper was still unsteady on his feet, but he made it to the recliner and knelt beside it.

From the opposite side of it, Kerra looked at him bleakly and drew his attention to The Major's lap. His torso was distended on his left side, indicating internal bleeding.

The Major said, "I sprung a leak. The surgeon warned me it was too early to leave, warned that my lung could collapse again. But Glenn—"

"Just be still," Trapper said. "Help will be here in no time. We'll get you back to the hospital. That doctor's good. He'll patch you up again."

Trapper was vaguely aware that uniformed men

had arrived and were clumping around the living room. Jenks must've had them awaiting his signal to move in. He appeared in Trapper's peripheral vision.

"Major?" Jenks placed his hand on The Major's shoulder. "My fault you were shot. I didn't have time to warn you, so I hit you in the head just to get you down. Petey wasn't supposed to—"

"We'll sort it all out later," Trapper said. "Is an ambulance on the way?"

Jenks nodded, but his attention was still on The Major. "Your friend Glenn Addison is in custody. I called him out to The Pit like Hank said, but for his own safety. I turned him over to arresting agents who were waiting there for us. Same as I did with Petey Moss. Sheriff Addison is fine. Cooperating fully. He specifically asked me to tell you that he loves you. Nothing ever changed that."

The Major asked, "Does he know about Hank?"

"Not yet, and I dread him having to be told. The sheriff's a good man. He might have cheated on an election or two, but he performed his duties well."

"Thanks for delivering his message."

Jenks gave The Major a reassuring pat on the shoulder then hurried away to brief and issue orders to arriving officers.

The Major looked at Trapper. "You saw my name on Wilcox's list?"

"He made sure I did."

"And you still handed it over to the FBI?"

"I had to. I didn't want to. I struggled with it, but—"

"But being you, you had to."

"I did, yeah."

The Major smiled shakily. "I'm proud of you for it." He took a rattling breath. "I hoped all this would go away without you ever knowing."

"Well, it didn't go away. And I do know. I know everything except the nature of your pact with Wilcox. Was it connected to that lucrative book and movie deal?"

"No."

Trapper bent his head low and blinked tears out of his eyes. "Just tell me...please tell me that you didn't bomb the Pegasus Hotel."

The Major fumbled for his hand and grasped it. "No, John. *No.* Is that what you thought?"

"It's what I feared. I've been through hell fearing it. When I started investigating the bombing, realized the three who took the blame were under orders from somebody else, I thought that maybe you were one of them, too, but had been lucky enough to get out."

"Why would you think that?"

"Because, except for Wilcox, you benefited from that goddamn disaster more than anybody. You built a career off it."

"Fate. Right place, right time. That's all it was."

"Then why'd you strike a bargain with Wilcox?"

"I swear on your mother's soul that I never had any dealings with him until three years ago when you started making headway on your investigation into him."

"Oh, Jesus," Trapper groaned, "I don't want to hear this."

"You did nothing wrong. You were doing your job. You're only to blame for being very good at it and being persistent. Wilcox reeled me in, told me I must, *must*, discredit you, dismiss your conspiracy theory, denounce you and anything you alleged."

"Or what? What could he do? Cancel your hero status?"

"Kill Marianne."

Trapper flinched.

"It's worse," The Major said. "He assured me that all the evidence would point to you."

Trapper looked across at Kerra, saw her horror, and said, "I've seen the names on his list. He could have made it happen." Going back to his father, he asked, "Why her? Why not just pop me?"

"Because he didn't know what you had on him, how much you'd uncovered and shared with your superiors. If you were killed, he was afraid of what you might be leaving behind for future analysis. But my denunciation of you would go a long way, he said. He told me to discredit you, or else. Even if you were acquitted for your fiancée's murder—"

"My reputation, my life, would have been destroyed. They *were* destroyed."

"I'm sorry, John. I took what I believed to be my only choice."

"Marianne knew nothing about it, did she?"

"No."

"That's a mercy," Kerra said softly.

"Here I've been thinking I was protecting you from Wilcox," Trapper said to The Major. "You were protecting me. The son of a bitch pitted us against each other."

Although his strength was waning, The Major squeezed Trapper's hand tighter. "It pained me when you said that this—I, Wilcox, the Pegasus—was your life."

"Aw, I was just spouting off."

"No. You weren't. In countless ways, what happened that day took over all our lives. Debra's. Mine. Yours."

Trapper, made uncomfortable by his father's remorse, turned and looked out the open front door. The ambulance was speeding through the gate, but Trapper willed it to go even faster. The Major was laboring for each breath, his complexion had gone gray, his lips bluish.

"I missed the spotlight," he was saying to Kerra, even as he gasped for air.

"You were good in it." She sniffed back tears and placed her hand on his shoulder.

"That's why I wanted...the interview." He seemed impatient with his increasing shortness of breath. It was obvious he wanted to say more. "My ego put your life at risk, and I'm more sorry for that than I can say."

"No apology necessary."

His eyes misted. "Vanity is my downfall. John knows. Fame is seductive and addictive," he said, struggling. "I went all in. Too often at John's expense."

"Look, I'm okay. All right?" Trapper said. Blood was frothing in the corner of The Major's lips. Trapper blotted it with his own shirtsleeve. "The ambulance is here. Stop talking. Save your breath."

The Major feebly raised a hand to touch Trapper's face. "You never gave up."

"That's *my* downfall. I'm pigheaded."

"In a good way, John. A good way."

Trapper's throat had become too tight to speak. The paramedics had come inside and were trying to push him out of their way, but The Major maintained a surprisingly strong grip on his hand. "John, please don't share Debra's diary. Not for my sake, but hers. Bury it with me."

Trapper wiped his nose on his cuff and smiled. "You don't have to worry about that, Dad. Mom didn't keep a diary."

Major Franklin Trapper was pronounced dead on arrival at the county hospital. For the second time in a week, the facility became the eye of a media storm.

Kerra was called upon to do three live stand-ups, the last of which was for the network evening news.

In his solemn baritone, the anchorman said, "A nation has lost an American icon. But you knew The Major personally. What are your thoughts right now, Kerra?"

"Although our time together was brief, I will feel the loss forever. If not for Major Trapper, my life would have ended twenty-five years ago." Tears threatened, but she swallowed hard and managed to hold it together.

"You were with him just before he died."

"I followed the ambulance from his house. He died en route to the hospital."

"We understand that The Major's passing is linked to the tragic murder-suicide that occurred earlier today in the home of prominent Dallas businessman Thomas Wilcox and the arrest of an area clergyman. Can you elaborate on that?"

"Only to say that the FBI has begun conducting a thorough investigation into Mr. Wilcox and Reverend Addison."

"Sources tell us that federal investigators are following a trail that goes all the way back to the bombing of the Pegasus Hotel. From your unique perspective of that historic event—"

"I can't comment on the government's investigation. Regarding the Pegasus bombing, my unique perspective is that of a five-year-old child, whose dying mother passed her off to Major Trapper. He saved my life. That's really all I can or am willing to say at this time."

"His son, John Trapper, a former ATF agent, took part in the apprehension of Reverend Addison, isn't that correct?"

"Yes."

"Mr. Trapper was injured. Do you know his current condition?"

"He suffered a head wound. He's been admitted to the hospital, but the injury isn't serious. He's listed in good condition."

"Has he made a public statement about the passing of his famous father?"

"No."

"Can we expect one soon?"

"No. Mr. Trapper doesn't give interviews."

On that disappointing note, the anchorman wrapped it up with her. She waded her way through a sea of reporters hurling questions at her before reaching the sawhorses barricading the entrance to the hospital's main lobby, where she was surprised to see Gracie.

"Guess what? *Entertainment Tonight* has called. The network has temporarily suspended the clause in your contract that prohibits you from—"

"This isn't entertainment, Gracie," she said and made to go around her.

"*The View* wants you tomorrow."

"I'll be busy tomorrow."

"Okay, I'll put them off. Maybe one day next week?"

"Until further notice, don't commit me to anything."

"Kerra, be smart here. Capitalize on this." She wagged her index finger at her. "I know you're holding back a lot of juicy stuff. If you never reported another story, you could make a career off this one."

The words were so painfully close to the ones Trapper had said to The Major, she recoiled. "That's the last thing I would want to do. Now, you must excuse me. Deputy Jenks has asked to talk to me."

He was waiting in the hospital lobby, in uniform, continuing the pretense that he was a high-ranking deputy sheriff and not a federal agent. He drew her aside, out of anyone else's earshot. He gestured toward her biceps. "I hope I didn't squeeze your arm too tight."

"When we were back there, why didn't you tell me you were an FBI agent?"

"Sorry, but you had to be convincingly frightened. I wanted Hank's confession to the Wilcox girl's murder before I arrested him."

"Trapper was told this morning that the FBI had a man working from the inside."

"Two of us, actually," Jenks said. "For the past couple of years."

"Is your partner also in the sheriff's office?"

Jenks smiled politely but didn't answer.

Abashed, she said, "I'm sorry. I shouldn't have asked, even though anything we say is off the record. You have my word."

"I believe you."

"Can I ask what put Glenn Addison on the FBI's radar to start with?"

"More people listened to Trapper than he was aware of," Jenks said. "Based on what he'd brought to light, we started sniffing out Wilcox, and things began to stink, especially when surveillance picked up the close contact he maintained with a sheriff, who happened to be The Major's good friend.

"Because of Trapper's kinship with The Major," he continued, "the higher-ups weren't sure he could remain objective if he were told about it. They sent us up here, but kept Trapper out of the loop."

"They shouldn't have."

"I tend to agree, but the decision was made by people above my pay grade. I was investigating the sheriff. Floored me when Hank approached me with a 'recruitment' pitch. He had some grandiose ideas."

"About?"

"Getting Wilcox's list and blackmailing people, monied people, into supporting his ministry and building him into a TV megastar. Motivational superman. The person with all the answers."

"God's mouthpiece."

"Essentially. This tabernacle was only the first step. He studied how Wilcox operated, saw how effectively he manipulated by instilling paranoia, and mimicked it."

"What happened today?"

"He called and told me he was going to drive The Major home from the hospital, needed me to go with him, and dispose of the body later. I could tell he was becoming more and more unhinged, that things were coming to a head fast, so I notified the cavalry and told them to stand by, then met him here in the parking lot. When I climbed into the van, I didn't expect you, just like Sunday night."

"Which was full of surprises."

"Tell me. Initially Hank told me to go alone. I was going to warn The Major of what was going on, advise him to leave town for a few days, give me and the bureau time to figure out if we had enough on Hank to make an arrest for Tiffany Wilcox's murder and make it stick.

"But Petey was sprung on me at the last minute. Hank thought he should go along as backup. Without blowing my cover, I didn't have time to warn The Major, except to make a lot of noise as we approached the house. I hit him in the head just to get him down, thinking I'd apologize later, and in the meantime, deal with Petey."

"Petey was trigger-happy."

"Till my dying day, I'll blame myself for not realizing what he was going to do."

By the look on his face, Kerra knew that to be true. "Petey was the one who asked how do you like being dead."

"Yes. Then the light went out in the bathroom. I had to choose between saving the person inside it or tending to The Major, and, honestly, I thought he was already dead."

"Thanks for not shooting me."

"I blasted everything I could but you. Hank wasn't happy we'd missed you and The Major. Once you were released from the hospital, Hank sent me to try again."

She listened, appalled as he told her about hiding in the closet of her motel room. "I couldn't let your producer discover me, or I'd have had to blow my cover."

"What if I'd returned to my room and discovered you there?"

"That's actually what I was hoping for. I intended to tell you who I was and what I was doing, and ask if you wouldn't mind cooperating with your government by vanishing for a couple days and letting Hank think you were keeping Petey company in The Pit." He chuckled. "Trapper saved me the trouble by kidnapping you."

Turning serious again, he said, "I was afraid since I'd failed twice to get you, Hank would send someone else. Somebody like Petey, who wanted to prove his loyalty, or like the guy he sent to do the Wilcox girl. Texas Rangers got that guy, by the way. He admits to acting on Hank's orders.

"But back to you. I was worried for your safety. I put the transmitter on your car so I could keep track. As it turned out, Trapper was cagier. He kept pulling disappearing acts with you." He paused, then added, "He's a pain in the ass, you know."

She laughed softly. "Yes, I do know."

"The bureau will be questioning you extensively about Wilcox, and you'll probably be subpoenaed to testify against Hank."

"That won't be a problem." She shuddered. "I think he's a sociopath."

"Well, if he's thinking of pleading insanity, he can think again. Turns out some of his flock proved less devoted when federal agents started showing up at their doors today with warrants. They'll turn on him in exchange for lesser charges. But all that will be overseen by people with ranks higher than mine. So, Ms. Bailey, if this is goodbye..." He offered his hand, and they shook.

"I can't say that it's all been a pleasure, Deputy Jenks.

He grinned with good nature. "I'll see you on TV." He started to move away, but she called him back.

"When did you make Trapper aware that you were FBI?"

"I didn't."

"Then how did he know that rifle wasn't loaded?"

The agent shrugged. "Far as he knew, it was."

Epilogue

Kerra let herself into her apartment, dropped her keys on the console table in the entry, and set her shoulder bag on the floor. Moving into the living room, she took off her jacket, pulled her blouse from the waistband of her skirt, and had the top two buttons undone before she saw Trapper.

He was standing in front of the glass wall, backlit by the glittering skyline, but she would know that silhouette anywhere.

"Don't stop there," he said. "Keep going. But leave the heels on."

After weeks without contact of any kind, her heart surged at the sight of him. But somehow she managed to keep her tone cool and uninterested. She stepped out of her heels. "How did you get in?"

"Picked the lock."

"How did you get into the building?"

"Told the doorman I was a building inspector for the ATF checking for fire code violations."

"He believed that?"

"When I showed him my ID."

"You're back with the bureau?"

"We'll see how it goes."

She wasn't fooled by his feigned nonchalance but knew it would be a mistake to comment on it. "Carson will miss you being upstairs."

"Come Saturday, he will have been married a month. He's going for a personal record. I told him he'd never make it if he continues to buy other women bad-girl bras. You still have it?"

"Yes."

"You wearing it?"

"It's hardly workday attire. I've spent all day with an editor—"

"Bet he liked it."

"*She* and I have been editing the hour-long special I'm doing on Major Franklin Trapper."

He dropped the teasing. "For the network?"

"It airs two weeks from Sunday and focuses on all the good he did, how he used his fame to benefit charities and educational programs. I appreciated getting your okay with a capital O."

In the chaotic aftermath of The Major's death,

following her conversation with Jenks, she'd gone in search of Trapper. A note, and only a note, addressed to her had been lying in the hospital bed to which he'd been assigned. *Okay* printed in block letters, his signature scrawled across the bottom.

"I saw some of your reporting," he said. "It was all good."

"Thank you."

"You gave a sanitized version of events."

"I told the public all they needed to know."

She had been obligated to contribute to the coverage of The Major's death and what had led up to it, of Thomas Wilcox's crimes dating back to even before the bombing of the Pegasus Hotel, and of the fall from grace of the vainglorious Reverend Addison.

Mention of Trapper had been kept to a minimum, and what she'd reported was a matter of record. Gracie had pressed her to "deliver the goods," but she'd threatened to quit if Gracie kept at her, reminding the producer and everyone up the food chain that, with her present celebrity, any other outlet in the industry would be thrilled to have her. They'd backed off.

Her reports had been comprehensive, but without any exploitation or invasion of the Trapper family's privacy.

"What's next for you?" he asked. "New York?"

"Trying to get rid of me?"

"Following this big hit, I figured you'd want to move on."

"I like the view from here." She motioned toward the panoply behind him.

"New York is famous for its views."

"I like this one."

They stared at each other. Somehow she resisted the urge to go to him and, as though holding herself back by force, folded her arms across her waist and looked down at her bare toes as she curled them into the rug. "The burial was private." When he didn't say anything, she raised her head.

"I couldn't go through all that falderal, Kerra."

"Nor should you have had to."

"Yeah, but it's what everybody expected. I think the folks in Lodal feel cheated of an extravaganza."

"You don't owe anyone an explanation."

"He's buried beside Mom. No headstone, just a plaque."

"No diary."

"No diary." He gave a rueful smile "Even he thought it was a good bluff."

"He laughed."

"First time in years we'd laughed together. Last time, too."

He paused there before going on to say, "I'm glad we had that laugh." Within minutes of it, The Major had died. Trapper had been in the ambulance with him.

Knowing how much he disliked sentimentality, she changed the subject. "Hank thought you were bluffing about the rifle."

"The one time I was completely straight with him..."

"If you'd been wrong—"

"I knew Jenks wouldn't have left a loaded rifle for Hank."

"But you only played a hunch that Jenks was the undercover man. If you'd been wrong, I would have shot you. You would have died right in front of me," she said, her voice cracking.

"True. I'm reckless. Beyond stubborn. A grab-bag of character flaws."

"Chief among them rudeness," she said, putting some heat behind it. "You show up here uninvited. You disappeared without saying goodbye."

"I'm sorry about that, Kerra. Soon as they stitched my scalp—"

"You pulled a disappearing act."

"Because the falderal was about to get underway, and I didn't want to be trapped inside the hospital when it did."

"I wanted to see you, Trapper. To know that you were all right, to comfort you."

"I didn't need platitudes and consolation."

"*I* did." She flattened her hand on her chest.

He opened his mouth to say something but seemed to think better of it. The tension went out of his shoulders. "I'm a shit. Ask Gracie. She wrote it down."

Moments ticked past. Kerra massaged her brow, got a grip. Looking at him again, she asked, "Is your head okay?"

"Carson told me you called to inquire."

"At the very least I wanted to know if you were upright and mobile, or undergoing delicate brain surgery."

"My head injury wasn't serious. I heard that myself on the news. Oh, wait. Wasn't that you reporting?"

She glowered at him.

He raised his hands to his sides in an apologetic gesture. "The scalp wound was superficial, couple of stitches. Goose egg went away in a few days." He paused for emphasis. "But I had to get my head on straight, Kerra."

It was an idiomatic statement, but rife with underlying meaning. Unable to stay angry with him, she said, "I understand."

He shifted his weight, looked around the room, and when he came back to her, picked up on Hank. "I'd warned him that if he ever hit me again, he'd be preaching through dental work. His jaw's wired shut."

"I hope they throw the book at him."

"It's as good as thrown."

"Glenn?"

"I saw him today. He's broken over Hank, but at least he's not behind bars. He was granted bail for health reasons, and, in terms of prosecution, he's way down in the pecking order. He's turning state's evidence. Probably won't serve time."

"I'm sure you had something to do with all that."

He didn't deny it, but he didn't admit it, either. She gave him a knowing smile. "The thing is, Trapper, you're not a shit at all. You only want people to think you are."

"Must be a damn good act, because most do."

Even though there was a lot she could say to dispute that, she forfeited the point. "In case you ever showed up uninvited, I kept something for you. Come here."

She led him into her bedroom, went to the closet, and switched on the light inside it. She dragged out a cardboard box and scooted it across the floor to the side of the bed. "I heard you put the house and land on the market and had all the furnishings auctioned off."

"Who told you?"

"I can't reveal a source."

"You're seriously going to play that card?"

"Is it true?"

"Yes. That place was never home to me, and, after everything, I knew I'd never go back."

"Sit down. Open the box."

He sat on the edge of the bed and lifted the lid. Inside were the photos from his bedroom in The Major's house.

Kerra sat beside him. "I asked Jenks to collect them before the auction. I thought you might want them. If not right now, someday."

Trapper stared down at the framed photos but didn't touch them. His chest rose and fell on a deep breath. "I want to believe, Kerra, but..."

"Believe what?"

"That he told the truth before he died. That he wasn't one of the bombers, and that the reason—the *only* reason—he'd tried to get to you through that locked door was to warn you."

"Why else would he?"

He ran his fingers through his hair. "I don't know. Maybe Wilcox—"

"Trapper, you've got to let it go."

"Dammit, don't you think I want to? Don't you think I want to believe that the man in these pictures, the dad I remember, was corrupted only by fate and fame as he said? But I'm having trouble accepting that."

"Why?"

"Wilcox wanted you silenced. You and The Major

are alone in the house. What does he do? He opens the gun cabinet and takes out that rifle. By your own admission, when you heard the shot, you thought he had fired it. By accident, maybe, but—"

"He couldn't have fired it. It wasn't loaded."

He gave her a sharp look.

She said, "I thought you knew that."

He shook his head. "How do you know?"

"Glenn Addison told me. The day I was released from the hospital. He and the Texas Rangers were questioning me. One of the details they were withholding from the public was that the rifle was found lying on the floor within The Major's reach. Until I told him otherwise, Glenn had reasoned The Major had taken it from the cabinet when he heard intruders. Not that it would have done him any good, he said. 'It wasn't loaded.'"

She placed her hands on Trapper's forearm and squeezed. "It wasn't loaded, Trapper. The Major had no intention of harming me. He was probably replacing the gun in the cabinet when he heard Jenks and Petey Moss. He came to warn me. Accept that." Lowering her voice, she said, "Accept that he loved you. Then start living *your* life. Not his."

He looked down at the picture on the top of the stack inside the box. Trapper was missing a front tooth. He was wearing a grass-stained softball uniform, kneeling beside a trophy that was taller than he. The Major was standing behind him, hands on his shoulders, grinning widely.

Trapper gave a wistful smile and replaced the lid. After scooting the box aside, he turned to her. "I have no choice except to love him. If it hadn't been for him, I wouldn't have met you."

Her breath caught.

"I had to show up here uninvited, Kerra."

She tilted her head inquisitively.

"You stopped calling Carson."

"He was becoming irritated." Huskily she added, "And I do have my pride."

He gazed into her eyes for an extended time, then softly asked, "If I make a pass, are you going to hurl me through that plate glass window?"

"Only a reckless man would risk it."

"Not reckless. Desperate."

"Then it's probably worth taking the gamble."

"Well, here goes." He reached out and brushed his thumb back and forth across her beauty mark. "I lied when I said I didn't need your consolation." He slid his hand down the side of her throat, moved her collar aside, and buried his face between her neck and collarbone. "I do. I need you. I want you like hell. It's a sickness. Carson says it's love. He thinks it's hysterical."

"What do you think?"

He raised his head to look at her. "What I *know* is,

if you don't invite me to stick around, I'll just have to carry you off again."

"Stick around for how long, Trapper? An hour? A night, before you dash away again?"

"No, I'd like to stay until I'm cured of what ails me." He rubbed his thumb across her lower lip. "But since the thought of being without you only makes me sicker, it could be indefinite."

"A vicious cycle. I don't see an end to it."

"Me either. You may want to take that into consideration before saying yes."

She pretended to ponder it until he cursed under his breath and kissed her with enough tenderness to stir her heartstrings and enough passion to set her hormones ablaze.

The kisses continued uninterrupted as they lay back, face to face. When he finally broke apart, she gasped, "I haven't agreed to anything yet."

"You know the alternative."

"You'd carry me off?"

"Without hesitation. But not in a stolen car. And first, I'd fulfill my sex fantasy."

"You'll have to be more specific."

"To fuck you in your newslady clothes." He put his hand under her skirt and slid it up her inner thigh, hooking his thumb in the band of her panties and tugging.

"Before you even got out of your coat and boots?"

"Hmm. That's part of it. I only wish you'd left the high heels on."

"Well, maybe this will make up for them."

"What?"

Leaning up, she placed her lips against his ear and whispered, "You're going to love this."

She finished unbuttoning her blouse and watched his smile stretch when he saw the bra she was wearing underneath.

LL